Rosehaven
LYNDA TRENT

Ⓢ
A SIGNET BOOK

NEW AMERICAN LIBRARY

"STAY THE NIGHT WITH ME," SHE WHISPERED.

"You're safe now," Logan said. "It was me they were after."

"Stay with me," Abigail repeated.

Pausing only long enough to pull the door closed, Logan took her hand and led her to the bed. Her thin chemise had slipped low, exposing the rounded fullness of her bosom.

Their eyes met and she felt a great spark of love leap out at her. Slowly he lowered his head, then took her lips in a kiss, his hands exploring her body, sending waves of hot desire coursing through her.

With her arms circling his neck, Abigail swayed into his embrace, kissing him with all the fury of her pent-up passion, urging him silently to take all she offered. . . .

PUBLISHER'S NOTE

This novel is a work of fiction. Names, characters, places, and incidents either are the product of the author's imagination or are used fictitiously, and any resemblance to actual persons, living or dead, events, or locales is entirely coincidental.

SIGNET, SIGNET CLASSIC, MENTOR, PLUME, MERIDIAN AND NAL BOOKS
are published by New American Library,
1633 Broadway, New York, New York 10019

First Printing, November, 1985

1 2 3 4 5 6 7 8 9

PRINTED IN THE UNITED STATES OF AMERICA

To Evan Marshall,
for knowing what to say
and when to say it

Prologue

A band of men sat astride their horses on the gentle, open knoll. All were silent and tense, not for fear of being overheard, but from concern about their approaching battle. The captain ran his finger under the stiff gray collar of his uniform and eased the scratchy wool away from his skin. His dark eyes were fastened to the twin rails of steel down below that gleamed silver in the afternoon sun. One of the horses, a red pinto, shifted and snorted impatiently. His rider, a boy scarcely sixteen years of age, leaned forward to pat the animal's neck.

"Logan," one of the men said, "here she comes."

The captain nodded, his vision fixed on the squat black locomotive. "I see her, Travis," he told his cousin. Without averting his eyes, he said, "You all know what to do. Harley, you and Martin take the caboose. Travis, you and Tobe take the mail car." The nature of their mission had long ago rendered any customary military formality unnecessary.

To the man who had shinnied up the telegraph pole at first sight of the train, Logan shouted, "Cut the wire."

The soldier followed orders, not only snipping the cable in two but also removing a section and chopping it into bits to preclude a simple repair. He tossed the pieces of telegraph cable far away and mounted his horse.

"Logan, she's slowing on the incline," Travis reported.

His cousin had already noticed. "Peterson, you take the livestock car. They seldom have a guard with the horses, but we don't want to take any chances. The rest of you divide up between the passenger car and the boxcar behind it. Anderson, see to our horses and keep them handy. As the Yankees come out, keep them covered from this side of the train."

He tensed in the saddle and felt his black mount fidget eagerly. The engine was almost even with them as it began struggling to climb the hill, great clouds of smoke billowed skyward. Logan gave the signal and they spurred their horses forward. He leaned low over the animal's neck for protection and raced toward the engine. As the leader, he took the greatest risk. This wasn't the first such raid for Captain Logan Sorrell and his men, but that didn't make his chore any easier or any less dangerous.

As he approached the ladder on the side of the wood car, Logan's horse obligingly shifted nearer, his black ears flattened in distaste of the thundering noise. Logan took a deep breath and lunged toward his target, over the churning wheels that could mean his death, and caught the metal rung. With his strong hands securely gripping the ladder, he pushed away from his horse.

For a perilous moment he clung by only his hands; then he found his footing and climbed up. He crouched on top of the almost full wood box, acclimating himself to the lurching of the train, then crawled toward the engine. As usual the roar from the steam engine masked all other sounds and he had been unable to hear whether shots had been fired, though he was sure they had been by now. With no further pause, he jumped down into the back of the engine compartment.

The engineer and the fireman wheeled to stare at him and the large revolver he held. Both men looked too surprised to react.

"Stop the train!" Logan shouted over the din of metal slamming into metal.

"What?" the engineer yelled.

In response, Logan raised the gun and pointed it squarely at the man's nose, improving his hearing. With a jerk, the engineer cut back on the throttle, and slowly the train lost momentum and rolled to a stop. The sudden silence was unnerving.

"Outside," Logan ordered, standing back from the door.

After the briefest pause, the two men obeyed. Soldiers in dark Union blue were already piling out of the train with their arms stretched high above their heads. Logan jumped down from the last step and prodded his captives ahead of him. Of the older man who was holding a group of the prisoners at bay several yards ahead, he asked, "Was anybody hurt, Martin?"

The old man spat and shook his head. "The boy nearly lost his hold, but I pulled him up. He's okay. We really caught them by surprise. Bet they didn't fire half a dozen shots before we got the drop on 'em."

Anderson rode up, herding the Confederates' horses in front of him. Logan motioned for the private to hold the horses there as he walked on down the train. His gun was still drawn and he maintained a watchful eye. At the livestock car he stopped and called for one of his men to help him slide out the ramp.

He walked up and unbolted the door, rolling it back. The horses inside snorted nervously and stamped their iron-shod feet. "Turn them loose," he told the man. "Then you and Peterson run them off."

The man nodded and started to untie the first animal and remove its halter.

"Captain!" the boy's voice called.

Instantly Logan put his head out. "What is it, Harley?"

"Travis wants you in the mail car."

Logan swung down and followed the boy to the next car back. Entering, he saw his cousin kneeling beside an open box.

"What is it, Travis?"

The man held up a canvas bag stamped "U.S." and dramatically poured a handful of gold coins into his palm. "Payroll," he said simply.

A wide grin spread over Logan's face. "Three boxes full? Jeff Davis should be able to use that."

He went back outside and told the engineer and brakeman to disconnect the train at the rear of the mail car. "Where's your commanding officer?" he demanded of a sullen Yankee corporal.

The man jerked his head to the left and Logan went to where Tobe held a big blond man at bay.

"Are you in charge of this train?" he asked almost amiably.

"That's right, Captain. Major Owen Chandler." He nodded curtly, his pale green eyes smoldering beneath his rigidly calm exterior. "And your name?"

"Nighthawk is all you need to know," Logan answered. "I see you're carrying payroll."

"Nighthawk!" The man took a step forward but gave way to the loaded guns. "I've heard of you."

"I imagine you have. On behalf of the Confederate States of America, I thank you for the gold."

"You take that gold and I'll have your hide!" All pretense of politeness vanished.

"Now, Major Chandler, you know we didn't stop this train just to pass the time of day." Logan's smooth Southern accent contrasted sharply with the major's clipped words. He saw the private return from driving away the Yankee horses. "Now load ours," he called out, and the man rode to obey.

"Major, those bright blue uniforms seem to be offending my horses." He smiled. "I'd be much obliged if you and your men would take them off."

"What!" the man bellowed.

"Strip!" Logan commanded, cold steel replacing the amiability in his voice. "Boots and all."

"We won't!"

"It's up to you. I want your clothes or your lives."

"Down to our long johns?" the major asked angrily.

"Major, if you and your men aren't buck naked in five minutes, I'm going to shoot you." His easygoing smile did nothing to soften his words.

Furiously the Union officer started unbuttoning the brass eagles that secured his coat. "I'll get you for this, Nighthawk."

"Just toss your clothes in that boxcar there. That'll be fine," Logan replied.

In a remarkably short time the Yankees stood naked and embarrassed in front of the guns. A few moved with tender-footed embarrassment to grumble to their comrades.

"Sergeant," Logan said to Tobe, "are all their guns and ammunition loaded into the mail car?"

"Yes, sir."

"Then set fire to those last three cars."

Chandler took a warning step nearer and Logan calmly pressed the cold barrel of his revolver against the man's bare chest.

"Don't be a damned fool," he suggested mildly.

As the fires were lit, Chandler stared intensely at Logan. In a hoarse whisper he said, "I'll remember you, Nighthawk, and if it's the last thing I do, I'll hunt you down and hang you myself."

"You do that, Major Chandler." Logan wasn't concerned in the least with such a threat. He had heard the same many times before.

Chandler glanced sharply at the horses being loaded—a large black, a red-and-white skewbald, the others pretty much nondescript. "I'll remember. And I'll get you."

Logan motioned for his men to get on the train. Martin and Tobe went to the engine as they had on other missions and started stoking the boiler. Logan swung up onto the mail car as the private locked the horses in and slid the ramp back under the belly of the boxcar. Behind it the rest of the train was now engulfed in rolling billows of flame and black smoke.

As the train started to inch forward, Logan grinned and gave Chandler a mock salute. "Better start walking. The nights are still mighty cool."

Chandler, indistinguishable in the mass of naked men, glared at Logan. "I'll find you, you bastard," he promised.

The train gathered speed and Logan stepped inside. His men were clustered around the boxes of gold, everyone trying to figure out just how much was there.

"What do we do now?" Travis asked.

"We head hell-for-leather to the east. When we run out of fuel we blow up the train, same as before."

"What about the gold?"

"If we can, we'll take it to Montgomery. Otherwise, we'll have to bury it and come back after it later. Lock the boxes again and give me the keys."

"There's a fortune here," Travis mused thoughtfully as he replaced one of the padlocks. "We could divide it among ourselves and all of us walk away rich."

"You know you don't mean that," Logan warned sharply. "After fighting nearly three years, the South needs this more than we do."

"Sure, Logan. I was just thinking out loud."

"I know. Still, it wouldn't do for the men to hear talk like that." He glanced out the window. "At least it's nearly spring. That always makes a man feel like he's going to make it, having winter behind. What month is this, March?"

"Early April."

Logan nodded. Even with the gold, he wondered how much longer his precious South could last. When they had left their homes and families three years before, none would have guessed this nightmare would last so long. He lowered himself into a jouncing seat and tried to get some rest.

1

Selma, Ala., May 12, 1865
To Col. B. W. Dearborn, Washington, D.C.:

Nighthawk still moving west toward Meridian, Miss
STOP *Will continue pursuit per your orders* STOP

Owen Chandler, Maj.

Abigail McGee straightened her aching back and drew her sleeve across her sweat-moistened brow. Although it was still early in the day, the Mississippi sun was already hot and she ached from hours of toil. The past month had been dry, and dust from her garden filmed her high-topped shoes and soiled the tail of her homespun skirt. Wearily she batted the dust from the dark blue fabric. She would have to start hauling water from the creek or the plants wouldn't survive.

Dropping back to a kneeling position, Abigail weeded another shoot of corn out of the encroaching grass. All her seeds had been lost when her barn roof went bad the winter before. By not plowing she had been able to glean the plants that had sown themselves from the previous years; but they were scattered randomly throughout the rows, and she could find them only by crawling about on her hands and knees.

Beyond the scrub-oak trees that rimmed her pasture, a billow of black smoke curled into the harsh blue sky. Slowly Abigail stood and unconsciously wiped her hands on her skirt. Her only neighbors lived in that direction.

Picking her way through the sprigs of new corn, Abigail walked to the low rail fence. The yellow dirt of the hard-packed road unfurled like a ribbon down a low rise and around the bend. More smoke choked upward and a breeze plumed it away from her. Could that be from a forest fire? she wondered.

A movement drew her attention back to the road. She tucked a strand of dark auburn hair out of sight beneath her sunbonnet and narrowed her violet eyes against the glare of sunlight. As the band of men rode toward her, she felt dread tighten in her stomach. Their uniforms were so battle-stained she couldn't tell if they were blue or gray, but she concluded, from the fact that they wore any uniform at all and still had horses to ride, that they were the enemy.

Running away was pointless, for she was certain they had seen her as soon as they had come into her view. So she rested her hand on the rail and waited.

" 'Morning, ma'am," the officer in charge said in greeting.

She nodded in silent acknowledgment.

His shallow blue eyes raked her small house, the bare chicken yard, the old barn, and came at last to the garden. With forced cheerfulness he said, "We're thirsty and hungry, ma'am. Could you spare us a bite to eat?"

Abigail shook her head. "The creek is over yonder. Drink your fill. As for food, I don't have enough even for myself." Her thoughts darted to the fresh pork she had hidden in the springhouse below the pasture. If the soldiers took it, she would have nothing to eat until the garden yielded its meager produce.

The officer dismounted and motioned for his men to search the barns and house. "Begging your pardon, ma'am, but we have to eat, too."

Abigail's hand tightened on the rough cedar railing that separated them. "The war's over," she ground out in a carefully modulated voice.

"But we still have to eat." His eyes met hers implacably.

Refusing to drop her gaze, Abigail glared at him. Lowering his eyes first, the captain nodded toward her garden. "Sowing a crop, I see," he tried to say lightly.

Abigail wasn't in the mood for small talk and she certainly wasn't going to let him off that easily. "What seeds your army didn't steal last fall were ruined when my barn leaked during the winter. I can't plow because a bushwhacker stole my horse. The plow went to *my* army to be melted into cannonballs to shoot at *your* army. That's not a garden—it's an exercise in futility." As always when she was deeply moved, the Scots-Irish burr of her parents' homeland colored her speech.

"I'm sorry, ma'am," the man said, dropping some of his stern manner. "I truly am."

"I know. You've a wife or a sweetheart or a mother back home and you'd not wish her to be on all fours culling weeds from a garden. I've heard it before."

"Captain!" one of the men yelled as he came out of her kitchen door. He gestured toward a pail as he hurried over. "It's fresh lard, Captain."

The Yankee's eyes grew cold again as he looked from the pail of yellowish-white substance to the woman. "I do believe you're right, Corporal. Well, ma'am, looks like you do have food for us after all."

Abigail forced a smile to her stiff lips. "You're welcome to it." She crossed her arms over her chest as the corporal dipped the tip of his finger in the bucket. "I was just going to use it to make soap. But I would rather you had it instead."

"Soap? Out of good lard like this?" the captain demanded as the corporal lifted his finger to his lips. "With food so scarce?"

She shrugged. "The hog died of cholera."

The corporal's reaction was violent as he spit the lard into the dirt and wiped his finger hastily on his pants leg.

"Here!" the captain snarled, shoving the lard at her. "No *lady* would try to feed tainted food to a man!"

"You're right, Captain. Only to the enemy." She took the heavy pail, and this time the smile reached her eyes.

"Anything in the barn?" he yelled to one of his men.

"Not a thing."

"Mount up!" he ordered as he swung up into the saddle and glared down at her. "You Southerners are no better than you ought to be!"

She dropped a contemptuous curtsy to him and watched as they rode out of sight around the grove of sweet-gum trees. Her smile faded as she glanced back at the pillar of black smoke.

Quickly she went into her house and replaced the perfectly good pail of lard in the cupboard. The men wouldn't be back. She hurried across the packed dirt of her yard and onto the road. The smoke wasn't spreading like a forest fire would have, and that could only mean the worst.

Of the three tracks scored in the road, two from the steel rims of wagon wheels and the other from the horses that pulled them, she chose the nearest one to avoid the soft sand that would slow her down and fill her shoes. Keeping her elbows pressed against her side as if she expected a blow, Abigail hurried toward her neighbors' farm.

The small frame house came into sight first, then the barn, which was engulfed in flames. Her steps increased to a trot and then to a hard run as she realized what was happening. "Mattie!" she gasped. Then, louder, "Mattie!"

Rounding the house, Abigail saw her friend with her younger children knotted closely around her. The eldest boy, a towheaded lad less than twelve, was tossing a bucket of water at the flames in an attempt to save the nearly gutted structure, but the heat from the blaze was so intense that he couldn't get close enough to do any good.

Abigail hurried to the woman who stood staring in stoic rigidity at the barn as tears coursed down her weathered cheeks. "Mattie?"

"Leave it be, Young Tom," the woman said in a heavy voice. "It's gone. No need to waste water."

The boy glared at the barn, then looked down to dig his toe in the dirt as he tried to hide his own tears.

"Are you all right?" Abigail inquired. "Did they hurt you?"

Mattie Grayson looked at her for the first time. "I'm as all right as I can be, seeing as how my barn is burning to the ground."

"But why . . ." Abigail gestured at the senseless waste.

"It was the chickens," Mattie replied dully. "I didn't hear them soldiers coming in time to drive the chickens into the woods like I always do. Those bluecoats swooped down on 'em like hawks, gathered up all the eggs, and set fire to my barn because I lied about having those chickens." She dabbed at her eyes with the corner of her apron. "All on account of a few scrawny hens and a middle-aged rooster."

"None of you is hurt?" Abigail asked as she looked from her friend to the young children that clutched about her.

"They didn't lay a hand on us, but Young Tom is taking it hard. His pa told him to take care of us and he's likely taking this to heart." Mattie sighed. "Even his pa couldn't have done any better. I tried to tell him that, but he thinks he's a man now, and wouldn't listen."

"A barn can be rebuilt," Abigail consoled. "Besides, without livestock you don't really need one. When Big Tom comes home from the war—"

"We won't be here," Mattie interrupted. "I've got a sister in Jackson. Me and the children are going to move in with her until this craziness is over. Then . . . well, then we'll see."

"The war *is* over," Abigail said softly as she looked at the burning hull.

Mattie shook her head. "I don't rightly think it will ever really be over."

Abigail put her arm around Mattie's shoulders and they watched the flames devour the barn's black ribs. After a while the roof crashed down in a shower of sparks and the blaze sank to lick at the few remaining timbers. The outline of a wagon could be seen inside the inferno, but soon it too melted away in the greedy fire.

Young Tom circled the building, keeping the fire contained and away from the house and field.

No one spoke until only coals glowed in a nest of blackened beams and ashes.

"You won't be back, will you, Mattie?" Abigail asked at last.

"I sure don't see how I can. There's been so much heartache here. I don't reckon I could ever see this farm and not remember all the bad times." She looked over at a grassy knoll in the pasture where three grave markers, carved from thick oak slabs, stood as grim reminders of the suffering. "Big Tom wasn't even here to bury Baby Emma."

Abigail felt a knot tighten in her throat and she looked away. Her own husband, William, had been buried at Shiloh, probably in an unmarked grave with countless others. After three years she was resigned to his death, but she had always had Mattie and her boisterous brood to give her support. "I'm going to miss you sorely," she whispered brokenly.

"Come with us," Mattie urged. "You don't have anything to keep you here. Come to my sister's house."

"Your sister is an angel for sure, but I would be an extra mouth to feed." She glanced down at the round-eyed children. "You'll be hard pressed as it is."

Mattie knew it was so, and she averted her eyes. "Still, we can make room for you and all. I hate to leave you here all by yourself."

"I'm not afraid. I have my part of the hog meat hidden down by the creek, and I found some corn seedlings sprouting this morning. I'll be all right."

Mattie gave her a look that said she knew false optimism when she saw it, and said, "If things go wrong with you in any way, you know my sister's name?"

"Sure I do. I've visited with her here several times."

"I want you to promise me, if things get too bad, you'll come find me and we'll see each other through."

"I will," Abigail said. Both she and Mattie knew she wouldn't, but neither could bear to say good-bye.

Abigail and Mattie went into the house and piled the family's few belongings onto three quilts, then tied the corners together to make bags. The furniture and other bulky items would have to be left behind.

"You pick whatever you want," Mattie said, looking at the bed where she had borne most of her children. "Whatever you don't want, leave behind for whoever moves here next. Maybe it won't be too long, with the menfolks coming home and all." Now that the time had actually come to leave, Mattie was avoiding Abigail's eyes, and silence grew long between their bits of tense conversation.

"You'd better get on the road. It must be close to midafternoon." Abigail helped Young Tom hoist the quilt of cooking utensils to his narrow shoulders. "What will you do tonight?"

Mattie managed a brave smile. "If we haven't come to a house and if no wagon comes along to give us a ride, I guess we'll sleep out in the open. Big Tom has done it for years. I guess we can manage. Tomorrow I'm sure we'll get a ride to Jackson. Wagons travel that road all the time." Mattie swung the larger load onto her back and motioned for her two older daughters to share the remaining bag between them.

Abigail ached from not crying, but she couldn't send her friend off with sobs. "Take care, Mattie. Give my greeting to your sister and to Big Tom when you see him." The two women gripped each other tightly. War wasn't hell only for the men.

Abigail followed them to the road and waved until they were out of sight, then let her arm drop dejectedly. She felt as sad and as lonely as when she had seen William trudge away on the same road four years before. Now, however, there was no one left to cling to.

With iron determination Abigail lifted her chin and squared her shoulders. Mattie and her children would be better off in Jackson; they should have gone years before and as her friend, Abigail couldn't wish for Mattie to stay.

She walked over to Mattie's garden and critically inspected the crops. Her neighbor's seeds had survived the lootings and the harsh winter, and now healthy young plants sprouted. Abigail hauled water from the well and poured it around the seedlings. When the plants were a little larger, she would transplant them to her own garden.

In the shed behind the house, Abigail found a small cache of potatoes. Although they were wizened and knotted from lying on the rack all winter they were a feast to Abigail, who didn't know how they had escaped the sharp-eyed Yankees.

She put two of the potatoes in her skirt pocket for her supper and the others she piled in a small wagon that had belonged to one of the children. Along with the cured hog meat, the potatoes might be enough to see her through until the other vegetables were ripe.

Along with a shovel from Mattie's shed, Abigail hauled the wagon out across the back field that separated their farms, and down to the creek. When the trees closed ranks behind her, she sighed with relief. If anyone had seen her, the potatoes would surely have been confiscated at once, for there was yet no difference between the days of war and the days of peace. The Confederate armies had surrendered to the North only the month before.

She walked beside the swift ribbon of water, the wagon jolting and rattling behind her. Later she would retrace her steps and smooth out the tracks left by the wagon wheels, just in case. She didn't want anyone to guess where she planned to dig her new root cellar.

When she came to the tiny shed that spanned the narrow stream, she looked in to see that her hams were all still there. She checked that meat more frequently than a miser counts his fortune. All was in order, so she went on deeper into the woods. The stream curved back onto her land as if it held the small farmhouse in its cupped palm. The place she had in mind, near a small footbridge that connected one pasture to another, was not too distant from the house for convenience, but was far enough away that no one was likely to suspect that food would be stored there.

Letting the wagon drift to a stop, Abigail tested the ground with the tip of the shovel. The place she had chosen was high enough above the creek to be dry and was fairly clear of large trees whose roots would make digging difficult. When the soil turned up easily beneath the blade, Abigail started to dig in earnest.

In no time she had a trough dug back into the hillside in such a way that any rainwater would drain away from the potatoes. Carefully she started laying them in the trench and piling dirt over them as she went. She ran out of trench before she ran out of potatoes, so she plunged the shovel back into the dirt.

The edge of the shovel scraped against an object much harder than the soil. Abigail poked the ground a few times, listening to the metallic clink each time she made contact, then knelt to brush away the dirt and moldering leaves. To her astonishment, she uncovered the top few inches of a square metal box secured with a large padlock. "PROP. OF U.S. GOVT." was stenciled on the lid in black paint. As she scooped the soil away from its cold sides, she discovered an identical box beside the first, then another next to that one.

All were too heavy to lift, so Abigail sat down on the ground and stared at them. How long had they been buried there, and why? Something of value must be inside, since all three were locked and well hidden. She looked over her shoulder at the railroad track that snaked through the woods. She was sure the last train had passed through months before. She couldn't, however, recall ever seeing a train stop just here. She tugged again on the handle of the nearest box, realizing that all three had been intentionally buried here, and wondering by whom.

She stood and chopped at the lock with the shovel's broad blade, until the rusted lock finally broke and fell away. Gingerly she knelt by the box and pried open the top, whose hinges creaked from rust. Inside were several canvas bags, all stamped with the Union Army's insignia.

Abigail lifted a pouch, and her mouth dropped open in stunned recognition even before she opened the drawstring flap. Gold coins, more than she had seen in one place in her entire life, fell into her lap, caught the glimmer of sunshine that filtered through the bower of trees overhead, and seemed to glow with a life of their own.

She blinked, yet the coins still remained. Moving as if in a dream, she sifted them through her fingers, feeling their slick coldness and hearing their musical clinks as they fell back to her skirt.

Jerking her head up, Abigail looked around her. If men would set fire to a barn over some scrawny chickens, they would surely kill over a fortune such as this! Seeing no one, Abigail forced herself to be very still while she listened. The only sounds she heard were the stream's babble and the thunder of her pounding heart. When she was convinced that she was truly alone, she looked back into the box and fingered the other packets. The bulge of coins was clearly discernible through the canvas. Abigail sat back and stared again. She had just discovered enough money to last the rest of her life, *if* she could spend it!

Slowly Abigail began replacing the coins in the bag, one at a time. She knew that if she suddenly started spending money, word would spread faster than nightfall and her safety, as well as the safety of her fortune, would be lost.

She would have to remember to keep up the appearance of being as destitute as her neighbors, even though she badly needed the necessities this money could provide. She wished Mattie was still here to share in her abundance. But if Mattie had not gone, Abigail would have had no potatoes to dig a cellar for and would never have found the gold. She resolved to somehow send some coins to Mattie as soon as she figured a way to do it safely.

For herself, she needed a horse, a plow, and seeds. Buying these things wouldn't raise undue curiosity if she could come up with a convincing story as to where she got the money for them. To protect the horse from thieves, she could build a pen in the woods where the animal would be much less conspicuous. Abigail smiled as her fingers caressed a coin. She already had a horse in mind—a bright bay owned by the family over the hill. It was both harness- and saddle-trained and it was young.

Abigail tied the bag shut, keeping a handful of coins in her lap. She wasn't sure what a plow would cost, but with horses so scarce, it shouldn't be much. Seeds were outrageously expensive, but if she played her role well, no one would wonder at her buying. Especially if she bought a handful here, another there. The horse would be her most difficult purchase because it was worth at least fifty dollars before the war. The farmer would probably ask four times that now. She smiled and narrowed her eyes thoughtfully. That farmer had bought his way out of serving in the army and had a bad name with his neighbors because of it. She would enjoy getting the better of him in a horse trade.

Lifting her skirt, Abigail deposited the money in the secret pocket sewn in her petticoat and buttoned the flap over it. When her mother had emigrated from Ireland she had carried her entire dot, or dowry, in just such a pocket, and no one had ever been the wiser until after she was safely wed to Jamie McTavish, fresh off the boat from Scotland. As her mother had often told her, no gentleman would search a lady's petticoats, and if he were a rogue, well, she was done for anyway. Abigail smiled at the memory of her mother's purring brogue and ruddy, earnest face. Both she and her darling Jamie were dead now of a typhoid epidemic, and Abigail missed them greatly.

She packed down the dirt and scattered last winter's leaves over the disturbed soil. This place had kept the gold safe for quite some time, by the looks of the box, and she saw no reason to move it. Carefully noting the exact location, Abigail went back the way she had come, pushing the wagon ahead of her and brushing away its tracks with a leafy branch. At the stream she paused and looked back. All her life she had been honest to a fault, and she knew the gold belonged to the federal government.

Then she thought of her William in an unmarked grave at Shiloh—wherever that was—and she tossed her head. All that gold put together could not buy back her dear William. Any reservations she had had about keeping the gold for herself vanished.

2

Abigail rested her hand on the splintery plank of Fred Carothers' feed lot and tiptoed to see between the boards and into the lot. The bay horse was drinking from the trough, but upon hearing her, he turned his head and pricked his ears. Droplets of water trickled from his muzzle and awareness sparked his eyes. Abigail smiled and nodded her head decisively. This was the perfect horse for her needs.

" 'Morning, Mrs. McGee," a deep voice said warily behind her, for no one quite trusted anybody yet with the surrender still so recent. "What brings you over today?"

"Good morning to you, Mr. Carothers. I thought I'd see if your wife would be interested in a quilt pattern I ran across in an old chest yesterday. Is she in?"

"She's in the house, yonder."

Abigail stepped forward, then looked back at the horse. "That's surely not the spanking bay I saw you riding last fall, is it?"

"It is for a fact."

She peered at the animal. "Is he ailing? I never knew a young horse to winter so poorly."

"There's nothing wrong with him," Carothers said, looking more closely at the animal.

"He's rather thin, isn't he?" Abigail said with her eyes wide and innocent.

"I like a lean animal."

"No one would argue that, of course." She turned toward the house but looked back again. "I believe I noticed him favoring his near back leg. Is he lame?"

"That horse is as sound as I am!"

"Well, you'd know best about that. Perhaps he's only flatfooted. A new pair of shoes should fix him up." She knew this was a defect that no doctoring could remedy and would devalue the animal. "I'll just go in and see Mrs. Carothers now."

She left the man staring suspiciously at the horse. He was falling into her trap and needed no further urging.

His wife was a spare-framed woman whose severe features belied her gentle ways. Abigail had never grown close to Ida Carothers because their farms were too far apart for casual visiting and William had never been able to abide Fred. But when the older woman's sunken black eyes became almost joyful at the sight of a visitor, Abigail wished she had made a greater effort.

"Come in, come in," Ida Carothers urged. "You didn't walk all the way, did you?"

"My horse was one of the first things to be 'liberated,'" Abigail answered. "You're lucky that your own animals were spared."

Ida glanced out the window to where her husband was repairing the catch pen. "Having a man on the place has been our salvation. Fred has had to send more than one bunch a-packing." Her gaunt face was thoughtful as she said as if by rote, "Fred's ailing, you know, though one would never guess it to see him."

Abigail made a solicitous murmur, though she knew the man's greatest problem was the yellow streak down his back. "You're a fortunate woman for sure. Not only do you have a horse to pull a plow, but a husband to do the hard work."

Ida turned back to her guest. "I heard about poor Mr. McGee. You have my deepest sympathies."

"Thank you kindly, Mrs. Carothers. It was at Shiloh, you know."

"Yes, so I heard. Please call me Ida. Don't you have a family to go to?"

"No, I was an only child and my parents are dead. All the rest of my family are in the old country. Even if I could afford the voyage, I wouldn't go. My home is here."

"I understand that, I surely do." Ida's long face nodded mournfully. "Perhaps you could live with your husband's family."

"I'm afraid that is out of the question." William's parents had been enraged at the idea of their son marrying a poor girl and they would rather burn their house to the ground than offer their daughter-in-law a place in it.

"How have you managed? A woman alone has such a difficult life."

"I've been alone since the beginning of the war. I can make it. But to tell you the truth, I desperately need a horse." She leaned forward imploringly. "Do you suppose your husband could sell me one?"

"Perhaps, but do you . . . that is . . . ."

"I have a bit of money. It's the remainder of my dot." When Ida looked blankly at her, Abigail clarified, "My dowry."

"I'll speak to him for you. I can imagine how difficult it must be for a woman alone, especially when it comes to dealing with matters of trade."

Abigail smiled. "Thank you. I would appreciate

it. William always did these things for me and . . . well, you understand. I do hope to buy a young horse. I expect it will take every cent I have, and I won't be able to buy another one anytime soon."

Ida's face lit. "We have just the horse for you! A bright bay with a half-moon on his face. Perhaps you noticed him as you walked by the pen."

"I'll look at him on my way back. I'm afraid one horse looks pretty much like another to me." As she spoke, she reached into her skirt pocket and withdrew several scraps of paper. "The reason I came by today was to share something with you. I found this quilt pattern in an old clothes press. Everybody in the county knows about your beautiful quilts and I thought you might be interested in it. See the note here at the bottom? It belonged to my mother's best friend—one of the Hamilton family of Savannah. Evidently it's been handed down over a hundred years."

Ida's eyes brightened avidly. "Would you mind if I copied it? It's such a lovely design."

"I'd be honored." Abigail spread the intricate pieces on the side table.

As Ida found the stiff paper she used for patterns, she said, "Did you see anyone on the way over?"

"No, why?"

"The Wilson plantation's slaves are all around here." She couldn't bring herself to call them by their new status of freemen. "They had as soon rob you blind as anything. I'm half-afraid to hang my clothes on the line. They're as bad as the Yankees."

"I have nothing to steal, although that's a measure of security I'd not wish on anyone."

"Just the same, you be watchful on your way

home." She carefully traced the pattern onto her paper and added a note detailing the origin of the pattern and the name of the woman who had shared it with her. "I declare, it's like the end of the world. All this killing and fighting and stealing. The end of the world."

Abigail looked around the well-furnished parlor and smelled the unmistakable aroma of beef stew. "Times are hard, Ida." She gathered the worn cutouts and replaced them in her pocket. "I had better be going," she said.

"So soon? You just arrived."

"True, but I have a long walk home and I have chores to do before dark. You will urge your husband to sell me a horse, won't you? I would appreciate it."

"I'm sure I can convince him. You just take a look at that bay as you pass."

Abigail smiled her appreciation and headed for the feed lot.

Fred Carothers, who was nailing a loose plank in place, looked up as Abigail approached. "Leaving so soon?"

"It's a long walk back home. Not that I mind it—I like to walk." She gazed at the reddish-brown horse. "A little sulfur and molasses will have him back on his feed," she said helpfully. "And I'd add some tobacco to it in case it's distemper." She nodded farewell and left the man staring after her.

Logan Sorrell rode silently, his face, like those of his remaining men, drawn with weariness and hunger. The war had lasted much longer than anyone could ever have predicted. As he shifted his weight in the saddle, he thought back to the days before the madness struck.

He and his brother Andrew and his cousin Travis Dunn had sat on the comfortable veranda of Rosehaven debating how many weeks it would take to drive the Yankees out of the South. No one had guessed the weeks would ravel into years and that defeat would lay at the end.

Logan leaned forward to pat the proud neck of his fine black mount. Miraculously, Caliban had come through the artillery and cannon fire unharmed. He had been the finest of his father's stables and had served Logan well, but now Logan planned to reward him by retiring him to pasture and brood mares as soon as possible. Only one task remained to be done before they could head on home.

But was Rosehaven still standing? Was Andrew's neighboring plantation, Fair Oaks, there as well? Logan shook off the nagging worry. Of course they would be there. He had been born in Fair Oaks, just as his mother had been born in Rosehaven. The two plantations were unalterable landmarks of grace and beauty. He couldn't imagine the land without the noble houses that had been part of his family for generations.

By the time he arrived, Andrew would surely be home as well. Andrew's wife, Marie-Claude, would have resumed her frequent dinner parties, so popular throughout St. Charles Parish, and would be organizing a cotillion to celebrate the return of the men from the war. Logan recalled the day his brother married the beauty of the parish. Royalty couldn't have had a more elaborate celebration and Fair Oaks couldn't have had a more beautiful new mistress to carry on the family traditions.

With a frown, Logan also recalled the night he had enlisted as an officer. Marie-Claude had disclosed an affection for him that would have been much better left unsaid. Especially since she was Andrew's wife. He shifted again in the saddle. Since she had poured out her heart to him in the magnolia-scented garden the night he left, he wondered if everything could go on as it had, though he knew it must. Logan would no more leave Rosehaven because of his sister-in-law's indiscreet declaration than the old house would get up and walk off its land. He knew he would have to avoid being alone with Marie-Claude until her infatuation died a natural death, which it perhaps already had. Logan felt as if he had been gone a lifetime, and he guessed Marie-Claude had changed over the past few years as well.

His cousin Travis nudged his tall gray forward and they rode silently for a while. Travis and Logan looked enough alike to be brothers and were often mistaken as such. They were only two months apart in age and the sons of twin sisters. Their fathers had been distant cousins who bore a resemblance to one another as well. Though Logan was slightly taller and broader of shoulder, both had the thick black hair and ebony eyes of their Creole mothers.

"How soon do you think we'll be there? Tomorrow? Next day?" Travis asked, studying the muddy road before them.

"Tomorrow is my guess." Logan's voice was deeper and more mellow than Travis' and had a softer cadence. During the war Travis had developed a habit of speaking more rapidly, and Logan had noted a harshness, as if anger was barely checked just below the surface. Considering all they had seen, Logan wasn't surprised. Had he not been so tired himself, he also would have been angry. As it was, Logan only wanted to go home.

Travis spoke of his resentment concerning General Lee's surrender. His words were not new; Travis had said the same thing many times during the past month.

Logan sighed as he had on past occasions. "Lee did what he had to. We were outnumbered and underfed. Another winter would have killed us all and the Yankees could have saved their bullets."

"It's a long time until winter."

"What's done is done. For one, I'm glad to be going home."

"If there still is a home," Travis said disparagingly.

"Don't talk like that."

"You've seen everything I have. The Yankees have burned and pillaged all through the South. Your Rosehaven and my Magnolias may be just piles of ashes."

"Then we'll move into Fair Oaks with Andrew and Marie-Claude," Logan said with forced lightness. "You know Marie-Claude wouldn't let a Yankee burn her home."

"If I was a Yankee, I'd be afraid to try," Travis said with a sudden grin. "When she's mad, Marie-Claude can set a man on his heels with just a glance from those steely blue eyes."

Logan didn't answer. He had seen too many homeless women in Sherman's wake. He was sure it would take more than a reproving look to turn aside a Yankee troop. "Rosehaven will be there," he muttered to himself as if it were an incantation.

"At least we'll have money to rebuild if it's not," Travis answered.

Harley Dobson, a teenager barely old enough to

shave, urged his horse within speaking distance of Logan. "How much do you figure is in those boxes?" he asked with the eagerness of youth.

Logan glanced at the boy's freckled face and lank pale blond hair. He was too young by far to have seen all he had, much less to have done the things war had forced him to do. But then Logan doubted anyone was ever old enough for war. "I don't know. More than enough."

"You'll be a rich man," Travis added. "Once you grow to be one, that is."

Harley scowled. He hated Travis' teasing, especially since he had ridden as far and had fought as hard as the older man. In his opinion, there was a world of difference between the two cousins in spite of their similar appearance and Harley much preferred Logan.

He let his spotted horse drop back to ride with the others. As usual, Tobe Tanner was talking about his wife, Rosa, and their brood of black-eyed, midnight-thatched children. Harley grinned. "To hear you talk, Rosa's the prettiest woman to come out of Mexico."

"She is for a fact," Tobe acknowledged in all seriousness. "Best cook as well."

"Maybe we ought to ride on to Texas and take a look at this perfect woman," Harley said to the eldest of the group.

"Hell"—the old man spat out past his tobacco-stained whiskers—"I never knew a Texian that didn't have the biggest, the best, or the prettiest of everything. Just ask 'em."

"She's not the biggest," Tobe corrected. "Rosa's a tiny little thing. Not much bigger than our oldest child."

"Now he's claiming the smallest as well," the old

man complained good-naturedly. "You Texians are all alike. If it's not one thing with you, it's another."

"Well, Martin, that's just how it is. I can't help it if Texas has everything worth having," Tobe replied in a serious voice. His laughing eyes met Harley's behind Martin's back.

The boy rode a little way, letting his horse's head droop lower to the muddy road. "Tobe, I've been meaning to ask you for a long time: how come they call you Tobe when that's not your real name?"

"If you were a Confederate named Abraham, wouldn't you go by something else?"

Martin chuckled softly in his almost white beard. "I gave him the name of Tobe just before you joined us. Named him after an old mule I used to own. As cantankerous an old cuss as I ever did see."

"A mule?" the boy asked. "Don't you mind having a mule's name?"

"I had a baboon's name before," Tobe growled. "A mule's name is moving up in the world."

The boy mulled over the unusual rationalization for a moment, then asked, "What about you, Martin? We've been riding together a long time and I never heard if that's your first name or your last."

"Nope, and you never will, neither. Martin's good enough. Another name along with it would just be confusing."

"It's all he can do to remember that much," Tobe put in. "He probably can't remember the rest himself. He must be nearly fifty years old." A broad grin split Tobe's weathered face, showing strong white teeth.

Harley returned the grin. He had listened to

Tobe and Martin trading insults from Meridian to Appomattox. The bandied words were as much a part of the sounds of the troop as the clopping hooves and the occasional jingle of the horses' bits. But beneath the surface was a comradeship that was missing in Travis' barbed gibes. Harley looked at the two men ahead. Of all the group, Travis Dunn was the only one he would be glad never to see again. The others were almost like family to him.

"I wonder what we'll do now," Tobe mused as they rode past a fire-gutted farmhouse.

"I guess we'll go our own ways," Martin answered. "Though I was thinking of going on to Texas with you. I never saw a perfect woman, or paradise either. Maybe I'll drift over to Oklahoma."

"You can't go 'over' to Oklahoma. It's north of Texas," Tobe corrected. "You'll get lost as soon as we disband."

"There you go again. I was riding all over the country before you rode your first rattlesnake."

"Rattlesnake! Why, we raised the finest horses you're ever going to see," Tobe exclaimed as he leapt to the bait.

Harley grinned. He came from a large, rather boisterous family, but home was going to seem peaceful after riding with Tobe and Martin.

Logan ignored the good-natured squabbling. He knew friendship lay at the core of it. Instead, he fixed his dark gaze on an approaching buggy. None of them made any effort to give way to the conveyance.

The man driving the high-stepping sorrel was dressed in a fine suit with a shiny brocade vest and a ruffled shirt. The woman beside him was decked out in flounces of watered satin in a shade of garishly bright pink. Her frizzy blond hair was done up like a lady's. Her bonnet was trimmed with too much lace and too many ribbons. And the deeply tanned skin of her face and hands gave her away as surely as did her cheap dress.

"Damned scalawag," Travis growled, making no effort to lower his voice as the man guided the buggy into the grass in order to get around Logan and his men. "I wonder what cotton field he found her in?"

Logan glanced at Travis. "Calm down. Haven't you had enough fighting?"

"A Yankee that would take up with white trash is no threat to me." He glared after the buggy and was pleased to see a red flush in the woman's cheeks. They had heard him.

"He's a Yankee, all right," Logan agreed. "No Southerner still owns clothes like that, nor a rig and a horse."

"Scalawags are even worse. A Yankee is bad, but he was born that way. A scalawag is a turncoat. A traitor."

Since Logan's conscience wouldn't let him disagree entirely, he kept his silence.

"I'll bet that a year ago she was no better than a slave and not worth half as much," Travis grumbled. "Do you think the carpetbaggers have slithered as far south as New Orleans? I don't relish the idea of having them as neighbors."

"We'll see soon enough," Logan evaded. He was praying the reports he had heard were exaggerated. Surely the destruction couldn't have been as severe way down in Louisiana as it had been in Virginia. If it were, his world was a shambles indeed. "Don't go hunting trouble," he said as much to himself as to Travis. "If trouble's out there, it'll find you soon enough."

"I just hope nobody found that gold," Travis worried.

"It's well hidden."

"Maybe we hid it so well we can't find it either. It was awfully dark that night."

"I can find it," Logan replied confidently. "That gold has been on my mind for a long time. I can ride right to it." A smile lifted the corners of his lips. Those boxes were heavy enough to make rich men of them all, war or no war, or at least to get them on their feet and off to a new start.

After taking the gold off the Union train in Mississippi, they had been forced to bury it to avoid capture. They had tried on several occasions to return for the gold, but each time a sabotage job of higher priority pulled them away. Now that the war was over, it didn't seem right to give the gold back to the enemy, so they had decided that it belonged to them. Since they had risked their lives and suffered immeasurable losses they deserved the money. Logan had gone over the details of the gold's location each night as a lullaby to soothe himself to sleep. He was positive he could go straight to it.

Abigail stood in Carothers' feed lot and shook her head sadly at the bay horse. "He seems a bit thinner today, doesn't he? Did you tonic him?"

"There's no need to doctor a well horse," Fred Carothers stated in exasperation. The McGee woman and Ida had developed a friendship and she had been over four times in the past three weeks. If he hadn't known they were working on a quilt, he'd have sworn the woman came just to run down his horse.

Abigail laid a small hand on the muscles swelling in the animal's neck. "I saw a horse go like this once. He belonged to my father. He hasn't been cribbing, has he?"

Carothers recalled the dips and valleys chewed in the top rails of all his stable pens. "All horses crib now and then."

She gave him a look that plainly said she knew better than that. "Mr. Carothers, I know I'm being foolish, but I'd like to buy this horse."

"You'd . . ." Fred began to speak, but stopped himself in contemplation. Ida had suggested he sell the horse to her friend, and even had said that Abigail had money to pay for it, but he hadn't believed it. "Why would you want a horse that you've never said a good word over?"

"I feel sorry for the poor beast." Abigail patted the sleek neck as her pansy-colored eyes blinked at the farmer.

"Maybe I don't want to sell him." Fred was a horse trader by profession and he had missed the haggling with other traders on market day. "Then again, maybe I do."

"A smart man like yourself?" Her lilting accent made the words a tickle beneath his chin. "You'd not want your horse to die here. What if he has something the others could catch?"

"I'm telling you there's nothing wrong with that horse!"

Abigail smiled. "You'd not object to me taking a wee glance at his teeth, would you?"

"He's just shy of five years."

She deftly parted the lips and looked at the horse's teeth. They were in good shape and the seven-year molar had not yet come in. "How old did you say?" she asked as if she hadn't heard him.

"Not quite seven years," Carothers altered gruffly. "For a minute I had him confused with that chestful gelding."

"I'll give you fifty dollars."

"How's that?" Fred Carothers leaned forward as if to indicate that he must have misunderstood her words.

"Fifty dollars, I said. And I'll ride him home to save you having to deliver him."

"Mrs. McGee, I wouldn't sell a blind horse, dying of pleurisy, for just fifty dollars, these days."

"You have one down with pleurisy as well?" she asked innocently.

"No! I was giving an example. I wouldn't take three hundred dollars for this horse!"

"Good. Because I'd not offer it. Sixty dollars."

"Sixty! This horse is broke to the saddle and to draw a wagon."

"But can he plow? What I really need is a good plowhorse." She walked around him. "Is he mean-tempered?" The horse snuffled at her sleeve in a friendly inquiry.

"There's not a mean bone in his body."

"I can see most of his bones," Abigail mused loudly enough to be overheard.

"Prime condition!" Carothers affirmed as he ran his hand over the horse's glossy rump. "Sound as a dollar."

"Flatfooted as a frog," she countered.

Carothers lifted a hoof and gestured at it. "He's no such thing. There's not a horse on the place that has better feet!"

"Oh dear," she commiserated. "Sixty-five dollars."

"I sold his brother for two hundred!"

"Did you sell him to a poor widow who has all she can do to keep body and soul together? Who has to spend the rest of her dot to buy a plowhorse because her other one was cruelly stolen?" Her violet eyes reproached him gently.

"Dot?"

"Dowry," she amended, and added, "It's all I have left in this world now that poor William lies buried at Shiloh." She could see she had finally struck his weakness. "Poor, dear William. And me with no son to protect me nor a daughter to comfort me." She peered up at him through her lashes to see the effect of her words.

He was avoiding her eyes. With a groan he said gruffly, "I couldn't take less than one-seventy-five."

"Are we still talking about this horse?" she inquired politely. "I wasn't interested in more than one."

He glared at her. "My price is firm."

Abigail circled the horse. He stood well, his powerful legs parallel and squarely beneath him, his back relaxed, his tail not tucked. His chest was deep and clearly ridged with muscles in the front, showing stamina. His rump rose slightly higher than his withers, promising speed, though she was never likely to need that. His head was broad with intelligence between his clear, dark eyes, and his muzzle was tapered.

She shook her head and pretended not to have heard his last statement. "I couldn't ever buy a horse without trying him out first."

"You want to plow my garden?" Carothers asked sarcastically.

With a laugh as if he had made a polite sally,

she said, "I've seen him drawing your phaeton. I would like to ride him."

"I don't have a sidesaddle. Ida doesn't ride."

"That's quite all right. I can ride astride."

He shot her a disapproving look but went to saddle the horse. He returned soon and bent and offered Abigail a foot up in his cupped hands.

Abigail, who could have mounted by the stirrup as easily as any man, took his lift graciously. She rode the horse in a trot around the pen, then nudged him to a canter. The glossy black mane billowed back from the curving red neck and she marveled at the obediently checked power she felt. The horse's gaits were as smooth as rocking in a chair, and she was determined to have him.

Walking back to where Fred Carothers waited, she said, "He does seem to favor that near hind leg, doesn't he?"

Carothers helped her down then rode the horse around the fence. "There's not a thing wrong with him."

Slowly shaking her head, Abigail patted the horse. "He's breathing rather hard, don't you think?"

"No harder than any horse ever breathes after being ridden."

"Perhaps," she said doubtfully. "Perhaps."

"Do you want him or not?"

"I do, poor thing. Seventy dollars."

"One-forty."

"Eighty."

"One-thirty."

"Ninety." She gave him her best helpless-widow look.

"One-twenty and that's my final say."

"Then one-twenty it is." She took his hand and

shook it before he could change his mind. "Turn your head, please."

"How's that?"

"So I can get my money." She lowered her eyes modestly. "It's on my person."

Carothers turned around abruptly and Abigail beamed her triumph. She had expected to pay twice that for the animal. She counted out six double eagles, rearranged her skirt, and handed them to him.

"Thank you, ma'am," he said, obviously relieved to see her go. "I'll unsaddle the horse and he's yours."

Abigail's countenance took on a wide-eyed innocence. "I assumed the bridle and saddle went with him."

Half an hour later, negotiations were complete and she rode away on her new horse, which she had named Gypsy, the stirrups of the included saddle adjusted to accommodate her height. She reached out to stroke the velvet-furred neck and hummed a lilting tune her mother had brought from Ireland.

All around her, the countryside blossomed with summer wildflowers. Birds called and butterflies skipped over the mounds of clover. War seemed very distant at the moment, and of no concern to her for the first time in years. Abigail found her spirit bounding with healthy youth. She was going to make it after all. If only her William had lived to share her good fortune. God rest his soul.

After her husband left to fight for the Confederacy, she yearned for his return with an ache from deep within her. They had laughed and loved that short year they were together, and her William was the only man with whom she had

ever shared her bed. Many a night she had clutched
a pillow to her breast and pretended he was there
to hold her and to love her.

In time, after the news of his death, Abigail had
accepted the fact that he would never come home;
but the physical desire, the longing for shared
intimacy, had never abated. Most of the time this
had been no problem because her mind was occupied with survival. Now that she had money, she
would have to find other thoughts to help her
through the lonely nights.

Her path took her within sight of the road and
she saw a group of ragged travelers, the women
carrying their younger children. They were former slaves and all had expressions of bewilderment on their faces. Their masters couldn't or
wouldn't feed them any longer, and more of their
kind had taken to the roads to make their way
north, where Yankee soldiers had promised they
would find a land of milk and honey. Carpetbaggers offered land and a mule. Yet the only things
these gullible freemen had actually received were
poverty and homelessness.

Abigail felt pity well up, not only for the travelers who had no idea where to go nor how to get
there but also for their former owners who were
doomed to failure because there was no longer a
work force to produce a livelihood. Slavery was
wrong, but its abrupt cessation was profiting no
one and was filling the road with people who must
steal or starve.

She rode into the sheltering woods and let the
horse slow from its ground-eating fox trot to a
sedate walk. Like a lodestone, the buried gold
drew her thoughts. She didn't know how much

the boxes contained, but she was certain she would never again worry about money.

To the east of her land lay a fine house, once a great plantation. The owners had died several years before the war and the land had been divided up and sold to pay the old master's debts. But the house remained, along with forty acres, and was for sale. Abigail thought of the grand lawns and gardens and the graceful house that nestled in the middle of it all. She would have to hire help to tend the grounds, she thought, and the house was awfully large for just one person; but eventually she hoped to remarry.

She had loved William, but he was gone and she was not. Time had mellowed her grief but not her loneliness. As a poor widow she had had only her looks to entice a man, but as a wealthy landowner she could have her pick. Her odds of finding happiness seemed greater in the latter circumstance. And if no man came who was able to win her heart, at least she would be much more comfortable in the big house rather than in her present farmhouse with its winter drafts and ill-drawing chimney.

The gold would change all that, but she needed to know exactly how much there was. She reined her horse toward the thick woods behind her house. Although prudence cautioned her to wait until dusk to dig up the money, she knew she wouldn't be able to count it all before dark. And since no one usually traveled through those woods, with the road so near, she decided to take a chance.

Dismounting, she tied her horse to a sapling by the curiously bent tree and took her shovel from its hiding place nearby. Soon she had uncovered the three boxes and slowly, with suppressed excitement, raised the lid of the first one. As before, she caught her breath at the sight of so many bags of gold. Taking the one on top, she began to pull open the drawstring.

"Hold it! Stop right there!" a deep voice demanded.

Abigail jerked rigidly and whirled to stare at the dark-haired man in the worn uniform of a Confederate officer and at the gun he had pointed straight at her heart.

3

"Who are you!" Abigail gasped fearfully.

"I'm not going to hurt you. Just put down that bag of gold and back away."

"I'll not be doing any such thing! This gold is mine!"

"No, it's not. Now back off from it or I'll shoot you."

Abigail saw all her hopes for a safe and comfortable future vanishing, and anger replaced her fear. "You'd steal from a helpless widow? For shame, sir! You discredit your uniform!" This line had helped her bluff marauding soldiers from both sides in the past.

He stood firm. "The gold is mine. Keep the bag you're holding and leave the rest," he said calmly.

"I'll do no such thing. Get off my land." After dropping the bag of gold coins, her hand found the handle of her shovel and she gripped it like a weapon. "You have no right here! Leave!" She made a threatening motion with the shovel.

The man made an equally threatening gesture with the gun. "I said I won't hurt you. Now, don't make me a liar."

Abigail jerked her chin higher. "If you take this gold, it will be over my bleeding and dead body." Her words were melodramatic, but she wasn't sure subtlety would reach him.

The gun barrel wavered and Logan Sorrell's

dark eyes grew troubled. He had no intention of shooting a woman, even such an unreasonable one, but he had no time to argue. Harley had seen in the distance what appeared to be a troop of Union soldiers heading their way, and he and the others had stayed back to divert them away from the gold until Logan had had time to dig up the strongboxes. "That gold doesn't belong to you!" he growled threateningly as he glanced over his shoulder, hopeful that the Union soldiers were only a local detail.

"Nor to you!" she retorted. "It's stamped with a northern mint mark."

"How do you know that, when you just now dug it up?"

"This isn't my first trip to these boxes," she said haughtily.

His frown deepened. "You've been spending this money?"

"And why not? It's on my land and it's mine." She decided he wasn't likely to shoot her or he would have done so by now. "I insist that you leave. Get off my land." Abigail's adrenaline was high and her heart thudded in her throat. Again she drew back her shovel as if to hit him.

Suddenly a noise came through the underbrush, then four mounted men rode into the clearing. "It's Major Chandler!" the youngest burst out. "I think he saw us!"

They reined to a stop at the sight of the woman brandishing a shovel at their captain.

"Who's that!" demanded the one who resembled the man with the gun. "Let's get the money and get out of here!"

Logan turned to answer his cousin, and saw Abigail's movement just in time. Reflex brought his free hand up to grab the handle of the shovel as she struck out at him. He yanked hard, bringing her body against his. Gripping her firmly with one arm, he holstered his gun, then tossed her weapon aside. "Get the boxes," he ordered to his men.

As he squeezed her against his chest, he was immediately aware of the softness of her flesh. Her body had turned as he pulled her to him so her back was against his chest and his forearm crossed the heaving swell of her breasts. He hadn't touched a woman in a very long time and his body's reaction to the contact was unexpected.

Helpless tears gathered in Abigail's eyes as she watched the four men smash the locks and empty the sacks of gold coins into their saddlebags and pockets. The captain's horse was brought forward and the remaining gold was poured into his battered leather bags, stamped "CSA."

The boy, his horse and pockets loaded, was looking back the way they had come. "Hurry!" he hissed. "They can't be far behind."

"I'll set them on you!" Abigail threatened. "I swear I will!"

"Shoot her," the other dark-haired man said emotionlessly.

"I don't shoot women," the captain snapped, then added, "Neither do you."

"Let's go!" the boy urged.

When Logan loosened his grip on Abigail, she seized the opportunity and sank her teeth into the arm that had been grinding against her breasts. Shouting an oath, the captain flung the woman from him and she stumbled and fell into the decaying leaves and freshly turned earth. Ignoring the pain, he reached for his horse's reins and with a wry smile tipped his weather-beaten hat as he said, "Good-bye, ma'am."

Abigail's reply evoked a broad grin as he vaulted onto his black horse. Together the men thundered away, leaving Abigail standing beside the empty strongboxes.

Fury shook her and she knotted her fists to keep from screaming imprecations after them. In the opposite direction she saw the Union Army troop that was chasing them. Her first impulse was to ride to the Yankees and show them which way the others had gone, but as she mounted her horse, reason prevailed. If she told the Yankees, they might catch them and take the gold and she would still have nothing.

She leaned forward and clapped her heels against Gypsy's round belly and held to his mane as he leapt forward in pursuit of the Confederates. Her mount was fresh and she soon had the men in sight. They were heading for the old plantation house and the road beyond.

Abigail swerved toward a shortcut she knew and leaned low over the horse's neck as limbs and vines brushed her back and legs, threatening to wipe her off. She broke out of the woods just as the band arrived.

"This way!" she yelled, pointing to her right. "I'll hide you."

"Don't trust her," said the dark man who closely resembled the captain. "We can outrun Chandler."

Abigail glared at him. To the leader she remarked haughtily, "You may be dirty thieves, but I am a Southerner, and those Yankees are my enemies too."

Logan paused for a moment, then spurred his horse to follow the woman. Logic and good judg-

ment weighed against his decision, but his several
years of experience as a saboteur had taught him
that his instincts could be trusted. More important,
the additional burden of the gold had slowed them
and he wanted to avoid any further killing if he
could. Logan's men dutifully followed, but Abigail
could tell from the expression on the face of the
man who had protested that he did so begrudgingly.

Abigail led them beside a curving wood and
over a shallow stream. Beyond, the trees were
very closely spaced and the underbrush was dense,
but she didn't hesitate. Following an old cow trail,
she rode on as fast as possible through the thick
undergrowth. Abruptly she reined her plunging
horse over a small knoll and into the stream that
snaked back through the woods. Keeping to the
water, she splashed upstream, the men following
closely, then veered sharply to the right onto the
bank, then again to the right through a narrow
passage between a large oak and a gigantic boulder and into a shallow cave. The men followed
her in, looking around suspiciously.

"You'll be safe here," she informed them as she
dismounted onto the packed dirt. "The Yankees
will never find this place."

"How do we know this isn't a trap?" the dark
man snarled, unable to keep quiet any longer. He
was the last one to step down from his mount.

Abigail ignored him. To the captain she said,
"Now that I've saved your lives, give me the gold."

He examined her more closely. She was a beautiful woman—a fact he had noticed right away. He
couldn't make out the color of her hair under her
gingham sunbonnet, but her eyes were a most
unusual shade of deep blue. In the dim light they
appeared violet, with a dark rim accentuating them

even more. Her skin was as creamy and flawless as a lady's, though her hands told of the hard work she had been doing. Even her patched and faded dress couldn't disguise her graceful waist and rounded breasts. Unconsciously he rubbed his arm where she had bitten him, the same arm that had grazed those supple mounds. "What are you doing out here in the middle of nowhere?" he asked, having ignored her demand.

The way the captain was looking at her was unsettling. His black eyes seemed to penetrate her clothing, and her entire body warmed a few degrees under his obvious stare. Men had ogled her before and she had been infuriated each time, but the captain's perusal was somehow endearing. For a moment she was sorry she had bitten him. Then the question he asked broke her reverie and she tensed again, shoving intimate thoughts from her mind and hardening herself for the task at hand. "I live here!" she exclaimed. "If you had bothered to look, you'd have seen my house. It stands across the creek and past the small meadow. The gold was practically in my backyard!"

"Your accent is unusual," he answered. "Where are you from?"

"My mother was Irish and my father a Scot, but that's neither here nor there."

"I can't give it to you," he said almost regretfully. "We have each earned our share of that gold. It's not yours." He turned to look back the way they had come.

The muffled voices of their pursuers came to him on the breeze and he motioned for the woman to move to the back of the cave and signaled for silence. As Abigail had predicted, the Yankees had lost the trail after it entered the water, and they now cursed their bad luck. Logan wasn't sure how far away the voices were; but even if the men came upstream, it seemed unlikely that they would notice the well-hidden cave.

Logan and his men had often been in similar situations as they performed their tasks as hit-and-run saboteurs under the orders of General Nathan Forrest, but at those times Logan had been the one to carefully choose their escape route. Trusting the woman, who certainly appeared to be more of an adversary than a friend, had been a reflex rather than a judgment decision. A quick check over his shoulder assured him that his men were alert and ready to draw their weapons if need be to defend themselves. Long minutes passed in the quiet darkness of the cave. Then, as he held his breath, he heard Major Owen Chandler bark out the order to abandon the search of the creek and retrace the path back into the woods.

Before the men could relax their vigil, Abigail stealthily reached forward and eased the revolver out of the older man's holster. The gun was surprisingly cold and so heavy that she had to use both hands to point the muzzle at the captain's dark head. "I'll be taking the gold now," she said.

Logan glanced at her, then spun to face her. "Where did you get that gun?" he hissed.

"I lifted it from him," she said as she nodded triumphantly at Martin.

"Is that right?" Logan asked the old man. "That's your gun?"

Martin felt his empty holster and nodded.

With a relieved sigh, Logan relaxed and walked forward.

"Don't come near me! I'll shoot!" Abigail's eyes were wide and her finger tightened convulsively on the trigger. She had no intention of shooting anyone, but she had never dreamed he would call her bluff.

Logan reached up and caught her wrist to push the weapon harmlessly aside. "Martin ran out of bullets for this gun yesterday," he said, as a loud blast erupted from the gun.

All the blood drained from his face as he yanked the gun out of her hand and turned on Martin. "You said you'd run out of ammunition for this old relic!" he accused.

"I thought I had," the man protested, "but then I found a few shells in the bottom of my saddlebags when we was filling 'em with gold."

The low, resonant growl that rumbled from deep in the captain's throat reminded Abigail of an angry bear. Rushing to the front of the cave, he looked downstream. "Do you think they heard it, Travis?"

"I don't see how they could miss it," his cousin replied.

"I didn't mean to—" Abigail began to say when she had recovered her voice.

"Mount up!" Logan interrupted as he leapt upon his horse, then gave the signal to ride as he sent his animal plunging out of cover and into the woods beyond.

"Wait for me!" Abigail cried out. She wasn't about to let that gold out of her sight.

The men were already well into the woods before she could sweep aside her full skirt and get her foot in her nervous horse's stirrup. As she swung up into the saddle, the animal bolted after the other horses, almost unseating her. She crouched low and held tightly, letting the animal find the way. Having ridden alongside the other horses even that short distance, Gypsy didn't want to be left behind.

After several long minutes of being terrified that she would be knocked from the saddle and lose both the gold and the horse, the animal broke into the open. Abigail dared to look up, and saw the men several yards ahead of her, galloping through the plantation's pastureland. To her left was the house she had so fleetingly planned to have as her home, and the sight strengthened her will. Kicking her heels against the horse, she urged him to run faster.

For the last hours of daylight she chased the men, her horse neither losing nor gaining ground. They avoided the road and headed southwest over farmland and through woods. But by the time dusk had given way to full darkness, she had lost sight of them and had reined in her tired horse for the night. As she sat, feeling his ribs expand and contract between her knees, she strained for a glimpse of them, but she could see nothing. Her hope of ever having that gold again slipped from her, moment by moment. Every muscle in her body was shrieking for rest from the unaccustomed ride, and she simply couldn't go on, even if she had been able to see.

Then, to her relief, she saw a spark of light, followed by a low blaze. They were tired too, and had made camp for the night. Abigail forced herself off the horse but clung to the saddle until her legs could support her. None of her bones or muscles wanted to cooperate. When she could finally walk, she unsaddled the horse. Afraid to let him roam free, she unbuckled the reins from the bridle and made a tether of them to tie him to a tree within reach of the stream they still followed.

Groping in the dark, she found a flat place to sleep. She removed her bonnet and unpinned the heavy auburn braid. Leaving her hair loose for the night, she lay down, using the saddle for a pillow and the saddle blanket's clean side for cover. Hunger rumbled in her stomach, but she ignored it. Tomorrow she would find food, and with luck, get the gold. She couldn't give up.

Rolling her head, she looked back the way they had come. Another fire, quite a distance back, pierced the darkness, and she sighed. She had hoped those Yankees would have given up by now. Quite probably they couldn't see the Confederate soldiers' fire because of a stand of trees or they would swoop down and apprehend them. Maybe they could see it, but they were as tired as she was and couldn't move another inch without rest. She wondered vaguely why the Union Army seemed to be chasing them.

Curling up, she resolutely closed her eyes. Dawn would come too early for comfort, and she couldn't risk losing the band of men before she retrieved her fortune. The ground beneath her was cold and uncomfortable and she heard noises that her safe house had kept at bay. Bravely she told herself that if Mattie could sleep outside with all her children, there was no reason she herself couldn't do the same. Nevertheless, sleep was slow in coming.

Before first light, Logan awoke and sat up. Nearby he could see the bulky shadows of the horses, and all around him lay mounds of bedrolls covering his men. He reached out and shook the nearest shape.

Tobe raised his head sleepily, looked around as

Logan had, and silently sat up and stretched before waking the man next to him. In short order they were all busy, each with his separate morning chores that had become a routine. Weak sassafras tea was brewed to wash down the last of the stale biscuits they had bought from a bakery back in Meridian.

"If I don't get meat soon, I'm going to lose my teeth," Martin grumbled, breaking the silence.

"What's meat?" Logan chided. During the past year he and his men had all eaten meat of questionable origin and had soon learned not to ask where it came from. Even that had been scarce for several months.

"Your teeth are going to fall out anyway," Tobe said conversationally. "Old age."

"Crazy Texian," Martin observed with no malice.

Logan studied the eastern sky and gauged the time before full light. Dull clouds pearled opaquely and the air felt heavy. Rain. He suppressed a groan. Riding in a downpour and sleeping in mud were experiences he was eager to do without.

When Travis finished tying his bedroll, he too glanced at the sky. "We're in for a wet day. Maybe we can spend some of this Yankee gold on a dry bed tonight?" His tone was almost boyishly wistful.

"Depends. We may have lost Chandler and his men, and we may not have. How he ever got on our trail in the first place is a real mystery to me. My guess is he's just lying back there waiting for us to lead him to the gold. If luck is with us, he doesn't know we already have it."

Travis fastened the bedroll to his saddle. "That man bears a grudge worse than any I ever saw."

Logan grinned at the memory of Chandler and his men wandering buck naked in search of clothes.

"I wonder how long it took them to get something to cover up with."

"I don't know, but they have those blue uniforms back on now. Those Yankee quartermasters must work day and night to keep uniforms coming to the troops. I never saw a Yankee in rags." He held up a tattered sleeve from which the gold braid was long since parted.

Logan looked back the way they had come. Pale light streamed down and lay over the meadow. Near the far end, a horse grazed and a figure was stirring. Farther up the slope he could see the wisp of smoke from a campfire. "Would you look . . . Travis! Do you see what I see?"

Travis followed Logan's stare and his black eyes narrowed. "She's still back there, and that fire must be Chandler's." His tone was harsh and he turned to kick dirt on their own dying fire.

Logan tried to pierce the hazy air to see what the woman was doing. Finding Chandler on his trail was no surprise, but to see the woman there as well was amazing. He watched her stretch to saddle the big bay and reach under him to catch the cinch. He looked down at the purple bruise on his left forearm and back to the woman. She was spunky—he had to give her that much. No woman he knew would have tried so hard to catch them. Marie-Claude would never have even begun, but then Marie-Claude was a lady. As he tied the battered coffeepot into his knapsack, he wondered what sort of woman would make such a desperate ride, and whether her eyes were really violet.

Tobe was also watching the woman as he fumbled through his belongings. His fingers found a piece of peach leather he planned to eat at noon, but knowing she couldn't possibly have had even weak tea and biscuits, he set aside the dried fruit. After a moment he added a few matches from his pocket to the food and laid his offering on a flat rock in plain sight. She was bound to be hungry and he hated the idea of a woman sleeping cold with no fire to keep animals at bay. How would he feel if that were Rosa over there? Satisfied with himself, he mounted and followed Logan.

Abigail reached the camp soon after the men left. She had awakened with a start and had instantly panicked when she realized it was already light. Forcing her stiff muscles to obey her command, she scrambled to her feet and whispered a short prayer of thanksgiving when she saw that the men with her gold had not yet broken camp. Her first thought was to hurry and overtake them, but she realized that with no weapon and no plan, such a move would be foolish. If they didn't see her trailing, they might not ride so hard and she could follow them until she had figured a way to get the gold back.

She almost rode straight through where their camp had been, but something urged her to look around. Right away she saw the strip of dried peach pulp and the matches. She followed the riders for a moment with her eyes, then dismounted and snatched up the treasure.

As she continued on after them, she savored the peach leather one small bit at a time until it was gone, then dismounted for a quick drink from the stream. The day promised to be wet and miserable, but at least her gnawing hunger was satisfied for the moment. And with the matches she could have at least a small fire that night to help her dry out. She studied the matches thoughtfully. If they were even the least bit damp, they would never light. Letting her horse follow the others, Abigail tore off a bit of petticoat, wrapped the precious matches, and slipped them under the arched pommel of the saddle and back into the hollow between saddle and horse blanket. They might not stay powder-dry there, but that seemed to be the best spot to shelter them.

Again she nudged Gypsy to keep pace with the others while she maintained her distance. Her body was sorer than she could ever remember, but the horse was rested and lengthened his stride eagerly. Over her shoulder she saw nothing, but suspected the Union troops might still be following them. Until those Yankees gave up or lost the trail, she knew they were all in danger, so she reminded herself to stay alert.

She shifted in the saddle and fastened her thoughts firmly on the gold that was her only hope of salvation. By now she was firmly convinced it was her property. Somehow she would get it back.

Unbidden, her thoughts wandered to the captain. But instead of the anger and resentment of her conscious mind, she was recalling the way he had held her against him, firmly but without excessive force, with an underlying gentleness. He could have squeezed the breath from her lungs, even the life from her body, but he hadn't. She regretted having bitten him, and, especially, that she might have killed him when the gun went off. She didn't want to injure anyone and he obviously meant her no harm, for she hadn't the slightest doubt that he was the one who had left the food and matches. For a robber, perhaps he wasn't such a bad sort.

4

Raleigh, Miss., June 12, 1865
To Col. B. W. Dearborn, Washington, D.C.:

Nighthawk elusive STOP *Still confident of capture*
STOP *Will wait for payroll retrieval before arrest
as ordered* STOP

Owen Chandler, Maj.

By sundown Abigail was again exhausted. All
she had eaten was the sympathy offering and an
occasional drink of water. A dull headache throbbed
in her temples and she felt curiously light-headed.
By now she wasn't sure she could quit following
the band of men even if she chose to, because they
had avoided towns and she was thoroughly lost.
Behind her, as surely as her shadow, were the
Yankees. The only positive note for the day was
that the threatening clouds had rained themselves
out by noon and the sky had cleared within the
last hour.

The Confederates had stopped beside a stream
only a thousand yards or so ahead, and Abigail
waited until she saw their campfire before she
dismounted. She had thought about the situation
all day and had not come up with a single good
idea. She was outnumbered five to one. She had
no gun. The gold was too heavy for her to carry
on just one horse. And besides, even if she took

the gold, she couldn't escape because she was lost. This all seemed so stupid, so incredibly stupid. She had known from the outset that the odds were heavily against her, yet she had stubbornly pursued these soldiers—or bandits, or whatever they were—to the point of no return. She couldn't even go to them and ask the way home because the captain probably thought she had intended to kill him the day the gun went off. All she could do was bide her time and pray for a miracle.

Somehow she got the saddle off the horse and wiped him dry with the blanket. Luckily he was young and strong and didn't seem nearly as tired as she was. She again made a tether out of the reins and led him to drink.

Kneeling upstream, she cupped water into her hands and drank, then splashed the cool wetness over her face. Longingly she looked at the water in the fading light of evening. A bath would be wonderful, even in the cold spring water. Deciding she might not get a better chance, Abigail unlaced her shoes, rolled down her stockings, and shucked off her clothing. Gingerly she stepped into the water as she shook her hair free of its bun.

The stream flowed around her slender ankles, then her knees, as she waded farther out. When she was hip-deep, she paused to brace herself, then dived in. The cold engulfed her, almost making her gasp. Her arms and legs stiffened with the chill and she swam to stay loose and warm up. Having no soap, she scooped a handful of coarse mud as a substitute and rubbed it over her body, then plunged back into the water.

Shivering but feeling infinitely cleaner, Abigail waded out and wrung the excess water from her bright auburn hair. She had no comb, so she ran her fingers through the wet tresses until there were no more tangles.

Looking down at her soiled dress, she sighed. She hated to be dirty but she had nothing else to wear, so she slipped the garment over her head. Bending over the water, she scrubbed her chemise and bloomers as best she could, then carried them back to the saddle, walking very carefully in the growing darkness.

After gathering sticks for a fire, she built a small pyramid on the opposite side of a giant live oak, hopefully out of sight of the others, then coaxed it to flame with just one of the matches. Carefully she arranged her undergarments so they were close to the fire, then sat down in exhaustion.

Across the clearing she could see the faint glimmer of the men's campfire. Obviously they were eating something, and the mere idea made her mouth water. A snatch of laughter, as one joked with another, clashed with the tranquillity about her, and a wave of loneliness forced her to look away.

The soft, dry wood she had chosen burned hot, and soon her underclothes were dry. Abigail stepped out of the circle of firelight and removed her dress. The night air was cool on her bare skin and her long hair tickled against her hips. She stepped into her bloomers and tied them around her slender waist, then pulled the lawn chemise over her head. By now, she mused, the men would be lying down to sleep, their stomachs full of food and their saddlebags full of gold. She yanked up her petticoat and tied the ribbon securely. From habit she patted the secret pocket and fingered the gold coins she had left over from buying the horse. They seemed to be very few in number when she thought of those saddlebags.

Abigail again critically surveyed her grimy blue dress and concluded that she could not bear the thought of wearing it dirty another day. If she washed it now, the fire would dry it by morning. Had she not been so far away from the band of men, who hopefully didn't know she was back there, she would never have considered moving about wearing only her underthings, much less sleeping in them. With her boots loosely laced on her bare feet, she gingerly stepped through the darkness, back to the stream, and soused the garment up and down in the water, working by feel since it was too dark to see what she was doing. When she thought she had done as well as she could, she stood and wrung the water from it. She might be tired and hungry, but at least she was clean.

A thousand cicadas sang reedily in the grass and the smoke made a sooty smudge above her to black out the stars as she spread the dress near the fire and lay down on the horse blanket. The saddle made a comfortable pillow, all things considered, and she was warm next to the fire. If she hadn't been so hungry, she would have been quite comfortable.

Her thoughts drifted back to the little house she had shared with William. Already that part of her life seemed to be from another world. Surely she had never really been confident of the future and so well fed that William had teased her about gaining weight. She ran her hand over her flat stomach and felt the faint ridges of her ribs. No need to worry about gaining weight these days.

Again she wondered about those Yankees behind her. She couldn't understand why they seemed to be so dead set on catching the very men she was after. Surely they had been sent word that the war was over. By now even the ships must have received the news, and they would be the last to know. Perhaps the men she chased were desperate criminals of some sort and she was doing a very foolish thing in trying to retrieve her gold.

But that couldn't be true. Their leader, the captain, had not mistreated her and his eyes had that haunted look she had seen on many a man who was by nature gentle and by circumstance a soldier. Of the others, one was a boy and another an old man. The lieutenant, the man who resembled the captain in a most uncanny way, was a different matter. She hadn't liked him at all, but of course she wouldn't like anyone who had eagerly suggested that she be shot.

Abigail drew a deep breath and closed her eyes. Soon they would get careless and she would have the chance to get back her gold. As she dozed off, she decided to take one of their horses as well. Her own animal couldn't carry her and the heavy gold.

Logan lay with his arm bent behind his head, his saddle serving as a pillow. He had been amazed to see the dull red glow of a fire in their wake and had wasted no time in focusing his spyglass in that direction to determine whether it was the woman or the Yankee major. Throughout the day they had carefully guarded their flank and had seen no one. He studied the dimly lighted area for several minutes, noting all he could. The fire appeared to be hidden behind something, though the illumination from it extended several feet on both sides. He saw no one nearby.

After stepping aside several yards he looked again and this time saw someone wearing white moving about behind the obscuring object. It was the woman! Shifting the telescope to his rested eye, he could see that she was wearing only her underclothing and was waving her dress like a flag. He had not informed the others, concluding that she must be getting ready for sleep and was, thus, of no immediate concern. He was, however, curious as to how she had started her fire without matches. She had no food, he was certain. How much longer would it be before she gave up and went home? Travis came over and sat down beside him. Together they gazed into the ruddy embers of their own fire, discussing the woman who trailed them. "I still say we should have shot her. She tried to kill you."

"You know you don't mean that, Travis. And that gun went off by accident."

Instead of answering, he asked, "Do you think the Yankees are still following us too?"

"I'd bet anything you care to name. They're back there, all right. You saw Chandler. Anybody else might have given up, but not him."

"He may not have a pea for a brain, but he sure is single-minded." Travis' voice was amused.

Logan laughed softly. "He is for a fact." Although Logan kidded with Travis about the Yankee major, he was indeed concerned. They had taken the gold from Chandler's train months ago and had not seen or heard from him until they had been mustered out of the army just after Lee's surrender at Appomattox. The major had been trailing them for weeks now.

"You know one reason we won't lose him? It's that woman. I was thinking that they may even be close enough to see her on the long slopes. If they know she's following us, all they have to do is follow her."

"They have no reason to think she's interested in us." Logan's tone, however, showed he was worried about exactly that.

"Why would a woman be traveling this hard by herself?"

"Let's try to lose her tomorrow. Better turn in."

Travis stood and walked the short distance to his bedroll.

Logan still gazed over at the distant fire. He was sure they could get away from her, but he couldn't keep from worrying about her. A man would be hard pressed to travel all day with no food, and he couldn't imagine a woman trying it. Unbidden, her image rose in his memory. She was a beautiful woman. Not delicate and fluttery like Marie-Claude or the belles he had courted before the war. Rather she had an earthy beauty, born of health and strength. Since neither characteristic had ever been a criterion for beauty in his opinion, he smiled. He had encountered only two kinds of women: the lovely belles who made gracious wives and sweethearts, and the girls of the night such as worked for Sally Hankins in her glittering pleasure hall in New Orleans. Neither of these types of women was tenacious enough to last the day he planned for tomorrow.

He went to sleep confident that the following sundown would find the woman heading home.

Well before dawn, Logan and his men saddled their horses and prepared to ride silently away. The neighboring fire had died to embers, and with the aid of his spyglass Logan could see no sign of the woman moving about.

Tobe looked in the same direction as his captain and shook his head woefully. He felt so sorry for her he didn't know what to do. A woman had no business out here by herself. She just wasn't safe so far from home. He tried to imagine his precious Rosa doing such a thing, but couldn't. That woman must have set great store by that gold for her to go to so much trouble to get it back.

Before he mounted, Tobe surreptitiously left his portion of the new potatoes they had baked the night before where she was sure to find them. He had been hungry before and knew she must be miserable.

Logan motioned for his men to follow and angled into the woods rather than heading out on the clearer path. He couldn't make as much time this way, but he doubted the woman would expect him to go in this direction. When he reached the river, he followed it to a natural ford and the horses splashed across and back into the trees. She would likely wake up, find them gone, and go home. At any rate, she wouldn't catch up with them.

Abigail woke up as dawn was turning the sky to opal. Her first thought was that at least rain wouldn't threaten as it had the day before. Riding in a drizzle until noon hadn't been pleasant.

She stretched, and standing looked over at the other camp. Instantly she was wide-awake.

They were gone! She stared for a few seconds, then yanked on her dress. How could she have let this happen? Surely some sixth sense should have warned her.

Quickly she saddled Gypsy and swung onto his back. Surprisingly, she wasn't as sore as she had been the day before. The long hours of work at her farm had left her muscles firm and supple.

The horse, too, was eager to be on the road and he loped down to the other campfire ashes. Abigail looked around for some sign of a trail and saw instead the small stack of red-skinned potatoes.

Dismounting, she picked them up and sniffed the skins. Cooked! She thrust them in her pockets and got back on the horse. Biting into one as if it were an apple, she chewed thoughtfully. She saw no trail, but that told her something. They must have gone into the woods. Now that she had a day's supply of food, she felt much more confident of overtaking them, although she still didn't know just how she would manage to get the gold back.

Noon came and went before she stumbled across their trail. She had tried logic and reasoning to figure where they might have gone, but perseverance was responsible for her success. Soon the carefully covered tracks she followed turned out into the open where she could ride more comfortably. Abigail sighed with relief and nudged her horse into a lope. Since she wasn't heavy and her horse wasn't burdened with the extra weight of all that gold as were the others, she knew she could catch up.

Logan looked back, more to survey the land they had just crossed than for any other reason. What he saw instead made him jerk around in the saddle to stare. "How in hell did she find us?" he roared.

His men turned and looked back to see a lone

rider just cresting the small hill they had passed several minutes before. Harley and Martin exchanged grins. "Damned if she ain't persistent," the old man chuckled. "Maybe she's part coonhound to track like that."

"She didn't look like any coonhound I ever saw," Harley allowed.

Travis frowned at her, then at Logan. "Do you think that means Chandler's still back there too?"

"Since she tracked us, you know he must be back there. We've been careful about not leaving a trail, but I'll bet she hasn't." Logan rubbed his eyes tiredly. "You know, it was a lot easier during the war. We'd strike a target and then head back for our lines. We didn't have to worry about covering our tracks." When Logan looked back, he said, "She apparently has no intention of catching up with us. She's just headed for cover. How do you suppose she's doing it? Keeping up, I mean. She *couldn't* have had time to bring food along. She must be starved."

Tobe shifted uneasily. "She may have a little food. Some potatoes, maybe."

Logan Sorrell glared at his sergeant. "How do you figure that, Tobe? Wait a minute, you didn't eat any potatoes at noon like the rest of us."

"Well, after all, Captain, she is a woman and all. I just couldn't stand the idea of her alone and tired and hungry as well."

"You left food for her!"

"What if it had been Rosa?"

"Damn it, she's not Rosa! She's trying to steal our gold or lead Chandler to us—or both!"

"Maybe we ought to bring her up here with us," Martin said.

"What!" Logan exclaimed as he reined his horse to a stop and glared at the old man.

"If we had her riding with us, she couldn't lag behind and leave a trail for Chandler," Harley agreed.

"And I wouldn't worry so about her," Tobe added.

"Worry about her! She's after us! She tried to shoot me!"

"Logan's right," Travis said. "She's nothing but trouble. I think we should try to lose her."

"I've been trying," Logan fumed. "Shaking her is like shaking loose your own shadow."

"All the more reason to bring her up here," Martin reasserted. "She'll do less harm with us keeping an eye on her. She don't have a gun and she won't be getting mine again. I'll guarantee that."

"Do you think we lost Chandler?" Logan asked Travis, hoping for what he knew couldn't be true.

"Not a chance in hell." Travis looked back to where the woman had ducked out of sight. "She's hiding now, but I'll bet while she was catching up with us, she left written signposts all along the way."

"I'll go get her. The rest of you keep going and we'll catch up." Logan pulled Caliban away from the other horses and trotted off at a right angle from them. He didn't want the woman to see him ride back toward her. She might spook and head straight back to Chandler. He carefully picked his way back through a dense pine forest.

Abigail had seen the men stop and talk together but she didn't know if they had seen her. She had decided not to overtake them, for she knew her best chance was to merely follow until someone became careless and gave her the opportunity to recapture the gold. By now she had decided to take all their horses, as well, so no one could chase her.

As she looked through the verdant foliage of the protecting underbrush, she noted that one of the men—the captain, she thought—rode off into the woods up ahead. Momentary side trips such as that were common when one was away from the conveniences of home. But then a tense knot clenched in Abigail's middle. Maybe he had seen her and was coming after her. Before she could decide what to do, she saw him cross a tiny clearing only a few yards away. She wheeled her horse and dug her heels into his side. The startled horse bolted and she held tightly, looking over her shoulder at her pursuer. Whatever he wanted, she was having none of it.

"Wait!" he called after her.

Abigail glanced back, noticed he was gaining, and slapped the ends of her reins on her horse's churning rump.

With an oath, Logan raced after her. If she kept going, they would soon be in sight of the Union soldiers who likely followed her. "Stop!" When she rode harder, he spurred Caliban and felt the mighty horse call forth more strength and speed.

By riding hard on her right flank, Logan made her course a large circle that brought them almost back to their starting point. Caliban's long legs stretched and he drew alongside the straining bay. Logan leaned forward and caught the reins, pulling both horses to a halt.

"Take your hands off my horse!" she demanded indignantly.

"Why in the hell did you run away from me?"

he stormed at the same time. "Don't you realize you could have run into those Yankees?"

"They aren't after me!" she retorted.

"These days, no one with a horse is safe."

She hadn't considered that. Looking back, she was glad to see the soldiers were nowhere to be seen.

"Are you going to keep following us?" Logan demanded. "Why don't you go home?"

"There's nothing to go home for. I planned to buy seed and a plow with that money."

"I'll give you more than enough for that if you'll just leave."

"I can't. I'm lost." She glared back at him. "It's your fault. I didn't lose my sense of direction until you started doubling around through the woods."

"I'll give you directions."

"I won't go!"

"Then you'll have to ride with us. Lagging behind is leaving too clear a trail for Chandler."

"The trail your horses left is more obvious than mine."

"We've been very careful to cover our tracks. You were just lucky to find us. But I'll bet Chandler's not far behind you."

"Who is he?"

"He's a Yankee major and he bears a grudge like no one I ever saw."

"You know him? Why is he after you?" She craned her head around to see if he was in sight yet. "Did you steal the gold from him?"

"Never mind about that. Come on. Let's catch up with the others."

"No, thank you, I'd rather not. See, I don't particularly care if this Chandler catches you." She smiled at him sweetly.

"Is that what you plan? To help them find us?"

"No, I'm waiting to catch you off guard. Then I'll take back what's mine." And your horses, she thought to herself.

"I'm afraid I can't allow that," he said as he tightened his grip on her reins. "Let's go."

"Aren't you afraid I'll get another gun and not miss you this time?"

"The gun going off was obviously an accident, but you won't get another chance anyway."

"Wait! How do I know I'll be safe traveling with you? I don't know anything about you ... except that you're being chased by a bunch of Yankee soldiers."

The woman's facial expression was bewildering to say the least. Behind the anger that flashed in her lovely eyes, Logan could see that the fear she voiced was genuine. He didn't want to take her by force, but he would have to if he didn't do something to change things. In an attempt to put her more at ease, he bowed from the waist. "Logan Sorrell of Rosehaven, Saint Charles Parish, Louisiana, ma'am, at your service. And whom do I have the pleasure of addressing?" His manner was straight from the genteel parlors of Southern aristocracy.

"I'm Abigail McGee," she answered, flustered by his sudden politeness.

"I'm the former captain of that group," he explained. "We want to go to our homes, not ravish women. Believe me, I can guarantee your safety with us. With Chandler ... well, who knows?" He gave her a look of direst apprehension. The ruse worked.

Abigail glanced behind her with concern. True, there had been a few actual rapes that she knew of, but still, they *were* the enemy. "I suppose I'll join you," she said as if accepting an invitation to tea. As they started to gallop back to the others, she added, "It will give me a better chance to get the gold."

"Lay a hand on our gold and I won't vouch for your safety," he threatened.

"I can take care of myself," she snapped. "Believe me, I'm quite good at surviving."

Logan looked at her with his peripheral vision. "Will your family worry about you?"

"I have no family living. My husband was one of the first in our country to join the gray," she told him with saddened pride.

"What if he comes back and you're gone? Perhaps you should ride home as soon as possible."

"I've told you, none are living. William never left Shiloh."

"I'm sorry, ma'am. You're awfully young to be a widow."

"So are many women in times of war. Now you can see why I sorely need the gold. 'Tis my hope of surviving."

"A woman like you will marry again," Logan pointed out. He had no intention of giving her the gold, but to deprive a widow seemed harsh. "When the men come home, you'll have suitors and then a husband to take care of you."

"You think I'd marry a man just to have him see to me?" she demanded in outrage. "Trade my name and my body for security? Never! If I marry again, and I think it not likely, it will be for love."

Logan turned in the saddle to study her. "I didn't mean to upset you." In his experience, women expected to marry and be cared for. This was as much a reason for marriage as the procre-

ation of children. Yet she looked insulted that he
had mentioned it. He couldn't figure her out and
she intrigued him. "Nevertheless," he said, putting on a stern demeanor, "you can't travel with us
for long. At the first town I'm putting you on the
road back to your home."

"I'll not go."

"We'll see." He wasn't at all sure how he could
force her to go home. Nothing in his experience
had prepared him for this.

By dusk they joined the others. A low fire was
warming a pot of beans by the time Logan had
unsaddled his horse. He turned to help the woman,
but she had already stripped off the saddle and
was rubbing the horse with the blanket. To reach
the large animal's back she had to tiptoe and stretch,
making her dress mold tightly across her full
breasts. Logan looked away quickly. He had been
without a woman for a long time, but this was no
camp follower. Besides, he had promised her safety.

He reached for her horse's reins but Abigail
intercepted his hand. He gestured at the creek. "I
was only going to water him."

"I'll see to my horse." Years of watching both
armies pillage her farm had sharpened her wits.
If she were in the captain's position, she would
simply turn her horse loose and drive him away.
With no horse, she could scarcely follow them.

"Suit yourself." Logan shrugged.

They led the animals to the water and watched
from the bank as the horses waded a few feet into
the stream, lowered their heads, and drank. Abigail held to the ends of the reins as her horse
stepped in farther and drew in great drafts of
water. Because the sun was setting, she removed
her bonnet and carried it by the strings.

Logan's eyes rested on the dark flame of her hair. For some reason, he assumed that it too would be an unusual color, as her eyes were, and he hadn't been wrong.

"That's quite a horse," Logan complimented, to curb his thoughts. "You don't see many that fine that aren't branded by one army or the other." He didn't want to continue wondering how long her hair would be if he removed its pins, or whether it was as thick and luxurious as it seemed.

Abigail led Gypsy from the water and stroked his velvety nose. "Indeed, I was fortunate to get him when I did or I'd have been left behind the day my gold was so cruelly robbed." She almost admitted that she had used some of the buried gold to buy the bay. If he learned that, he would probably take the horse away as well. She glared at Logan in the thickening twilight.

He gave her an exasperated look and pulled his own horse back to the bank. Silently they walked back to the fire and tethered their horses in the tall grass with the others.

The gray-bearded man was kneeling by the pot of beans, ladling measures into the men's metal plates. Abigail tried not to stare, though the sight of food made her stomach rumble and her mouth water.

Logan was watching her, and when Martin handed him the plate, he silently offered it to her. Abigail's head snapped up and she tried to read his dark eyes. "That's your own," she pointed out.

"There's enough. Take it." When she still hesitated, he said, "The war may have taken our way of life, but not our manners. I would be a poor excuse for a man if I didn't give a plate of beans to a hungry woman."

Abigail took the plate but still looked up at Logan. "Are you the one who left me the fruit and potatoes?"

"No," he answered bluntly. "I had hoped you would get hungry and go back home. There's your benefactor over there. He left food for you without my knowledge." He pointed to a man about his own age. "Abraham Tanner over there is the one for you to thank. He's sensitive about his first name, so we call him Tobe." One by one he introduced her to the others.

Abigail made note of their names and walked over to the man Logan had first mentioned.

"Have a seat, ma'am," the man said with a broad Texas accent.

She sat on a rock and balanced the plate on her knees. "Thank you for leaving me the food, Mr. Tanner," she said as she started to eat the beans. "I hope you didn't get into trouble because of it."

"None to speak of. The captain talks mean but he's a good man. By the way, I'd be obliged if you'd just call me Tobe. Everyone else does."

Tanner's soft speech and gentle manner quickly put her at ease, but Abigail was still wary of the others. She looked over at Logan Sorrell and the man he had called Travis Dunn. She asked Tanner, "Are they brothers? Even though they have different last names, they bear an uncanny resemblance."

"Cousins." As a rule Tobe Tanner was shy around women. Most of them seemed to intimidate him, but with Abigail he felt more comfortable, although he wasn't aware of the difference.

"Where are all of you from?" Abigail had traveled little, in fact most of it had been during the past few days, and she was curious about people from different places.

"Logan there, and Travis, they're from near New Orleans. The boy, Harley, is from a Louisiana town to the west of there, and as near as I can figure, Martin is from Shreveport. He don't talk about it much. And I'm from Texas. We was all a part of the same regiment from Louisiana."

"How did you happen to join a Louisiana regiment?"

"My Rosa, she was about to have a baby when my county formed up. I couldn't go off and leave her like that, so I stayed behind for a few weeks, until she was back on her feet and feeling sprightly. Then I rode off looking to join up wherever I could. This was the first one I come to. They were already headed toward Tennessee when I met up with them." He finished off the beans and waited until Abigail was done. "Had enough, ma'am?"

She nodded and thanked him. She felt as if she would never be full again, but she had seen the amount of food left in the pot and was aware that the captain had not yet eaten. When she realized he was waiting for his plate, she stood up guiltily. In her parents' family the men had always been served first.

She went to the stream, rinsed the plate, and scoured it with sand before rinsing it again. Shaking the water from it, she started back for the campfire, but before she had left the deep shadows, a velvety voice spoke. " 'Evening, ma'am."

At first Abigail thought Logan had followed her, and her heart quickened. The next words dispelled the idea.

"Travis Dunn, ma'am, at your service." The words were mocking, as if he meant something far less polite.

"Mr. Dunn, you startled me," she acknowledged. Something about his manner made her wary.

The man stepped away from the trees and came toward her. She couldn't make out his features in the dark and she unconsciously backed up.

"Logan was telling me you're a widow," he went on.

"That's right. I am."

"You must be lonely, a woman like you."

"Like me?"

"Yes, ma'am. You strike me as the type to really miss a man. Especially at night." Dunn spoke quietly so that his words would not be overheard by those around the campfire.

Abigail's mouth dropped open and words failed her. Even the Yankees hadn't been so forward! She'd had a few looks that she found unsettling, but no one had ever been so blatantly overt as this.

Travis took her silence for acknowledgment. "I'm a lonely man. No wife to warm my bed, nor even a sweetheart. Why don't you come with me down the creek and let me show you the moon?"

"I've seen the moon, thank you," Abigail retorted. "And I've seen the likes of you." He reached toward her and she whacked his hand with the plate. "Keep your distance, Mr. Dunn, and you'll be a happier man." She heard him mutter a curse as he rubbed his abraded knuckles, but she hurried back to the safety of the others.

"Here's your plate," she breathlessly said to Logan. "And I thank you." Had he sent Travis out after her? For the first time since she and Logan rejoined the group, she realized she might be in danger from all those men, even Tobe Tanner. After all, the war had been long, and who knew when they had last been with a woman? She backed away from Logan and glanced to where she had left Dunn. Perhaps she had made a grave mistake in joining them. The least threatening seemed to be the boy, so she sidled over to him and sat down. He grinned at her guilelessly. "Your name is Harley, isn't it?" she asked to make conversation.

"That's right. Harley Dobson from Opelousas, Louisiana."

"Call me Abigail," she said. She decided she needed a friend right now. Logan was staring at her with an undecipherable expression and Travis Dunn had not yet returned. "Where are we headed?" she inquired as she screwed up her courage. Logan rose suddenly and Abigail started, but he turned and walked briskly into the darkness.

"Back to Louisiana. We're going to New Orleans first to see the captain and Travis' plantations, then Tobe is going with me on over to Opelousas, where my folks are. I don't know about Martin. Maybe he'll go on to Texas with Tobe. If it wasn't for my folks, I think I'd go to Texas with him. He says it's really great there."

"What sort of man is this captain of yours?" Abigail poked aimlessly at the fire with a stick, as if the answer to her question held little interest for her.

The lad's face beamed proudly. "He's a good man. I've seen him risk his life more than once to save his men. I'd follow him anywhere." His voice dropped low so she had to lean closer to hear him. "Watch Lieutenant Dunn, though. They may be cousins, but they ain't nothing alike. The others don't believe me, but there's something funny about

Travis. Twisted like. But don't ever tell him I told you so."

Abigail nodded. "I'll watch out for him." As he spoke, Abigail watched his eyes. They weren't those of a boy, in spite of his youthfulness. Harley had clearly experienced things no boy should have. "I'll heed your advice, and your warning is safe with me." Even without the supporting evidence of the incident by the creek, she would have believed the boy with the old man's eyes.

Martin joined them and sat down slowly, as if his joints would have been happier in a rocking chair. "Good evening," he greeted her in his gravelly voice. "You must be tired after such a hard ride."

"I am, a little," she conceded.

"Yeah, we all are. I'm getting too old for this. It's been a real adventure, but the years have taken most of the fun out of it." He pointed his finger at Harley. "Don't you go telling Tobe I said that, you hear?"

The boy grinned. "I won't."

"I'm sorry I took your gun. I hope that didn't cause you any trouble."

The old man chuckled. "That damned thing going off like that surprised us all. No harm done, though. But I wouldn't try that sort of thing again, if it was me."

Abigail smiled at the old man, her confidence rebuilding. He seemed more like a grandfather than a soldier. She wasn't afraid of him at all. "Where will you go after you reach Louisiana?"

"I don't know. I guess I'll tag along with Tobe for a while. He's liable to get lost and never find that wife of his without my help." Martin winked at Harley.

Abigail's eyes followed Logan as he reappeared and stepped toward the fire to get some beans. He was taller than she had thought at first and he moved with a sensuous grace. The apprehension she felt about him only seemed to heighten her interest in him. Crouching, he ladled food onto his plate as the firelight gilded his skin and accentuated the blackness of his hair and eyes. She noticed tired lines in his face that she hadn't seen earlier. He, too, had seen too much. Yet his eyes still held a gentle quality.

Feeling her gaze, he looked up and their eyes met across the fire. Abigail felt her pulse leap unexpectedly, for he was looking at her not as a soldier bent on taking her gold or claiming her body, but as a man who had seen too many dreams shattered and too much loneliness and hardship. Abigail's heart reached out to him in sympathy despite her efforts to the contrary. She looked away quickly.

"We split up at dawn," Logan instructed his men. "Chandler's bound to be back there, and we have to lose him before we can continue on to New Orleans. I recall a place south of here where we can meet. It's an odd formation of rocks beside a lake. Sort of looks like a giant turtle shell." He glanced back at Abigail and regarded her thoughtfully. "Ma'am, I do wish you would just turn around and go home."

"That's out of the question," she replied.

Ignoring her, Logan continued. "The rocks are due south. We'll meet there in three days. Any questions?" When they shook their heads, Logan said, "Ride as if we're scattering for home. They can't follow us all. If they follow you, ride easy for the first day, then double back around and lose them." He stood and looked again at Abigail, then walked away to tell the others.

Martin sighed heavily. "Damn that Chandler. I wish his mama and daddy had never met." He stretched, and said to Abigail, "We'd better rest while we can. I have an extra blanket you can use."

"Sleep close to the fire," Harley said, his eyes noting Travis' return. "You'll be warmer there."

Abigail had seen the boy's glance toward the lieutenant and she nodded. "It *is* a bit chilly. I think I'll stay here by the fire."

5

Abigail mounted her horse and reined the eager animal around. Martin and Harley had headed off together, but as they rounded the nearby outcropping of sweet-gum trees, they separated. Travis was riding due west and would soon be out of sight. Abigail nudged Gypsy to a trot to match pace with Logan's horse.

As he heard her approach, he looked around and frowned. "You heard me say to scatter," he said sternly.

"That I did. However, I'm not under your command, nor was I born yesterday."

"What's that supposed to mean?"

"Maybe you and the others know about these rocks by the lake, but I don't. If I let you out of my sight, you and my gold will be gone forever."

"You won't be able to keep up."

"I have so far."

He scowled at her with a look that seemed more perturbed than angry, then kicked his big horse to a lope. Again Abigail encouraged her horse to keep up, and the bay stretched his long legs obligingly.

Logan led them in an arching curve to the southeast for several hours before letting his horse slow to a less tiring pace. He had tried to ignore the woman beside him, but had been unable to do so. She rode well and had kept up with him without complaint. Curious, he had wondered about the fact that she rode astride the horse rather than sidesaddle. Although he had thought sidesaddles must be damned uncomfortable, he had seldom seen a girl over the age of six straddle a horse. No lady would even consider riding like that.

Out of the corner of his eye he watched her move gracefully with the horse, the reins held expertly in her left hand. He again noted that her hair was auburn—a color he had never particularly cared for until now. He had preferred blonds with porcelain-blue eyes, but this woman was altering his opinion. He tried to determine the color of her eyes but couldn't without looking directly at her. He remembered they were dark, but were they actually violet as he recalled? Surely he was mistaken. No one he knew had eyes that shade. Feeling a bit uncomfortable with his train of thought, he renewed his efforts to ignore her.

Abigail, on the pretext of watching a cardinal flit by, glanced at Logan. She didn't dare look her fill, but she also couldn't resist glancing at him. Never in her life had she seen so handsome a man, nor one with such a royal bearing. His hair was as black and as glossy as a crow's wing. And as a puff of wind ruffled his hair, she noted that he had not plastered it in place with pomade as most men did. From the healthy shine she could tell that it had been well cared for. His eyes were also dark, but they held the gentleness of a summer's night rather than the brittle blackness of his cousin's. Also the shape of his mouth and the turn of his lips promised sensuousness rather than lust. She was glad he was clean-shaven, for she disliked beards and mustaches. She wished he would speak. His voice was deep and mellow like an orator's she had once heard; his Southern accent was musical in her ears.

Late in the afternoon as they stopped on the crest of a knoll for the horses to rest, Abigail pointed down the far slope. "There's a town."

Logan nodded. He was trying not to talk to her.

"Could we go down there?" Abigail couldn't keep the wistful note from her voice. "I had to leave home so suddenly that I didn't have time to pack. I need a change of clothes, a hairbrush, some soap."

Logan imagined Abigail lathering her curvaceous body. "I have soap you can use," he said brusquely.

"I need a bedroll if we're going much farther."

"You needn't go any farther at all," he pointed out. "All you have to do is follow that road northeast and it will take you home." He gestured toward a main thoroughfare that bisected the small town.

"No."

"You don't know what you're getting yourself into. Those Yankees could still catch up with us. Haven't you heard what they do to women?" he bluffed.

"No, what?" she asked with interest.

"I couldn't tell you. It's too terrible. But I wouldn't want anything like that to happen to you . . . or to anyone."

"Then if you are going to protect me from them, you'll be coming into town with me." She nudged Gypsy forward. She knew it was a gamble, but she couldn't figure any other way to convince this man that what she needed was important. If he didn't come with her, she would have to back down and follow him. He had the gold.

Logan knew he should ride off in the opposite direction, but his men needed food, and this might well be the only town around in which to buy it. As he slowly started downhill, he reminded himself that getting supplies was the only reason to go there. The woman could obviously take care of herself, unlike the ladies back home. He could tell from her tone that she didn't fear what the Yankees might do to her. What sort of woman, he wondered, would be so casual about a thing like rape? Dismissing the answer he conjured up as absurd, he moved on faster to catch up with her. She just wasn't that type.

The town was small but apparently thriving, judging from the businesses that lined the main street, among which were two general stores, an apothecary, a bank, and a two-story hotel. The streets were thick with dust but were flanked by boardwalks. Several of the stores even had awnings to protect their customers from the sun and the rain. The townspeople who bustled about seemed accustomed to strangers traveling through, for they paid no heed to the man and woman when they rode in.

Abigail dismounted at the first general store she came to and tied her horse to the rail. Logan did the same, his eyes warily searching the passing people. After a moment he unbuckled the heavy saddlebags and draped them over his shoulder. To leave them on his horse was asking for trouble. He followed Abigail inside.

The store was large and cool. Gaslights lit the rows of shelves even though daylight streamed through the front windows. Abigail passed the bolts of yard goods and went to the rack of women's ready-made clothes. Up until now she had always made her dresses to save money, but her present circumstances made that frugality impossible, and she was glad. She had always wanted a store-bought dress.

Logan had gone to the other side of the store to buy food, but Abigail kept him in sight as she selected a russet-colored dress almost the same shade as her hair and a white bonnet trimmed in forest green. She also chose two pairs of bloomers and some white cotton stockings. Unable to decide between a comb and a hairbrush, she added both to her stack of things, then went to join Logan at the far counter.

She felt extremely extravagant, but she couldn't do without any of the items. She had considered paying for them herself, but since the gold Logan had draped over his shoulder was hers, she decided to have him pay. She hoped he wouldn't embarrass her by refusing. Logan, however, seemed not to notice, or if he did, he didn't care. He counted out the money from his pocket as if it were perfectly natural to do so. Abigail noticed he had also bought two blankets. She reached out to touch the dark brown wool. They were good quality and would be warm.

"Those are for you. I didn't want you to catch a cold," he said without looking directly at her.

"Thank you," she replied.

"No need to thank me. If you get sick, you'll slow us down."

She smiled and didn't answer. Beneath the gruffness in his voice she detected kindness.

After the clerk wrapped their purchases in heavy brown paper and securely tied them with string, Logan automatically took them both, even though Abigail had reached for hers. She was unaccustomed to such gallantry and felt awkward following him out to the street.

"I also brought you some saddlebags," he said as they walked. "I thought you would need them to carry your clothes and your share of the food. They had meat," he added. "I didn't ask what kind."

Abigail's steps faltered and Logan grinned. "It looks like beef, though."

She hurried to catch up with him. "Where are you going? The horses are in the other direction."

He measured the time until sunset and nodded toward the hotel. "I'm staying in town tonight."

"Aren't you afraid this Major Chandler will catch you?"

"He's looking for five men, not a man and a woman. If you want to ride on, however, I won't stop you."

Abigail didn't grace that remark with an answer. She followed him into the hotel and looked around curiously, as she had never been in one before. Her family had been too poor to stay in hotels, and the one time she and William had traveled from her parents' home in Walnut Grove to their farm, they had stayed with his elderly aunt.

To Abigail's eyes the hotel was grand. The registration desk was polished oak, as were the floors, and brightly colored rugs muffled the guests' footsteps. A number of comfortable-looking chairs stood about the lobby, each with a shiny brass spittoon strategically placed for the hotel's male guests. The wallpaper was a floral design of burgundy and brown and the ceiling boasted a large chandelier composed of tiers of gaslights. Abigail stared at it in awe. She had never seen such a magnificent light in all her life.

Logan glanced around the lobby and quickly concluded that the place would suit their needs. The carpets were worn but clean and the place looked respectable. He went directly to the desk.

The manager scarcely glanced at him, as travelers were common. "Ten dollars a night," he said in a bored voice.

"Ten dollars?" Logan repeated. "For a bed?"

"I assume you'll want a private room." The man flicked his eyes over Abigail.

"No, I only—"

"We'll take it," she spoke up. With a smile she put her hand on Logan's arm and said to the manager, "We've only been married a short time."

"That's not—"

She leaned nearer to the front desk. "Since he left Gettysburg, he's been a bit vague." She tapped her temple and nodded. To Logan she said, "Pay him the ten dollars, dear."

He scowled but tossed an eagle to the man as Abigail signed the register as Mr. and Mrs. Mc-Namara.

As they climbed the stairs, he growled, "What the hell did you do that for?"

"You're not leaving my sight," she said, smiling up at him for the benefit of the manager, who had craned his neck around the corner.

"Aren't you concerned about sharing a private room with a man? And why McNamara? I mean, what—"

"It was my grandmother's name on my father's side. They were a fine family and one to be proud of. And, no, I've shared a room with a man before."

Logan found the room and unlocked the door. Had she meant her husband? he wondered. "After you, Mrs. McNamara."

When Abigail entered, all she could see was the big iron bed. Up until now her thoughts had centered on keeping an eye on the gold and she hadn't considered the sleeping arrangements. With neither a sofa nor a chair in the tiny room, the floor was the only alternative to the bed.

While Logan deposited their parcels on the dresser, he studied Abigail. She had been quick to ask for just one room and had even told the manager they were married. "Is that the side you prefer?" he asked, hoping she would clarify her intentions.

Abigail swallowed nervously. She had been testing the mattress for softness while she contemplated her dilemma. She also hadn't thought to buy a nightgown or even a nightcap. "Yes . . . of course . . . this side," she said as she patted the feather mattress again and turned her head to hide the rising blush. Then: "The horses," she murmured to stall for time. "We have to see to them."

"I'll do that while you're bathing."

She looked back at him with a mixture of apprehension and expectation. "A bath?"

He nodded, uneasy at the look on her face. Her eyes really were violet. "I'll order a bath sent up while I take the horses to the livery stable." As an afterthought he added, "I'll bathe at the barbershop before I come back."

"That's fine, but leave the gold here," she said. After he arched an eyebrow in doubt, she added, "The saddlebags must be awfully heavy and the gold will be safer here with me. Who would suspect a woman would be guarding so much?"

"You're right about its being heavy, but why should I trust you? You might take it and run."

"And miss the chance for a bath and the comfort of a real bed? Not a chance. Besides, if the gold is as heavy as you say, I would raise quite a stir dragging those saddlebags down the stairs, thumping and clinking the coins on each step."

"Well, all right, but you watch it closely. I'll be with your horse, so you can't get far."

"That's fair," she conceded.

He took a change of clothes from his bedroll and left without another glance at her. Abigail closed the door behind him and turned the key in the lock. Leaning against the door, she wondered what had ever possessed her to get herself in this situation. He would be back eventually, and there was only the one bed. She reached over and tugged on the saddlebags, then realized that trying to take the gold now would be futile. This just wasn't the right time.

Slowly she untied her dusty bonnet and pulled it off. As she smoothed her dress, she noted that it, too, was travel-stained. She sighed tiredly and wondered if the gold was worth all this exhaustion and deprivation. She was normally fastidiously clean, and washed both her hair and clothes more often than any other woman she knew. Now the mirror above the dresser revealed a woman that could only be described as dirty.

An unexpected knock on the door caused her to jump. After learning that her bath had arrived, she unlocked the door and gladly stood aside for the two men carrying a copper-and-tin bathtub and the woman with a pail of hot water.

After several trips downstairs for more water, the trio had the tub filled with steaming water. The men left and the woman said, "Will there be anything else, ma'am? We have someone here who does clothes, if you need anything washed."

"You do?" Abigail had never considered that a hotel provided anything except a bed. "Yes, I do want my clothes washed."

"It'll be extra," the woman said.

Remembering the gold, Abigail nodded in agreement. She was going to be clean, whatever the cost. The woman helped her undress, and then Abigail, under the pretense of unknotting the string that held up her petticoat, removed the gold coins from the hidden pocket.

Decorously keeping the towel around her, Abigail gave the woman her clothes and locked the door when she had gone. Tossing the towel across the footboard, Abigail stepped into the steaming water and eased down.

Never had a hot bath felt so good. The maid had clearly thought it an extravagance for Abigail to use the bath alone and not save the water for her husband's return, but Abigail had been adamant that the bath be removed in half an hour. She slid lower until her breasts were submerged, and closed her eyes blissfully. So this was what it was like to be rich! She thoroughly enjoyed it. How marvelous to have someone else fill her tub and remove it when she was through.

She took the pins from her hair and let the thick masses unfurl. With the square cake of soap she washed and rinsed her hair, then lathered the rest of her body, enjoying the feel of soap and hot water against her skin. When the water started to cool, she stood up regretfully and reached for the bucket of rinse water. Ladling the warm water over her head, she rinsed away the last of the soap before patting her upper body dry and stepping from the tub onto the soft rug.

By the time the hotel's employees had returned to bail the water from the tub and take it away, Abigail was dressed in the russet-colored gown and had toweled her hair almost dry. As she brushed the rest of the moisture from her hair, she stood by the window and looked out on the town.

Lights were coming on, not only down the street but also out in the fields. Houses that she had not noticed in the daylight were lit like lightning bugs in the dusk. Farther down and across the street a saloon was thriving, though its music scarcely reached her window.

With her hair dried and spread across her back like a cape, each strand glistened. Abigail combed a hank forward and examined it critically in the lamplight. William hadn't liked that shade of hair and had told her so on several occasions, and she had not been overly fond of it herself. But she wondered what Logan Sorrell thought of the color, quickly realizing she shouldn't care if he liked her hair or not. She tried to summon her anger but found that none was left. He had treated her well under the circumstances—even chivalrously. Ordering a bath and giving her the privacy to enjoy it was certainly the mark of a gentleman. Had she not stopped him, he would have asked for separate rooms.

She looked back at the bed and wished she had some alternative. The feather mattress had been soft when she'd felt it earlier, and it looked irresistibly inviting. Perhaps she could lie down just for a few minutes before he returned.

As she dragged the worn saddlebags to the end of the bed and flopped them over the footboard, she recalled how easily Logan had carried the heavy load. The thought of his strength caused a warmth to grow inside her as she speculated on how Logan looked beneath the dusty gray uniform. Regardless of his muscular build, he moved with a lithe grace that Abigail had quickly noted. As she thought of him soaking in a hot tub as she just had, the glow began to spread, but Abigail fought it back quickly. The very last thing she wanted was to be enamored of the man who was stealing her gold.

Pulling back the covers, Abigail lay down, fully clothed, on the cool sheets. A sigh escaped her lips. After nights of sleeping on the cold ground, the bed was bliss. The ticking was stuffed fuller than her bed at home and she felt as if she were floating on a cloud of feathers. She unbuttoned the neck of the dress to make it more comfortable and wriggled her bare toes against the cover. She tried to stay awake just to savor the comfort, but sleep gradually overtook her.

Logan rolled his dirty clothes into a bundle and tucked them under his arm as he paid the barber for his bath and haircut. He had been lucky to catch the barber as he was closing, and had had no trouble convincing him to stay open late and to take his time.

While he had soaked in the hot water, he considered the situation before him. The woman had come with them of her own free will and didn't seem to be afraid that she was the only female traveling with five men—soldiers who hadn't been around a woman in a very long time. She had even implied she wasn't worried about his threat that the Yankees might accost her. He had let his imagination run free and had envisioned what it would be like to kiss her sensuous lips and caress her curvaceous breasts. But in the end he had decided that he wasn't sure what her intentions were. As Logan stepped onto the boardwalk, he glanced at the hotel directly across the street and to the room he shared with Abigail McGee. Until he returned to their room he wouldn't know what to expect.

As he passed the desk, he left his soiled clothing with orders to have it washed and ready by morning. Going up the stairs, he renewed his musings about Abigail. Her insistence on sharing his room put a new light on things. He had been giving her the deference he would a lady, but no lady would ever consider sleeping with a man who wasn't her husband. He had shared a bed with a woman from time to time, but none of them had been ladies.

By the time he unlocked the door and entered their room, he was smiling. Perhaps they could work out an exchange for some of that gold. Even covered with road dust, the woman had been prettier than any of Sally Hankins' girls.

He shut the door behind him and locked it. Abigail had left the lamps burning and she lay quietly upon the bed. As he drew nearer, he saw that she was asleep. Her dress was open at the neck, exposing a curve of creamy flesh. He sat on the bed and pulled off his boots and socks. When he stood to shrug out of his coat and shirt, she shifted in her sleep, causing the bodice of her dress to gape provocatively.

Logan unbuckled his belt and unbuttoned his

pants as he gazed down at the sleeping woman. He had not lain with a woman in a very long time and his body ached with longing. Naked, he slipped between the covers and propped up on one elbow to look at her.

Her hair was fanned out over her pillow, rippling in natural waves. Gently he touched the silken tresses and his yearning grew. Never had he felt such soft hair. The auburn strands sensuously curled about his fingers, stirring in his imagination just how her hair would curve over her breast and whisper against his skin as he caressed her pliant flesh.

Her eyebrows and lashes lay against her pale cheek like a fringe of lace. Her skin was clear, unmarred by freckles or other blemishes. Her nose was small and straight. Behind her slightly parted lips Logan could see her pearly teeth. Drawn as if by a magnet, he bent and tasted the lushness of her lips.

She stirred and smiled as if in a pleasant dream. Encouraged, Logan opened the buttons down the front of her dress. Brushing the fabric aside, he caught his breath on seeing the perfection of her breast. Proud and full, it was peaked by a coral bud that pouted prettily as his fingers brushed against it.

Logan found his breath coming fast as he tried to restrain himself. The woman wasn't merely pretty—she was beautiful. If she were dressed in expensive gowns, she would be more beautiful than any belle in New Orleans.

He drew the back of his hand over her nipple and she sighed with pleasure. Slowly he bent his head and again claimed her moist lips.

Abigail dreamed a man with hair as black as the

captain's was loving her. She tried to call him by William's name, but she knew this man wasn't her husband. He was kissing her in a way William never had, and his hands were touching her in a way she had never before been touched. Desire coursed through her, unleashing wants and needs she would have checked had she been awake.

She moved eagerly toward the man in her dream and heard him laugh low in his throat like a man finding rare pleasure. She dreamed she encircled his shoulders and ran her fingers through thick, damp hair. All the time he kissed her and stroked her breast.

Abigail moaned and held him closer as she groggily drifted upward from the realms of sleep. She held to the dream and willed herself not to wake, but awareness was creeping over her and gradually she knew that this was no dream at all.

Her eyes flew open and she found herself staring at the captain's cheek. He was kissing her deeply, his tongue coaxing hers and teasing the sensitive skin of her lips. His hand cupped her breast and kneaded it gently, sending tremors of desire through her entire body. Worse, she discovered she not only was enjoying his loving but also responding eagerly.

With a muffled cry she shoved him away and struck at him. Her hand bounced harmlessly off his shoulder but she hit him again. He made a startled sound and ducked, then lunged at her, pinning her hands to either side of her head. He found himself staring down into the angriest eyes he had ever seen. To keep her from jerking loose and hitting him again, he held her tightly. She continued to struggle, though her efforts were in vain. "What the hell are you doing?" he demanded, his mind still foggy from her seductive response to his attentions.

"Me! How dare you ... attack me like this?" Her voice trembled with outrage. "Turn me loose."

He drew back and relaxed his grip. At once she slapped him as hard as she could. With an oath he grabbed her hand again and this time he held her firmly. "Be still, dammit!"

"And allow you to rape me? I will not!"

"I'm not trying to rape you. Calm down before you get us thrown out of here."

"I hope you *are* thrown out!"

"If I go, the gold goes with me."

Abigail still squirmed but she lowered her voice. "You are no gentleman," she hissed. "Attacking a woman in her sleep!"

"I didn't attack you. I only kissed you." This wasn't entirely true, so he added, "I thought you wanted me to."

Her mouth dropped open. "Wanted you to ... to molest me? Never!"

"You're the one who wanted to share a room," he reminded her. "You said you'd shared a room with a man before."

"I had nothing like this in mind! And the man was my husband." She quit her useless struggling and glared up at him.

As beautiful as she had been asleep, Logan found her even more desirable awake. Her oddly colored eyes flashed in anger and had darkened to the shade of twilight skies. A pulse pounded in her slender throat and her quick breath made her breasts rise and fall most temptingly. But her distress was obviously real and he managed to curb his desires. "I think," he said carefully, "that we have had a misunderstanding here."

"Not we. You. Now, get off me." She was all too aware of her bare breasts pressing against his hard chest. A furring of black hair tickled against her, affecting her in an alarming way. His shoulders and arms rippled with muscles. His clean-shaven face was all too near her own. "Where are your clothes?" she demanded.

"Over there."

"Turn me loose. I'll not hit you again." She had to get away from him because her traitorous body was still excited from his touch.

"You're sure of that?"

"I promise."

Cautiously he released her wrists and sat up. Abigail pulled her dress over her breasts and clutched the bodice together. "Put on your clothes," she commanded.

"I will not. I've had to sleep in my clothes nearly every day since this war began. This is the first bed I've even seen in months. I plan to get a good night's sleep and I can't do that fully clothed. I'll leave you alone if you'll do the same."

"You can be assured of that. But I thought soldiers prided themselves on being able to sleep anywhere, in any way," she disputed. She couldn't bear the idea of lying beside his magnificent body all night. Not when her own pulses still raced and she found it so difficult not to stare at him.

"If you're tired enough and have no choice, you can sleep in the mud or even on horseback. I've done it myself. But not tonight. Not when I have a soft feather bed and a dry room." He had almost added "a beautiful woman" to the list of luxuries, but that was clearly not offered. He belatedly flicked the sheet across his lap. "Do you plan to sleep in your clothes?"

"Certainly! I have no gown."

"Do you always sleep in a gown ... that is, when you have one?"

"Of course I do!"

"Even after living alone all this time?"

She had never considered not sleeping in one and was startled by the arousal that thought triggered within her. "Yes!"

"Even before your husband left for the war?"

Abigail abruptly sat up and turned her back to him as her fumbling fingers tried to close the buttons. Naturally, she had worn a gown with William. Anything else would have been shameful—wouldn't it? This man brought up questions she would rather not think about.

"I'm sorry," he said contritely. "That was rude of me."

She glared at him over her shoulder. "The rudeness was to fall upon me in the night and attack me as if I were a ... a common slut!"

Logan caught her arm and gently pulled her to face him. To his surprise a tear trembled on her long lashes and her eyes were brimming. At once a protective surge melted through him. As their eyes met, Logan felt something new tremble to life, something that made him realize that his opinion of her had been so very wrong. "I don't think you're like that." Looking at her, he wondered how he had ever considered that she might welcome his advances. "I'm sorry I offended you."

Abigail tried to draw her eyes away but they returned to the apology on his lips. He was so handsome, so vibrantly alive. Unbidden her gaze traveled over his muscled chest and down his taut stomach to the bunched sheet that covered his manhood. A fiery blush stained her cheeks and she hastily looked away. She had never seen any man naked except William, and the two men were nothing alike. William had been boyishly slender and bare-chested, whereas Logan exuded a virile strength.

Thinking she was offended all over again, Logan reached for his pants. Abigail stopped him by catching his arm. His skin was warm and smooth beneath her fingers and she had to try hard to get words to form.

"I don't want you to be uncomfortable. If . . . if you promise to stay on your side and not touch me, you may sleep however you please." Her haunted eyes begged him to understand she really wanted his comfort but that she couldn't yield to him.

Logan paused, then let the pants drop. "If you will feel safer, I'll sleep in my clothes."

"That's not necessary." She swallowed nervously, unsure of her own motives. His nearness sent a tremor through her, yet she wasn't afraid of him. She had to continually repress the emotions Logan evoked in her or she would want him to kiss her and touch her in a way that made her weak with wanting him. And that, of course, was out of the question.

After a moment's pause, Logan lay down and curled his arm behind his pillow. "And you? Are you going to sleep like that? Fully clothed and buttoned up to your chin?" His voice gentled as he remembered the tear on her lashes. She was probably still mourning her husband, and here he was treating her like one of Sally Hankins' whores. He felt as deeply ashamed as she could have wanted him to be.

"I don't mind sleeping like this," she said primly.

"I won't touch you. I give you my word."

"Unlike you, I'm accustomed to decency." She hadn't meant for her words to sound so sharp, but she was fighting hard to keep her earlier dream from becoming reality.

"Suit yourself," he answered in a rebuffed voice. "Will you turn out the light or shall I?"

"I will." Hastily she stood and turned the knob on the lamp. The room melted into darkness.

Gingerly she lay down on the far edge of the bed. When he made no move or sound, she said, "Good night, Captain."

After a moment he responded, "Good night, Mrs. McGee."

6

In spite of the bed's softness, Abigail found she couldn't sleep. The ticking was too sensuously full of feathers and tended to shift her body closer to Logan's. The velvety sheen of moonlight through the windows was extremely seductive. Logan slept soundly, neither snoring nor thrashing about, and Abigail felt his even breathing alarmingly exciting.

Rolling over to face him, she studied his features as he slept. Her body still glowed whenever she recalled his touch and she didn't doubt that he had been at least as aroused as she was. Yet he had stopped when she showed she was unwilling. She wasn't at all sure her William would have done that, despite all his protestations of love. In fact, she was almost sure he wouldn't have, for he had told her more than once that a man in a state of arousal must be satisfied or he would suffer the agonies of the damned. Logan, however, didn't seem to be suffering any discomfort as he slept soundly. Aside from looking regretful, he seemed to have suffered no discomfort at all.

Perhaps he had not been as eager for her as she had thought. Perhaps his actions had merely been overtures to see how she would react. From infancy onward she had been taught that a man would take anything he could get—the moral being that a man was either randy or dead. That theory had fit nicely with William's injunction that she should

never promise more than she was offering, but
neither explained how a man could refrain from
raping her once he had not only kissed her but
also fondled her bare breast.

A frown puckered Abigail's brow as she wondered if her lack of beauty was the cause of such
improbable conduct. Maybe she simply wasn't desirable to him. A lot of men disliked reddish hair
and her eyes were most definitely an odd color.
Abigail found herself longing for hair of spun
gold and eyes of cornflower blue.

Realizing the direction her thoughts had taken,
she blinked and sat up. She should be *glad* she
wasn't attractive to him, for he otherwise might
have done unmentionable things to her body.
Against her will, Abigail found herself wondering
just what he might have done, and her heart raced
at a few of her imaginings.

Catching her breath and her thoughts, Abigail
rolled out of bed. She couldn't sleep, and lying
beside Logan was creating all kinds of problems in
her libido. She went to the window and looked out
at the deserted street. Soon dawn would break.

Common sense told her to take as much gold as
she could carry, get her horse, and leave town.
She even went to the saddlebags and unbuckled
one of the flaps, but then she stopped. This was
too much like stealing and she had always been
honest. To take the gold while he slept was to
confirm that she was no better than the sort of
woman he had thought her to be.

Had he really believed she would welcome his
advances like a common trollop? She had done
nothing to give him that impression. Nothing but
lie in his bed, dressed but without undergarments,
and return his kisses with a fervor that couldn't

have been entirely subconscious. She was very glad that he was asleep so she didn't have to meet his eyes at that moment.

Using the darkness as a screen, Abigail hastily put on her camisole and bloomers, then her petticoat, finally buttoning the dress properly to her throat. She also rolled the white stockings up over her legs and put on her shoes. In the future she would be careful to show him she was as proper as any other lady he knew.

By this time dawn was sending a rosy glow through the curtains and was softening the starkness of night. Abigail looked at the sleeping man. He fascinated her. Why did the sight of him deep in sleep make her long to smooth his tumbled hair?

Turning to the window for solace, Abigail stared down at the street. To her far right, a group of men in dusty Union garb was riding into town, but these days there was nothing unusual about that. Her thoughts were too full of Logan to notice that the man on the sorrel horse looked vaguely familiar.

At that moment, Logan awoke, thoroughly alert as usual. For a moment he blinked in the dim light and wondered what seemed to be missing. The woman! She wasn't in the bed. He rolled over, half-expecting to see his saddlebags gone as well, but to his amazement, the gold was where he had left it and Abigail was standing by the window. He relaxed a bit. "You're still here," he stated.

She jumped and looked back at him. "Where else would I be?"

"You could have taken the gold and left," he pointed out. Her remarkable hair still hung loose down her back, and in the dawn light her graceful form was silhouetted. He remembered the kisses she had returned so freely and how full and warm her breast had been in his hand. All night he had dreamed of finishing what he had begun, and of her eager loving. Now he was embarrassed at having taken such liberties with her.

"I'd not steal it back, although it is my own," she said stiffly. "Whatever you may think, I'm not that sort of woman."

The sound of her voice, with its musical accent, stirred him and he frowned to hide the fact. He decided he had better work a little harder at being detached. "Whatever you say. Now, turn around so I can get dressed."

She stared at him defiantly, so he sat up and started to throw off the cover. Immediately she wheeled to face the window. "I wonder, Captain, that *you* are still here," she said to the room behind her. "After all, you had only to leave me behind in the middle of the night. You and my gold could be far from here by now."

Logan was silent for a minute. Then he answered brusquely, "I needed a good night's rest." She would never know how long he had struggled to fall asleep. "Besides, I couldn't abandon you here. I feel responsible for you in a way."

"Oh?"

"I mean, if you hadn't followed us, you would be safe at home and not lost. No gentleman would leave a woman stranded like that."

She felt stung that he had said "woman" and not "lady." Again she scolded herself for returning his kisses. "I can take care of myself."

"Not the way you're going, you can't. Didn't anybody ever tell you not to go to bed with a stranger? Who knows what could have happened last night."

"Thank goodness you're a paragon of virtue," she retorted. Anger flushed her cheeks at his daring to voice her reproaches aloud.

"That's true," he said with no humility.

"I suppose my virtue rests solely upon your honor and decency."

"No need to thank me." He bent to retrieve his boot from beneath the bed. She tipped her head back and glared up at him. "If it was up to you, I'd be a ruined woman now!"

"You spent the night with me. You're 'ruined,' as you call it, already."

"Where I come from, there's more to being done for than having a night's rest."

"Not the way I heard it. What would your family and friends say?"

"My family's dead, as you know, and as for Mattie, she'd say I was right to keep the gold in sight."

"Mattie?" He pounced on the name. "Who's Mattie?"

"My neighbor, Mattie Grayson. At least she was. Now she's gone to her sister's in Jackson."

"Hah! Then there *is* someone to take you in."

"She's not my kin, only a friend."

"Nevertheless, I can send you there and not have to worry about you."

"I won't go."

"You can't follow me forever. Once we lose Chandler, I'll be heading straight to my home—or whatever may be left of it. What do you plan to do?"

"When I get my gold, I'll buy a farm and settle wherever that may be. One bit of ground is as good as another to me."

"Are you deaf or simpleminded? I'm not giving you the gold."

"You'd persist in stealing from a helpless widow?" She raised her voice to match his.

"The helpless widow stole from me first!" he roared.

"Has ever a woman been more cruelly slandered! It's glad I'll be when our paths part forever!"

"No one is stopping you!" He gestured toward the door, his arm swinging widely. "Go! Part paths now."

"No!" she shouted as she jerked up her chin. "As you've pointed out, my reputation is ruined. You owe me."

"I owe you nothing! Look, you don't know a soul in this town and neither do I. As far as anyone knows, last night never happened. Now, you go your way and I'll go mine."

"*I* know," Abigail stated with dignity.

Logan sighed and tried to hold his temper against all odds. "All right. Aside from the gold, which you can't have, what is it you want?"

Abigail thought for a minute. "I never thought about it," she finally answered.

Logan groaned and sat on the bed to pull on his boots.

"I mean, I lived with my parents," she went on thoughtfully. "Then, when William and I were wed, I followed him without question. He already had bought the land before I ever saw it. When he joined the army, I assumed he would be back and we would pick up our lives as before. When word came he was dead, I never considered leaving. But now," she said with growing excitement, "I've already left. I can go anywhere, can't I? There's no one to stop me."

He stared at her. "You can't roam around by yourself."

"I'm not by myself—I'm with you and the others."

"You're not *with* me. As for the others, there might be one there you'd favor more than you obviously do me." He was still a little hurt by her rejection the night before. He couldn't remember ever having been stopped before by any woman.

"Nonsense." Her mind was on far more intriguing matters than a wounded male ego. "I could travel with you as far as you're going."

"You're not invited."

"Then I'll follow you."

Logan put on his worn coat and buttoned it as he looked at her. Aside from the risk of her putting Chandler back on their trail, he didn't want her taking chances like that. Yet he couldn't have her ride with them. He couldn't imagine her wanting to do such a thing.

"Why are you staring at me like that?"

"I was just trying to figure you out. I never knew a woman who would just take off like this and follow after a band of strange men and not . . ." He stopped short of describing the obvious.

"Your life must have been excessively dull if everyone you knew was so predictable. My mother traveled alone all the way from Ireland when the potato famine wrecked her family's land and hopes. The war has done for my farm what the famine did for hers."

"That's entirely different. I doubt she joined a band of soldiers."

"I'm not journeying to a strange land," Abigail countered. "Will you let me ride with you, or must I follow?"

Logan was quiet a minute as he studied the excitement in her amethyst eyes. "I'll have to think about it." He wasn't sure how he would do it, but he was going to get her on a coach and back to her friend in Jackson.

In the meantime there was the matter of breakfast. The hotel had a small restaurant adjoining it, and as they ate, Logan watched Abigail covertly. She just didn't fit any pattern he knew. As far as he could tell, she had no desire to, either. He began to suspect his training in women was sadly lacking.

After paying for the meal, Logan hefted the saddlebags across his shoulders and then held the door open for her. Whatever he was going to do with her, he had to do it soon. As they walked down the boardwalk, a tailor's shop caught his attention and his steps slowed. For years he had worn the scratchy wool uniform and had been glad of it, especially in the winter, when another layer or two of wool would have been welcome between himself and the elements. Now, however, summer was coming on and already the fabric was itchy against his skin. Also, Chandler was looking for a band of soldiers, and a change of clothes might help them escape his tenacious tracking.

He guided Abigail across the rutted street and was soon trying on a new suit of clothes. "What do you think?" he asked her as he stepped out of the small room in the back of the shop where he had changed clothes.

"You look very . . . nice," she answered truthfully, if with an understatement in her inflection. The walnut-hued coat made his shoulders seem even broader, and the soft shirt he were contrasted with his tanned skin. The buff breeches clung to his muscled thighs as the ill-fitting uniform had not, and she was all too aware of his masculinity.

Logan also bought a change of shirts and small-clothes for himself, and then decided to get a change of clothes for his men as well. The quicker they discarded their uniforms, the easier it would be to lose Chandler for good.

Abigail noticed the tailor's face as Logan casually asked for four more outfits. Logan was obviously accustomed to wealth and thought nothing of the expense involved, but the tailor was used to the poverty brought on by the war. Logan had probably bought more clothes already than the man had sold at one time in the past year. When the tailor's eyes narrowed ferally, Abigail spoke up. "Do you really think we can afford more clothes, dear?" To the tailor she added, "My husband's brothers are home from the war and we would love to outfit them. Do you have something less expensive?"

Logan glanced at her in surprise.

"A shirt of cotton perhaps? Linen is fine, but cotton is just as durable, and less expensive."

The tailor shrugged and showed her a shirt of coarser-grade fabric. "I have this one, but it's not as soft."

"How much?"

"Twenty dollars."

"For this?" Abigail asked in outrage. " 'Twas the shirt I was pricing, not an entire outfit."

"This is good sturdy cotton," the tailor argued. "Twenty dollars is a real bargain."

"A bargain, is it? And me able to buy calico at a dollar and seventy-five cents a yard? I thought that to be as dear as angel wings, but evidently this cotton was picked by Gabriel and spun by Saint Patrick himself."

"That price doesn't seem unfair," Logan tried to interject.

Abigail silenced him with a look. "At this rate, dear, we'll be through all our savings before we ever buy the seeds." Turning back to the tailor, she said, "I'll give you fifteen dollars. Take it or leave it."

"The price is twenty."

"Very well." Abigail dropped the shirt to the countertop and turned to go.

"Al right, all right. Fifteen dollars," the tailor agreed hastily.

Abigail smiled charmingly. "We'll have three others just like this one. Now, about the pants."

In half an hour Abigail walked out of the store beside Logan with a satisfied smile on her face. Logan shifted the package to his other arm and adjusted the weight of the saddlebags. He looked at Abigail and said, "You needn't have bargained with him like that. We had more than enough money to meet his price and still buy the entire county." He had never seen a woman dicker like that with a shop clerk and he was a little amazed by her obvious talent.

"How long do you think it would take before he spread word of you making such a large purchase and not even trying to get a better price?"

"Before the war I often paid that much for shirts," he objected.

She stared at him incredulously. "That was foolishly extravagant."

"Not at all. The shirts were of excellent quality."

"They must have been spun gold at that price. I can see you're sadly lacking a woman's conservativeness. I would never pay so dearly for a shirt."

"I don't see anything wrong with it." He knew

Marie-Claude had paid even more for Andrew's clothing.

"These days, everyone is close with their money. Perhaps you had money to burn before the war, and enough gold over your shoulder now to buy this county, but you'd be wise to keep that a secret. They're men here who would shoot you for less."

Logan smiled at her in amusement. "I can hold my own."

"That's just like a man," she snorted. "You figure a thief would just walk up and ask politely for the gold? No, they'd wait for you in a dark alley or put a bullet in your back." Her voice had dropped to an ominous warning. "If you're not more careful, you'll lose all my gold and your skin as well."

"I'll avoid alleys."

"And what of barren hillsides and lonely roads? It's a good thing we're traveling together so I can help protect my wealth."

"That's where you're wrong. We aren't traveling together," he said as he strode through the door of a square building. "You're taking the next coach to Jackson."

"That I'm not!"

Paying her no heed, Logan went to the ticket window. "One to Jackson," he told the old man. "When does it leave?"

"It's loading now. You might' near missed it."

"I'll not go!" Abigail protested.

"Yes, you will."

"I'll cause a scene!"

"Go ahead. You'll only embarrass yourself."

Abigail realized he was probably right. One middle-aged matron standing nearby was already giving her a chastising look. "What of my horse?" Abigail demanded. "You can't steal him from me."

"I'll buy him. What did you pay for him?"

"Five hundred dollars," she lied. She saw no reason to pass her bargain on to this man who was so determined to cheat her out of her gold.

"Five hundred . . ." Logan gasped.

"I needed Gypsy most desperately. Of course, a horse will be of little use to me with no money for seeds or a plow."

"How much would that cost?"

"Twenty dollars would buy me a start of corn. Now, don't look at me like that. You were willing to pay that for a shirt only a few minutes ago."

"I'm not objecting to the price. I was just wondering who would plow for you."

"I'll have to do it myself," she replied with dignity. "My people are used to hard work."

"Which people, Irish or Scots?" he teased. She didn't look as if she could hold a plow upright, let alone break clods with it.

"Both," she retorted. "Unlike your people, we don't sit back on our porches and have others do our work."

"Neither did I! You have a strange idea about plantation life if you think that's all there is to it. I was riding the fields from dawn to dark."

"You were *riding*," she pointed out haughtily.

"Here. This is enough money to buy another horse and put in a crop." He surreptitiously dipped a handful of coins from the saddlebag.

"Are you daft? Put that out of sight!" Abigail hissed as she covered his hand with hers and scooped the gold into her skirt pocket. "You'll have us robbed right here in the coach station."

"I notice you took it," he hissed back. "Get in the coach, it's about to leave."

"I don't want to go."

"People are staring. Get in."

"No, I'll—"

Before she could protest, Logan pulled her to him and kissed her. His lips closed over hers, effectively cutting off her words, and he felt her sway toward him involuntarily. Her lips were soft and her breath clean in his mouth. He could feel her breasts molding to his chest and he had to remind himself the kiss was only for the benefit of the other passengers.

Reluctantly he pulled back, then steadied her. His breath was ragged and his muscles ached as if he wanted to hold her again, but that was ridiculous. When she opened her eyes, he had to look away lest his very soul become caught in their depths. Yet that was ridiculous, too. She meant nothing to him. "Good-bye, Abigail McGee," he said softly.

She made no reply, but let him hand her into the waiting coach. Thoughts were jumbling into her head and she found it hard to breathe, let alone to speak. Besides, words weren't necessary.

She leaned toward the window and watched Logan walk over to the driver and give him her ticket. Every move he made touched a chord in Abigail's heart, and she imagined she could hear his deeply mellow voice as he exchanged a greeting with the driver. A tight lump caught in her throat and she blinked back the tears from her eyes. Suddenly she realized that not only was the gold important to her, but the man as well.

"Excuse me," she said to her fellow passengers as she climbed back over their feet and knees and out the door.

Her heel caught in her skirt as she stepped on the metal rail and she fell forward, only to be rescued by two strong arms. Startled, she looked up into the palest green eyes she had ever seen.

"Are you all right, madam?" the man asked. Even had his uniform not given away the fact that he was a Yankee, his clipped speech pattern would have.

"Yes. Yes, I only tripped."

He glanced into the crowded coach. "May I help you back inside?"

"No, no. I'm not leaving. Thank you anyway." She tried to pull her arm free, but he held it with a firm grip.

"You just arrived, then? It's not safe for a woman to be traveling alone. Especially these days." His pale eyes raked over her as if estimating her bodily charms. "Most husbands wouldn't allow a wife to be alone on the road."

"I have no husband—I'm a widow," she stated with an edge to her voice. "Unhand me."

"A widow, you say?" His voice held interest and his eyes were calculating. Removing his hat, he made a mock bow, giving her a glimpse of pale scalp beneath his thinning blond hair. "Perhaps I may escort you somewhere. My name is Owen Chandler, Major, Minnesota Third Regiment."

"Owen Chandler?" Abigail gasped. She threw a quick look toward Logan's back. So far neither man had seen the other. Grabbing Chandler's arm, she wheeled him about before he had a chance to see Logan. "Mercy, I do feel rather faint. Perhaps I could use some assistance."

"Gladly. Where will you be staying?"

"At the hotel." She started hurrying him away, then remembered that fainting ladies hardly ever trotted and forced her steps to slow.

"Are you? That's a coincidence. So am I. Room 209."

"Two-oh-nine?" she repeated hoarsely. That was across the hall and down one door from where she and Logan had stayed. "When did you arrive in town?"

"Early this morning. I don't believe I caught your name."

"Moira McNamara," Abigail improvised quickly. "From Georgia."

"You don't sound Georgian," Chandler said flirtatiously. Taking her elbow, he grazed the side of her breast with his knuckles.

Abigail glanced at him sharply. That had not felt like an unintentional touch.

"Perhaps you would like to come up to my room and have a glass of sherry. Only to recover from your faintness, of course."

"I couldn't possibly." She tried to peep over her shoulder to see if Logan were still in sight.

"Surely you trust me. After all, we are both civilized."

"Certainly, Major." She was scarcely listening to him. "By the way, are you here alone?"

"My troop is here, but they have their own rooms. No one would ever know you were there."

Abigail looked at him blankly.

"In my room," he added. "For the medicinal sherry."

"Oh, yes." They were well away from the coach yard now and almost to the hotel. What if Logan had returned to the coach and discovered that she was gone? Perhaps he would go back to the hotel to look for her. "Oh, look!" Abigail exclaimed, grasping at straws. "What a darling bonnet." She pulled Chandler around toward the window display.

"If you like, I could buy it for you," he said suggestively.

Abigail again felt his fingers brush against her breast. She clenched her teeth, but forced a smile, as if she might consider selling herself for a bonnet. "I would like that."

He opened the shop door and she preceded him in. As the clerk took the bonnet from the display, Abigail saw Logan across the street. He was glaring about as if searching for her. Then he turned on his heel and strode toward the livery stable. Abigail glanced at Chandler, who was also peering through the window. He gave no indication that he had recognized Logan, but she couldn't be sure.

"Oh!" Abigail shrieked as she threw herself at Chandler in a feigned swoon. She had never fainted in her life, but she had a pretty good idea how to fake it.

"My God!" Chandler exclaimed as Abigail's weight fell against him. He grabbed at her, but she was so limp she slipped through his hands and dropped to the floor. "She fainted!" Surprise knocked the glimmer of recognition from his mind. To the shopkeeper he said, "Get some brandy."

"Where would I get brandy?" the frightened woman cried. "This is a milliner's shop, not a saloon."

Abigail roused weakly, clutching at his sleeve. "You get it, Major," she moaned. "Hurry. I think I noticed a saloon out back and down the street."

"Why, yes, she's right. Just out my back door there and to the left," the clerk said helpfully.

"Hurry," Abigail gasped as if she were dying.

Chandler stepped over her and raced out the back door. Abigail scarcely waited until she heard the door slam before she leapt to her feet, almost frightening the clerk into a real swoon. She dashed out the front and across the street, holding her long skirts up in a most unladylike fashion.

Logan was standing in the central aisle of the livery stable, next to his black horse. Caliban was already saddled and the bags of gold had been strapped in place. "Abigail!" he snapped. "Why in hell aren't you on the coach!" He wasn't aware that he had called her by her first name.

"Chandler's here! He saw you!" To the stable-boy she said, "Saddle my horse there. Quick!"

"Chandler!" Logan glared back the way she had come. "Where?"

"It's a bit of a story and we haven't much time."

Logan took the saddle from the boy and threw it on the bay's back. As soon as he tightened the girth he lifted Abigail and tossed her into the saddle.

"You'll let me come with you?" she asked needlessly.

"I can't leave you to Chandler," Logan answered as he swung up into his saddle and wheeled Caliban around. "Come on."

Abigail leaned low over Gypsy's neck and dug her heels into his ribs. The animal lunged forward in stride with the big black and raced through the doorway. People scattered in their path and several yelled curses at them, but Abigail looked neither left nor right. She was following Logan and that was all that mattered.

7

Abigail, tired and dusty from the day's ride, shaded her eyes against the lowering sun and looked at the unique rock formation. As Logan had said it would be, the limestone-and-granite outcropping was adjacent to a sizable lake, and she needed very little imagination to see that the designated rendezvous point resembled a giant turtle. The more she looked, the more remarkable it seemed. A flat boulder formed the head and two smaller ones the front feet. The domed "shell" was rounded from centuries of rain and wind.

"It does look like a turtle," she marveled as they rode nearer. "A huge terrapin."

"It's the most obvious landmark around here." He rose in the stirrups, more to stretch his legs than to gain a better view. "I hope the others would be here by now."

Abigail gazed across the sun-spangled water to a stand of pines that wandered in broken file to the lake. "I don't see them over there, either."

Logan dismounted and stretched before leading his horse to drink. Abigail rode into the shallows and let the reins fall loose on Gypsy's neck. "You don't think Chandler captured them, do you?"

"I don't imagine. He was following us or he wouldn't have been in town."

She looked back the way they had come. "Do you think he picked up our trail again?"

"I don't think so, but who knows? I never expected him to track us this far." He led his horse out of the water and started to unsaddle him. "At any rate, we got a long head start. Even if he saw us ride out of town, he would have to muster his men and saddle up before he could follow us. I think we've lost him this time."

"I hope so."

The horse waded a few steps farther in the clear, shallow water as Abigail leaned over to watch the puff of mud clouds created by the animal's hooves. Minnows floated in layers around the bay's black legs and a glossy black bug skittered over the calm water's surface.

"I'll bet there are fish in this lake," Abigail mused. "Big ones."

"Probably so."

"You don't happen to have a fishhook, do you? Fried fish sure would be good tonight."

He grinned across at her. "As it just so happens, I do have a hook and line. Let's see if we can outsmart Brother Fish."

Abigail rode her horse out of the water and was unsaddling him when Logan saw her and came to help. His large hands caught the heavy saddle as she was dragging it off the horse.

"You can't lift that. Let me help," he said automatically.

Their hands brushed and Abigail looked up to find herself practically in his arms. They stood in stunned silence as the magic of their nearness swept over them. Abigail was the first to look away. Ducking under his arm, she said, "I'm quite capable of unsaddling my own horse."

"I know, you come from strong people." His voice sounded gruff and strained.

"I do appreciate it, though," she added shyly.

"Why didn't you wait for me to unsaddle your horse?" Logan asked. "You should have known I would do it."

"Why?"

"Because ladies don't see to their own horses. Men do that."

"Why?"

"What do you mean, 'why'? I'm stronger than you are."

"I've cared for him every day since I bought him. I'm not used to having someone look after me."

Logan was careful not to look at her as he concentrated on rubbing the horse dry with the blanket. "Not after your husband's death, you mean."

"Not ever. We were farmers, as were our parents before us. I worked as hard as he did." She watched Logan tether his horse in the spring grass. After a while curiosity won out and she said, "Don't the women in your family work?"

"They oversee the cooking and cleaning, of course. My sister makes preserves and pickles cucumbers and tomatoes. My mother enjoys cooking some of the delicacies she learned as a child. Her mother was French and taught her to cook."

"You're French?" Abigail asked with interest. "I've never known a Frenchman before."

"My family is Creole," he said proudly. "One of the oldest in New Orleans."

Abigail nodded sagely. "My family on my mother's side has traced itself back to Brian Boru."

"Who's that?" Logan had taken the hook and line from his bag of personal items and was turning over rocks in search of worms.

"You've not heard of Brian Boru?" Abigail exclaimed. "Did you never go to school?"

"Certainly I did," he defended himself. "I just never heard of Mr. Boru."

"He was a great Irish king. Maybe the greatest of them all."

"So you're royalty?" He baited the hook and climbed up the slope of the turtle's back.

"Not exactly. There was a slight complication. Brian Boru was indeed the king and he was the father of my ancestor. However, that ancestor's mother was never the queen. She was a scullery maid. Though a very fine one," she explained, climbing after him.

Logan was surprised to see her on top of the rock, but he made no comment, as she didn't seem to think her athletic prowess was remarkable. He tossed the baited hook over the edge of the rock and into the deep water. Abigail sat beside him and spread her skirts over the lichen-coated rock.

"What about your father's side?" Logan asked as lazy ripples circled out from the line.

"I know less about his people. They were highlanders and what he called a 'braw lot.' My mother said that that meant they were a wild bunch and likely sheep thieves." At Logan's surprised glance she said, "They were always teasing like that. It meant nothing."

Logan nodded with no understanding at all. He couldn't imagine his mother calling his father a sheep thief. They had the most amiable of relationships, and if they shared little to talk about, well, that's the way life was. A woman had her realm, a man his.

"I can remember them out on the fells ..."

Seeing his confusion, she interpreted, "Hills, that is. We grew sheep and used the wool to buy whatever we couldn't raise. At lambing time we would all go out to help the sheep birth. They are stupid creatures and have to have someone with them at such times."

"Your mother helped birth sheep?" He couldn't believe he had heard her correctly.

"Of course, and so did I when I was older. You can't imagine anything so dear as a newborn lamb. We cared for the orphans in our kitchen if Papa couldn't get a ewe to adopt them."

"In your kitchen?" He was certain she must be joking, but she seemed quite serious. Her face was turned to the lake and was glowing with pleasure at the memories. Her eyes were bright and her rosy lips parted in a smile. Logan looked away quickly.

"Someday I hope to have sheep again, though they are more than a bit of trouble." She looked over at him. "What of your family?"

"My parents live with my brother, Andrew, and his wife, Marie-Claude. Our plantations adjoin. Mine is called Rosehaven and once belonged to my grandmother. I inherited it, since Andrew, as the elder son, was heir to Fair Oaks."

"What lovely names. Are they as beautiful as they sound?"

"More so. At one time Rosehaven was regarded as the finest plantation in the parish." He gazed thoughtfully at the water as he recalled other plantation homes that had been deliberately burned to the ground by enemy troops. "I'll be glad to get home."

Abigail puckered the fabric of her dress and tilted her head as if she didn't care what he might answer as she said, "You didn't mention a sweetheart. Is there no colleen waiting back home?"

"Not a special one." He thought he felt a fish tug at the line and he leaned forward expectantly.

A pleased smile beamed on Abigail's lips as she smoothed her skirt. "What a pity."

"My father's sentiments exactly. He wants to see me with a houseful of children. Especially since Andrew and Marie-Claude don't seem to be inclined to have any." He frowned and shook his head. "I shouldn't have said that."

"What?"

"It was indelicate."

"Why? Having babies is as natural as rainfall."

"Maybe so, but it's not something a man and woman discuss."

"Have you ever been told that when you say you agree with something when you don't, you've a small frown right between your brows? It's there now."

The frown deepened. "I've never noticed that."

"Nevertheless, 'tis true."

"You must be spending a great deal of time watching me to have taken note of that."

Abigail blushed and looked away. "How do you expect to catch a fish if you keep talking so?" She turned her back on him and pretended to have a great interest in studying the pattern of wind rippling over the water.

By the time the sun had settled on the treetops, Logan had caught three good-sized catfish and Abigail was frying them in his small skillet. As soon as each filleted strip was done, they ate it while another cooked.

"I've never tasted such delicious fish," Abigail

stated when they had finished eating. "And I never used to like it."

Logan lay back on his bedroll and propped his head on his saddle. "I don't think I've been this full since the war started."

"I know for a fact that I haven't." Abigail left the shelter of the rock and went to the stream to scour the pan with sand. "There have been times I wondered if I could keep body and soul together."

"Oh?" Logan asked. He knew the war had been hard on the soldiers but he had assumed the women were safe at home. "Didn't you put in a garden?"

"Well, of course," she replied through the dark. "But every soldier that went by took a pass through it. The bummers were the worst of all. They followed both armies and looted everything of value they found. When the armies spared me a pan of beans, the bummers usually got it, and like as not took pan and all."

Logan tried to pierce the ring of firelight but the gloom was too thick. "Was it really that bad?"

"Between Mattie and myself we managed. Salt was one of the hardest staples to come by." She rinsed the pan and went back to the fire. Leaning it against a rock near the fire, she let the heat dry it. "We discovered an ingenious way to get it. We dug up the floor of our smokehouses and boiled the dirt. Then when we needed salt we used that water for cooking."

"Ingenious," Logan agreed. He studied her face and tried to imagine the women of his family doing such a thing. But perhaps they had.

"What were the battles like?" she asked.

"Not at all what I expected. There was very little enthusiasm after the first few. Usually we were camped within sight of the Yankees and often we were close enough to call out to each other. We even traded goods when the commanding officers weren't watching. Naturally they frowned on us fraternizing with the enemy. Then the next day we would get up, break camp, and try to kill each other."

"Did you kill anyone?"

"I don't know. I guess so. There was so much confusion at the time, it was hard to tell for sure. Yeah, I guess I did."

The fire crackled softly and a thousand cicadas tuned up for their nightly chorus. Logan twirled a twig between his fingers before flicking it into the fire. "During a battle we were surrounded by noise. Mostly the sound of rifles. After the roar of a cannon being fired, you could hear the ball whistling down and could tell just about where it would hit. The rifles make more of a cracking noise, like sticks breaking, and the hand-to-hand combat was a rattling sound like a bunch of fishing poles rapping together. The worst sounds were the horses." He was quiet as if he wouldn't continue, then said, "They screamed just like humans, and they didn't stop. When a man got shot he might cry out, but then he would usually get real quiet. Not a horse, though."

Abigail had already heard more than she had wanted to hear, but she didn't stop him. Talking seemed to be purging him of horrors.

"After the battle, we picked up the wounded and the dead, but there were never enough embalmers. Everyone steered clear of the tents where the bodies were, because a lot of them were superstitious and the others didn't want to be reminded that the next battle might leave them in the same shape. Most of the time, we had no way to prepare the bodies other than to cross their arms over their chests and pin their socks together. Even at that, the burials were done with as much dignity as we could muster. We marked the names on the ones we knew and just put a cross over the others."

Again the silence grew long and Abigail longed to reach out and comfort him. She wished she could have spared him such experiences. Only later did she realize that her William must lie in just such a grave as he had described.

"Of course we didn't fight all the time. Most of our time was spent marching from one place to another. Weeks or months might go by between battles—but you always knew one was coming." He picked a long strand of grass and tied it in a series of knots. "Luckily I was chosen to head a regiment whose primary purpose was sabotage. One of our assignments was to stop traffic on the rail line behind your house. When we carried out the order, we found that the train was carrying a Yankee payroll. We buried it, thinking we could get it later and turn it over to Jeff Davis, but we marched out before we could do that." He smiled mirthlessly. "We were good at our job. My code name was Nighthawk."

"Nighthawk," she repeated, thinking how the name suited him, with his black hair and eyes and regal appearance.

"I don't know who thought up the code names. I guess our colonel did."

"So that's why Chandler is after you?"

"That's part of it, but the grudge I think he bears is personal." This time Logan's grin was genuine. "When we captured the train we burned the boxcars on the tracks, ordered the Yankees to strip down to the skin, and burned their clothes. Then we put our horses and the gold in the car that was left and stole the engine. Chandler might have forgiven us the part about the train, but he was real partial to that blue uniform. And his dignity."

Abigail smiled at the mental picture of a Yankee regiment traipsing naked through the bushes. "I'm beginning to see why he's after you."

Logan tossed the knotted grass into the fire and watched it writhe to ashes. "You know, I don't really hate Chandler. I don't even know him. I just detest what he stands for."

"It must be very hard to go to battle and kill a man if you don't hate him," she mused aloud.

"If you know your choice is to kill or be killed, the decision is easier. Thank God it's over," he said fervently.

Abigail bent her knees and clasped her legs to her chest as she gazed into the fire's molten landscape. "Do you think it will ever truly be over? Won't you always wonder when you meet a man whether you fought with him or against him? I think I would."

"No, I don't think I'll ever be able to let my guard down." He turned to regard her profile. "Did you really boil the dirt from your smokehouse and cook with the water?"

She nodded. "Most of the sand settled out, but not all of it. Everything tasted gritty, but we had to have salt. Did you really force Chandler and his men to strip?"

"We sure did. Otherwise they might have reached help too fast. You should have seen that bonfire. I've seen that done to boxcars before. After the fire burns out, nothing is left but the iron wheels and axles sitting on the tracks. The next train through has to stop and move them before it can pass."

"That must be a sight."

"You know, I can't picture you behind a plow."

"Nevertheless, I was." She held out her small square hand, palm up.

Logan took her hand and ran his thumb over the calluses on her palm and fingers. She had indeed done hard work. Their eyes met and he couldn't help but think how much she resembled a startled fawn at that moment. Her eyes were dark in the dim light from the fire, and apprehensive, as if she might run away if he moved too quickly. Her cheekbones were highlighted by the faint shadows that lay softly in the hollows of her cheeks. And though her neck was in near-darkness, he could see the pulse that beat strongly there.

Abigail jerked her hand away and stared at the fire. Her fingers still tingled from his solicitous touch and her breath came too fast for comfort. "Where do you suppose the others are?" she asked to relieve the tension between them.

"I wish I knew." His voice was harsh, as if he too had more on his mind than small talk. "If I know Martin, he may have wandered to Canada by now, unless he ran across one of the others. I can't figure out where Travis is, though."

"Maybe they will come tomorrow."

"If they aren't here by noon, we'll have to leave without them. Chandler will eventually pick up our trail, and we can't afford to lose the lead we've gained."

Abigail hesitated, then reached into her skirt pocket and retrieved the handful of gold coins he had given her as she boarded the stagecoach.

"Here," she said with obvious effort. "Take these back."

"What? You're giving gold to me?"

"This was for the purchase of my horse, and now I don't have to sell him."

He made no move to take the money. "So why aren't you keeping the money on general principles? You've been claiming it's all yours the whole time we've been together."

"I've given that a bit of thought today, and it's best that you keep it. My pocket is deep but the gold could fall out and be lost. It will be safer in the saddlebags. Besides," she added, "I've now saved you twice from Chandler. Once in the cave near my land and this morning at the milliner's shop. I figure that entitles me to a fair share of the gold without me having to take it from you."

"What if the others don't agree?"

"Then you will convince them."

"I will?"

"Aye, Captain. You will." She nodded at him decisively as if no sane man could argue the point further.

"Maybe you should call me Logan, now that we seem to be partners in crime."

"I'll do that." She had thought of him as Logan for quite a while now. Magnanimously she said, "You may call me Abigail."

Logan smiled and stretched his feet out to the fire. Although her bedroll was a couple of feet from his, he felt very close to her—comfortable, as if he had known her forever. "Maybe you will decide to settle near Rosehaven."

"Perhaps." This was practically an admission that he would speak up for her share of the gold.

"The land is good there. I'd be glad to help you

find a place." He paused, then added, "I hope you decide to do that. I'd like to see you."

"Would you now?" she asked in surprise. "Whatever for?"

"You're a beautiful woman. I'd like to ask you to walk out with me."

Abigail laughed wryly. "Now you've gone to dreaming. I may not know anything about the kind of life you led, but I know what your people would think of me."

"My family? They will like you." All but Marie-Claude, he amended silently. "You remind me a little of my grandmother."

"Thank you. I was praying I would remind you of a grandmother," she retorted dryly.

"She was small like you, and full of spunk. She kept everybody hopping, from my father and aunts down to the boy that fetched her kindling."

"She's dead now?"

"Yes, nearly ten years ago."

Abigail knew she should let the matter drop, but she said, "Nonetheless, your family will not welcome me as an acquaintance. Our backgrounds are too different. I wouldn't be able to talk to them."

Logan looked at her thoughtfully. In his heart he knew she was right. But that didn't change the way he felt.

"There. You see? That tiny frown is back. I'm right."

"I still want to see you."

"For what purpose?" She drew a deep breath. "I'll not be your light-o'-love. What other relationship could a man and woman have? We cannot be friends or we'd be the talk of the county."

"Parish," he corrected.

"See? I don't know even the simplest of things about your life. Perhaps I should move on."

He was quiet but the lines of shadow on his face told her he was struggling hard within himself. "At least come to Rosehaven with me and see. You could be wrong, you know. Even if you aren't, I want you to stay. I'm a grown man and my own master. No one dictates what I may or may not do. I just spent four years fighting a war to prove that."

"We lost," she replied simply.

His eyes met hers as he considered his reply. What she had said was correct. His family might like her, but they would never accept her. But what he said was also true. When he made his choice for a wife, no one would convince him otherwise.

Wife? he thought, startled.

"Get some sleep," he ordered brusquely. "We've ridden hard today."

Abigail sighed and raised her hands to her hair. She wished he hadn't seen her point quite so readily. With the lowering of the sun, she had removed her bonnet and now she pulled the pins from her hair and placed them carefully inside it. Hairpins were as hard to come by as needles, and she didn't want to lose them.

Taking her hairbrush from her bedroll, she drew it through her hair, stroking the gleaming waves out to arm's length. She liked Logan—that was the truth of the matter. Never in her life had she ever made friends with a man. She and William had been in love and their marriage was an amiable one, but when Abigail wanted to exchange confidences or simply to pass the time of day, it was Mattie Grayson she sought. William had been her husband, fellow worker, and provider, but never her friend.

She looked over at Logan and was surprised to find him watching her. "Can a man and a woman be friends?" she asked.

"Up until now, I would have said no."

"But now?" she prodded.

"Now I think maybe they could."

"Why are you looking at me like that?"

"I was watching you brush your hair. I used to watch my sister do that, but hers is nothing like yours."

"Hers is dark?"

"As black as the night. And not nearly as long or as thick as yours."

"I always wished my hair was dark or maybe blond. Anything but auburn."

"I was just thinking how much I like it the way it is."

A satisfied smile tilted Abigail's lips, but she made no reply. Those were words to treasure, since she had spent most of her life willing her hair color to change.

She lay back and pulled the blanket over her. "Have you looked at the stars?"

He eased lower and gazed up. A dusting of diamonds showed the arching Milky Way against the black velvet of eternity. "It's a clear night."

"I've never spent so much time outside. And I never slept out, not even during lambing season. Now I wish that I had."

"You don't mind it?"

"I would prefer a feather bed like the one in the hotel, but I'm enjoying looking up and seeing the stars and the moon."

"The moon is late rising tonight," Logan said

comfortably. "I guess we'll see it in the morning sky."

"My mother used to make a wish when the moon shared the sky with the sun."

"Is that an Irish custom?"

"I don't know. She often made up sayings and customs to fit the occasion." She thought for a few minutes. "Logan, will Chandler catch us?"

He felt a warmth wash over him when he heard her use his name so easily. "Not if we can help it."

8

"They're not coming."

Logan had been restlessly pacing all morning and Abigail knew he was worried that Chandler might show up at any moment. "Maybe we should leave," she suggested.

He frowned and kicked at a tuft of grass. "Seems like at least one of them would have come by now."

"If we ride in the direction you planned to take, maybe we'll see them."

"Why would they ride on without meeting like we planned?"

"How should I know? I've been with you, not them."

"Well, we can't sit around here waiting for them, it's past noon. Let's ride on," he said, as if it had been his own idea.

"We could do that," she said agreeably.

Logan finished scattering the remains of their fire to make it look as if the camp were several days old, then peered back a couple of times as if he were reluctant to leave the appointed rendezvous before the others arrived; but Abigail rode on without a qualm. She figured the men hadn't been captured, because they hadn't been with Chandler in the town.

Logan kept more or less to the edge of the woods, where they would be less visible than on the roadways. Abigail didn't object. Her big bay leapt readily over ditches and worked his way as smoothly through the grasses as he would have on the road's packed dirt.

After a few hours, they paused to rest the horses and let them drink. Abigail sat on a mossy log and arched her back to relax her muscles.

"This William," Logan said unexpectedly, "was he an older man?" He was looking directly at her but his expression was unreadable.

"No," she said in surprise. "He was twenty-two when he died. How odd," she reflected. "I'm older now than he lived to be. I never thought of that before."

"What did he look like?" Logan's voice sounded begrudging.

"His hair was as pale as fresh butter. Nearly, at least. I believe he got it from his mother's side— they were British. But he was nice for all that. He was more than passing fair to look upon."

"You sound as if you were quite fond of him."

"Of course I was. I married him, didn't I? No one would ever be able to force me into a loveless marriage."

He grunted, propped his foot on the stump, and leaned his forearms on his knee. "How long were you married?"

"About a year, before he was gone. I don't count the two years following, since for all purposes he died the day he and Big Tom Grayson walked off to join up with the army. That's Mattie's husband," she added. "Why are you asking me this?"

"Just passing the time of day," he snapped. Her answers had sparked an uncomfortable jealousy in him.

A crackling in the brush caused them both to

freeze in alertness. The sounds ceased, then came again, this time closer.

"Maybe it's a deer," she whispered.

"Get behind the log." His big army revolver was in his hand as he pulled her over to shelter her behind the fallen tree.

Abigail crouched low, one hand on the bristly moss of the tree, the other clasping her skirts to prevent them from billowing in the wind. "Is it a deer?" she whispered.

He shook his head silently and pushed her head lower.

Peeping over the top, she saw a gray horse and then the rider. She let out a sigh of relief.

"Travis!" Logan exclaimed. "Don't you know better than to slip up on us like that? I could have shot you!"

"It wouldn't have been very smart for me to announce myself ahead of time. What if you two had been Chandler?"

Logan holstered his gun and helped Abigail to her feet. "Where are the others?"

Travis shrugged. "I thought they would be with you."

"We haven't seen them."

The mounted man flicked his eyes over Abigail, who unconsciously crossed her arms over her breasts.

"Why didn't you come to the meeting place?" Logan asked.

"I was . . . diverted. A lonely widow at a farm not far from here needed consoling."

Abigail frowned and walked over to the horses. She was certain the widow must not have been very picky if she took up with Travis Dunn. Even though he had an uncanny physical resemblance to Logan, the similarity stopped there. Within minutes of meeting him, Abigail could tell that he was a man who neither liked nor respected women. She resented his candid admission of promiscuity in her presence.

"How long has she been with you?" Travis asked, nodding toward Abigail as if she couldn't hear him.

"All the time. She wouldn't split off without a saddlebag of gold like the rest of us had. Can't say I blame her."

"You'd better watch her. She'll likely take the gold and be off while we sleep." He watched her move farther away.

"Not Abigail."

"Abigail?" Travis asked with raised brows.

"It's her name," Logan said defensively, then added, "It's a good thing she was with me."

"I daresay." Travis glanced at her graceful form beside the horses some yards away.

"Chandler showed up in town. If she hadn't diverted him, I would have been caught."

"That was lucky." Travis' dark eyes narrowed as if he wondered just how she had done the diverting. "Is he still back there?"

"It's possible. That's why I didn't dare wait longer for the others. Do you think they're lost?"

"You know Martin. And Harley wouldn't know any better than to follow him like a pup. Tobe may be halfway to Texas by now."

"Not without dividing the gold fairly, he wouldn't. You always did underestimate him. Harley, too."

Abigail had mounted and led Caliban over to Logan. "We ought to go," she said.

He swung up into the saddle and they rode toward the southwest and New Orleans. After a while they paralleled a road from which they heard voices and a refrain from "Orleans Cadets." Riding nearer, they saw three horsemen traveling down the road as if they hadn't a care in the world.

Logan rode out to intercept them, the others close behind. "Where have you been?" he demanded.

"Look," Harley said belatedly. "There's the captain. 'Afternoon, ma'am. Lieutenant."

"I guess we got lost," Martin said in greeting. "I didn't see any odd-shaped rock."

"You didn't pass the lake?"

"Sure I did."

"And you didn't see a rock shaped like a sunning turtle sitting there as big as a house?"

"I thought that rock looked more like a monkey or something," Tobe put in when Martin looked blank.

"Didn't look all that odd to me, Captain," Harley agreed. "I thought it looked pretty much like any other rock."

Logan groaned but reined his horse around to head down the road.

"If we had known you meant that monkey rock, we would have surely stopped," Tobe said agreeably.

"I don't know how you figured that looked like a turtle," Martin added.

"Just looked like any old rock to me." Harley nodded.

After they rode awhile Martin said, "We were just planning how to spend all this money. What about you, Logan?"

"I guess I'll plow it back into Rosehaven. Who knows what may need to be fixed by now."

Travis volunteered, "I'm going to head straight to Sally Hankins." To Martin he said, "Sally has some of the best girls in New Orleans. Some white, some octoroons so light they might—"

"That's enough," Logan interrupted, nodding toward Abigail. "If you ask me," he said in a kinder voice, "you would do better to spend it on the Magnolias. It won't be easy to run a plantation these days."

Travis snorted. "There will be time for that later. In the meantime, I have four years of living to make up. Hell, I may buy Sally Hankins' place, girls and all, and move in there." He nudged Martin. "Wouldn't that be something? Living in your own whorehouse?"

The older man glanced at Abigail's flaming cheeks and made a noncommittal grunt.

"I know what I'm going to do," Tobe spoke up. "I'm going to buy my Rosa the prettiest dress in Texas and all the tamales she can eat."

"She must have a powerful hunger if she can eat her way through all that gold," Martin observed.

"What do you mean by that?" Tobe demanded.

"Nothing. You can't tease a Texian. They're too damned hotheaded," he muttered to his horse.

"I'm not hotheaded!"

"You're a Texian, ain't you?"

"Just don't you go running down my Rosa." To his own horse Tobe added, "The old geezer is probably a damned Yankee spy."

"Crazy Texian," Martin mumbled.

Logan was ignoring the banter and said to Travis, "You know, I almost dread seeing Rosehaven after all the ruins we've passed. Maybe it's burned to the ground too."

Travis was silent a minute before he said, "It's just a house. You can rebuild."

"You don't believe that."

Travis didn't dispute him.

"If our plantations are gone, or even if they're not, what do you suppose will become of our way of life? These past months I've been thinking about that a lot. We weren't taught to do anything but run a plantation, Travis. Whatever we find when we get there, that way of life is gone forever."

After a moment Travis grinned. "You can move in with Sally and me." He laughed and spurred his horse ahead before Logan could reprimand him again.

Logan looked over at Abigail, who was pointedly ignoring Travis' remarks. "He didn't mean to be offensive," he said apologetically.

"No?"

"In some ways the war has been harder on Travis than on any of us."

"Does that excuse him?"

"No, but it explains him. We all have scars from this, some deeper than others."

She didn't reply but she knew Travis would never have made such off-color statements in front of his own people. At least she didn't think he would. "He's not like you," she observed aloud.

"No? Most people confuse us all the time."

"You just look alike. He's like a bad copy." Watching the man ahead of her, she added, "He frightens me."

"Travis? Don't be silly. I've known him all my life. We even shared the same cradle when our mothers visited each other. How could you be afraid of him?"

"I just am, that's all." She continued to watch him warily.

*   *   *

The campfire burned low and steadily and in the distance an owl hooted over its successful hunt. The men and Abigail sat on their bedrolls, not yet sleepy, but lulled by the supper they had eaten. Reminiscences floated around the circle of firelight.

"I recall fighting somewhere around here," Harley said. "Can't quite remember where. It's sure a lot more peaceful these days."

"I recollect that," Martin agreed. "Seems like it was north of here a piece. Old Whistling Dick was there." To Abigail he explained, "Whistling Dick was a cannon. It had a real peculiar whistling sound that you could recognize just like it was a human voice."

"Why was that?" she asked.

"I don't know. I don't know a thing in this world about cannons except to stay out from in front of 'em."

"I remember that battle," Tobe joined in. "That was the last time I went to a real honest-to-God barber. Remember? He came out from Hattiesburg to where we were camped and set up to do business. He must have made a small fortune that day."

"Have you ever noticed," Travis mused, "how many freemen are barbers?"

"I've noticed, but I don't rightly know why that is," Martin agreed. "It is an uncommon amount, though."

"Maybe a barbershop is cheap to set up," Harley suggested. "All you need is a razor, shaving soap, and maybe some bay rum and pomade."

"I think the boy has been looking into it," Travis teased. "Are you planning to set up a business?"

The boy scowled and didn't answer.

Abigail watched the exchange silently.

"That was some battle," Martin said, steering the subject away from his young friend. "Beecher's Bibles was raising Cain that day."

"What kind of Bible is that?" Abigail asked.

"It's a nickname for a Yankee rifle," Logan explained. "They're Sharps, and very accurate."

The crackling of the fire and the songs of crickets filled the silence that followed. The owl called out again from farther back in the woods. Tobe absentmindedly hummed a refrain from "O, I'm a Good Old Rebel."

"I guess we'll have to learn new songs now," Travis commented.

"There won't never be a sound as sweet as 'Dixie,'" Martin affirmed.

"I'd give anything if we had won," Harley murmured. "Losing sure goes against my grain."

"It's going to change our lives," Logan replied. "The South will never be the same again."

"Lee shouldn't have surrendered," Travis spoke up.

"We couldn't fight without bullets," Logan argued. "We've all seen soldiers using their rifles as clubs because they had no ammunition."

"You know," Travis said, "we shouldn't have to take this defeat."

"Do you plan to start a new war?" Logan smiled. "This one is over."

"No, but think about it. We've passed several carpetbaggers in the last few days. All of them look fat and sassy. They must have money."

"So do we," Logan pointed out.

"I was thinking more along the lines of sabotage," Travis said. "Like the raids we pulled in the war. Nobody stopped us."

"Tell that to Anderson and Peterson," Logan answered dryly.

"They died in battle, not a raid." Travis leaned forward conspiratorially. "We could still do our part to disrupt the Yankees by robbing these carpetbaggers and the banks they frequent."

"Rob a bank?" Tobe asked. "That's illegal."

"Even in Texas," Martin added, and grinned at Tobe.

"I'm serious," Travis affirmed. "We could take the Yankee gold and use it to help the South get back on its feet."

"Like Robin Hood?" Harley asked.

"How would you know Yankee gold from Rebel gold?" Tobe objected. "I don't want any part of it."

"That's an idea," Martin said thoughtfully. "The Yankees sure as hell aren't going to help us get ahead. Lincoln made some grand promises, but he's dead now."

"How would you use the money?" Harley asked. "Would you give it to the poor?"

"There's too many poor people," Travis scoffed. "You could pour out gold all day and not do any real good. I would give it to the generals or use it to get Jeff Davis out of that prison at Fort Monroe."

Harley shook his head. "I'm not interested. I've had all the war I can stand."

"Me too," Tobe echoed. "I'm sorry we lost, but I'm glad it's over."

"How about it, Logan?" Travis asked. "You aren't talking much. Are you with us?"

"No. No, I'm not, and neither are you. Aunt Lucy would skin me if I let you get into a mess such as that."

"Mother will never know."

"You mean you're really serious about this?"

"Of course I am!"

Logan studied his cousin's earnest face. "Travis, you're not going to do this. All kidding aside, I can't let you. Robbery is against the law. You'll end up in prison or worse."

"I've heard the prison at Belle Isle doesn't even have a shelter to get under," Tobe told him. "The men eat crackers and fat meat ground up with corn cobs and sawdust. You want to eat sawdust? I don't."

"That's an army prison," Martin said as he stared thoughtfully at the fire.

"I don't plan to get caught," Travis retorted with a frown at Tobe.

"You're not going to do it," Logan repeated. "No man of my regiment is going to steal."

"You seem to be forgetting we were mustered out." Travis' anger was barely held in check. "You aren't our commanding officer anymore."

"I'm still your kin," Logan replied, "and I won't let you do it." He ended the discussion by standing and holding out his hand to Abigail. "Care to go for a walk?"

She didn't hesitate. The fanatical note in Travis' voice had frightened her, as did the black anger smoldering in his eyes. This man was dangerous and she was eager to be away from him.

She fell into step by Logan, not touching him but yearning to. "Is his plantation near yours?" she asked after they had walked awhile in silence.

"Within the same parish, but his is farther west."

"Do you think he meant what he said? About robbing banks?"

"No, Travis has always been more apt to talk than to do."

"I think he meant it."

Logan didn't respond. He wasn't all that sure that Travis was just blowing off steam either, but he didn't want to admit it. He pulled a limb aside for her to pass.

As before, they had camped by a stream. Abigail walked along a cow trail that led beside the water. A series of submerged tree trunks and rocks made a miniature rapids that sang to the night, and an almost full moon silvered the leaves on the trees.

"Are you afraid to be in the woods at night?" Logan asked.

"Of course not. There's nothing here in the dark that isn't here by daylight."

"I was almost hoping you would say you are, so I'd have a reason to put my arm around you for protection."

"Why, Captain, are you flirting with me?" Abigail asked, a smile curling her mouth.

"Not Captain, just plain Logan Sorrell. We've all been mustered out. Remember?"

"Not plain to my eyes," she answered. "And you don't seem to me to be shy enough to need an excuse." She stopped walking and tilted her head to regard him.

"I never quite know how to talk to you," he pondered aloud. "You don't play by the rules."

"I don't know the rules," she said softly. "I only know that if a man is taken with a woman, he must give her a sign. Otherwise no one gets anywhere."

"You're also uncommonly outspoken."

"Yes, that's always been a failing with me. Do you mind too much?"

He put his arm around her and smiled down at

her moon-pearled face. "I don't mind at all. It just takes some getting used to, that's all." He touched her smooth cheek and stroked the firm line of her chin. "Would you mind if I kissed you?"

"Yes. I would mind a great deal." Her eyes flashed and she pushed him away. "When a man kisses me, I want him to just do it, not ask my permission. If you've not got it in your heart, don't do it."

"I didn't mean to make you angry," Logan said in confusion.

"I know. You only meant to give me honeyed words and stilted phrases, as if I were a languishing magnolia blossom cosseted on a shady porch." She turned and stalked away, her arms folded tightly about her. "I'm a real woman, Logan, not some porcelain doll. If you—"

He grabbed her, whirled her around, and kissed her, not even giving her time to uncross her arms.

Abigail gasped at the unexpected embrace when she was able, and at once his lips again closed over hers. His tongue, warm and insistent, flicked over her lips and she opened them instinctively. A small sound escaped her and she swayed toward him as her arms encircled his shoulders. His hair was thick and rich beneath her fingers as she urged him to kiss her again and again.

Her heart raced and matched the rhythm of his own as her breasts melded against the strength of his chest. A curious weakness threatened to buckle her knees, but he held her securely as if she were as light as thistledown. Indeed, she felt no heavier than that as her soul winged upward to meet his. She was as light-headed as if she had gone out in the sun without wearing a bonnet, but this was a delicious feeling. One that made warmth course through her veins and left her craving more of him.

At last he lifted his head and she clung to him as if he were the pillar of her strength. "Is that more what you had in mind?" he asked hoarsely.

She managed to nod, but words failed her. His kisses were like nothing she had ever experienced before. As naturally as moonbeams she lifted her head and pulled him toward her for another deep embrace.

He smiled as if surprised but pleased with her eagerness. This time his hands stroked over her back, traveling the shallow groove of her spine and passing back up her ribs. He felt the outer swell of her breast and rubbed his thumb over it. When she didn't pull away but kissed him deeper, he ran his hand beneath her breast and cupped the fullness in his palm until her nipple grew taut. He ran his thumb over the quickening bud and longed to tear away the fabric that impeded him. Memories of her coral-and-ivory beauty tormented him and he pressed his body longingly against her.

Abigail felt the hardness of his desire and an almost desperate longing surged through her. She wanted him more than she had ever wanted William. She wanted to lie with him in the spring-scented night and become his woman.

The intensity of her desire startled her and caused her to pull back. Leaning her forehead against his chin, she fought for control. He held her without speaking, as though he understood the turmoil of her emotions and was trying to conquer his own.

At last she lifted her head. "It's not that I don't want you," she whispered. "Don't ever think that."

He shook his head. "A woman wouldn't, couldn't, kiss like that and not want to be loved."

The all-important word hung between them and enfolded them in all its depth. Logan gazed down at her loving face and knew beyond a doubt that this was the woman he had been born for. The knowledge almost staggered him.

But did he have a future to offer her? As far as he knew, Rosehaven might be burned to the ground and his land high in weeds. No, before he spoke his mind, he had to know what he had to offer her.

Carefully he said, "When we love, I don't want it to be like this—on the rubble in the woods with my men barely out of earshot. When we love, I want it to be all you've dreamed of. I want it to be perfect in every way."

Abigail nodded happily. His words and the velvety way they were spoken made her melt inside and affected her as seductively as his passionate kiss and touches. She never considered he might mean anything more permanent than his words implied, and to her amazement, she found merely loving him would be enough. She would rather have a night of Logan's love than a ring of pure gold from anyone else.

Soaring with happiness, she walked with him back to the fire.

9

"I don't think Chandler is still back there," Martin speculated as he narrowed his eyes to peer back through the gathering dusk.

"He's there," Logan grumbled. "I can feel him."

Abigail stirred the pot of beans and glanced anxiously in the direction of town. "Shouldn't Tobe be back by now?"

Logan paced across the circle of firelight, glaring at the darkening sky. "I've been expecting him for over an hour."

"Do you think Chandler has him?" Abigail had to ask the question that was in all their minds.

"I don't know." Again Logan strode across the grass, then stopped. "Maybe I should go look for him."

"Tobe's grown up. He can find his way back. It's not like the boy," Travis said with a snicker.

Harley turned his head away before Travis could see that the barb had hit its mark. Most of the time, Harley enjoyed the fun that the men poked at one another, even when he was the butt of the joke. But Travis often went overboard, as if he intended to hurt people's feelings. The best thing Harley could do was to try to ignore him.

"I agree with Travis," Martin said. "If nothing has happened, Tobe will find us. If Chandler has him, you couldn't do anything anyway."

"He couldn't find the turtle rock," Abigail reminded them.

"We found it," Martin answered. "We just didn't think it looked very remarkable, so we rode on. Tobe will see our fire."

"Seems to me he's had more than enough time to ride back and see if we lost Chandler," Harley murmured. "I'll bet he's lost."

Logan merely frowned and tried to pierce the gathering shadows. He was worried too, but if anybody rode back to look for Tobe, it would be him. Mustered out or not, he still felt vitally responsible for all his men. "Whoever would have guessed that Chandler would be so damned persistent! We've tried every trick I know to lose him."

"We even made up a few new ones," Travis agreed. "That Yankee sure bears a grudge."

"You know what I think?" Martin asked. "I think he's after the gold—for himself, I mean. All he has to do is tell his commanding officer that we spent it all. Then he retires as a rich man."

"That makes sense," Travis agreed.

"Look!" Logan pointed to a lone rider loping toward them. "It's Tobe." A vast relief washed over him.

The man rode up and dismounted. "I saw him. He's in town."

"So close?" Harley asked. The town was only two miles away. "Maybe we ought to move on, Captain."

Tobe answered for Logan. "We may as well rest first. He doesn't know we're this close or he wouldn't have checked into the hotel."

"That's true," Logan agreed.

"I found out how he's trailing us," Tobe said.

"The hotel is built in with the saloon. I went in and acted like I belonged there, keeping my back to him, of course. I heard him ask the bartender if he had seen a bunch of men come through. He said one of them was riding a paint horse of an odd color—red and white." When everyone's eyes turned to Harley, he squirmed uncomfortably. "That's how they managed to follow us. Chandler has been trailing that spotted horse."

"I was afraid of that," Travis said dourly. "I told you when I first saw him that that boy would bring us bad luck."

"I've carried my own weight!" Harley hotly retorted in his own defense. "It's not my fault my only horse was red-and-white-spotted! I had to ride something."

"That's enough from both of you," Logan snapped. "We have too much to worry about to fight among ourselves."

Harley continued to scowl, but he backed away. Travis threw him a taunting grin.

"We're going to have to split up," Logan said. "Let's divide up the money and go our separate ways in the morning. Harley, I want you to ride hard tomorrow. One man traveling alone can outdistance Chandler and his troop. Don't go straight home. You ride due west and loop back home when you're sure you've lost them. Got that?"

"Yes, sir." His voice showed that he was still smarting from Travis' remarks. "And I'm sorry about my horse."

"Don't worry about it. That Yankee major has a remarkable talent for tracking. If he hadn't been following your horse, he would have figured some other way," Logan said kindly.

The boy frowned at the spotted horse. "I never

liked him anyway. Looks like a circus pony or something a little kid would ride. No man would ride a spotted horse—especially a red-and-white one. Damned old skewbald horse."

"Watch your language, kid. You're not old enough to have a foul mouth," Travis goaded.

"Leave him alone," Logan barked. "We've all said things in front of Abigail that we shouldn't have."

Travis raised one eyebrow as if he questioned whether Abigail fit into the category of lady, but he wisely refrained. He might be angry at Chandler's persistence, but he wasn't foolish enough to fight with Logan. He noticed Abigail had caught his implication because her cheeks were pale with suppressed emotion. Good, he thought. The fury inside him boiled often, and it felt good to see some of it bleed off onto others. Thinking back, he couldn't remember a day when he hadn't fought to hide this mounting tempest. He supposed the war had affected them all that way. The reminder caused his anger to leap and crackle in his brain. He turned away and pretended to be watching the sunset as he struggled for control.

While Abigail had silently stirred the beans, she had developed a plan to get at least a share of the gold. With her anger at Travis in check, she decided to speak. "How much of the money will I get? I assume you've all talked it over and decided by now. The captain said he'd speak with you about it."

Travis was the first to respond as the others stared alternately between Logan and Abigail. "Logan, what's she talking about?"

Logan glanced up at the sudden change of subject. "Abigail and I did talk about it several days ago, but I . . ."

"We certainly did," Abigail began when Logan paused. "We discussed how all of you had risked so much to get the gold in the first place and how I really wasn't entitled to claim it all because I merely found it buried on my farm."

"Yeah, that's right," Martin quickly agreed. "We earned it and you didn't." Tobe and Harley nodded along with him.

"But then I pointed out to the captain that I had led all of you to safety in the cave near my farm, and when we were split up, I warned the captain that Chandler was in town and we got away again. He said I deserved a share of—"

Logan interrupted. "Now, wait a minute. I said I appreciated your help and that I'd see what the others thought, but I didn't make you a promise."

"As far as I'm concerned, she's been more trouble than help," Travis said, directing his words to Logan. "She led us to safety in that cave, but then she tried to shoot you and we had to make a run for it with Chandler less than a mile away."

"Now, wait," Tobe argued. "At first she thought that gold was all hers and now she's admitting that she isn't entitled to the whole thing. Sounds to me like she is being reasonable."

Logan wanted to defend Abigail's position, but he knew he was biased and, thus, chose to sit back and wait for the others to work this out.

"How much of your gold are you willing to give her for being *reasonable*?" Travis asked Tobe, his voice filled with sarcasm.

Before Tobe could answer, Martin rose to his feet and motioned for quiet before he began. "We've been on the run from Chandler for so long now, I couldn't even tell you how long it's been. The only way I'd share my gold is to get that bastard off our trail."

Abigail suppressed a satisfied smile. They had taken the bait. Carefully she asked, "How much would that be worth to you?"

Travis laughed heartily. "I'd give you a thousand dollars, myself, but I don't think I'm risking a thing."

"Well, what about the rest of you? Will you match his thousand?"

"Don't be silly, Abigail," Logan insisted. "We're splitting up tomorrow."

"Perhaps it's not very practical, then, but would each of you give me a thousand *if* I could get Chandler off your trail?"

The proposition was so absurd that each man nodded his agreement.

"Abigail, you'll have to go with me tomorrow. I can't let you ride off alone," Logan said.

"Whatever you say, Captain."

They went to bed as soon as the sky was black. Abigail lay a little farther away from the others than usual, but no one commented on it. Probably no one but Logan noticed, she figured, and with the growing interest between them, he might be glad of the distance. She had found it very difficult to keep up the pretense of indifference toward Logan for the sake of the others.

Although she usually fell asleep as soon as she lay down, tonight staying awake had been easy. Her mind was filled with quickening thoughts and she was hard pressed to feign sleep.

After an hour she cautiously lifted her head. Martin's steady snores told of his sleep. All the others lay still. Slowly she sat up and looked around. No one moved, and when she felt sure they were all asleep, she stood and quickly coiled her hair up on top of her head and then covered it with her concealing bonnet, even though it was nighttime.

Holding her skirts so they wouldn't rustle against the grass, she tiptoed to the horses. A glance back told her that all the men were still asleep. Carefully she untied Harley's spotted horse, bridled the docile animal, then led him away from the camp. Stopping next to a fallen log, she stepped up and vaulted onto the horse's bare back.

Turning his head toward town, she walked the horse far enough away from the sleeping men that they wouldn't hear her leaving, then kicked him into a lope. After having ridden Gypsy, Abigail found the paint to be not only rough-gaited but also hard-mouthed. She could only wonder why Harley hadn't tried to get rid of him.

The town soon loomed out of the darkness, and as she approached, she slowed her pace. Although the hour had to be pushing midnight, lights still burned in some of the houses, and the saloon was as lively as if it were early in the evening. Abigail looked around curiously. She had always assumed people were asleep at this hour of the night, though it suited her plan perfectly to find them awake.

She rode the horse down one dark alley after another until she was near the saloon. After sliding off the broad back, she tied the horse out of sight and dusted her skirt. Lifting her head with more confidence than she really felt, she walked out onto the boardwalk and into the saloon.

A gray haze of smoke hung thick in the air, and loud shouts and raucous laughter made a din around her. Abigail's steps slowed uncertainly. She had never been around so many men, and certainly never in a saloon. A quick survey told her that none of those present was a Union soldier, at least she assumed so since she saw no uniforms. Suddenly she felt far too shy to carry out her plan, and she was on the verge of retreating when the bartender saw her.

"Here! You! What are you doing in here?" he demanded.

"I . . . I'm not . . ." she stammered.

"I can't hear you. Speak up." He leaned toward her threateningly.

Abigail edged closer to the polished bar. The men nearest her glanced disapprovingly, but for the most part, she was ignored. "I said I'm looking for someone," she stated more clearly. "Major Owen Chandler."

"Well, you can't look for him in here," the man snapped. "This is a saloon. We don't allow ladies in here."

Abigail glanced around the smoky room. A woman dressed in bright red and another in yellow caught her eye. "They're in here," she objected.

"Charlotte and Ruthie aren't ladies," the bartender said, and grinned. "Now, you go on and get out of here."

"Not until I find Major Chandler."

"Chandler? He's upstairs in Room 210, but you can't go up there, either."

"Why not? Surely that's not a part of the saloon up there, too."

"This is a men's boardinghouse. I can't let a woman go traipsing up there. No telling what might happen. Now, will you go without a fuss?"

"Certainly. You had only to explain matters to me." With dignity she swept out into the night.

Frustration raged within her as she rounded the corner and stepped into the deep shadows beside the saloon. He was just up the stairs, if only she could get to him. But on the other hand, a part of her was relieved that her path had been barred. As she recalled that her share of the gold and Logan's safety depended on her plan, her ambivalence was replaced by courage. She couldn't afford to be weak-hearted now. Feeling her way down the wall, she found what she was searching for—a door.

She turned the knob and felt it give beneath her hand. It was unlocked! She pushed it open and peeped into a dim and shadowy kitchen, now deserted for the night. Beyond the open door on the far side of the kitchen, she could see across a narrow hallway and into the saloon. A smile tilted her lips.

Not giving herself time to reconsider, Abigail slipped into the kitchen and closed the door behind her. Quietly she crossed the room and stole a quick look into the hallway. The bartender had his back turned and no one else in the saloon had a view into the kitchen. To her left was a flight of steep and narrow stairs, probably intended for the use of servants.

She hurried down the hall, then paused to look up the steps. If she was going to back out, this was her last chance. Resolutely she put her hand on the wall to aid her balance, lifted her skirts, and climbed the steps.

At the top, Abigail stopped to catch her breath and regain her composure. Her heart was racing and she was feeling a little light-headed from the excitement. Swallowing the lump in her throat, she started down the hall. In front of the door marked 210, she stopped. This was Chandler's room. She mentally rehearsed her lines, drew what she hoped would be a calming breath, and knocked on the door. Never had she felt more like running away.

The door swung open and she found herself staring up into Chandler's curiously pale green eyes. She tried to summon a smile, but her face seemed to be frozen.

"Well, well," he intoned. "Who are you?"

Belatedly Abigail recalled the obvious function of the women in the saloon. "Are you alone?" she asked.

"Not anymore. Come in, come in." He stepped aside and gestured for her to enter the room.

When he didn't immediately recognize her, Abigail's courage returned and she stepped lightly into the small, darkly furnished bedroom. As she scanned from one side of the room to the other, she noted that Chandler's room wasn't nearly as nice as the one she had shared with Logan. Chandler had carelessly tossed his coat across a chair and his bedcovers were rumpled, as though he had been lying on top of them. His untidy habits reminded her of William's and she concluded that, after all, Owen Chandler was a mortal man and not the ogre she had imagined him to be.

"What brings you up here?" he asked curiously.

Abigail smiled broadly and affected a thick Southern accent. "I just thought y'all might be lonely." She hoped to disguise her distinctive brogue.

"You weren't wrong there." He gave her a calculating look that sent a chill through her.

She allowed him to lift her chin and stroke the curve of her cheek as she continued to smile.

"Your timing is perfect," he said silkily. "I was

just about to go to bed." He raked his eyes over her body. "Funny, I didn't see you downstairs."

"I just came to work," she lied. "You're my first customer." She wondered whether this was something a saloon girl would say, so she added, "This evenin', that is."

"You surely don't look like any tart I ever saw," Chandler said as he ran his hand over her shoulder and down toward her breast.

Abigail moved away and gave him a flirtatious wink. "I'm new here. My fancy clothes aren't made yet. But," she said daringly, "I just *love* Yankee officers, and when I heard y'all were here, I just came a-runnin'."

He grinned, obviously swallowing her entire line. "And I just *love* you little Rebs," he teased back, failing miserably at a Southern accent. "Come here."

"Now, Major, don't you be impatient." Abigail pouted. "Remember, I'm just a young girl." From his lecherous leer she figured she had hit the right tack, but she had to struggle to continue smiling. "Very young," she added for good measure.

"How young are you?" His voice held a harsh note of lust.

"I'm not supposed to tell," she said with wide-eyed innocence. "If I do ... well ... it's just better that I don't."

"Take off your bonnet," he told her. "We may as well start there. Why are you wearing it, anyway?"

"My bonnet?" Her hand touched the concealing fabric. Her long auburn hair was as distinctive a feature as Harley's skewbald horse.

"You don't plan to keep it on, do you?" he laughed. "That would look odd indeed." He reached for her.

With a girlish giggle, Abigail dodged back. "I just might do that."

"And your shoes as well?" Chandler laughed with passion husking his voice.

"Why, shame on you, sir," Abigail rejoined, again darting out of his way. She was finding it difficult to keep out of his reach.

His fingers found her bonnet strings and he tugged sharply. The bonnet came away and her hastily coiled hair came tumbling down. The sight of her unbound hair made his eyes glint dangerously. "I believe you may be as young as you say you are, after all."

Abigail brushed her hair back from her face, her violet eyes large. At that moment she felt more vulnerable than she ever had before, and much more foolish. Why had she ever concocted such a foolhardy scheme! She made her mouth smile and said, "Y'all didn't think I was lying, did you? A good little girl like me?"

"Come here, girl," Chandler commanded. "If I have to chase you, it will go worse for you."

Slowly Abigail approached him. She couldn't possibly outrun him, but a swift knee to his groin might even the odds. He yanked her close, knotting his hand tightly in her hair, then ground his lips against hers. Pain made her wince and she tasted blood as her teeth cut her lip.

When he lifted his head, she managed a weak smile. She wasn't going to go through all this and not accomplish her goal.

He put her bonnet back on her head, leaving her hair flowing loose beneath it as a child would wear it. "There, now. You look as pretty as a picture." He tied the ribbon in a bow beneath her chin. "Why don't you take off that dress now."

"Y'all sure aren't anything like the Rebel men that come through here yesterday," Abigail mused aloud as she toyed with the top button of her dress. "Animals. That's all they was."

"Rebels? Soldiers? What did they look like?" His voice was razor sharp and his pale eyes became alert.

"The leader was a dark-haired man. I didn't catch his name. Ruthie might know. I just know about the boy with them." She giggled again. "He was riding a red-and-white-spotted horse, of all things. You don't see many like that."

She twirled the end of a strand of hair. "All that boy wanted to do was talk, talk, talk. Well, maybe not quite all," she tittered girlishly.

"Did he happen to say where he was headed?" Chandler asked.

"Let me think. Yes, I believe he did. He said something about heading up to Shreveport, Louisiana. Yes, I'm sure of it. Shreveport, he said."

"Shreveport! That's northwest of here."

"I wouldn't know about that," she said demurely. "Do you know the boy?"

"Let's just say I know the horse. Did he say the others were also heading that way?"

"Lands, yes. Thick as thieves they were." She had to remind herself to maintain the Southern accent. "Mercy sakes alive," she added for emphasis.

Chandler's grin spread. "You surely are taking a long time getting that dress unbuttoned. Maybe I ought to give you a little help." The lust was back in his eyes.

"You know what I was thinking?" Abigail stopped him, one small capable hand squarely in the middle of his chest. "I was just thinking a big man like you might relish a shot of bourbon."

"Whiskey? Now?"

She batted her eyes and averted them shyly. "The truth is, I've never tasted strong drink. I thought maybe if I brought you up a bottle, you might give me just the tiniest taste." She gazed at him through her eyelashes. "Please?"

"Well, now, that might be arranged. If you're good, that is. A real good girl, I mean." He leered at her.

"Oh, I can guarantee that," she assured him. "I'll just run down and get a bottle while you"—she winked at him and tickled his nose with a tendril of her hair—"get more . . . comfortable." She glanced at the bed, then back at Chandler.

"You do that." He started to unbuckle his belt, his flat eyes regarding her hungrily. "Run along now, and hurry back."

"Yes, sir. I will." She turned to go, and he swatted her buttocks playfully. She twittered and wagged her finger at him as she backed out of the room.

Once the door was shut between her and Chandler, Abigail let out a sight of relief. Closing her eyes a moment, she told herself she was all right. He had believed all she told him. Quickly she bolted for the back stairs and ran down them as quickly as she dared.

The kitchen was still dark and empty and the racket from the bar covered the noises she made while bumping her way to the outside door. She let herself out into the night and felt her way back to Harley's horse. Now for the second part of her plan.

She was unable to remount without a log to give her height, so she led the horse through the back streets. After several minutes she stumbled by pure luck on a small stable next to what appeared to be a very opulent house. She opened the door wide to let in enough moonlight to see four stalls, three of which had horses inside. She tied the paint to the outside of one of the stalls and opened the gate as she caught the occupant's halter. Leading the horse into the moonlight, she looked him over critically; she had gone to too much trouble to trade one distinctive-looking horse for another. This one was well-shaped and dark in color, chestnut or possibly a dark bay. Either way, he wasn't a peculiar color that anyone would be apt to notice and remember.

Abigail put Harley's horse in the stall and pulled the bridle off. In the distance behind the sleeping house, a dog barked. Not taking the time to remove the halter, Abigail bridled the horse and looked around for a way to mount him. The dog barked again, more certainly this time.

She backed the horse close to a buggy and stepped up onto the seat. By pulling on his mane, she maneuvered the horse closer and climbed onto his back.

The animal unexpectedly reared, and she tightened her grip, not daring to turn loose. He came down snorting and prancing, so she leaned low over his neck and slapped her heels against his sides. The horse jumped forward, shaking his head angrily and bouncing as if he were winding up to buck. Abigail pulled the reins tight, keeping his head up so he couldn't throw her, and again kicked him.

With a leap the horse raced through the open barn door. As he headed for the open street, his ears flattened. Abigail held tightly and prayed she wouldn't fall off. After he had run a short distance, she tried to rein him to a stop, but the horse jerked his head and stretched his muscled neck instead as if he had no idea what that signal meant.

"Oh, damn!" Abigail gasped as they flew down the street in the opposite direction. "He isn't broken to ride!"

The horse was, however, eager to run, and he clattered over street and yard indiscriminately. Abigail pulled his head to one side, more by sheer strength than from finesse, and he veered in that direction. She tried the other side, and that, too, proved somewhat successful. Gripping the horse with her knees, she rode him out of town.

"What in hell do you mean, you saw her leave!" Logan demanded of Travis. "Why didn't you stop her?"

"She's a grown woman and not our prisoner. I thought you'd be glad to see her go. Now we don't have to give her any gold. Besides, she took that damned paint horse."

Logan muttered a purple oath and turned away rather than punch his cousin in the nose. Where she had gone and why were obvious. She was going to try to earn a share of the gold by attempting to throw Chandler off their trail. She had even taken Harley's telltale horse as bait. Logan's heart ached at her bravery, but his words cursed her foolishness.

As Logan's anger raged, he clenched his teeth to keep from hitting Travis after all. He couldn't believe that Travis had watched Abigail leave without trying to stop her! Logan couldn't recall ever being this angry.

She was out there somewhere, his reckless love,

leaving a clear trail for Chandler to track. And what if he caught up with her, then what would happen to her? Logan groaned in real agony. Fear for her safety twisted like a knife in his middle.

The sound of hooves drew his attention, and not daring to hope, he ran toward them. A horse raced out of the night and circled the fire twice as the woman on his back pulled on the reins. Logan jumped up and caught the bridle as the horse plunged past. He held tight and brought the animal to a nervous halt.

Abigail slid off his back and the animal quieted. She tried to smile up at Logan, though she felt more like falling in a heap. "I brought Harley a horse. He isn't quite broken, but Harley can train him. Boys enjoy that sort of thing."

Logan handed the reins to Travis and caught her to him. "Are you all right?" he demanded roughly, holding her so close she could scarcely breathe. "That was a damned fool trick."

"I'm fine. Let me get some air," she cried out. "There. I really am fine. Really."

"You stole an unbroken horse?" Travis interrupted.

"I was able to ride him. Harley can too," she snapped. "Someone had to do something."

"You could have been killed!" Logan upbraided her. "You're still shaking all over."

She clung to him and felt his strength protect her. "I did it. I threw Chandler off our trail."

"Swapping the horse should help," Logan admitted. "But we still need to get moving. Can you ride?"

She nodded. "As long as it's not that son of Satan. But there's no great rush. Chandler thinks we're heading northwest to Shreveport, not southwest to New Orleans."

Logan stiffened in her arms. "Now, what would make him think that, and how in hell do you know what he thinks?"

Abigail looked up at his distraught face. If he was this worried about her exchanging horses, he was going to be really upset if he knew the whole story. "I'll tell you later," she evaded. "Much later. But I did what I said I'd do. I threw him off our trail. I've earned a share of the gold from each of you."

Logan studied her. He wanted to know what she'd done, but he suspected it might be better if he didn't. Not just yet. "I don't know how you did it, but I'll take you at your word. But, Abigail, don't ever do anything like that again. Promise me!"

"Yes, Logan," she said innocently. "Whatever you say."

"As for the money, you've earned it. A deal is a deal." Logan turned to the others and added, "Right?"

Travis was the only one to argue that she hadn't proved anything, but in the end he relented and counted out fifty double eagles for Abigail's saddlebags, as did the others.

As they mounted to ride away in the pearly dawn, Abigail leaned over to Logan and thanked him.

"I'm going to have to watch you closer or there might not be any grandbabies to listen to the story of how I met you," he whispered to her. Before she could open her mouth and reply, he said, "Harley. Saddle your new horse and let's get going."

Had Logan said grandbabies? A warmth spread

over her and made her smile. She was glad she had taken the risk to ensure his safety. Logan was worth risking everything. Still smiling, she coiled her hair and covered it with her bonnet.

10

Crossroads, Miss., June 21, 1865
To Col. B. W. Dearborn, Washington, D.C.:

Nighthawk and accomplices in Shreveport, La STOP
Will arrest all and return them to Washington for
trial STOP

Owen Chandler, Maj.

Buggies and wagons clotted the narrow dirt streets of Hammond, Louisiana, and everywhere Abigail looked, she saw people. She rode close by Logan and glanced at him now and then to reassure herself. His expression was eager, as it had been since they crossed the Pearl River and entered Louisiana. She assumed this town must be as familiar to him as New Orleans, as his plantation lay between them.

He leaned near her and pointed toward a large shop that resembled a livery stable. "I bought my first buggy over there," he said with glad recognition. "It was a landau painted black with red trim. I drove it behind a pair of grays. They were fine horses—probably the best team I ever owned."

"Where are they now?" she asked.

"I sold them at the beginning of the war. Even then, Dixie needed all the horses she could get. The buggy is still in my carriage house. I'll show it to you tomorrow when we get to Rosehaven."

"Are you certain you don't want to ride on tonight? There's still a bit of daylight."

"No, it's another fifteen miles or so and we wouldn't get there until after dark. No one is expecting us, so we would have to wake everyone up. Besides, I want you to see Rosehaven in daylight for the first time."

Neither of them wanted to admit the plantation might no longer be there.

"There's Goodlett's Boardinghouse," he informed her needlessly, for she could read the prominent sign. To his men he said, "We'll stay there tonight."

"I could use a bath," Travis said amiably. "I'm enough to scare old Jeremiah. If he and the other servants are still at Magnolias." He looked thoughtful for a moment. "Surely they'll be there. I can't imagine Magnolias without Jeremiah and Mamie and Julep and the rest. Why, they've been there longer than I have."

"I, too, would like a bath," Abigail said thankfully. "I feel as if I brought most of Mississippi's dirt with me. Logan, do you think they will have a copper tub like the other hotel?"

Travis raised his eyebrows at his cousin, but Logan ignored the silent innuendo. "If there isn't, we'll find one and buy it," he promised grandly.

"Hush, Logan," she scolded. "No need to broadcast our wealth."

"Afraid someone will take your new fortune away from you?" Travis grumbled. He was still resentful that Abigail had called his bluff.

"I earned that money. A deal is a deal," she answered. Travis was the only one of the men who begrudged her the money for what she'd done. The others had expressed their gratitude. "Had it not been for me, Travis, you wouldn't be so close to home now. You'd still be traipsing around Mississippi trying to lose Chandler."

When Travis didn't respond, Logan said, "You never did tell us what happened the other night when you swapped Harley's horse."

"Nor will I. Some things are a woman's secret."

Logan looked at her curiously but didn't question her. He had decided there were some things he was better off not knowing, though curiosity piqued him.

As they rode into the boardinghouse yard, two boys ran out to take care of their horses. Logan spoke to the proprietor, Samuel Goodlett, and was able to get four rooms. Breakfast would be provided, but as Goodlett's wife was in childbed, he asked that his boarders take their evening meal at the establishment down the street. Logan was glad to oblige.

"When Papa and I came to Hammond," Logan explained to Abigail as Samuel showed them to their rooms, "we always stayed here. Samuel's father and grandfather owned it before him. You can always be sure of a clean bed here."

Samuel grinned back at Logan. "And as of last night, there's a new Goodlett son to carry on after me."

"That's good," Logan said. "A man needs continuity in his life. A way of knowing he will somehow continue on through his children."

"Especially these days," Samuel agreed as he opened a door for Martin and Harley. "Thank goodness the war is over and my boy won't have to go through all that."

"Amen to that," Tobe agreed. He and Travis took the next room.

Samuel showed Abigail and Logan to the two

front rooms overlooking the street. "I think you'll be comfortable here, ma'am. I'll have the boys bring up the tub and water if you like."

"Please," she breathed in anticipation. "Could I have my dress done up as well?" She had been impressed with the laundry service in the previous hotel.

"Yes, ma'am. There's a laundress just a block over. Give your things to one of the boys and he'll see to it."

"I hope you have two tubs," Logan said. "I can use a bath myself."

"You're in luck. We added a second one last year."

"Are we the only boarders here?" Logan asked. "I was afraid we would find you full, with all the traffic on the roads."

"Normally we would be, but you caught us at a . . . slow time." Samuel glanced uneasily at the door opposite Abigail's. "There is one other guest. You aren't likely to want to meet him, though."

"Why is that?"

"He's a carpetbagger. A man named Prescott. News that he's staying here may be the main reason I have these vacant rooms."

"Oh?" Abigail prompted.

"He's here in town to buy up cheap property."

"There's not much around here by that description. This is all rich bottomland," Logan said.

"Times have changed," Samuel told Logan in a low voice. "I've seen plantations going on the block for nine, even eight hundred dollars. Plantations that have been handed down two or three generations."

"Why?" Logan demanded.

"Taxes. The plantations are being taxed to death.

Also, there's no slaves to work the fields, so no crops are being planted."

"With no crops, there would be no income."

"Exactly. And no way to pay the taxes. So these carpetbaggers are flocking in to buy land while it's cheap. Some say they plan to live here, but most are looking to resell it at a high profit when the economy improves. I even heard of a plan to use some of these to homestead the new freemen. Each family would get a few acres. I can't see it working out, though. Why, those people have been slaves all their lives. How are they going to know how to run their own place? And how will they live until a crop is produced, with no one to feed them?" Samuel shook his head dolefully. "These are fair troubled times."

Logan drew a deep breath before he asked, "Have you heard any news about Rosehaven?"

Samuel again shook his head. "The last I heard, it was still standing. I've had no reason to go out that way."

"It is off the road a ways. Maybe the Yankees didn't see it." His voice rose hopefully.

"Maybe. It's hard to say. They were all over this area. But maybe."

Logan and Abigail exchanged a long look. "We'll see tomorrow," she said encouragingly. "No need to borrow trouble." After all the destruction they had passed, she had very little hope, but she couldn't bear the worried look in Logan's dark eyes.

Abigail was glad of Logan's strong arm as they walked back from dinner. The streets were packed with people who seemed to be doing nothing but blocking traffic. Some were Union soldiers loung-ing away the hours either before or after their assigned duties. Many were homeless blacks with nothing more to do than while away the day.

The boardwalk ahead was blocked by a young black man dancing the buck and wing to claps and whistles from his companions. Logan's face grew set with anger but Abigail drew him off into the street to avoid a confrontation.

"They know to show respect to a lady," he growled.

"It doesn't matter," Abigail placated. "I would rather walk around than cause a scene." A gaudily dressed man bumped against her as he hurried around them, scarcely giving her more than a sneering glance. Logan doubled his fist, but Abigail pulled him back to her side. "An accident, Logan. 'Twas but an accident." Her own anger was sparking to life and she was eager to reach the safe harbor of the boardinghouse.

"I don't understand it," Logan muttered as he took note of a painted woman standing in the street ahead of them, obviously intent on plying an ancient trade. "This isn't the way I left it. Has the whole world gone mad?"

"Only our part of it, perhaps. Had we won, the insanity would be evident in the North instead of here. War always breeds madness." Abigail watched as the man who had hurried past them stopped in front of the prostitute; then she averted her eyes. "Things will be different at Rosehaven," she said, unconsciously repeating the refrain that Logan had used so often.

"At least it's bound to be less crowded." He maneuvered her back onto the boardwalk and glared his way through a group of Yankee soldiers. "With Hammond like this, what must New Orleans be like?"

Suddenly an elderly man stumbled out of a shop and thudded heavily into Logan. Through the doorway, a younger man who was clearly the aggressor waved a fist, saying, "Don't come back in here, you old fool!"

Logan steadied the man as he yelled, "You're a Yankee thief! A robber!"

"What's wrong?" Logan demanded as the old man tried to lunge once more at the younger one.

"He sold my plantation on the block! I didn't owe but a hundred dollars in back taxes. He sold it to more of that Yankee scum like himself!"

"You don't pay your taxes, you lose your land," the other man yelled from the safety of the store. "That's the law!"

"I could have paid it if you'd have waited for my tobacco to ripen! I told you that!"

The man shrugged. "I have a business to run. I can't wait around for harvest time. Besides, I had a man willing to pay cash."

"Who?" the old man yelled back. "Who stole my land and home!"

"His name's Prescott. It's on the town records if you want to look it up." The man stepped back inside and closed the door.

"Prescott?" Abigail exclaimed. "Isn't he the one Mr. Goodlett mentioned?"

"Samuel Goodlett? Over at the boardinghouse?" the man asked. When she nodded, he seemed to collapse into himself. "I've heard of Prescott. He bought out one of my neighbors, too. I guess he'll own all of Tangipahoa Parish before he's done." His voice cracked painfully. "This might as well be the end of the world, near as I can see."

A muscle tightened in Logan's jaw. "Can't anything be done about this?"

The man gave him a searching look, then dropped his gaze. "Not lawfully. Not in days like these."

"Have you no bairns? No children?" Abigail asked anxiously. "Where are your kin?"

"I've got a son in Baton Rouge," the man answered dully. "I guess I can stay with his family until I figure out what to do."

"Here," Abigail said as she fumbled in her pocket, then pressed a gold piece into his palm. "This will see you there safely."

He squinted at her. "I can't take this! Times are too hard, and beside, you're a woman."

"Please. I want you to."

"It's all right," Logan reassured him. "We can spare it."

"Bless you," the man murmured. "Bless you both." To the closed door he muttered, "Those white trash will get what's coming to them. You'll see."

"That's right," Logan soothed.

Again the man gave him a questioning look, then regained some of his dignity and walked into the crowd.

"Poor old thing," Abigail murmured. "All lost for want of a hundred dollars. I've more than that in my pocket."

"Now who's broadcasting it?" Logan asked, glancing around to see if she had been overheard. "And even if he had been able to pay this year's taxes, the next would have wiped him out. That's evidently the way they have been set up. The idea is not to collect the increased taxes, but to get the prime land into Yankee hands."

Abigail put her hand in the curve of his elbow and felt the tension in his muscles. She knew he was worrying about his own plantation, but there was no way she could comfort him.

Soon they gained the comparative isolation of the Goodlett boardinghouse porch and Abigail sank gladly onto the double swing. Logan sat beside her. Outside the picket fence, all of humanity seemed to be aimlessly parading.

"I'm sorry I had to subject you to all this," Logan said. "I had no idea it would be this way."

"How could you know? Do you suppose all the towns are like this? Where did all the people come from?"

"There were a lot of large plantations around here. Also, New Orleans was probably heavily garrisoned, since it's a major port. We aren't that far away." He gazed at her. She looked so dainty and feminine, so in need of his protection, and Logan thought it strange he hadn't noticed that when they first met. Of course conditions had been somewhat strained then. He had ample reason to know she wasn't nearly so fragile as her delicate features indicated. A tendril of red-tinged hair showed beneath her bonnet, and her eyes were the pansy shade of a thunderstorm. Logan looked away before he gave in to the temptation to kiss the coral blush of her lips.

A wiry man with slicked-down black hair came through the picket gate, letting it bang shut behind him. He stared at the couple in the swing but gave no sign of greeting before entering the house. Again he let the door slam in his wake.

"That must be Prescott," Logan observed.

"He looks the part of a villain," Abigail confirmed. "He has a mean, spiteful look about his eyes."

Logan smiled at her. "Even when you're saying

derogatory words, you have the most beautiful voice I ever heard."

Abigail stared at him in surprise.

"There's a touch of heather in everything you say."

She laughed self-consciously. "It's a good thing my mother isn't here to hear you say that. She would have preferred that I spoke in shamrocks, not heather."

He thought a minute. "With a name like McGee, was your . . . William . . . Scottish?" He found he couldn't quite call the man her husband.

"Aye. His family and Papa's were from the same region, though William's family had been in this country for two generations. He had no accent to speak of and he teased me about my own."

Jealousy pricked Logan, though he had asked for it. "I like the way you talk."

"I wasn't planning to change it."

Travis came up the front walk and joined them on the porch. Leaning on the rail, he said, "Have you ever seen so many people?"

"Only on the battlefield," Logan answered. He had been hoping to have more time alone with Abigail.

"If you'll excuse me," she said, standing up, "I'll go inside now."

Logan watched her go and wondered why she always seemed to be avoiding Travis. "Have you ever noticed the color of her eyes?" he asked his cousin.

"Whose? Abigail's? They're sort of blue, aren't they?"

Logan smiled. "She's quite a lady, isn't she?"

The question was obviously rhetorical, so Travis merely grunted and looked back at the street.

"When we get to Rosehaven, I'm going to ask her to marry me."

That got Travis' attention and he stared at Logan. "Abigail?"

"Of course. All I'm waiting for is to see if I have a home to offer her."

"Marie-Claude should love that," Travis remarked dryly.

"What does she have to do with it? She and Andrew have Fair Oaks."

"Neither of us are blind, cousin. Marie-Claude may be married to your brother, but it's you that her eyes follow."

"Nonsense." Logan frowned as he recalled the unpleasant scene in the garden. Marie-Claude had made it clear that she was his for the asking. If Travis knew, did Andrew?

"Besides, I always thought you would marry one of the Dupree girls."

"Why would you think that?"

"Well, you escorted them all over Saint Charles Parish."

"I drove them to a few parties, but so did you. Besides, I never took just one out at a time, and twins or not, I couldn't marry them both."

"Personally, I thought Letty had a slight edge over Dolly."

"You marry her. It's Abigail that I want."

Travis paused, then said nonchalantly, "Andrew may not be too pleased, either."

Logan looked up sharply. "Why?"

"This is rather delicate, but you did see the area she comes from—not a really fine family for miles, and likely her house was no better than our slave quarters. Not to mention the fact that she's Scots-Irish."

Logan slowly stood to face his cousin. His black eyes snapped with suppressed fury as he said very distinctly, "If Andrew says anything along those lines, or if you ever do again, I'm going to knock you from here to Sunday." He paused to be sure his words had sunk in, then strode angrily into the house.

In the unaccustomed privacy of her bedroom, Abigail removed her dress and stretched, reveling in the sensation of being unrestricted by clothing. Her sleeveless low-necked chemise was so light it felt nonexistent, as did her ribbon-trimmed bloomers. She carefully folded back the covers on the bed and ran her hand over the smooth sheets. She was discovering she had a real penchant for luxury.

Outside, night had fallen and the streets were quiet, the people having mysteriously dispersed to their various homes. Occasionally she heard the jingle of harness as a wagon passed, but the town was drawing in its skirts for the night.

She yawned and stretched again. The old-fashioned tester bed beckoned like a magnet. Using the small stool, she climbed in and rolled onto her back. As the feathers billowed and shifted beneath her, she spread her arms in abandon, relishing the comfort.

All of a sudden her door burst open, and she sat up with a startled scream. More men than she could count were crowding into her room, all of them dressed in flowing white sheets. Abigail's mouth dropped open in stunned fear as she stared at them and they stared back.

The leader, whose peaked hood was decorated with red-rimmed eyes and mouth and a lolling cloth tongue, held up his hand. At once the men stopped crowding into her room.

"Who are you!" she managed to gasp. "What are you doing here!"

The men were eerily silent and this frightened her almost as much as their outlandish costumes.

"What do you want?" she cried out, trying to keep fear out of her voice but failing.

She heard a commotion in the hall, then Logan shoved his way into the room. Glaring from one hood to the other, he backed toward the bed, keeping his body between Abigail and the Klansmen. "What's going on here?" he demanded.

The leader turned to glance at the shorter man on his right, who shook his head in a barely perceptible manner. Turning back to Logan, the leader spoke one word in a sonorous voice. "Prescott."

As Abigail clutched the cover to her, she stretched out a wavering arm. "Across the hall."

Still maintaining silence, the men left. Abigail gulped, remembered to breathe, then whipped her head around to face Logan. "What are they?" she gasped as she heard the sound of another door crashing open, followed by a startled curse.

"Klansmen," Logan answered. "I had heard they were in Tennessee, but I didn't know there were any here."

They heard shouts from Prescott, then a scuffling as the robed men dragged him out of his room and down the stairs.

"What will they do with him?" Abigail whispered.

"I don't know." Logan went to the front window and opened the shutters as Abigail pulled loose the bedspread and wrapped it around her body.

She hurried to his side as the men reached the street. Forming a circle, the silent men shoved

Prescott from one to the other. He stumbled time after time, only to be jerked up and shoved again. His frightened cries had aroused the neighbors, and several of the people had crowded toward the boardinghouse to see what was causing the commotion.

"I think they're just going to scare him," Logan said.

"Who are they?"

"Townsmen. People who are tired of seeing their land stolen and their women insulted. The law won't help them, so they have decided to take matters into their own hands."

"But that's wrong! Why won't the laws protect us?"

"Have you forgotten? Those are United States laws and we are no longer citizens."

Abigail stared at him. She hadn't thought of that. "If there is no longer a Confederacy, what citizenship are we?"

"As near as I can tell, we haven't any," Logan replied.

They watched as the Klansmen shoved Prescott to the center of the circle, where he collapsed sobbing on the ground. They ringed him in terrifying silence for a moment, all standing impossibly tall beneath the cone-shaped hoods—the only movement being their wind-ruffled sheets. Then the leader gave a whistle and they turned and mounted their horses. Another whistle and they raced out of sight down the street.

Abigail turned to Logan. "Don't leave me," she whispered. "Stay the night with me."

He reached up and caressed the rounded flesh of her bare arm. "You're safe now. It was Prescott they were after."

"Stay with me," she repeated.

Pausing only long enough to shove the door closed, Logan took her hand and led her to the bed before gently unwrapping the sheet from around her.

She stood before him, her eyes anxiously asking for confirmation that he found her desirable. Her thin chemise had slipped low, lying upon the tips of her breasts and exposing their rounded fullness.

Logan let his fingertips stroke the warm globes as he feasted his eyes. "You're beautiful," he said softly.

Abigail reached up and untied the ribbon that laced through her chemise. As the thin fabric loosened, it dropped to her waist. Her breasts were as large and well-shaped as he remembered, and the peaks were tipped with coral buds that pouted rosily under his gaze. Her waist was slender and supple, yet not too thin for beauty.

When he made no move, she untied the ribbon that held her bloomers and pushed them away to pool at her feet. Her hips were gently rounded and her legs gracefully long. The nest of auburn curls at their junction drew his gaze.

She was determined that he should make the next move, so she waited, letting him gaze his fill. At last he began to remove his shirt. Now Abigail stared as his clothing dropped piece by piece to the floor. She had never dreamed a man could be so beautifully made. Her glimpse of him in the hotel hadn't done him justice.

He held out his hand and she took it as if this were a pagan ceremony to bind them. Their eyes met and she felt a spark leap at the love she saw there.

Slowly, as if afraid she would vanish, Logan stepped toward her. Her nipples grazed his chest and he felt the sensation clear to his soul. He lowered his head, then took her lips in a kiss that began sweetly but quickly leapt into passion.

Her arms encircled his neck; then she swayed into his embrace as she kissed him with all the fury of her pent-up passion. Their mouths widened and she met his tongue in silken desire.

Murmuring with emotion, he lifted her and laid her in the bed, stretching his length to touch and cover hers. Abigail moved beneath him as his large hand found her breast. Love sang in her veins, and she stroked her palms over the hard muscles of his back. His hot maleness pressed against her belly and she shifted, urging him silently to take all she offered.

Logan eased between her parted thighs but waited as his lips found the rosebud of her breast and his tongue urged it to tender tautness. His hand slid over her flat stomach and lower to the curls.

Abigail's eyes flew open as he touched her in her most secret place. William had never done that! Logan's knowing fingers dipped and caressed, sending waves of hot desire coursing through her. A weakness and an ecstasy fought for supremacy and she was aware only of the heights she soared toward.

As she reached the peak of her endurance, he entered her and in two long movements sent her blissfully into a completion she had never before known. Abigail cried out and held him as one pulsing wave after another roared through her.

Spent at last, she relaxed her grip and lay back to see him smiling down at her. A golden glow seemed to cradle her as she touched the beloved planes of his face. Again he began to move within her and her eyes widened with surprise. She had assumed he had finished.

Logan placed a trail of kisses over her temple, down the shell of her ear, and to the pulse that raced in the sensitive hollow of her neck. Abigail moaned as the delicious fire again smoldered to life.

She ran her hands over his powerful rib cage and cupped the rounded muscles of his buttocks, pulling him deeper into her. Logan moved steadily, deeply, his body learning her most sensitive areas and new ways to please her.

Abigail flicked her tongue over the curve of his neck, as he had done to her, and he sighed in response. Encouraged, she raised her hands, following the hardness of his body, to stroke his broad chest and then to lace her fingers in the crisp black fur that tickled against her breasts. Logan murmured love words to urge her to greater daring and to show her ways she had never dreamed of for pleasing her man.

This time when the fires leapt to blazing and carried Abigail spiraling upward, she felt Logan with her all the way. When she swirled up and into the sunburst of her passions, his cry matched her own, and together they melded into one being.

As the world slowly reformed around them, Abigail nestled comfortably in the warm security of his embrace, his leg still between hers and her long silky hair entwined around them both. Never in her life had she known such safety or such satisfaction.

11

Even the horses seemed to step out more eagerly, as if they sensed the end of their long journey. Spirits had been high since they left Hammond. As they circled the west end of Lake Pontchartrain, Abigail marveled at the expanse of water.

"It's a sight bigger than the pond on my farm," Tobe admitted, hiding the twinkle in his eyes.

"There you go again," Martin said as he rose to the bait. "Of course it's bigger. It's a lake, ain't it?"

"On the other hand, my pond may be deeper. It's hard to tell, just looking down on it."

"Bigger, deeper—I wish just once you'd admit to something average."

Tobe thought for a minute. "I had an average dog once, but I sold him."

Martin groaned.

Travis nodded toward a group of sycamore trees. "That's where old man Benson's farmhouse used to be. We're almost out of Saint John the Baptist Parish." To Abigail he added, "It burned when we were boys. Isaac and Obadiah Benson were smoking a grape vine and set the barn on fire. Before they could put it out, the fire spread to the house."

"The next parish is Saint Charles," Logan said. "Home." He smiled at her in a way that excluded everyone else, and she blushed like a schoolgirl.

To Abigail's eyes the land around them looked pretty much as it had for miles, but Logan and

Travis kept exclaiming over its virtues. Her love for Logan was such that she began to think perhaps the trees were larger and shadier, the grass greener, the people better cared for than had been the case in previous parishes and counties.

Gradually Travis grew quieter, as did Logan, and Abigail sensed they were nearing the plantations. They turned off the road and headed up a worn lane. The three grooves made by wheels and horse seemed to stretch forever. Abigail found she, too, was holding her breath and straining to see beyond the hedges and flowering oleander bushes.

"Wait until we round this curve," Travis said to no one in particular. "We'll be almost in the front yard of Magnolias. See? You can see the trees it was named for."

Abigail could indeed see perhaps a dozen large magnolias, the white blooms now gone from the dark, rubbery leaves. "Have you family here?" she asked to make conversation and relieve the strain.

"My mother is there, and of course the servants. Old Jeremiah has always been here. My grandfather bought him the year Magnolias was built."

They rounded the curve and drifted to a stop. No one spoke. No one needed to.

A pile of charred rubble lay heaped around the blackened trunks of the huge trees. A partial wall still stood, its empty windows showing the barn and outbuildings beyond. Four chimneys reached like grotesque fingers toward the sky; the fifth had collapsed with the roof.

Slowly Travis rode near, his horse picking its way among the rubble of brick and ash. He dismounted with the lurching movements of a sleepwalker and stood staring at what had been his home.

Logan got off his horse and handed the reins to Abigail. Going to his cousin, he said, "I'm sorry, Travis."

Travis bent and picked up the blackened knocker that had once been on the front door. He still didn't speak.

"Aunt Lucy is probably at Fair Oaks with Mother," Logan offered.

Still Travis was rigidly silent. He turned the knocker over and the bar slapped together, making a tinny sound that was only a ghost of its former voice.

"We all knew Jeremiah and the other servants would be gone," Logan said to break the silence. "I imagine most left as soon as news came that they could. Even Jeremiah."

Travis raised his red-rimmed eyes and studied the house as if he couldn't quite grasp what had happened. Logan touched his shoulder, but Travis violently shrugged away his arm. He looked back at the discolored knocker, then threw it into the heart of the rubble with as much force as he could. At last he spoke, but his words were reedy and tight, as if they had fought their way around a knot in his throat. "I'll get those Yankee bastards!"

"Travis, you can't undo what's been done."

"I'll kill them." His voice rose in volume. "I'll see them in hell!"

"You can rebuild. Make it better than ever," Logan tried to console his cousin.

"This is Magnolias!" Travis yelled, as if Logan didn't understand. "This is all that's left of one of the most beautiful plantations in Louisiana! The staircase was imported from England"—he gestured at a sagging mass of blackened wood—"the mantels came from Spain and Italy. Not a one of them like another."

Logan glanced at the protruding corner of cracked and chipped marble. He felt sick at heart even though he had never lived at Magnolias. The room in which Travis had been born no longer existed. "Let's go."

"Go? Where do I have to go? This was my home. This was what I fought for years to protect!"

"Get on your horse. We're going to Rosehaven, then on to Fair Oaks and see about our family." When Travis continued to stand and stare wild-eyed at the rubble, Logan said in his command voice, "Mount up."

Still moving like a man underwater, Travis obeyed. From the saddle he again faced the ruin of his future. A dull pounding had started behind his ears and a red haze seemed to color the scene. He blinked but myriad voices, all seething hate, seeped into his brain. "Get back your own," they shrieked silently to no one but him. "They owe you!"

Travis blinked again and shook his head. Somewhere within him a core of strength tried to unwind to help him tamp down the anger that he dared not acknowledge, let alone unleash. Then the voices subsided and became a black murmur he could almost ignore. "Let's go," he snarled.

No one spoke as they rode down the lane that twisted around thickets of sweet-gums and pin oaks and bridged several narrow streams. A cold, lead weight had settled in Logan's chest, and he dared not look at Abigail or his men. He had not felt quite like this since his boyhood when he had been plagued by nightmares due to a nursemaid's overactive imagination during bedtime stories. Now he was in the middle of a nightmare from which he couldn't escape. To tell Travis to rebuild his home was easy enough. But what if it had been Rosehaven?

Logan glanced at Travis' pale face and grim features. He was taking it better than Logan would have expected. Aside from his quite natural outburst of anger, he had seemed to accept his loss. Logan tried to prepare himself for an equal blow.

Abigail rode closer and reached out to touch Logan's knee as if she had heard his thought. Her troubled eyes met his and she wordlessly let him see that she was there, that she would be his strength if he needed her. Until now she had been reluctant to show her affection for Logan in front of the others, but now she no longer cared. Silently she reached out to him.

Logan looked at her hand and then to her eyes. He should be the brave one, the tower of strength, not her. She continued to meet his gaze and extend her hand. Slowly Logan took it and she gripped his firmly, conveying her desire to help him. Logan hadn't realized he was holding his breath, but he let out a heartfelt sigh. Together. That was the solution. Together they could overcome anything. He tightened his grip on her hand and was deeply glad that Abigail was woman enough to be both protector and protected.

They crossed a meadow deep in summer's grass and splashed across a shallow stream that would eventually feed the Mississippi River. Another forest of pin oaks and scrubby pines stunted by storms from the Gulf of Mexico had to be traversed, but then they were again in a meadow.

And ahead lay Rosehaven.

Abigail was amazed by its beauty. A double row

of live oaks, each much larger than she could reach around, flanked an avenue of luxuriant shade wide enough for three buggies abreast. At the end was the house. Untouched. Whole. Mellowed red bricks rose two stories behind soaring white Ionic columns. Two porches, one above the other, encircled the house on both levels, offering deep shade to laze away a day or a lifetime.

As they rode up the grassy lane at a canter, Abigail saw the once carefully tended gardens that had now grown wild. A tangle of roses of every shade she could imagine made a bramble surrounding a tall white fountain, its water now stilled. Yew hedges, a few of which still retained some semblance of the fanciful shapes of their pruning, grew in tight clumps of the deepest green. Weeds grew in profusion among the walkways, threatening to choke out the day lilies, pinks, and touch-me-nots that had been planted with a careful hand.

Abigail glanced at Logan and saw a muscle tighten in his jaw. Something was wrong.

They stopped in the front yard, where a graveled surface battled the weeds. The windows were dark, but with more than an hour of daylight left, that was not unusual. However, Logan stared at the quiet house as if to question its silence. Surely someone must have heard them ride up. Surely someone must be there.

He dismounted and wrapped the reins around the porch rail. When the others joined him on the front steps, he took Abigail's hand protectively. The house was much too quiet, too still. Keeping ahead of her, he crossed the porch and tried the front door.

It swung open with only the tiniest creak, but Logan frowned. In over fifty years that door hadn't been allowed to creak. He warily entered the familiar vestibule. Oak wainscoting soared to the ceiling where a dusty chandelier of five layers of prisms hung. Dusty? In front of them a separate staircase curved up each side of the room to meet wishbone fashion in a broader stair to the second floor. The mahogany rails weren't dusty, but a general air of neglect, like that of an aging person who has ceased to care, permeated the entryway.

And the house was silent.

Logan went to the double doors on the right and pushed them open. They struck the walls with a bang, causing everyone to jump. Logan sniffed the still air. Was that the smell of collard greens cooking? Someone must be there. He took out his pistol and motioned for Abigail to stay behind him. His men also pulled their guns from their scabbards. Bushwhackers, the Southerners who looted their own countrymen, were known to take up temporary residence in deserted houses.

A door shifted in the back wall and Logan nodded toward it. Travis swung wide, coming up from behind, while Logan reached out for the doorknob. Jerking it open, he pulled an aged black man into the room. Five guns pointed at him before Logan exclaimed, "Jeremiah!"

The man was quaking from fear, his rheumy eyes darting from one man to another. "Master Logan? Is that you? Master Travis?"

"Jeremiah!" Travis gasped. "What are you doing here? Put away your guns. This is Jeremiah from Magnolias."

"We had to come here, Master Travis. Magnolia's done burned to the ground."

"Yes. We saw it. Where's Mother?"

The old man swallowed nervously and looked at

Logan. "The Yankees. They done it. They allowed as how we was hiding silver plate. We was, o' course. Julep and me, we buried it in the chicken yard. It's there now. Safe."

"That's good, Jeremiah," Logan said. "But where's Aunt Lucy? Did she go to Fair Oaks?"

"Oh, no, sir. Couldn't none of us do that. We come here." The old man nodded his grizzled head as if Logan should have known that.

"Why couldn't you go to Fair Oaks? I'd think Aunt Lucy would want to be with my parents."

"She did for a fact, but your folks, they was here. At Rosehaven."

"Fair Oaks burned too, then?" Logan tried to probe patiently, as the old man was clearly senile or at least vague in his recollection.

"No, sir, Fair Oaks is just fine. That's where Miss Marie-Claude and that Yankee lives. Y'all couldn't expect your mamas to go there." He looked from one cousin to the other.

"What Yankee?" Travis growled. "What the hell are you talking about?"

"Master Andrew, he fell at Manassas. Leastways we think he did. Miss Marie-Claude, she sent that boy called Taffy to see was he dead. Taffy come back and said that some say he was and some say he wasn't. Anyways, Taffy couldn't find him alive, so he come on home." Belatedly he said to Logan, "I'm right sorry, sir, to have to give you the news."

Logan nodded. "Go on."

"Well, sir, it wasn't six months later that a Yankee man come to New Orleans. Old Beast Butler had just got shut of it and General Banks took over. This Yankee, a fella name of Smith, Amos Smith, he was a reconstructionist." Jeremiah rolled out the word with dignified disdain.

"She married him?" Travis demanded. "A damned Yankee!"

"Yes, sir. She did for a fact."

"And her not even knowing for sure if Andrew was dead?" Logan gasped.

"That's right. 'Course, none of us family went, but I reckon she married him up right. Leastways they's living at Fair Oaks."

"Then where is everyone?" Travis snapped impatiently.

"I's getting to that. This here's the bad part." He paused as Logan and Travis exchanged a look of foreboding. "Come last summer, they was a outbreak of yellow jack. It was like that bad one back in fifty-three. Julep got it first and poor old thing didn't last but a little while. Then Miss Lucy come down with it and the next day both your papa and your mama. Before the week was out, your sisters had it too. Those of us what was had it before, we worked as hard as we could, but there weren't nothing we could do."

"They died?" Travis said hollowly. The angry voices were back in his brain, eating at his reason. And this time they wouldn't still.

"Yes, sir. We buried them in the graveyard alongside the old master and mistress. We done it as best we could, and Lige, he said some words over they heads. We done our best."

Logan crossed the room to the bay window and looked up at the family cemetery on the hill. Because of the flowering crape myrtle and the black wrought iron that surrounded the plots, he couldn't see the graves. Then the whole scene blurred, and he looked down at the windowsill.

Abigail had followed him. And when she put her arm around his waist, giving him her strength, he pulled her to him and held her close until he could blink back the tears. At last he said to Jeremiah, "Where are the others?"

"They left. They said you weren't never coming back and that I was a old fool to stay on, but Miss Lucy, on her dying bed, told me to stay on and keep the place up against you coming back."

"I appreciate it, Jeremiah," Logan said tiredly. "If you hadn't been here, we would never have known for sure what happened." He drew a deep breath and squared his shoulders as if he were about to take on a physical adversary.

"We're home now," Travis growled, "and things will get back to normal. Are the crops in?"

"No, sir. I was by myself by then. I planted some collard greens and taters and a few other vegetables. You know I never learned no field work." He hesitated, then said, "Lige said it wouldn't matter nohow, once they put that paper to the column out front."

"What paper?" Logan asked, turning abruptly.

"The one what's nailed to the column out front. I can't read, but the soldier what done it said it means we can't live here much longer. Now y'all home, it don't matter, do it?"

Logan strode across the room and out to the porch. In the fading light of sunset, he read the dreaded words. "Taxes!" he ground out. "Rose-haven's being auctioned for back taxes!"

"We can pay them," Abigail said hastily. "There's still time, isn't there?"

"No you can't," Travis said harshly. "You start flashing gold around, and questions will be asked."

"But they're auctioning off my home!" Logan cried out. "What do you expect me to do?"

"The paper says the sale is still a month away. That gives us time to think."

"First we have to find out how much is owed," Abigail said. "Maybe it's not much, like with that man we saw in Hammond. You could explain having a hundred dollars."

"Rosehaven being sold for taxes," Logan murmured.

"You could always rebuild," Travis quipped with only barely concealed sarcasm. "Bigger and better."

Logan's head snapped up at the unexpected slam, but Travis only smiled innocently. Martin and Tobe exchanged a look but kept quiet.

"Let's see how much is owed," Abigail soothed. She too had heard the attack in Travis' words. "We'll figure out something between us."

Night was falling swiftly, so Jeremiah went to light the candles while the men took their horses around to the barn. Abigail stood on the porch and inhaled the rose-scented air. Homecoming had not been what any of them expected. For the first time in days she thought of her own small home back in Mississippi. At the moment it seemed very far away.

12

Abigail walked through the tangled remains of the garden. More varieties of flowers than she could name were clotted with the choking weeds. Some woman had obviously loved this garden and had likely spent many hours strolling through it in happier days. Abigail had never had a real flower garden. She had planted daisies on either side of the front steps of her home in Mississippi, but as pretty as they had been, they were nothing like the flowers she saw about her. She knelt and tried to free a bright orange cluster from the encroaching chickweed.

"Impatiens," a deep voice said.

Startled, Abigail turned to the figure seated on the bench in the deep shade of a willow. For a moment she thought it was Logan, but her smile died as Travis rose and came forward.

"Those are called impatiens," he repeated, almost as if to himself. "I recall the day Martha Ann planted them. That was Logan's sister, the one who lived here. They were her favorites. You'll find them all over the place. Of course she kept the rose gardens too, since that's where Rosehaven got its name, but she didn't prefer them like our grandmother did."

"Your grandmother planted them?" Abigail asked to be polite. She felt uneasy being alone with Travis, but she couldn't let him know. He might assume that she was vulnerable and cause another scene.

He nodded. "She always said roses were the flower of passion, that a person who loves roses loves life. I heard her say it many a time." He turned his head slightly so he could see her, but not squarely. "Do you like roses?"

"They're beautiful. I also like the impatiens and all the others." She took a few steps up the path so she would have a head start if she had to leave quickly.

"No preference? I wonder what Gran would have said about that." His sardonic chuckle indicated that he was pretty sure he knew.

Abigail wondered if she had been insulted. Why should she like one better than another? Just because his grandmother was choosy didn't mean that she should be. "My parents had a wild rose. Mama said it was grown from a clipping taken from County Cork. It was a lovely thing."

"Yes," he said thoughtfully. "I wonder if your parents had more than one wild rose." His black eyes traveled familiarly over her, lingering on her bosom.

She knew the underlying meaning of his statement. Unobtrusively she eased farther away.

"Marie-Claude always loved the roses here. She says they don't grow anywhere else like they do at Rosehaven."

"Who?"

"You remember hearing Jeremiah talk about her. She was married to Logan's brother."

"Oh, yes. Marie-Claude."

"She was over here as often as possible."

"I suppose Logan and his brother were close."

"Not overly so. They weren't much alike. Marie-Claude was here much more often than Andrew."

"She and Martha Ann were friends?"

"No, Martha Ann was barely civil to her. She was much too astute for that."

"What do you mean?"

"Isn't it obvious? Marie-Claude is a beautiful woman. The sort that can have any man she wants. Now, why do you suppose she spent so much time at Logan's house?"

"Logan and Marie-Claude? I don't believe Logan would ever do such a thing."

"No? It's been my experience that a man takes anything that's offered, especially if it comes in such a pretty package." His lips tilted upward as if he were enjoying her discomfort.

"Not his own sister-in-law!"

Travis shrugged. "Bloodlines don't mean much to some people. Marie-Claude is also our third cousin. On our mother's side."

Abigail tried to hide her shock. "Be that as it may, the lass is now a new bride. She'll not still be lusting after Logan."

"What a charming way to put it. Still, she and Andrew had only been married five years. Some considered them still newlyweds. And Andrew and Logan were brothers." He paused for effect, then added, "If Andrew is in fact dead. There seems to be some doubt."

"Disgraceful! How could she remarry, not knowing if her own husband were dead?"

"One of Marie-Claude's most endearing characteristics is that she goes after what she wants. And gets it. Yet, at the same time, she's the most feminine of women."

Abigail frowned. "She doesn't sound it."

"Oh, but you've never seen her. She has hair of purest spun gold and eyes as blue as sapphires. Her skin is alabaster white and her lips are rubies, her teeth pearls."

"She seems to be made entirely of rocks and stones," Abigail observed.

"She is as soft and warm as a kitten," Travis assured her. "And as affectionate."

"Most kittens scratch and bite."

"I imagine she does too, at the proper time."

Abigail blushed at his suggestive comment and turned away. She had no desire to continue this discussion. "Where's Logan? Have you seen him?" she asked abruptly.

"He's up the hill at the cemetery."

"I believe I'll go up and console him." She turned to go, but Travis' words made her pause.

"Marie-Claude will probably want that job. If she had known for sure that Logan would come home, she would never have married that Yankee. If you ask me, there was an understanding between them. I imagine Logan is grieving for more than the deaths of his family."

Abigail swished her skirts angrily and swept away. She didn't believe a word of it. The night before last, she had lain in Logan's arms and they had loved the night away. Surely he wouldn't have done that if he thought he was about to be reunited with his paramour. Would he? Travis said a man would take whatever was offered, and she had certainly offered herself. Had Logan told Travis that? She grew flushed at the mere idea. No! Logan wouldn't tell!

She let herself through the yard gate and went into the pasture. Easily she climbed the gentle slope of the hill. Ahead she could see Logan's profile inside the low fence, his head bent forward as if he were deeply grieving.

When she reached the iron gate, she hesitated. Perhaps he would rather be alone. She couldn't go back, though, without being seen. Feeling awkward and foolish, she stood at the entrance until Logan turned to look at her.

Silently he held out his hand and she went to him. Five graves lay in a neat row just downhill from several older ones. Crude wooden crosses had been erected at the head of each, but since none of the former slaves could read or write, no names had been etched on the markers.

"I don't know which is which," he said dully. "This might be Papa or it might be Mahitaba. She was my youngest sister. Not yet twenty." His voice took on a bitter note. "She never even had a chance for a life of her own."

Abigail silently slipped her arm around him.

"I should have been here. I should have taken better care of them," he said unreasonably.

"How could you have helped? Have you had yellow fever?"

"I had it the first year of the war. Seems like we all came down with something. Everything from measles to yellow jack. I could have helped doctor them."

"It would have done no good," she said gently. "If it hadn't been their time, they would have survived as you did. Jeremiah said he and the others did all they could."

Logan nodded tiredly. "He would have, too. I trust Jeremiah. He lost family as well." He gestured toward a separate area where a picket fence surrounded three new graves. "Julep was his daughter."

He fell silent for a while. Only the sighing leaves of the sheltering oak broke the stillness. Overhead a bird dipped and swooped in search of a meal. Pale yellow and white butterflies skipped among the patches of white clover that dotted the hillside. "I had thought nothing would be changed," he mused. "Oh, I really knew it would be, but I never believed it. I expected Martha Ann to be bustling around as usual, keeping everybody on their toes. She had more energy than any two people I ever met. I thought Magnolias would be there forever, and probably Aunt Lucy as well. I can't imagine Fair Oaks without my parents or without Mahitaba's laughter. She was always so happy. And Andrew. He was the serious one—didn't laugh often, but he was as smart as they come." He paused. "I sure can't imagine Marie-Claude married to a Yankee and them living at Fair Oaks."

Abigail frowned and bit her lower lip. The inflection of his words showed her that Marie-Claude must be more to him than a sister-in-law.

He sighed. "I'll hire a stonemason to put up some permanent markers. One for Andrew, too. But just to be sure, I'd better see if Andrew's death has been confirmed." He shook his head. "I just can't believe Marie-Claude would do such a thing."

Abigail abruptly looked away. She was fast tiring of hearing that name. Could Travis have been telling the truth about Logan and Marie-Claude? Why else would Logan look and sound so sad when he spoke her name? She lifted her chin proudly. She had never been a second fiddle and had no intention of being one now. Perhaps something had been between them in the past, before Marie-Claude married Andrew, but that was then and this was now. She decided Travis' words had simply made her see more in Logan's speech than was really there.

"I've been wondering what you plan to do," she said.

"I don't know yet. This afternoon I'm going to ride into town and see what taxes are owed. Maybe I can weather this through."

She nodded. "I'm thinking of moving on." She glanced at him to see if he showed signs of caring.

He looked at her sharply. "You're leaving?"

"Aye. Tobe's tales of Texas intrigue me. I've a mind to travel on with him and perhaps find me a farm there."

"Why?"

"He says there was less fighting there. If so, there may be less scars on the land. He says the people are friendly and there's plenty of good farmland to be had."

"You'd leave me?"

"You have Rosehaven," she said deliberately. Would he prove to her that Travis had been lying? "You don't need me."

"But I *want* you."

"I always said the two of us couldn't work out."

"Don't go."

"I told you I wanted my own place. You should have listened."

"Don't leave me."

She met his eyes and was pleased to see the sincerity there. Logan was a strong man, both physically and mentally, but she knew that he needed her. "Perhaps Tobe doesn't plan to leave right away," she amended. She didn't want to hurt him, but Travis had almost convinced her that there was something between Logan and his former flame. She needed more reassurance from Logan. "But don't expect me to stay when he goes."

Quietly Logan said, "I guess I did expect it. I seem to have been wrong."

Abigail longed to take him in her arms and kiss away the raw pain she saw etched on his features. Only the uncertainty of his feelings for Marie-Claude prevented her. Abruptly she said, "I'm going back to the house. Will you walk with me?"

"No. I'm going to ride into New Orleans to take care of my business there." His voice was hard and clipped. "Tell Jeremiah I'll be home late."

"I'll tell him." She hadn't expected Logan to leave at such a crucial moment. She forced herself to walk away, but as she did, she felt as if a major part of her had been left behind.

Abigail sat on the dark veranda listening to the night song of the crickets. She knew she should go in out of the damp air, but she was reluctant to do so. Her afternoon had been occupied cleaning the house. And while much remained to be done, the house was in better shape than when they arrived.

Logan had returned from town shortly before supper, but she had managed to avoid him. Her heart felt sick when she wondered whether part of Logan's business of the day had involved a reunion with Marie-Claude. Perhaps her probing had put the notion in his head! In the moments when her jealousy waned, Abigail longed to swallow her pride and love Logan at any cost.

Never had any man filled her with such a mixture of doubt and desire. Her love for Logan wasn't at all serene and confident as her love for William had been, but, rather, was like a raging torrent. To make matters worse, she wanted him more almost daily.

Following their night of torrid lovemaking in Hammond, he hadn't come to her bed. True, only one night had passed since then and he had been distraught over the loss of his family; but she had expected him to come to her for comfort. She had been too proud to go to him. Now she wondered if Marie-Claude figured in his absence, and she burned to know if Travis had lied simply to upset her, or if he was trying to warn her.

Logan had made no reference to their loving, nor had he then or later made any declaration of affection for her. Much less one of marriage. Abigail had assumed that one, if not both, would have been forthcoming. She mentally derided herself for loving more than was prudent.

With a sigh she thought of William. Forthright and simple, William had been the very soul of security. Had he lived, she would never have truly hungered for anything, though wealth would not have been part of their future. In time babies would have come, some with his yellow hair, perhaps some with red. After the years had passed, she would have grown old with him in peaceful comfort and eventually been buried beside him in the churchyard.

Why, then, did she feel more longing for Logan than regret for her lost serenity with William? Why did she feel more alive after the last few weeks than she had in all her life? And why was she haunted day and night by the memory of Logan's sensuous kisses and caresses, when by all rights she should shun him as a rake and a despoiler of virtue?

Because Abigail knew she had lost no virtue in

their coming together and she had learned more about loving in that one night than she had ever experienced before.

The front door opened and Logan came out. He stood on the porch in his shirtsleeves, his back illumined by the light from inside. Abigail leaned back into the porch's deep shadow and waited for him to leave.

He gazed out at the night. Moonlight glowed on the curving drive and on the leafy domes of the avenue of live oaks. The broad entrance was a tunnel beneath their stretching boughs and the hedges were wild blots against the silvered grass. He drew a deep breath and said without turning, "Why are you avoiding me?"

He heard a faint gasp, then added, "Answer me, Abigail. I know you're there."

"I was not avoiding you," her softly burred voice replied from the shadows. "I was merely sitting and watching the moonlight."

Turning toward her, he strolled along the deep porch. As he neared, her pale face became visible. He sat beside her on the padded couch and gazed at her profile while she continued to watch the moonlight. "Searching for leprechauns?" he asked.

"None of the wee folk are around here, and there's not an Irish family about. And they don't like for people to call out their name so freely."

"Then what are you doing?"

"I was thinking of William," she said, sticking to a partial truth.

"Oh." He felt oddly deflated. Yet what could be more reasonable? She was too young to be a widow and had obviously loved her husband. Perhaps, he thought painfully, she had pretended he was William when she had loved him so thoroughly. He was a little surprised that the mere thought could hurt him so much.

After a while he said, "You never told me how you threw Chandler off our trail."

"I went to the hotel that Tobe told us about and asked to see him. When the barkeep refused, I slipped in the back way and up to his room."

"You went to his room? Alone? That was dangerous." Logan felt dread tighten his muscles.

"I pretended to be a barmaid, and in the process of flirting with him, I said you had been in town but had left for Shreveport."

"You did what?" he demanded. "A barmaid! He could have raped you! Did he touch you!"

"Not really," she hedged.

"Either he did or he didn't. Which!"

"He did but then he stopped. I'm not so foolish as to risk myself." Her voice had a doubtful ring, as if she weren't too sure of that.

"Don't you ever do a fool thing like that again."

"I'm quite all right. No harm came to me. In fact, I gave a lovely performance."

"I'll bet you did. I suppose you're going to tell me he won't remember those eyes of yours or that hair? Your accent alone is as good a trail as he needs to track us."

"I used a Southern accent," she said in honeyed tones. "He didn't know I have a slight one of my own."

"He 'dinna'?" Logan asked.

She frowned. "I did a better job of it at the time. I wasn't really trying just now."

He drew a deep breath and tried to smile. She was right or she wouldn't be here now. "As long as he didn't make any advances toward you."

"Well, I didn't exactly say that," Abigail said. "I said no harm came to me."

"What happened?" he asked warily.

"Believe me, Logan, you don't want to know. It would only fash you, and besides, the matter is done with. Let it be."

He watched her and wondered if "fash" was as ominous as its sound. Rather than ask, he decided he was better off not knowing.

"I found out about the taxes," he said to change the subject. "I owe nine thousand dollars and they will accept only gold."

"Nine," she gasped, unable to finish the phrase.

He nodded and rubbed his eyes tiredly. "Rosehaven is only worth about twenty thousand."

"Will you pay it?"

"I don't know. That would take every bit of my gold, and next year more taxes will be levied. Without money to hire labor, I can't put in a crop. I could live here a year, but it looks as if I would lose it then." He glanced at her. "I would chance it if you would stay."

Abigail looked quickly back at the tunnel of oaks. "I've said I'm going."

"Yes. You have." He had thought that their night together in Hammond meant more to her than it obviously had. How could she have held him and kissed him so ardently and then move on as if only a handshake had occurred between them?

"I wish you could have seen Rosehaven before the war," he mused aloud. "Everything was different then. Our people were well-fed and content. The place was beautiful. Martha Ann had made this a gracious home and it was a place to be proud of."

Abigail smiled. "It's still beautiful. I've never seen so grand a house."

"But now it's gone." He was on the verge of asking her to marry him, but prudence stopped him. His life was upside down and he had nothing to offer her—no security or even a guarantee of a roof over her head by the next year. He couldn't propose. Not with no more to offer her than himself.

He said, "Look through Martha Ann's clothes, if you like. She was about your size, maybe a little rounder. You may have whatever you want."

"I couldn't do that."

"They will only go to waste."

"Marie-Claude wouldn't want them?" Abigail asked, a strange note tightening her voice.

"No, she's taller than you are."

"I'm not surprised."

For some reason she sounded miffed. Logan wondered why. "Do you want the clothes or not?"

"I'll look at them." Belatedly she added, "Thank you."

"You're welcome."

A stiff silence knifed between them and the air seemed to thrum with the tension. Logan tried to make out her features in the night shades. "I guess you'll be moving on soon," he said awkwardly.

"Aye. As soon as Tobe is ready."

"I've asked him to stay a couple of weeks. The horses need a long rest after being ridden so hard the last few days. I hope that's not too inconvenient for you."

"I'll manage."

Her voice was tight and he thought he detected a tremble.

After a while she added, "If you aren't going to pay the taxes, what will you do?"

He shrugged. "I have no idea."

"Perhaps you should pay them. This is your home. With a good woman beside you, the place might pay."

"The woman I want doesn't seem to want me," he said dryly.

"Things change."

He *had* heard a tremor in her voice that time. Perplexed, he said, "Even if I stayed, I shouldn't pay the taxes. Everybody would wonder where I got so much money in times like these. I'd be asking for trouble with everyone from bushwhackers to carpetbaggers. A constant line of thieves and extortionists would line up at my door. Not to mention that word might get back to Chandler somehow."

"You'll buy a smaller place?" she suggested. "You could stay here that way."

He shook his head. "Rosehaven is my home. If I'm not going to live in it, there's no need to stay around. I wouldn't want to see trash buy it for a third of what it's worth and move in." He thought a minute. "I may as well move on."

"Perhaps you would like Texas," she said in an offhand manner, as if it didn't matter to her one way or the other.

"I may as well ride that way as any other," he replied with careful nonchalance.

"Then you might as well ride with us, I suppose." She looked at him squarely. "It will only be you going, I guess."

"Yes, I imagine so." He thought Jeremiah wasn't likely to want to go. He was old and would probably prefer to join his friends in New Orleans. He had no idea what Travis planned.

"Then you'd be welcome." If he chose to come

to Texas with her, then she could forget her rival and welcome Logan with open arms.

He hadn't missed the smile that softened her features. Gently he raised his hand and traced the rosebud velvet of her cheek. In the dark her eyes were mysterious pools that threatened to trap his soul. The prospect was alluring. "Now, will you tell me why you have been avoiding me?"

"You've imagined it."

Bending closer, he nuzzled her temple, where a tendril of her hair curled temptingly. "I didn't imagine you saying you wanted to leave me. Do you really feel that way?" He willed her to deny it so he could propose and end this purgatory.

"I could never live here," she answered. "Rosehaven is your home, not mine. I would never fit here."

"That's not true." He nuzzled her ear and left kisses along the shell-like curve.

"Logan," she whispered as his nearness spun the web of magic that always caught her senses. "In town today, did you see Marie-Claude?"

He paused in the act of kissing her temple and drew back. "How did you know that?" He had seen her at a distance, driving past in Andrew's buggy behind Andrew's best bay. If Marie-Claude had noticed him, she had given no sign of recognition.

"You did!" How could he dare to be with Marie-Claude in the afternoon and come around kissing her own ear that night? Outrage gave her strength.

Abigail jumped up so fast that Logan almost tumbled over into the space she had vacated. "I'll be going in now," she informed him in a trembling voice. "I'm going straight up to my room. And the door will be locked!" She spun on her heel and stalked away.

Logan stared after her and wondered what in the world he had said or done to set her off again. Trying to understand her was so damned frustrating.

13

Logan straightened his tired back and stretched his long arms. Hoeing a garden full of weeds was a chore he wasn't accustomed to doing, but the exercise felt good and he enjoyed the warm sun on his back. He surveyed his work with satisfaction. The plants started by Jeremiah stood strong and healthy in the fresh-tilled brown earth. Before long they would be steaming in bowls on the dinner table. He found he actually enjoyed being part of the process.

Beyond the garden fence, his land sloped away into horse pastures whose expanse was broken only by rows of trees that followed the streams and fences. The fine horses were gone with the exception of Caliban, who grazed with his men's horses. But the grass was tall and rich and a herd could be rebuilt, using Caliban as a start.

The cotton fields that lay beyond the pastures had gone back to the wilds. Weeds covered the once carefully tended rows, weeds that had flourished, died, and flourished again, each winter adding nutrients back to the soil. The next crop that was planted would produce better than ever for the land having lain fallow for several years.

He rested his hand on the hoe handle as he gazed over the land that had seen his birth, youth, and adulthood, as well as that of his parents and theirs before them. How could he have ever thought of letting it go? He loved this land and he couldn't just walk away and leave it to Yankee scavengers or trashy scalawags. Not his beloved Rosehaven.

The taxes were high, but perhaps a mistake had been made. If he talked to the tax assessor, maybe a deal could be struck or an agreement could be reached. Logan believed most people were basically honest and he felt confident that two reasonable men could work out a compromise. The assessor was out of town now, but he would return, and when he did, they could talk.

He looked across to the servants' yard, where Abigail was hanging the wash. A breeze filled and billowed her skirt, then whipped it tightly against her legs. Recalling how those legs had entwined with his brought a hot longing to his groin. He wanted her body, but more than that he wanted her love, which seemed out of his reach.

She had continued to avoid him and had again coolly denied that she had. Logan had no idea why. Although he had given the matter a great deal of thought, he could remember saying or doing nothing that would warrant her behavior.

He supposed he was better off without her if she was that moody and unpredictable, but he couldn't stop wanting her. Or loving her. Even now when she was pointedly ignoring him, he wanted to go to her, release her fiery hair, and let it tumble about them both, and love her until she loved him in return. If he tried, he suspected he would get swatted with a wet shirt for his effort.

The sound of horse hooves drew his attention and he turned to see a woman riding up the drive and around the house. There was no mistaking either her or the tall chestnut she rode. Logan leaned his hoe against the fence, then wiped his hands clean on his pocket handkerchief. "Hello, Marie-Claude. What brings you to Rosehaven?"

She was as classically beautiful as he had remembered. Her hair of palest gold was swept up in an elaborate chignon under her small blue velvet riding hat and her eyes, almost the same shade as the sky, were irresistibly lovely. Carefully protected from any sunbeams, her skin was pale and looked serenely cool. The blue velvet riding habit she wore was cut of luxurious cloth and had been perfectly tailored to her trim figure; even her graceful hands were encased in soft white kid gloves that were still spotless after her ride. To look at Marie-Claude, no one would ever guess a devastating war had torn this land apart and had ended an entire way of life, for the genteel South lived on in Marie-Claude.

Abigail, too, had heard the woman approach and she watched her as she finished hanging the sheet on the line. She had no doubt who the woman was, and a sick pain gripped her heart. With this lovely vision as her rival, Abigail knew she didn't have a chance. How could anyone compete with such perfection? Just looking at Marie-Claude across the yard made Abigail feel awkward and homely. As she dried her hands on her water-spotted apron, she noticed how red they were from the washwater.

The same instinct that encourages a person to poke at a sore tooth made Abigail cross the yard for a closer look. Surely no one could be so pretty. On closer surveillance, she hoped she would discover that Marie-Claude had a wart on her face or at least bad breath. But no wart was to be seen, and from Logan's attentive expression, her breath was apparently sweet as well. Hoping for crooked teeth to be revealed, Abigail stepped a little closer.

"I was almost afraid to come," she heard Marie-Claude say in the sweetest of tones. "So very much has happened."

"Yes. So I've heard." Logan turned to Abigail, who was quite near now, and said, "Marie-Claude, this is Abigail McGee. Abigail, my . . ." He paused awkwardly, for the woman he wanted to introduce was no longer his sister-in-law. "Marie-Claude . . ." Again he stumbled, unable to remember her married name.

"Smith," Marie-Claude supplied. Looking back at Logan, she said, "Could we talk? I have so much to say to you." She earnestly beseeched him to grant her an audience. She dismissed Abigail with a glance.

"I've more work to do," Abigail said stiffly. She threw Logan a disapproving glare that he missed altogether, and went back to the basket of wash.

Logan held up his hands to aid Marie-Claude in her descent. She unhooked her leg from the side-saddle and gathered her yards of skirt before letting him lift her down. She placed her hands on his broad chest to steady herself and lowered her silken lashes as if his mere presence overcame her. Delicately she said, "I've seldom seen you in your shirtsleeves."

"You'll have to forgive me. I couldn't decide which jacket was proper for hoeing the garden." Looking at Marie-Claude was like reliving the past. He actually felt slightly guilty for being improperly dressed in her presence. The sensation was both familiar and uncomfortable. "You must be quite warm in velvet on a day like today," he said, though she didn't look uncomfortable at all. In fact, he didn't recall ever having seen Marie-Claude perspire, and he wondered how she managed that.

"Do you like my dress?" she asked as she pirouetted for his approval. "It's new. My husband," she said, gracefully blushing, "ordered it from Boston. After all, I couldn't ride out in calico." She glanced at Abigail, who was wearing one of Martha Ann's calico dresses.

"Come sit in the shade and tell me why you're here," he suggested.

Marie-Claude took his arm, though he hadn't offered it, and let her breast graze his elbow. "You're so fortunate to find a competent laundress," she purred after appraising Abigail's face and figure. "With Cuffee grown so proud, we have had a terrible time getting servants. She's Scotch, isn't she?"

"Abigail isn't a laundress," Logan said hurriedly. "She's . . . Abigail."

The woman in question tossed Logan a glare over her shoulder and stabbed a clothespin on the shirt she held over the line.

"It's a little difficult to explain," he finished lamely.

"Yes." Marie-Claude managed somehow to look both embarrassed and superior. "Yes, I expect it is."

Logan frowned, but he couldn't explain Abigail's presence without mentioning the gold. After he dusted off the bench, Marie-Claude settled upon it like a windblown flower.

"I'm so terribly sorry about your family," she began. "Such a tragedy to lose them all. Even little Mahitaba."

"Yes, it was. Your own life has also been touched, I understand," he said tactfully. When she looked blank, he added, "Andrew. Jeremiah tells me he was killed at Manassas."

"Yes, he was." Marie-Claude produced a lace handkerchief from her sleeve and touched the corners of her eyes, which seemed quite dry. "I don't know why you had to go. You and Andrew both owned over eighty slaves. No one could have made you sign up."

"If I hadn't, I couldn't have lived with myself. Andrew probably felt the same way. Conscription wasn't a consideration for either of us."

"I suppose," she sighed petulantly. "I know everyone blames me for remarrying, but what was I to do? Our slaves ran away, and with Andrew gone forever, there was no one to take care of me and protect me."

Logan looked past Marie-Claude to Abigail, who was hanging the last pair of trousers. She bent and easily lifted the large basket and balanced it on her hip as she straightened a fold of the sheet. Her movements were strong and graceful.

Marie-Claude lowered her lashes to her cheek and tilted her head so she would appear smaller than she really was. "You can see my predicament. When Amos came along, he was my salvation."

"I understand he's also rich."

"Goodness yes, though I don't like to talk about it. He asked me to marry him and I couldn't refuse. If you ask me, I think those old gossips are simply jealous." She cast her captivating eyes up at him and blinked once. "You do understand, don't you? Tell me you do."

"Yes, I understand." He found that he really did. Marie-Claude was like a camellia, soft and easily bruised. She wasn't strong like Abigail. She was every bit as much of a survivor, but while

Abigail drew on her own resources, Marie-Claude would always need a trellis.

"I knew you wouldn't scold me. Oh, Logan, if only you knew what I've endured. I've even been called a scalawag! And white trash!" She shuddered delicately. "Me, whose blood is bluer than anyone's!"

Abigail passed them on the way to the house and gave Logan another scornful glance, which he missed entirely.

"She seems to be rather ill-tempered," Marie-Claude observed. "Her breeding no doubt."

He figured Abigail must have heard Marie-Claude's snide remarks, and his frown deepened. "She's not bad-tempered at all," he defended her, though by now she was out of earshot. "As a matter of fact—"

"You can't imagine how terrible it's been around here," Marie-Claude interrupted. "First there were terrible battles. Then New Orleans was put under Beast Butler. Do you know what he did?" she demanded in feminine outrage.

"No." Logan watched Abigail go into the house. He could tell by the way she carried herself that she was hurt, and he longed to go to her.

"He put a proclamation up all over town that said any Southern women rude to his troops were to be treated as fallen angels plying their trade." She blushed furiously by the simple ploy of holding her breath. "Can you imagine such an insult?"

"What?" He hadn't been listening.

"I never thought I would see such hard times. It was about then that Amos came to town." She turned to Logan imploringly and took his hand with her fingertips. "I had no way of knowing you would return or I would have waited, somehow. But you never wrote to me."

"I wrote to my parents and my sisters. There was no need to write to you separately."

"Logan, Logan, don't be cruel. My poor heart is breaking." She again touched her eyes with the handkerchief.

"Nonsense. I'd say you got exactly what you were after."

"I have a loveless marriage. Not that Amos is actually mean to me, but I don't care for him."

"Then you shouldn't have married him."

"I *had* to! Oh, don't you see? If I hadn't, a heavy tax would have been placed on Fair Oaks and I would have had no home." As if suddenly inspired, she said, "I tried to save it . . . for you."

"By marrying another man when you weren't positive that Andrew was dead?"

She recoiled as if he had struck her. "Logan! For shame!" Her face indeed paled, for that technicality had crossed her own mind more than once. "Are you trying to break my poor heart?"

"No, hearts are sturdier than that," he told her. "Otherwise none of us would survive."

"I was only trying to keep a home for you," she wailed.

"Rosehaven is my home. Not Fair Oaks. Don't cry, Marie-Claude." He couldn't bear to see a woman cry because he never knew what to do about it.

"I can't help it. You have turned against me like everyone else. And you know how I love you."

"Stop that." He stood abruptly and turned away. "I told you never to say that again."

"I know you did, but it's true. I do love you. I've never loved anyone else."

"Nonsense. You loved Andrew, or at least he thought you did."

"I loved the ways he was like you."

Logan groaned at her. "You have to stop this. Otherwise I'll have to ask you to leave. For goodness' sake, Marie-Claude, remember who you are."

"You're right," she sniffed daintily. "I was a Beaumont and then a Sorrell. It's just that I can't bear for you to be angry with me."

"Listen to me, and this time hear my words. There was never anything between us, nor will there be. Ever. I told you that before, you evidently didn't believe me."

"I was married to your brother then. Now everything is different. He's dead and you're here with me."

"You're forgetting one small detail. You have a husband. One who is probably wondering where you are."

"Not him," she said as she made a shooing action with her handkerchief. "He's off on one of his business trips up the river. I'm there all alone with the servants." She gazed up at him through her tear-dewed eyelashes. "And I'm lonely," she pouted.

"I see." He held out his hand and she took it. Drawing her to her feet, he tucked her fingers into the crook of his elbow and strolled her back to her horse. "You mustn't be afraid of being alone," he said, thinking he now understood. "I'm sure your servants are to be trusted or your husband would never have left you behind. As for loneliness, you must have friends."

"None of our people will accept me anymore," she mourned. "Not even the Beardens, who are *nouveaux riches* and quite insufferable." Her kittenish pout drew a smile to Logan's lips.

"You must have made some new friends."

"Yes, but they are all Yankees, and when Amos isn't here they snub me." She added imploringly, "I need you, Logan."

"No, you don't. You're stronger than that. Why, our grandparents carved this land out of a wilderness."

"Great-grandparents," she corrected automatically.

"If they could face Indians and snakes and wild animals, you can manage a few Yankee women. Where's your fighting spirit?"

"Logan, how you do talk. Fighting spirit indeed! I'm a lady, not a soldier. And I'm tired of being snubbed. I want to go back to the way things were."

"I know. We all do," he said sadly as they reached her horse. "Those days are dead, I'm afraid."

"Don't say that!"

"It's true. We have to face reality and make a new future. That's the only way to survive."

"How unpleasant you are today," she complained sulkily. "You've changed."

"We all have." As he spoke, he realized that what he said wasn't entirely true, for Marie-Claude hadn't changed at all.

"Will you come see me?" she asked petulantly as he lifted her onto the sidesaddle.

"No," he answered pleasantly. "You have your own life, and I have mine."

"With that laundress, you mean?" Marie-Claude said spitefully.

"I told you that she isn't a servant. No more than I'm a gardener." He nodded toward the freshly hoed garden. "Times have changed and I plan to change with them. As for Abigail, yes. I hope she's in my future."

Marie-Claude's eyes dilated in fury but she merely straightened in her saddle. "You'll come to your senses and see that she's all wrong for you. I'm the one you were meant for. Not her."

"No. You were never the one." He knew his words were overly harsh, but he had to get through her shell of make-believe and false hope.

"You'll see. Somehow I'll prove it." Marie-Claude wheeled her horse and thundered away, clearing the rail fence neatly.

Abigail stepped back from the parlor window and rubbed her palm over her middle. Marie-Claude was all she had feared she would be. Travis' glowing description of her hadn't done her justice. Abigail had watched them shamelessly, though at first she had felt a twinge of guilt. She hadn't missed a single fluttered lash or dainty gesture. Although she couldn't hear what was being said, she saw that it was Logan who reached out to Marie-Claude and drew her to her feet. He had put her hand on his arm of his own volition, and when they reached the horse, he had lifted her up to the saddle as if she were a child and not a grown woman. Jealousy pierced Abigail's heart. He never did such things for her. She conveniently overlooked the fact that he had offered to carry the heavy load of wash for her, but she had sent him away.

Lifting her hands, Abigail frowned at them. They seemed to typify all she lacked by comparison to Marie-Claude. Her palms were square and her fingers short. Capable hands, hands strong enough to do whatever work was necessary, but not the hands of a lady. She had never owned a pair of riding gloves in her life, nor did she expect to. And she would never be a willowy blond with incredibly blue eyes who wore a velvet riding habit. No wonder Logan preferred Marie-Claude.

When she heard Logan enter the house, she turned and dashed for the stairs. Facing Logan's love-filled eyes was the last thing she wanted. Before he could call to her, she was gone.

She ran down the narrow hallway and into the small room that adjoined her own. She sat on a cushioned seat beneath one of the expansive windows and drew her legs up under her. Far below, she could still see Marie-Claude. The woman had slowed her horse to a less dramatic pace and was crossing the larger meadow.

Was Marie-Claude as heartsick for Logan as she was? Even in her jealousy, Abigail couldn't wish this misery on her rival. She felt as if her heart was indeed broken, because after seeing Marie-Claude, she knew she had no chance of completely winning Logan away. There would always be a part of Logan that wished for his way of life before the war, and that included the perfect Southern belle, Marie-Claude.

She heard Logan's footsteps coming down the hall, but she didn't turn her head. Tears were stinging her eyes and she couldn't trust herself to face him. He paused at the open door, then came in.

"I was looking for you," he said.

She ignored him.

"You mustn't pay any attention to what Marie-Claude said. She didn't know you could hear her."

"No?" Abigail congratulated herself on keeping her voice casual. "I have no idea what you could be talking about."

"She comes from a different world than your

own. Her family is one of the oldest and proudest in Saint Charles Parish."

Abigail swallowed and tried to blink back her tears. Marie-Claude's remarks were only a taste of what she could expect if she stayed at Rosehaven as Logan's lover. She was beginning to accept the fact he would offer her no more than a liaison.

"She isn't strong like you. She needs someone to protect her and to see to her needs."

Abigail knotted her capable hands into fists, but buried them in her skirt rather than strike out at Logan. He had come to the window and together they watched Marie-Claude ride out of sight. Neither spoke for a moment.

"I guess you've decided to stay here?" Abigail asked dully.

"Yes. This is my home. I want you to stay here too."

"As your laundress? No, thank you."

"Hah! I knew you heard that!"

Abigail glared at him. "What does 'Cuffee' mean?"

He looked away. "Most of our laundresses around here were slaves or freed Negroes."

"That's what I thought it meant."

He put his hand on her slender neck and stroked his thumb over the stray curls that had escaped her bun. "Why are you so set on leaving? Don't you like Rosehaven?"

"Rosehaven is beautiful. It's like a fairy-tale castle I read about when I was a child. That's why I can't stay. You saw what she thought of me. This isn't my place."

"You met under adverse circumstances," he objected. "If you had been in the front parlor or the music room, she would never have made that mistake."

"No, then she would have taken me for something different. I prefer to be confused with an honest laundress." She shot him an appraising glance. "That *is* all she thought, isn't it?"

"Yes," he said a shade too quickly and with a bit too much fervor.

"I don't believe you." She turned back to peer out the window. She could see Harley and Tobe walking along the creek, carrying a string of fish for their supper. Travis and Martin had been gone all day.

"I can't talk you into staying?"

"No." His hand fell away from her neck, and at once she was regretful.

"I'm not going to stop trying to change your mind. As long as you're here, I have hope."

Abigail didn't answer but she prayed Tobe would decide to leave soon. Though she dreaded leaving Logan, she was very much afraid she wouldn't be able to resist him for long.

14

Self-consciously Abigail sat in the front parlor trying to decide what to do with her hands. She was dressed in a gown of celery green trimmed in deep flounces of ecru lace. In her hand she gripped a fan inlaid with flowers of mother-of-pearl. Never had she felt so ill-at-ease.

"Bless me," said her company. "It does seem so strange not to see your womenfolk about the house. Rosehaven just isn't the same."

"No, it never will be," Logan agreed. "Care for some more cider?"

"Goodness, no. The girls and I are quite satisfied." The woman smiled beatifically upon her twin daughters, Letty and Dolly.

Both girls replaced their glasses on the tray at their mother's signal and smiled shyly at Logan. Abigail shifted in the satin-covered chair.

"I guess you'll be settling down," their father said in his booming tones. "After all this upheaval, it's time to turn to domestic matters, such as a family to carry on the name of Sorrell."

"Papa!" One of the twins blushed. The other merely twittered as if overcome by such blunt talk.

"I suppose it is, at that," Travis drawled, enjoying Abigail's discomfort. "Any candidates, cousin?"

Logan gave him an appraising look. He had told Travis in confidence of his intentions toward Abigail. What was Travis doing? Logan smiled back and said, "I'm not quite ready to make an announcement."

Abigail's eyes dropped to the fan in her lap. She unfurled it, then snapped it shut, trying to escape the curious and jealous glances from all four Duprees. Logan had not offered to explain her unexpected presence at Rosehaven and she knew the Duprees must be assuming the worst. Still, she couldn't quite explain it either. When she started chasing after the gold, she had never considered she would end up on a Louisiana plantation.

"Have you anyone in mind?" Travis pursued, daring Logan to name Abigail in the company of his parents' close friends and Logan's old flames.

Letty and Dolly lowered their lashes demurely and listened with rapt attention.

"Perhaps," Logan evaded. "Until I've spoken to her, however, I won't tell you her name."

Each girl gave the other a triumphant look, and Abigail writhed inside. If she hadn't known about Marie-Claude, she would wonder how he could choose, for Letty and Dolly were as much alike as two buttons. But neither could match Marie-Claude's poised beauty.

"Don't tarry too long," their father advised stentoriously. "More of our boys in gray are coming home each day. Take my word for it, my beauties will be snapped up in no time."

"Papa!" the twins cried in unison.

He chuckled and hooked his thumb in the pocket of his vest. To the room at large he said, "The boy knows it's true and that there's not another family in the parish his parents would rather have seen him allied with."

"Really, Mr. Dupree," his wife objected. "You're embarrassing us all." She smiled at Abigail, who tried valiantly to smile back. "I don't believe I caught your relationship to the Sorrell family. Are you a cousin?"

"She's from Mississippi," Travis blurted out.

"I don't believe I've ever heard of a branch of the family in Mississippi."

"I'm not a Sorrell," Abigail answered. She had not spoken a dozen sentences since the Duprees arrived. Although she wasn't usually shy, she found herself tongue-tied in their company. The Duprees belonged here, down to the marrow of their bones. And although Marie-Claude's implication that she didn't fit into this society still rankled her, Abigail couldn't disagree. She didn't want her presence to be an embarrassment for Logan. Had it been left to her, she would have stayed in her room.

Logan shifted uncomfortably and wished Travis would stop throwing barbed innuendos into the conversation. He and Travis had shared secrets all their lives. What was going on with him?

From where they sat, Logan was able to watch Abigail without appearing to do so. Sunlight from the window cast a glow in her cheeks and brightened the red highlights in her hair, which was wound in an intricate braid and coiled on the back of her head.

The conversation flowed to horse farms Mr. Dupree had seen in Mississippi and then to the training of horses in general. The Dupree women seemed quite bored, but Logan noticed Abigail's eyes were alert with genuine interest. Mrs. Dupree was trying to engage her in a conversation about recipes, and though Abigail responded politely enough, Logan could see she preferred the conversation of the men.

While the discussions droned on, Logan compared Abigail to Letty and Dolly. Before the war he had considered marrying one of the twins, but he had never decided which. Now he was amazed that he had ever given them a passing thought. Not only were they remarkably alike in thought as well as form, but they seemed excessively dull.

His father had told him to be careful in his choice of a mate. Many things were to be considered in a courtship, not the least of which was compatibility. Logan had been taught to look for a woman with a sweet docile nature, one who would ask no probing questions, one who was unquestionably obedient. Yet, since he had met Abigail, he had begun to doubt his father's wisdom. He found Abigail's straightforward speech and energetic ways much more compatible than Letty's simper or Dolly's studiously blank expression. Abigail was a woman with whom he could build a new empire from the ashes of the old. A woman who would stand proudly beside her man, not two paces behind. Logan liked that.

"I heard Logan say you're a widow," Letty said. "Such a pity."

"Aye. He was killed at Shiloh," Abigail replied.

"And you came to Rosehaven for shelter and protection?" Dolly assumed.

"Not at all. I never knew Rosehaven existed, nor the Sorrells," Abigail told her. "I had my own farm east of Jackson. And a good one it was, too, with rich bottomland and a lovely hillside where I planned to raise some sheep."

The Dupree women looked at her blankly.

"Abigail is Scots-Irish," Travis said. Buzzing voices in his head had been hovering around all morning, stoking his anger, urging him to lash out at someone. Anyone. He shook his head to clear his thoughts, then added, "She knows more about farming than any man I know. And sheep."

Abigail flashed him a surprised look. She had never confided in him. She noticed Logan also seemed to be wondering at Travis' knowledge of her past.

"Surely you had an overseer to look after such matters," Mrs. Dupree protested.

"It was a farm I had, not a plantation. After my William was gone, I was there alone and I ran it all myself." She lifted her chin defiantly.

"My goodness," Dolly murmured.

"Sheep!" gasped Letty.

"A farm!" their mother exclaimed as she peered at her astonished husband. "I don't believe you're a Sorrell at all!"

"That I'm not. I said so myself."

Mr. Dupree cleared his throat gruffly, because everyone knew no woman of breeding ran her own farm and aspired to raise sheep, much less spoke with a Scots-Irish burr. Not to mention the unspoken question of why she was here unchaperoned, if she were not a relative. "Speaking of farming," he said heartily, hoping to redirect the conversation to safer ground, "I expect to put in a full crop of cotton next year. We were fortunate in that no Yankee has cast a hungering eye on our home, and our taxes have consequently been fairly reasonable, though they are higher than they've ever been."

"We can't say the same of Rosehaven," Travis said. "If Logan doesn't pay within the month, it's to be sold."

"I can pay it," Logan snapped. He had missed not one word of the exchange and had correctly interpreted the Duprees' disdain. "Next spring I'll plant, too."

"You can pay those taxes?" Mr. Dupree exclaimed. "I saw that notice. You must have buried a fortune in silver plate to meet that and afford cotton as well."

"Better than that," Travis answered indolently. His anger and resentment grew, provoking him to shock the comfortable and self-satisfied Duprees, to shatter their silly smiles and hush their simpering voices. He needed to do something to prove his superiority.

"What?" both twins asked as they leaned forward as if pulled by the same string.

"Travis is joking with you," Logan growled warningly at his cousin. "Aren't you?"

"Why, we're all friends here," Travis said innocently. "The Duprees would never tell the Yankees where their gold is."

"How ever did you get Yankee gold?" asked Letty.

"Do they know?" Dolly chimed in.

"They know we stole it, but they don't know where it is," Travis said.

"That's enough!" Logan's voice was curt with command. Fortunately, Travis had discretion enough to obey. To their guests Logan said, "I'm afraid that's become a private joke with us. Of course we have no gold. At least, no more than anyone might have."

"It's precious little these days," Dolly complained.

"My parents had a bit put away before the war," Logan said to cover up.

"A wee bit," Abigail added. "Scarcely enough to mention. I'm surprised Travis did." She glared at him.

"He won't do it again," Logan said meaningfully. "Such words in the wrong ears could bring about grief for us all."

"How true," Mr. Dupree agreed. "These days there's a thief behind every bush. Silence is a good rule on such matters." He was thoughtful for a moment, then said very casually, "I hear there's a group of men hereabouts that aim to do something about those thieves. They call themselves the Knights of the White Camellia. So I hear."

"Oh?" Travis was suddenly alert. "Where do they meet?"

"I've heard they meet in old Bernhart's horse barn. Couldn't say for sure, of course. Thursday nights, the rumor goes."

"We wouldn't be interested," Logan answered before Travis could speak. "I've seen enough fighting to last a lifetime. I just want to put my life back together."

"I understand," Mr. Dupree said heartily. "Travis, maybe you'll drop by someday soon?"

"I'll do that."

"Good, good. Mrs. Dupree, girls, we had better go now."

As obediently as children, his womenfolk stood up and smiled their farewells on Logan and Travis. Abigail also received good-byes, but they were noticeably strained.

She gripped her fan tightly and managed to appear calm as the guests left. As Dolly let Travis hand her into the coach, Abigail heard her ask, "Whatever could she be doing, living here without a woman to chaperon her?"

"Hush," Letty scolded playfully. "What a wicked thing to say!" Both girls giggled archly and were silenced by a frown from their father.

Abigail kept her chin up until the barouche had pulled away. Then she gathered her skirts and ran down the steps and over the grass toward the woods.

"Abigail!" Logan called out. When she only ran faster, he muttered an oath against the Dupree twins. No one had misinterpreted their parting remarks. He had hoped Abigail was too far away to hear it, but obviously she wasn't.

He ran after her. Abigail's low cloth shoes let her run quickly over the sloping ground. The trees closed around her, but she continued to hurry along, tears blinding her. She knew Logan was chasing her, and she couldn't bear to face him just yet.

At the mossy bridge that arched over the creek, Logan caught up with her. "Abigail! Wait! Don't run away." He grabbed her arm and drew her to a stop.

She kept her face turned so he couldn't see the tears of mortification that raced down her cheeks. All her life Abigail had despised her own vulnerability, and had hated for anyone to see her cry. "Leave me alone!" she snapped, trying to hide her pain behind a mask of anger.

Logan easily saw through her. "Don't run away from me," he said with great gentleness.

Drawing a trembling breath, Abigail quit struggling. He was much stronger, and she knew that fighting him would be useless. "I was right, Logan," she sighed. "You heard what they said. I've shamed you in front of your friends."

"No friends of mine would hurt you." He never wanted to see the Duprees again.

Abigail misunderstood. "Then I suppose I imagined it all. I'm sure that they were very pleasant and hold me in a high regard. Perhaps they will come for tea and we can discuss methods of birthing sheep." Sarcasm dripped from her voice.

Logan knew no words could take away the hurt, so he drew her to him. Silently he held her close, cradling her body in a protective embrace. After a pause, she relaxed against him and put her arms around him. Sobs trembled through her body but she made no sound. "Don't cry," he soothed. For some reason her tears didn't make him feel responsible and guilty—only very protective.

"I'm not crying!" she lied. "If you think I am, you're wrong."

"What are you doing, then?"

"Breathing. It's a long run from the house."

"I see." He handed her his handkerchief. "You're the only woman I've ever known who wasn't prepared for . . . breathing. I've never seen you carry a handkerchief."

She took the freshly ironed soap-scented handkerchief and wiped her eyes. "Thank you," she mumbled.

He lifted her chin and gazed down into her dewy eyes. "You're also the only woman I've ever known who didn't use tears as a manipulative weapon. I never thought of that until now."

"I never cry," Abigail managed to deny. "Never!"

Logan took the handkerchief and wiped away a tear that trembled on her eyelashes. "Of course you don't."

She turned away and wrapped her arms across herself as if she were in pain. "You know what they thought of me," she ground out. "They think I'm white trash. That I'm here to pleasure you and feather my own nest!" She stared sightlessly at the dark water beneath the bridge.

"No they don't."

"They do. And they're right." Her voice was harsh, as if saying the words rasped her throat. "I followed you for gold and I gave myself to you. Willingly and without any hope that you cared for me."

"Abigail, I—"

"No, don't deny it," she interrupted. " 'Tis true. I'm a fallen woman, just as they say. I should never have left my farm."

"Starving for the sake of what some gossiping biddies might say wouldn't make any sense," he defended her. "You didn't sell yourself for gold and you sure as hell aren't living here to pleasure me!"

"I'll go away. That's what I should have done before." She didn't trust herself to look at him. "I'll go back to my farm."

"What about Texas? I thought you were going on with Tobe."

"I don't know where Texas is. I can find my farm again." Logan also knew where her farm was, and if he ever wanted her, he would know exactly where to look for her. "I'll leave today."

"No you won't. I don't want you to leave."

"You would have me stay here and be scorned by all your friends? Shamed if I ever left the house? I can't do that."

"I want you to stay as my wife."

Abigail stared at him, hope glimmering in her dusky eyes. Surely no man would propose to one woman if he were interested in another. Maybe all her fears had been groundless, but she wanted to be positive that she had Logan's heart on a first-hand basis. Did he want her enough to go out of his way to attain her hand? "No," she answered firmly.

Logan blinked incredulously. He had seen her expression brighten eagerly, then fade. "No?" he asked uncertainly. "You won't marry me?"

"You must not be accustomed to having your offers turned down, but no, I'll not marry you." She watched him from the corner of her eye.

"Believe it or not, I don't go around proposing to just anyone I can outrun," he said. His face was drawn with concern. "Why won't you marry me?"

"I'm not required to tell you that, and I'm surprised at you for asking." She jerked up her head and crossed over the curving bridge. Beneath the deep shade of a huge sycamore which grew beside the water, flanked by several tall willows, she stopped and stared down at the carpet of emerald moss at her feet.

Groaning in exasperation, Logan followed her. "You don't love me? Is that it?"

She gave him only a cool glance. He hadn't spoken of love for her, and wild horses wouldn't make her admit she loved him. To lie about it, however, was beyond her, especially under the circumstances. She pretended to be very interested in the moss and knelt to examine it.

Logan sat on the ground next to her and pulled her around to face him so that she reclined in his arms. "I don't understand you," he growled.

Before she could stop him, he kissed her, his lips mastering hers with a sensuous persuasion that force could never have equaled. Abigail felt his tongue caress her lips and tease the soft inner lining. Her mouth opened instinctively, inviting his passion.

As his arms held her securely, his mouth urged her to respond. The banked fires rose within Abigail and a soft moan escaped her throat. His hand found her breast and loved it through the thin cotton of her dress. Abigail's nipples peaked in response and she realized she was returning his kiss with as much ardor as his own. In surprise she pulled back.

"How can you kiss me like that and not care?" he demanded. "How can you respond to a kiss with so much emotion, yet say you don't want me?"

"I never said I didn't want you," she whispered. "Only that I won't marry you."

"That doesn't make any sense." He stroked the pulse in her throat and pressed his lips to the warm beat. "Will you stay with me and be my wife? No one in Louisiana will dare look down on you then."

"No," she murmured. "No. Don't ask me again."

"I'm going to ask you again. And again. I won't stop until you agree."

"You're a hard man," she sighed in his ear, her voice not matching her words at all. "A gentleman would take a lady's refusal. But then," she said, "I suppose I'm no longer a lady."

"And I have rarely been a gentleman." His tongue traced the inner curve of her ear and he felt her shiver deliciously.

He rolled her over his lap and onto the soft moss, his body stretching out beside hers. She made a token protest, but with her arms holding him tightly, Logan paid no attention to her words. His lips followed the line of her jaw to the warm hollow of her neck. Abigail made a purring sound as he tasted her skin lovingly, running the tip of his tongue over her smooth flesh. She moved beneath him, but not in objection.

Logan freed her hair and untangled it from its

bun. As the thick tresses curled over her shoulder, he wound his fingers through it. "Your hair is like tamed fire," he said hoarsely. "I wish you would leave it down."

"That wouldn't be proper."

"I would run my fingers through it every time you came near," he went on as if she hadn't spoken. "I'd wrap my hand in it and pull you into my arms." He wound it around his hand and gently tilted her face up to his. "In the spring I'd weave you a garland of daisies and in the fall a wreath of leaves as bright as your hair. You'd be my queen and bind me with your magic just as you are doing now."

Abigail gazed up at him, her eyes the soft shade of woods violets, her lips dewy from his kisses. "Logan . . ." she whispered.

"I'd make you happy every day of your life," he promised softly as he rubbed her hair along her cheek. "There may be hard times ahead, but we'll face them together. You and I. And every day I'll love you and every night I'll prove it."

"Yes," she breathed in spellbound delight. "Yes, Logan, I'll stay with you and be your wife." Her words surprised her almost as much as they pleased him. Yet what woman with the passions of both Ireland and Scotland in her veins could deny a proposal like that? she defended herself. His last words sank in and she blinked. Had that been a manner of speech, or did he really mean he loved her? She was afraid to ask. Instead, she drew him down to kiss her as she ran her fingers through his thick black hair.

His lips moved over hers, knowing exactly how to give her pleasure and awaken her desires. Abigail met him equally, urging him further. Her breast swelled under his hand and she moved eagerly against him.

Logan drew back and sat up, pulling her up beside him. Abigail swayed, dizzy from her passion. Her hair tumbled over her shoulders and breasts and pooled in her lap. Her lips parted and Logan leaned nearer to kiss her again. But she sensed a restraint now where none had been before. Her eyes questioned him silently.

"Not here," he said huskily. "Not tumbled in the woods where anyone might come along at any time."

"But—"

"I'll ride into New Orleans tomorrow and find someone to marry us."

"But I—"

"I know. A woman wants her wedding night to be special. I'm not going to give you cause to look back on this day and regret that we sealed our engagement like we almost did." He smiled in understanding, though he ached from unfulfilled desire.

Abigail let her hands drop into her lap. She already knew she would look back on this day with regret. She would have preferred the tumble in the moss.

Travis leaned on the stall door and watched Harley toss out the soiled hay. "What do you plan to do with all your gold?" he asked pleasantly enough.

"I come from a big family. I don't expect there will be any lack of places to spend it. Besides, I've been giving some thought to marrying."

"Marrying! At your age?" Travis hooted. "You're not much older than the baby you'll make."

Harley flushed as he jabbed the pitchfork angrily into the hay. "I was old enough to go to war. I'm coming home a rich man. That makes me plenty old enough."

"He's got you there," Martin called out from the next stall. "Hey, Tobe! When you come back this way, bring a bale of hay."

"I hear you," Tobe's voice floated down from the loft.

"What about you, Martin?" Travis asked. "Where are you going to spend your money? As far as I know, you don't have a family."

Martin glanced at him, then went back to shoveling out the hay in his horse's stall. "Nope. No family. I'm going to spend it all on wild women and song." He exchanged a grin with Harley and winked. "What about you, Travis?"

"I guess it will take all that and much more to get Magnolias rebuilt." Travis leaned on the top rail of the stall. "Unlike our young gentleman here, ten thousand isn't a king's ransom to me."

A bale of hay dropped unexpectedly from the loft and came within an inch of hitting Martin. He yelped and jumped back to glare at Tobe, who was squatting down by the square opening in the loft floor. "You damn fool, you nearly threw it on me!"

"You said you wanted a bale of hay," Tobe drawled. "There it is."

"I said bring it, not throw it at me."

"How was I to know you'd call for hay and then stand under the drop? You aren't getting senile, are you?"

Martin brushed the stray straw out of his gray beard and glared again at Tobe. "Crazy Texian," he muttered. Taking out his pocketknife, Martin cut the two jute strings that secured the bale, handed them over the fence to Travis, and started kicking the hay around the stall to make bedding.

Travis passed the hay ropes through a loop of wire that was used to gather them and said to Tobe, "I guess you'll be spending your money on Rosa."

"Yep. Her and our *niñas*. I'm going to make life sweet for her. She has had to work way too hard all her life. Now she can be a *patrona*."

"On ten thousand?" Travis asked in disbelief.

"Money goes further in Texas." Tobe shrugged.

"Nothing to buy but jackrabbits and cactus," Martin put in. "They don't cost much."

"That just goes to show how much you know about it," Tobe rose to the bait. "My part of Texas has trees as big as any you ever seen, and all kinds of wildflowers and rivers. It's a real paradise."

"Then how come God put it in Texas?" Martin countered.

"Sounds to me as if we could all use more money," Travis observed. "Harley's got his family and bride, Tobe has his estate to plan, and I know for a fact there's more wild women than Martin has money to bed."

"Well, we can't make it grow like potatoes," Harley retorted from the safe walls of the stall.

"No, but we could add to it," Travis said nonchalantly.

"What have you got in mind?" Martin queried as Tobe sat down and let his legs dangle over the manger.

"Like I've mentioned before, there's plenty more Yankee gold where that came from. There's a little town not far from here, and that little town has a bank. A place that size has to have at least fifty thousand. Now, we all know no Southerners have that kind of money these days. No, that's Yankee gold, pure and simple."

"Last time you brought this up, Logan told you to forget it," Tobe said. "Besides, it's not ours."

"Neither was the payroll gold before we took it," Travis answered.

"But that was wartime," Harley objected. "This ain't the same thing."

Travis' face darkened and his eyes glittered with hate. "Maybe Lee surrendered, but I never did. I'm going to hate Yankees all my life and do all I can to get back at them."

"Still," Martin said, "you're talking about bank robbery. Aren't you?"

"That's right. At least fifty thousand in gold, split four ways."

"Four? What about the captain?"

"Logan already said he didn't want any part of this. No point in mentioning it to him."

"Robbing banks is wrong," Harley said. "We could get put in jail."

"Why do you think Chandler was chasing us?" Travis replied. "He wasn't intending to scold us and send us on our way. We got away from him once and we could do it again."

"I don't know," Harley muttered uncertainly. "I mean, I could sure use the money, but something don't seem right about this."

Tobe frowned but kept quiet.

"Fifty thousand, you say?" Martin asked.

"Minimum," Travis answered. "Bank in a city like New Orleans has to have twice that."

"A hundred thousand?" Tobe said. "All in one place?"

"That's right. That's why almost all the banks

are run by Yankees. Southerners don't have that kind of money anymore. All our banks are closed down by law." He flicked his black eyes from one to another. "What do you say?"

"Count me out," Harley spoke up. "I didn't come through the war to end up in some stinking prison from foolishness like this." He raked the last of the hay out the stall door. "Tobe, shove down another bale."

"Stand back."

"What about you?" Travis asked Martin. "Are you as chicken-livered as they are?"

The old man rubbed his beard thoughtfully. "Fifty thousand, you say. Let me put my mind to it for a bit. It's not a thing a man ought to rush into."

"You think it over and let me know. You too, Tobe." Travis glanced up as a rectangle of hay tumbled through the hole.

"I'll think about it, but I can tell you now that my answer will be no, just like I said before," Tobe replied with no malice. "It's not for me."

"We'll talk about it later," Travis said as he saw Logan walking toward them from the house. "And remember. No need to bother Logan with this."

Martin nodded.

15

Shreveport, La., July 2, 1865
To Col. B. W. Dearborn, Washington, D.C.:

Lead on Shreveport erroneous STOP Leaving for
New Orleans today STOP Will keep you advised
STOP

Owen Chandler, Maj.

Abigail shoved aside the billowing yards of her
peach lawn skirt, only to have the fabric flare and
roll back. With a grimace she put down the flat-
iron and glanced around the room. Since no one
was around, she tucked the petticoats and skirt
between her knees, then straightened. That was
better.

Again she tested the iron and continued smooth-
ing the wrinkles from Logan's shirt. At least now
she could reach the ironing board without tripping over her skirt. She was beginning to wonder
how fine ladies ever got anything done for having
to battle their own clothes. But then, fine ladies
had a platoon of servants to do their bidding. She
was thankful she had not put on the hoop that
was supposed to hold the skirt out like an inverted
flower. She had discarded the hoop because it had
made the skirt too short for her. Had she worn it,
the entire affair—skirt, petticoats, and all—would
be belling up behind her now, revealing her legs

and bloomers to anyone who passed. Abigail couldn't understand why any woman would consent to wear a hoop, let alone choose to.

As she continued with her task, Abigail breathed in the fresh smell of hot starch that scented the air. She loved the clean aromas of starch and soap. Although cooking wasn't her favorite activity, she had never objected to ironing. Especially not Logan's shirts.

Running her hand over the smooth fabric, she imagined the way it fit across his sides and chest and pulled taut over his shoulders. She was going to enjoy being Logan's wife and seeing to his needs. His clothes would always be clean and pressed under her care, and his meals hot and hearty. Logan's wife.

The mere words had a magical ring to her and made a secret smile curve her lips. She wondered if he had told anyone. At times like this she sorely missed her friend Mattie. No one was there to listen while she recounted all Logan's peerless qualities. No one to nod agreeably while Abigail explained that he was indeed perfect and their love the greatest the world had ever known. Abigail missed having a woman friend in whom she could confide.

Her eyes grew dreamy as she imagined Logan as her husband. He had faults—she knew that, logically—but she loved him and knew that the two of them were a good match. Their relationship might lack the serenity of her first marriage, but sometimes serenity masked dullness. Dull was one thing Logan would never be. Sometimes he tried to put her up on a pedestal and admire her from afar, but she would have none of it. Logan needed a wife as strong and vigorous as he was, and Abigail McGee was just the woman to mate him.

The iron cooled as Abigail's reverie lingered on, so she took it back to the fire and exchanged it for one of the other two that were heating. She pushed the troublesome skirt back between her legs, then set her mind to the job at hand.

Logan entered the room behind her, but instead of announcing his presence, he leaned against the door to study her. She fascinated him. He could watch her for hours and never tire of the activity. Today she wore a dress the color of a ripe peach that made her skin look as rich as cream. Her hair was looped low on her neck in a convolution of braids that intrigued him. How on earth did she do that without a maid's help? Abigail was truly remarkable.

To watch her, one would think she was enjoying the work, rather than doing what must be done from necessity. Someday, he promised silently, he would have servants to do the work for her. Then Abigail could dress in luxurious gowns and live like a queen. With the setback of the war, this goal might take a few years to accomplish, but Logan had no doubt that he would be a rich man again. Not only survival but also success was in his blood.

He stepped up behind Abigail, then bent and kissed her on the nape of the neck.

Abigail jumped and cried out in surprise. She wheeled around brandishing the iron but realized in time that the lips belonged to Logan. "Good heavens," she gasped. "You nearly scared the life from me." Hastily she fluffed the skirt out from between her legs.

"I didn't think you'd mind."

She set the iron on the metal rest and put her

arms around his neck. "I'll never mind your kisses. I just had no idea you were anywhere around."

"What was that song you were humming?"

" 'The Riddle Song.' My papa used to sing it to me when I was a child. He said it was very old. The oldest song he knew."

"Someday you'll sing it to our children."

Abigail blushed happily. "Aye, that I will."

"I hope they all look like you. Beautiful, feminine, with lots of reddish hair."

"That will be a curse on all the fine strapping sons I plan to give you."

"Let's just be sure there's at least one daughter." He grinned. "A colleen who will wind me about her little finger."

"Listen to us," she laughed. "Planning our family, and not even a wedding date set."

"When do you want it to be?" he asked, brushing a curly tendril off her warm brow.

"I see no reason to delay," she answered. "Not when we've our whole lives waiting to start."

"That's exactly how I feel. I'll ride over to the church and arrange things. You decide what sort of dress you want."

"Another dress? That would be too extravagant! There are more here now than I'll ever wear out."

"Sweetheart, as the mistress of Rosehaven, you can have new dresses every season. It's expected."

Abigail saw a long future of hoops and cumbersome skirts stretching ahead of her. "But, darling, there's no need. I don't want new dresses."

"You'll need one for the wedding and several for your trousseau. I'll have a seamstress come out and take your measurements."

"A seamstress? Hire it done? What of the expense?"

"How often do you get married? We can afford it. I've had Jeremiah dig up the silver and I'll sell what we don't want to keep."

Abigail, who had had only one new dress for her first marriage, merely stared at him.

"You go through the silver this afternoon and decide what you want to keep. The rest will go to replenish our fortune."

"I'd really rather not spend it on clothing," she objected. "We may need a plow or a team of mules. Certainly we'll need seeds and wages for hired field hands."

He kissed her nose. "Let me worry about that."

She tiptoed and kissed the tip of his nose. "I'll worry about it too." When he opened his mouth, she added, "As your wife, I have the right, and it gives me pleasure."

"To worry?" he laughed.

She shrugged with Gaelic fatalism. "Who can understand the ways of a woman? Not even a woman at times." She had no intention of letting him shoulder all the burden.

"I can take care of you." He wasn't accustomed to having the women of his family take the stand of refusing clothes and insisting on responsibility.

"I know you can," Abigail agreed with a winning smile. "A braw lad like yourself could fight tigers for me and win. I have complete confidence in you." When he smiled, she nodded her head decisively. " 'Tis settled, then. No new dresses."

"I never agreed to that," he objected.

"Logan, what have we been saying here? Of course you did. And you've made me overly happy in doing so."

"I did?"

She tiptoed up again and drew down his proud

head. "Kiss me, Logan, and tell me you love me."

"I do love you, Abigail. I never knew how much I could love until I met you."

"And I love you. Watch and see. I'm going to make you the happiest man in all of Saint Charles County."

"Parish," he corrected.

"I remember. A small detail. Go now and settle with the priest. I found some berries yesterday, and for supper I'm going to make you a splendid blackberry cobbler."

He kissed her again and smiled. "Those berries will have to go a long way to be sweeter than your lips. Maybe I'll take these instead." He kissed her again and felt the warm swirling sensation her nearness always triggered. "Do you have to iron today?"

"Could we dally in the hedgerow if I don't? No, I remember now. You're saving me for our wedding night." She gave him a coy look of innocence. "In the interest of my purity, I'd better keep ironing."

"I'm already regretting having said that," he muttered wryly.

"Not nearly as much as you will before the wedding," she purred teasingly. She was already planning how she could slip into his room that night after the others were asleep. She doubted he would cling long to his chivalry.

"Maybe a quick trip to the hedgerow wouldn't be out of order," he suggested as he fondled her full breasts. "I can see the priest tomorrow."

She playfully swatted his hand. "And not make an honest woman of me? For shame."

He sighed in rueful resignation. "I should have

made love to you instead of being so damned upstanding."

"Aye. That you should have. But you didn't and now I've decided you were right." She smiled secretively. "However, sometimes I hear the fairies give a gift at midnight—if a person leaves his door unlocked."

"Why is it all right for you to talk about fairies and I can't?"

"Hush. I'm Irish and you're not."

He tilted his head to one side; his dark eyes gleamed. "This gift you mentioned. Do you think I'd like it?"

Her smile broadened. "I guarantee it."

"In that case, I guess I will leave my door unlocked." He pulled her to him and claimed her willing lips. She was intoxicating like a honey wine, and his senses reeled. Abigail McGee was no fainting, frail creature who would lie with him merely out of duty. He ached to take her then and there. Only the likelihood that someone would come in at any moment gave him the strength to release her. "I'm leaving now," he said hoarsely. "I'll tell the priest to hurry up with the banns."

"You do that."

He turned to go, but paused. "Do you have any idea how difficult it is for me to leave you?"

"I'll be searching for those gift-giving fairies while you're gone," she promised.

Logan was smiling contentedly when he left. Abigail's heart was light, and she quickly finished the ironing. She wanted to make him not only the blackberry cobbler but also a supper of all the best things she could find. Even collard greens, which she detested but Logan loved.

As she busied herself in the kitchen, she found

the bunglesome dress was also awkward when it came to cooking. One flour-sack apron didn't begin to cover the fine lawn, so in exasperation she tied two around her slender waist, one overlapping the other. Even at that, a light snow of flour sifted onto the skirt.

Abigail didn't hear the buggy arrive, so she looked up in surprise when Jeremiah came to announce that she had a visitor. She ignored his reproving look at finding her doing servants' work. "It isn't the Duprees, is it?" she asked.

"No, ma'am. It's Miss Marie-Claude. She's waiting for you in the front parlor."

Stifling an exclamation of dismay, Abigail whipped off the aprons. She washed her hands hastily and dried them on a linen towel. "Is my hair all right, Jeremiah?" she asked. "There's no mirror down here."

"Yes, ma'am. It looks just fine."

Abigail patted the bun nervously. Of all the people she didn't want to see, Marie-Claude was second only to Major Owen Chandler. "Thank you," she said to Jeremiah as she walked briskly from the kitchen.

After the heat of ironing and cooking, the breezeway was almost pleasant and the main house seemed fairly cool. In the wide hall outside the front parlor she hesitated in order to calm herself. She, Abigail McGee, was to be Logan's wife and the mistress of Rosehaven, and this miracle gave her precedence over Marie-Claude, whatever she had been to Logan in the past. With her head held high, Abigail entered the parlor.

Marie-Claude stood by the bay window, a porcelain figurine in her gloved hand. "Hello, Abigail. I was just admiring the little shepherdess. She seems like an old friend, since I've seen her so often."

"It is lovely." Abigail wondered how Marie-Claude could make her feel inferior with so little effort. "I'm afraid you've missed Logan. He rode into town."

"I thought he would be gone. Actually, you're the one I came to see."

"Oh?" Abigail was at once on guard.

Marie-Claude drifted gracefully to a lady chair and sat daintily on the front edge of the cushion. Abigail, who at the same time had sat on a matching one with her back against the padded backrest, shifted uncomfortably. She had so much to learn about the social graces and etiquette of a grand lady!

Marie-Claude glanced at Abigail's back against the chair and indulged in a small smile, as if she enjoyed catching her in an awkwardness. "Travis rode over to visit me yesterday." She rounded her blue eyes in feigned bewilderment. "He had the oddest news. According to Travis, Logan intends to marry you." Her voice tilted up slightly, as if she were hoping Abigail would correct her.

"That's right," Abigail said smoothly. "Logan has gone now to see the priest about posting our banns."

"Then it's true? Please don't think I'm being indelicate, but how ever will you live? Surely he's told you about the taxes owed on Rosehaven."

"Aye, he did, and I've read it for myself—the notice is on the front column. I could hardly miss it."

"But it's such a large amount! How can Logan pay? I know that must sound as if I'm prying, but dear Logan is my cousin and I do worry so about him." Her eyes flicked over Abigail as if Logan's business sense were not her only cause for concern.

"Logan knows what he's doing." Her words came out rudely, so she added, "He hopes to have the taxes reduced. When the tax assessor comes home, Logan will have a talk with him."

Marie-Claude's eyes widened but she hid her surprise. "And he does plan to marry you?" she asked, as if for a reconfirmation.

"Aye. As soon as possible."

The blond curls bobbed with distress. "Oh dear. Have you given this a great deal of thought? You know the old adage, 'Married in haste, we may repent at leisure'? Logan is so . . . headstrong."

"He is for a fact. It's one of his most endearing qualities."

"Have you known each other long? I don't believe I've ever seen you around the parish."

"I met Logan in Mississippi. I lived there all my life."

"I see."

"We've not known each other long, but we love each other. Marriage is not a decision either of us will repent."

"Oh, my. You're . . . Irish . . . I believe?"

"That I am, and Scottish on my father's side."

Marie-Claude shook her head dismally and reached out to take Abigail's hand in her gloved fingers. "I don't know quite how to say this."

"I find the best way to say anything is to do it straightforwardly. There's less chance that way of being misunderstood." She carefully withdrew her hand.

"Don't think I'm being cruel, but . . . well, none of our friends are Scots-Irish."

"That won't bother me as long as they speak English. I never learned French."

"That isn't quite what I mean," Marie-Claude sighed.

"I know exactly what you mean," Abigail said firmly. "You're saying I won't fit in."

"Exactly. How clever of you to realize it."

"And even more clever of me not to care."

"What?"

"Logan and I are in love. If his friends won't accept me, then we'll have to make new friends."

"With Yankees? With people lower than our class? There isn't anyone else." Her voice was sharpening and losing its syrupy edges.

"His true friends will accept the woman he loves. The others don't matter." Abigail's heart seemed to be forged of cold lead, but she tried to keep her voice calm and her face untroubled.

"How easy for you to say," Marie-Claude murmured. "It's Logan that will suffer."

"I can make him quite happy. Rest easy on that score."

"But you will have no social life at all. Not the sort he is accustomed to and wants."

"Logan's needs and wants may have changed drastically during the years he was gone. Now he wants me." Abigail tossed the verbal gauntlet before her rival.

"Does he? Are you quite sure? Or does he want children and a woman to manage his estate? That's quite different from wanting you personally."

"You can rest assured that Logan's love for me is quite personal," Abigail replied calmly, though she felt as if her face might crack from the strain of concealing her emotions.

Silence ticked away for several moments. Finally Marie-Claude said stiffly, "I see."

"We would be glad to meet your husband and have the two of you over," Abigail continued.

"I don't think that would be advisable, under the circumstances."

"Oh? And what circumstances are those?"

"You may be his fiancée, but I'm his mistress." The killing words were delivered with honeyed serenity.

Abigail felt as if she had been kicked in the stomach. When she could speak she said, "I don't believe you."

Marie-Claude made a careless gesture that was elegantly French. "Whether you do or not, it's true. We became lovers before he left, and we picked up again when he returned."

Abigail was trying hard to breathe. So that was the source of Logan's great gallantry! He had been receiving all the passion he wanted from Marie-Claude even while he professed to love Abigail! The room blurred, then steadied. "I'll ask him."

"If you don't mind demeaning yourself, go ahead. He'll deny it. Men always do." She laughed a tinkling laugh, as if they were having the most pleasant of conversations. "That's the way it's done here. Haven't you ever noticed the number of slave children that are so much lighter than their mothers? It's not hard to understand why that is. We women have not only to accept it but also to ignore it. Where else but here can a man install one or more lovers conveniently under his own roof and his wife never say a word about it? Why, to notice those mulatto babies is considered more disgraceful than the act that made them." She paused for effect. "So you see, you should be grateful. You and I are the same race, and I don't live in your house."

Abigail could only stare.

"You see? You can only lose by marrying Logan. Everyone—with the exception of my husband, of course—knows we're lovers. Ask Travis."

No need, Abigail thought painfully. Travis had already warned her. "And don't you worry about your husband learning of your infidelity?"

Marie-Claude smiled as if she knew a secret. "No one will tell him. You might say Amos is a very important man around here. No one wants to upset Amos."

Sighing prettily, Marie-Claude stood and looked around the room. "I've always liked Rosehaven. Perhaps someday . . . But then, I do tend to run on. By the way, I love your dress. Martha Ann always did look so pretty in it, though her coloring was darker than yours."

Abigail registered the cutting remark but her mind was too full of greater problems to pay any heed to it. She forced herself to stand, although she couldn't feel her feet and all her joints seemed to have stiffened. Wordlessly she picked up Marie-Claude's gossamer shawl and handed it to her in silent dismissal.

Marie-Claude looked down at Abigail and gave her a china-doll smile. "I see you understand. Do as you please, of course. I can't stop you from marrying Logan; but if you do, you'll be the laughingstock of the parish. And you'll ruin Logan's life. Think about it." She took her shawl and swept from the room in complete control of her belling hoop, petticoats, and skirt.

Abigail stood in the center of the room staring

after the woman who had just shattered her life. Her mind seemed to be splintering into thoughts as painful as shards of glass. When she could move, she turned and went slowly upstairs. She had many things to think through before Logan returned.

She was too numb to cry.

Within the hour, Abigail nudged Gypsy into a lope. One of Martha Ann's sunbonnets was pulled closely around her pale face. She wasn't sure where she was going other than toward New Orleans, but she had to do something.

As she sped down the dusty road, she saw a curving drive that led up a low hill. Over the entrance in black letters she read "FAIR OAKS." Abigail reined her horse to a stop. This was Marie-Claude's home, then. Somehow she had expected it to be farther away from Rosehaven.

Looking up and down the road, she saw no one. With great trepidation, Abigail guided her horse beneath the impressive sign and up the azalea-flanked drive. Her heart was racing and her chest felt tight at her daring, but she reasoned that if she were going to spend so much energy worrying about Logan, she might as well know all the details.

As the tall white house came into view, Abigail left the drive and headed through the bushes. Well concealed in the deep shade of a bank of crape myrtle, she skirted the house. A lush carpet of grass muffled Gypsy's hooves, and she was relieved that no dog barked. At the left side of the house, Abigail stopped and stood in the stirrups to peer into the side yard through the sparse upper twigs of the bushes.

Standing beside a porch swing that had been

suspended from one of the enormous oaks was Logan. He was alone. Stifling a surprised gasp, she held her breath. As she watched, he touched the swing, causing it to sway gently. His face was sad and he seemed tired. Then he turned and stared at the house. After what seemed like a very long time, he walked away, presumably to return to his horse.

Angrily Abigail blinked back the tears that scalded her cheeks. Logan had left her and come here of all places! No matter that Marie-Claude was nowhere to be seen, Fair Oaks was her home. Abigail wheeled Gypsy and kicked him into a run, returning to Rosehaven, where she busied herself in the kitchen preparing the evening meal.

After supper Abigail went to her room and finally released the bank of tears. Exhausted at last, she wiped her wet cheeks and lay on her back across the bed to stare at the ceiling. How like fate, she thought dourly, to show her the man she was made for, then to snatch him back.

At length she got up and undressed, leaving her clothes uncharacteristically in a pile on the floor. She pulled a soft white nightgown over her head and unbraided her hair. Standing before the oval mirror, she stared at her reflection. Her skin was pale and her eyes were red from weeping. All in all she decided she was not a pleasant sight. Slowly she brushed her hair as she did every night, catastrophe or not, and went to bed.

But sleep wouldn't come. She lay wide-awake, staring at the night world framed by her windows. Silver trees and pewter grass rolled out to a sky of jet. Her own world had no more color. She had often heard her mother say that no one could lament more deeply than a Scot and Abigail had to admit that the saying might be true. Certainly she saw no glimmer of light in the tunnel of life that stretched before her.

The large house stirred with the usual activity of its inhabitants going to bed, then gradually the pops and creaks of floorboards ceased, and the house settled for the night.

Still Abigail lay awake, longing for Logan or for the sleep that would give her some surcease from grieving. The news of William's death had not cut her so keenly.

The great clock downstairs struck midnight, then half-past. She imagined Logan lying in his bed down the hall, waiting for her to come to him. She had not had the strength or the opportunity to tell him she wouldn't. By now, she supposed, he would have fallen asleep.

When she heard the first tap on her door, she jumped. He had come to her. Feigning sleep, she lay quietly, willing him to go away. Instead, he opened the door, which she had seen no reason to lock, and came in. She kept her eyes shut and hoped he would go away rather than disturb her.

Logan struck a light to the candle on the mantle and looked down at Abigail. She was so beautiful and she looked gentle in her sleep. Her unbound hair spilled over the pillow and her gown was open at the throat to disclose a suggestion of her luscious breasts.

Love such as he had never known flowed through him. This was the woman he had sought all his life, and by a miracle, she was his at last. He could scarcely believe his good fortune. He only wished his family could have known her. In a moment of nostalgia, he had ridden to Fair Oaks and walked one last time on the grounds. He had felt comforted by silently telling his family about his love, and he had fantasized that the soughing of the trees was their approval.

Abigail, hearing no sound, opened one eye and found herself looking straight at Logan.

He smiled and reached out to stroke the velvet of her cheek. "You overslept our rendezvous," he said. "It's nearly one o'clock."

"I didn't sleep through it," she replied sadly. "I've been lying here thinking."

"Are you nervous? You know I won't hurt you." His heart went out at what he assumed to be modest shyness.

"I was not fearing you. Never that."

"Then what? I thought you said the fairies would be out tonight bearing gifts." He tried to tease a smile to her lips.

"The fairies died today," she told him sorrowfully. "There will be no gifts."

"I don't understand. Why do you look so sad?"

She sat up and clutched her up-drawn knees to keep from reaching out to him. "I cannot come to you, nor can I marry you." She almost choked on the words.

"What? I couldn't have heard you right."

"Yes, you did. I said I cannot marry you."

"You canna'? Why not? What are you talking about? I saw the priest today and our banns will be posted Sunday. By the end of the month, you'll be my wife."

"I won't be. I cannot explain."

He sat beside her and stared at her mournful face. In the weak light her eyes seemed very large and woeful. "Have you been crying?" he asked suspiciously.

"I told you I never cry," she denied.

"Abigail, everyone cries. But usually not unless they have a reason. Has someone said something to you? Travis! It had to be him. I can't understand what's happening to him. Sometimes it's as if he's a stranger. What did he say?"

"I've not poken to Travis." She could not admit to Marie-Claude's visit nor to having seen Logan at Fair Oaks. He had to think this was her own idea or he would never give her up. Besides, her pride prevented her from letting him know she had learned of his relationship with Marie-Claude.

"Surely none of the others upset you."

"No, no. It's none of them. It's that I've been thinking and I've decided not to marry you."

The lonely candle guttered and flickered but did nothing to break the silence.

"You decided what?" he said at last. "Tell me you're teasing."

"I would never tease about anything so serious. Our wedding is off." The words almost lodged in her throat, and more tears welled in her eyes. She blinked them away. "I cannot marry you."

"Why can't you?" he demanded.

"I will not."

He got up and paced to the mantel and back. Running his fingers through his hair, he said, "Abigail, make sense. What's going on here?"

"You understood my words, surely. How much more plainly can I say them?"

"Why? Tell me why you won't marry me." He rested his hands on the bed to either side of her and leaned forward.

Abigail turned her head.

"Look at me. Can you tell me you don't love me?"

Gazing into his troubled eyes nearly robbed her of all her strength and resolve. Taking a deep breath, she told the greatest lie of her life. "I don't love you."

Logan straightened and stared down at her. After several long minutes he turned and left the room, his shoulders slumped and his face lined in agony. The door shut behind him with a final-sounding click.

This time Abigail cried herself to sleep.

16

Abigail sat curled in the soft velvet of an arm-chair in the library, her feet folded beneath her and a book in her lap. She knew she should be doing one of the endless chores involved in seeing after a household of men, but after the scene with Logan the night before, she was indulging herself. All her life she had loved books, but she had owned very few. Those, she had read over and over until they were practically committed to memory.

Now she was virtually surrounded by books, and she found she couldn't concentrate. The first one she had chosen had contained the flowery script of Marie-Claude's pen. "To Logan with love, Marie-Claude," it had read. Presumably it was a birthday or Christmas gift, but Abigail could no longer pretend the "love" was sisterly. Especially not when the book was titled *Sonnets from the Portuguese*. What sister gave a volume of love poems to her brother? She looked down at the book she held. *Modiste Mignon* lay in her lap, but the words she read formed no mental images.

A bird called musically from the willow tree beyond the window, drawing Abigail's attention to the blue-and-green vista framed by the lace curtains. She saw Harley and Martin heading for the woods, their rifles in hand. Squirrel would be the fare for supper that night. Logan liked squirrel.

With a frown, she turned back to the book. Whether Logan liked a meal or not was no longer of importance to her. He had played her false with Marie-Claude, and she was well rid of him. She only wished she believed that.

The library door opened and she heard footsteps behind her. Abigail stiffened. She and Logan had studiously avoided each other all morning. She had no desire to be alone with him in the oak-lined coziness of the library.

A pair of worn boots stopped in front of her chair and she raised her eyes until she recognized their owner. "Tobe," she said with relief. "I was just reading. Were you looking for me?"

"Yes, ma'am." He moved uneasily.

"Is something wrong?"

"No, no." He sat on the chair opposite her and rested his forearms on his knees. "I've just been worrying about you."

"Oh?"

"Logan told us about you two planning to get married. I heard the news yesterday afternoon, and now it seems you've called it off. Why is that?"

"I really don't think—"

"You're going to say it's none of my business and you're right. It's not. Only the captain and all of us . . . well, we've gotten real close over the years. Then you come along and I thought for sure you were the best thing that ever happened to him. So I'm going to talk to you like I was your brother."

"Nothing you can say will change matters."

"Now, you just put down that book for a minute and let me try."

Abigail obeyed but her eyes told him she was going to disagree with anything he said.

"Logan, he ain't like Travis," Tobe said. "He don't take up with fancy women nor run wild in a town. He was more apt to use his free time in a card game or swapping tales around the fire. Nobody ever accused him of being a ladies' man.

"Then when you threw in with us, I started seeing a change in Logan. He got absentminded at times, edgy for no cause at others. About the time we all started wondering what was wrong with him, he commenced to grinning like a possum over nothing. Well, I saw that grin and I knew straight off—he's in love."

"You might have questioned whom he was in love with," Abigail said dryly. Logan had obviously been eager to see Marie-Claude as they neared his home.

"Well, it sure wasn't me or Harley," Tobe said, "and nobody'd look twice at old Martin. Who else could it be, if not you?"

Abigail was too proud to answer.

"Everybody saw it, and we were all happy for you. I remember the spring I won my Rosa's heart. I was so happy I thought I might die from it. That's what I saw in Logan's face yesterday. Today he looks like the world ended and heaven was full up before he got there." Tobe studied her pale face earnestly. "Did you two have a falling-out?"

"You might say that."

"Well, Miss Abigail, I don't know what caused it and it's none of my business, but you two really ought to patch it up. Never let the sun set on a problem between you."

"It's not always that simple."

"Don't you think I know that? Me and Rosa don't always agree. One of us will do something and the other will fly off the handle—and let me tell you, the fur flies. She hollers out something in Spanish and I holler it back. Then she takes off in English or a combination of the two." He grinned self-consciously. "Rosa's just pretty as a pup when she's mad. And she's not scared to let me know what's on her mind, either."

"Somehow I got the idea you two never argued," Abigail said in surprise.

"You just don't know Rosa. I think she enjoys a row once in a while. The point is, we don't never go to bed mad. One time we stayed up all night before we got the wrinkles ironed out, but we kept after it until we did."

"You're a lucky man, Tobe."

"Yes, ma'am. That I am. I want you and the captain to be like that too. You have it in you—I can read it in your eyes. Yours and his. Make up with him."

Abigail closed the book and hugged it to her. "It's not that simple."

"Are you sure? I know when a person's mad, it seems like everything goes wrong. Maybe if you just smiled at him. You know, like a woman does. There's not a woman I ever saw that didn't know how to do that forgiving smile."

"This goes deeper than a smile can mend." Before he could ask, she said, "I can't possibly talk about it. Please don't be asking me."

"I'm not going to. Whatever it is, it's between you two. Couldn't you make a step or so, though? He could meet you halfway, then. The captain's a proud man—as proud as any I ever met. Coming all the way might be more than he could manage."

"It's more than I can do, too."

"Pride gets real lonely around midnight, Miss Abigail."

"If you knew the reason, you would see why I won't make up with him," Abigail stated firmly. "Believe me, Tobe, 'tis no slight matter."

Tobe straightened and leaned back in the chair. Shaking his head, he said, "I could sure tell that. I never saw two people look more miserable. There ought to be something to do about it."

Abigail leaned toward him and covered one of his big rawboned hands with both hers. "I appreciate what you're trying to do, and I thank you for it. Logan's lucky to have a friend like you."

"He don't know I'm talking to you. If he did, he would tell me to tend my own fences. I just can't stand to see folks I care about hurt like this, and me not try to fix it."

Abigail squeezed his hand as if she were the comforter, and not the other way around. "Tell me about Texas," she urged him. Aside from Rosa, this was his favorite topic. "I've decided to settle there. That is, if I can ride west with you."

"You'd be welcome, but I'd rather see you and Logan get things patched up." He gazed up at the many-prismed chandelier and said, "Texas ain't really the land of milk and honey like I tell Martin, but it's as close to it in my mind as I'll ever see. I live in the part called the Piney Woods. It's just that. Pines as big as any I've ever seen. There's rolling hills, some of them as big as small mountains. The one I live near is called Button Mountain. I don't know why, unless a family named Button settled it, maybe."

"I hadn't expected mountains."

"You won't hardly know when you see this one. All the hills around are so tall and the valleys so shallow, it don't look much like a mountain. Not like the ones we crossed going to Virginia. Those were real big compared to ours. I hear there's even bigger ones out west, but I ain't never seen those."

Abigail nodded in understanding. To her they were all just pictures in a book or a frame. "Are there green pastures and good creeks?"

"There are for a fact. And you can get good land there fairly cheap."

She made a thoughtful sound. "I have a mind to buy a farm. Perhaps I could raise sheep. It's something I know."

"You have me there. I ain't never had much to do with sheep. We have a few goats and some cows, but that's about it. Pigs and chickens, of course."

"Of course," she agreed absently. If she were away from Rosehaven, she could put Logan out of her mind. Perhaps. At the moment the rift had caused a wound that seemed too painful ever to heal.

"I think Rosa would be pleased to have you for a neighbor. She's real friendly, Rosa is. I don't guess you speak Spanish?"

"Not a word."

"That's okay. Rosa knows English pretty well. Of course, our younguns speak one as well as the other."

"I'd like to see your bairns." Abigail smiled. "Not having a baby is my one regret in my marriage."

"They're a blessing for sure," Tobe agreed.

Logan entered the room in time to hear the last exchange. His anger swelled to hide the hurt. He had tossed all night and suffered the torments of the damned, and here she was discussing babies with Tobe. She wished she had had William's child.

Unreasonable jealousy made his anger flare. Logan let it. He preferred rage to pain.

"There you are, Tobe," he said shortly. "I've been looking for you." He ignored Abigail and she turned back to the book she was reading. More proof of her callous nature, he told himself. His heart was in shreds and she was reading a novel.

"We were just having a talk," Tobe said when Abigail refused to look at Logan, let alone smile. "I was telling Miss Abigail—"

She silenced Tobe with a glare.

"I have something I want you to do," Logan interrupted. "The fence is down in the horse lot and I would appreciate it if you would mend it. I have to go to New Orleans today and see the tax assessor."

"Sure thing. I'll fix it for you." Tobe stood and looked from Abigail to Logan and back again. When she kept her eyes firmly on the book, he sighed heavily. "I'll get right on it."

As Tobe left, Logan gazed at Abigail. She looked as serenely calm as a cat full of cream. As he watched, she blinked as if a beam of sunlight hurt her eyes. In other circumstances he would have suspected she was repressing tears. But that was ridiculous. She didn't love him, and probably never had.

A stab of pain made him wheel and stalk out of the house. He saddled Caliban and rode toward town. Yet Abigail stayed in his mind. He was torn between wanting her to leave so his torment would end and wanting her to stay forever. If she didn't leave, he thought, he might somehow teach her to love him. As long as she was there, a small hope glimmered. But logic told him the glimmer was merely a false hope—Abigail was as unreachable as the stars.

The tax assessor's office, in the section of New Orleans called the French Quarter, was located in what had once been the front parlor of a fine old home. The building, crowding upon the narrow street like its neighbors, was heavily ornamented with wrought iron on the balconies and supports like garlands of black lace.

Logan looked up and down the street as he tied his horse to the iron ring. Once this had been the elite section. Now several houses were boarded up, and all the passersby seemed to greet each other with Northern accents. The town was changing.

He pushed open the wooden gate that led to a cobbled brick tunnel. Beyond lay a tiny courtyard with a marble fountain that tinkled seductively. Logan crossed the square of sunshine and rapped on the French doors marked "TAX ASSESSOR." All the other doors off the courtyard, which had originally led to other rooms in the house, bore business placards as well. The upstairs bedrooms appeared to be vacant.

A young man answered the door and ushered Logan into a lush office. A Turkish carpet covered the floor, and two leather chairs stood before a wide oak desk. The windows were curtained with bottle-green damask trimmed in gold cording. A man with the beginnings of a paunch stood before one, several papers in his hand. At Logan's entrance, he looked up.

"I'm Logan Sorrell. We have an appointment."

"Oh, yes. Mr. Sorrell." He came forward, his blue eyes taking Logan's measure. When he smiled, almost effeminate dimples appeared in his cheeks, but the smile never reached his eyes. "I'm Amos Smith."

Logan started and his eyes narrowed thoughtfully. This was Marie-Claude's husband. He hadn't expected that. He took in the man's natty appearance, from his heavily pomaded hair and his black mustache down to his burgundy coat and tan trousers. Logan couldn't imagine this dandy as master of Fair Oaks in Andrew's place.

The silence grew tense before Logan said, "I've come to talk to you about the taxes on Rosehaven. I suppose you're familiar with the property?"

"Yes, yes. It adjoins my own place." He watched Logan wince. "I believe my home once belonged to your brother." Again the man's slick blue eyes slid over Logan. "I've heard my wife mention you more than once."

"I've known Marie-Claude all my life. We grew up together."

"Such a pity about your brother. Naturally, your loss is my gain in this case. Marie-Claude is a marvelous wife and Fair Oaks was a more-than-adequate dowry."

"Yes. It would be." Logan disliked the oily way the man spoke, as if he were needling and probing for weaknesses. "About Rosehaven. I believe there has been a mistake in the tax assessment."

Amos Smith sat at his desk and motioned for Logan to take a chair. He riffled through some papers, assuming an air of importance. "Here it is. Rosehaven, presently owned by Logan Sorrell, late a captain in the Confederate Army." He glanced at Logan as if for confirmation. Logan nodded brusquely. "The taxes are set at nine thousand."

"Yes, that's correct."

"Rosehaven is worth only twenty thousand. The

taxes owed can't possibly be nearly half its entire worth."

Amos swatted a mosquito on the back of his hand. "Damned swamp," he muttered darkly. To Logan he said, "In the case of Rosehaven, that is the correct amount."

Logan leaned forward angrily. "That's robbery!"

"You still owe nine thousand. Rosehaven may not be the largest plantation around, but it's a good producer and is in a prime location."

"It's off the road by nearly two miles!" Logan objected. "We get our supplies by boat on the river."

"I know."

"So why is it in such a 'prime location'?"

Amos had the grace to look discomfited. "We have someone interested in buying it. As an investment."

"Rosehaven isn't for sale!"

"If the taxes aren't paid by the end of the month, it will be auctioned. You people seem to think your world is carved in granite. When I came here, matters were in a deplorable condition. A dozen families ruled this area as if they were royalty. You people seem to think you're immune from taxes and from rules that govern everyone else."

"We are entitled to fair taxation!"

"Are you accusing this office of graft? I would answer carefully, as that's a very serious charge."

Logan bit back his words. He knew enough about how things had changed to realize that a false word could lead to his arrest. These were not days when a man could speak freely. Not if he were from the South and his adversary were from the North. Using all the control he possessed, he asked, "Who is trying to buy Rosehaven out from under me?"

"Sorry. I'm not at liberty to divulge that." Amos didn't look as if he regretted it at all.

"It's my home, dammit!" Logan exploded. "You can't levy a tax as unreasonable as that and expect me not to be upset or to try to find out what's going on!"

"Careful," Amos reminded him.

Logan left the chair in a lithe movement that brought him leaning toward Amos over the desk. "Don't push me, Smith," he growled. "You married my brother's wife and took over his house before anyone knew for sure whether he was dead. Now I find an exorbitant tax on Rosehaven, which just happens to adjoin Fair Oaks. Now, do you really think I'm too stupid to figure out who wants to buy it cheap at an auction?" Logan's black eyes snapped dangerously. He was holding himself in check, but with a great deal of difficulty.

Smith backed his chair away from the desk and rose, keeping the bulky furniture between Logan and himself. "I think you had better leave!"

"If I pay these taxes, what can I expect as taxes for next year?" Logan demanded. "Will they be outrageous again until you starve me out?"

"How can I know what next year's taxes will be? I'll tell you this, though: a smart man would sell out and move on. Times have changed, and the quicker you people realize it, the better off you'll be."

Logan made a low noise that resembled a growl. "Don't take anything for granted, Smith. You might be in for a surprise."

"Does that mean you can pay the taxes? Frankly, that would surprise me very much. So much that I would wonder just where you got the money."

The man's superior attitude and goading words dropped a red haze over Logan's eyes. He had come there expecting to have a rational discussion and find the excessive taxes were a mistake. Now he realized he couldn't win. He could use all his gold and pay these taxes, but he would be wiped out the following year. Rage boiled within him. He was trying to decide if it would be worth risking probable arrest to hit Amos Smith's dimpled cheek, when the door opened and Marie-Claude came in.

"Logan!" she exclaimed.

He wheeled, the glare still on his face and his hand doubled into a menacing fist.

"Imagine running into you here," she said in pretty confusion, as if seeing him unexpectedly had quite taken her breath away. "Hello, Mr. Smith," she belatedly greeted her husband.

"I didn't expect you," Amos said, relieved that her arrival had saved him from a fight he was sure he couldn't have won. "What are you doing in town?"

"I came in to do a bit of shopping. Fair Oaks is so dull these days. No company or balls." She gazed up at Logan with her wide blue eyes. "Don't you find things changed since the war?"

"Yes." Logan drew in a breath to calm himself. While he might have few qualms about punching Amos Smith in private, he wasn't about to do so in front of the man's wife.

Amos looked from Marie-Claude to Logan, and back again. He hadn't seen her Southern-belle performance since their wedding. Was something going on here? When she spoke to him at home, her voice was more often strident than not, yet now she was practically gushing. "We were just remarking how things have changed," he said thoughtfully.

"Well, it's a real shame," she declared. "You just can't imagine the parties we used to have. The couples promenading through the garden to cool from dancing." She blushed prettily. "You can't imagine the number of declarations of love that have been made in our yew garden."

Logan looked decidedly uncomfortable and said, "I'll be going now. I've said all I can." He didn't offer Amos his hand.

Amos regarded him suspiciously. Why would Marie-Claude say that? It was almost as if the words would mean more to Logan than to anyone else. Logan's abrupt departure seemed to bear that out. "The taxes stand as recorded. And they have to be paid promptly at the end of the month. No exceptions." He knew Logan wouldn't be so foolish as to attack him in front of a witness. A moment before, he hadn't been so sure.

A muscle tightened in Logan's lean jaw, but he nodded brusquely and left.

Amos stared at the door for a moment, then pivoted to his wife. "You seem to be quite friendly with Sorrell."

"For mercy's sake, Mr. Smith," Marie-Claude sighed petulantly, all pretense at dainty femininity over. "I've known Logan all my life."

"So he said."

"Did he?" A veiled expression crossed her beautiful face. Casually she said, "What else did he say?"

"He seems to think there was reason to doubt his brother's death when we got married. Is that true?"

"Certainly not," she stated, avoiding his eyes. "What a mean thing to say."

"Mrs. Smith, why do I get the idea that you lie to me?"

"How should I know? I suppose it's your sneaky little mind. You came out rather well, I should think. You have a wife whose blood is the bluest in town, one of the finest plantations around, and thus a revenue to see you elected senator. That's not bad for the son of a shopkeeper."

Amos flushed angrily. He was damned tired of hearing her flaunt her lineage and wealth in the face of his middle-class background. "I've paid for it dearly," he muttered. "And I haven't won the Senate seat yet."

"No, but you will. With the governor backing you, who would dare not vote for you?" She examined the point lace on the pale pink parasol that matched her gown.

"I hope you're right. Then I can get out of this godforsaken hole."

"You'd leave New Orleans?" she gasped.

"In a New York minute. I've seen more swampland and mosquitoes and Negroes than I ever want to see again in my life."

"But this is my home!" she protested.

"You're welcome to it!" Then he remembered their handsome neighbor who had no wife to keep him at home. "But your place is with me. When I go to Washington, you'll go as well."

"But—"

"That's final!"

Marie-Claude's eyes shimmered blue fire, and she was about to berate him soundly even if his male secretary was in the next room, when a knock on the door forestalled her.

"Come in!" Amos snapped.

The door opened and a tall blond military officer entered. His dark blue uniform was brushed as neatly as if he had just stepped out of a bandbox. Marie-Claude stared at him. She had never seen such pale green eyes, and she found the man excitingly handsome, in a cold sort of way.

"Owen!" Amos exclaimed in welcome. "Owen Chandler!"

"Amos!" The army major crossed the room and clasped his friend's hand. "They told me at headquarters you were here. It's good to see you!"

"This is my wife, Marie-Claude. This is Major Owen Chandler."

"Mrs. Smith," Chandler said in smiling appreciation of her beauty. "It's a pleasure."

Marie-Claude lowered her eyelashes demurely. He was indeed a handsome man and his blond coloring and height were a perfect complement to her own. What a pity he was her husband's friend. "Charmed, Major Chandler. Are you assigned to New Orleans?"

"What are you doing here?" Amos asked, as if Marie-Claude hadn't spoken. "Don't tell me you're stationed here. You couldn't deserve such a punishment."

Marie-Claude glared at her husband.

"No, I'm passing through. I'm on assignment to apprehend a war criminal, and he came this way. While I was in town I thought I'd come by and look you up."

"You must stay with us at Fair Oaks," Marie-Claude urged sweetly. "Our home is yours."

"That sounds like a plantation." Owen grinned. "You haven't gone Rebel on us, have you, Amos?"

"Smile when you say that," Amos said in mock severity. "I married this little belle, and the plantation came with her."

"Not a bad bargain," Owen said as he assessed Marie-Claude's charms.

Some of the light had gone from her eyes. In a noticeably cooler voice she said, "How long will you be in town, Major?"

"Not long, I imagine. As I said, I'm tracking a war criminal."

"That sounds dangerous," she replied. "What sort of criminal is he?"

"He robbed a payroll train."

"Oh?" That didn't sound very interesting to her. "Do you expect to capture him here?"

"So far, he's been as elusive as the very devil," Chandler admitted.

"How do you know he's in New Orleans?" Amos asked.

"The same way we've followed him since we got on the trail in Mississippi. We don't know his real name, but his code name is Nighthawk. He's a big man with black hair and dark eyes. He's traveling with about half a dozen men."

"That could fit half of New Orleans," Amos observed.

"The way we've trailed him and his men is by their horses. The leader rides a big black. If you saw him, you'd notice it. One of the others rode a red-and-white pinto, but he either left the band or traded horses near the state line. This seems to be the direction they're headed, however. There's not another big town around here."

At the mention of the black horse and the man's physical description, Marie-Claude's eyes widened. The man he was looking for sounded a lot like Logan. But surely that was only a coincidence.

"He sounds dangerous," she murmured. "How ever will I know if I see him?"

"He has a small scar on his gun hand. It's on his thumb and it's shaped like a curved fishhook."

She turned so that her hat brim hid her face. Logan had a scar exactly like that. He had cut himself when he and Andrew were playing mumblety-peg on her sixth birthday. "Goodness," she said in a voice that trembled. "I hope I don't see the rogue."

"Not much chance of that," Owen reassured her. "He isn't likely to run in your circles." He and Amos exchanged a laugh at her feminine flutterings.

She let them believe she was fearful of meeting such a desperate criminal. Silently she tried to think of a way to warn Logan. Now that Amos was home, the servants would be only too glad to report her solitary rides. She was surprised they hadn't met him at the door with tales of her meanderings. Another ride over the open fields in broad daylight wasn't to be chanced. She wanted to warn Logan, but not at the risk of implicating herself. "This robber—Nighthawk, was it?—did he kill anyone?"

"No, he was real slick. He had held up other trains before mine. That was his assignment, to sabotage our rail system."

"But if it was an assignment, surely you can't hold him personally responsible."

"She's a Rebel through and through," Amos apologized.

"He did more than just carry out his assignment," Chandler answered her abruptly. "He embarrassed me in front of my men." His eyes were flat as he recalled that day. Because Nighthawk had not only robbed a payroll but also humiliated an entire company of men, a ranking officer included, Chandler had received a severe upbraiding. His colonel chastised him for allowing a Rebel to steal a large payroll shipment and had reassigned him to other duties so that he would not be in charge of any more money. This had left a blot on what had been a spotless record. By the end of the war he was still a major, despite the relative ease of promotions during wartime. Chandler had felt certain he would be retiring as at least a full colonel, if not a lieutenant general, until the incident with Nighthawk. With only eighteen months left in the army, catching Nighthawk and getting the gold back were his only hope for any advancement.

"I'm going to get Nighthawk if it's the last thing I do," he affirmed.

"What will happen to him?" Marie-Claude asked.

"I'll personally see that he hangs." He smiled again, but this time his lips only stretched in a grimace of geniality. He noted her gasp, but ignored the reaction. The woman was obviously of a delicate nature and very sensitive to matters such as this. In deference to her he softened his tone. "We know he's here, and I'll find him. In the meantime, I'd be honored to stay at your home." He gave Marie-Claude a little bow. She was damned pretty. What a pity she was married to his old friend Amos.

17

Jeremiah had just finished clearing the table and Abigail was folding the tablecloth. The heavy white fabric had been mended in several places, but with so fine a stitch that the small holes were all but invisible. Abigail wondered whether the woman who had made the repairs was Logan's sister or perhaps a servant. Certainly she herself was unable to mend so adroitly—another proof that she would never have fit in as mistress of Rosehaven. She finished folding the cloth, then put it away in the tall linen press.

Harley came in and helped her spread the protecting day cloth over the table. "Tobe said for me to tell you that we're leaving tomorrow. Are you really going with us?"

"Yes. I plan to settle in Texas." She avoided his curious eyes.

He looked around the elegant room with its gleaming china cabinet, rosewood furniture, and gaslight chandelier. "I sure don't think I'd ever leave a fine place like this. Nor the captain either, if I was a lady."

Abigail gave him an exasperated look. "Did Tobe put you up to matchmaking for me?"

"He only mentioned what a shame it is that you're set on turning down the captain."

"There's more to it than that, and I won't talk about it. You can pass that on to Martin as well." With a slight frown, she asked, "Is Tobe really going tomorrow?"

Harley nodded. "I've been expecting it for several days. He's been looking west and humming 'Lorena.' That's a sure sign he's missing Rosa."

"Are you leaving too?"

"Yes, ma'am. My home is west of here. I'll drop off there, and Tobe and Martin will go on to Texas."

"So will I."

"You're sure?"

"Tell Tobe I appreciate what he has tried to do, but I'm going to be ready to ride when he leaves."

"He said we'll go at dawn."

"I'll be ready." She turned away. Leaving Logan was harder than she had expected.

Just then the front door banged open, and she saw Travis lurch into the entry. He reared back drunkenly and belted out the first lines of "I'm a Good Old Rebel."

She went to the doorway of the dining room just as Logan came out of the library. A dark frown clouded his face.

"Travis!" he said. "You're drunk again."

"Only the least bit, cousin," Travis admitted. "Not so you'd hardly notice."

Abigail hung back as Logan confronted the man. She feared Travis even when he was sober.

"Where have you been?" Logan demanded.

"To Sally Hankins' house of ill repute," Travis announced grandly. "You should have come with me. Sally bought the Monsels' town house in the French Quarter." His voice became doleful. "Poor old man Monsel's dead now. Remember all the good times we had in that house, Logan?" He brightened. "I can guarantee you I had an even better time tonight!" He reeled against the stair rail and surveyed the route to his bedroom.

"Is that the only place you went?" Logan asked. "You didn't go to Bernhart's barn, did you?"

"What do you mean?" Travis scowled.

"This is Thursday. Mr. Dupree said the Klan meets there. Did you go?"

"That's my business!" Travis leaned on the rail and glared at Logan. "If General Nathan Forrest thinks the Klan's a good idea, it must be. God knows we need it."

"You keep away from them. They're a bunch of hotheads and you'll end up in trouble."

"I can take care of myself. You don't know what you're talking about." He grinned and straightened but his eyelids drooped to half-mast. "Afterward we adjourned to Sally's. I'm telling you, Logan, you should have been with us. Sally has a new girl who's specialty is—"

"Be quiet!" Logan barked. "Abigail is standing right there." He frowned at Travis.

Abigail, who had been listening unashamedly, blushed. "I was just on my way upstairs." Head held high, she crossed the entry and went up the steps. If Travis was drunk, it was no concern of hers. She was curious, though. Up until now, she had never heard a woman of the night being discussed, much less that she had a "specialty."

She couldn't help but wonder what on earth that meant.

Behind her, Logan said, "Harley, help me get Travis up to his room."

"Harley," Travis said in booming confidence, "have you ever visited a real top-notch whorehouse?"

Abigail missed Harley's answer, but through the closed door she heard Travis singing a bawdy ditty as he passed her door on his way to his room.

She lit a lamp against the approaching night. At least she would never see Travis again.

Reluctantly she took her saddlebags from the bottom of her wardrobe and laid them on the bed. Her heart beat heavily as she removed her things from the lavender-scented drawers and packed them for the journey. This time tomorrow she would be sleeping by a campfire on the hard ground. She didn't welcome the prospect.

She rolled the two wool blankets into a bedroll, then wrapped them with an oiled slicker. Most of her gold she placed in the bottom of the saddlebags. The rest she stacked on the side table beside her chair. Sitting in the lamp's glow, Abigail quilted the remaining pieces into a belt to wear around her waist. Still more she planned to sew into the slits in her horse blanket. She had never heard of anyone stealing a horse blanket.

Rosehaven grew quiet as Travis' voice trailed off into sleep. Logan was right. If he continued to mix Klan secrets with drink, Travis would get into more trouble than he was worth. She hoped none of it would reach Logan.

Her packing finished, Abigail blew out the lamp and sat in the dark. She felt tired, as if she hadn't rested in weeks. She didn't want to leave Logan, and the worst part was that she knew it wasn't necessary. All she had to do was go down the hall and tell him she wanted to stay.

She closed her eyes and leaned her head back against the chair. She could no more do that than she could fly to the moon. If she stayed with Logan, she would die a little each time he had "business" in town. Marie-Claude would waste no opportunity to flaunt her liaison with Logan. In time Abigail knew that her deep love would die and she would be left a bitter shell. As an incurable romantic and a dreamer, she couldn't bear to kill her shining love. Better to take it with her, bruised but intact.

She was feeling thoroughly sorry for herself when she heard hoofbeats below her window. Moments later she heard a hail of pebbles against the end of the house, and she opened the French door to the balcony and went out to see what was going on. A full moon washed silver over the horse and woman in the yard, and Abigail froze in the shadows as Logan also came out onto the balcony.

"Marie-Claude?" he called out uncertainly. "Is that you?"

"Come down, Logan. I have to see you," she hissed loudly. "Well, come in the house. Why are you standing out there in the night?"

Marie-Claude glanced back over her shoulder. Her movements were jerky with apprehension. "I don't dare. Come out here."

Abigail wrapped her arms across her middle. She had inadvertently eavesdropped on a lover's tryst. Marie-Claude had more gall than any woman she had ever known. Imagine her coming to Rosehaven to ask Logan out into the dark with

Abigail in the very next room and Marie-Claude's own husband at home at Fair Oaks!

Logan straightened and pointed toward the nearby gazebo. "Meet me in the summer house," he said.

When he was gone, Abigail went back to her room. She didn't want to witness the lover's embrace. She tied her bedroll securely with two leather thongs and lay it and her saddlebags by the door. Dawn couldn't come soon enough to suit her.

Logan went down the stairs reluctantly. Marie-Claude was a fool to risk coming here and he intended to tell her so. He hadn't missed the speculative look on Amos Smith's face that afternoon. The man was jealous and likely had more than one reason to be. Logan had enough problems without adding a jealous husband to the list. Especially when he had no intention of dallying with Marie-Claude.

She was waiting for him in the summerhouse, and through the open sides he could see her pacing nervously. She wore no bonnet and her hair was curled into a bouquet of ringlets. Her dress was ivory, trimmed with gold threads such as she would wear for an evening's entertainment. Even though she was obviously agitated, Logan noticed she had taken the time to put on spotless kid riding gloves. He smiled in spite of himself. Marie-Claude certainly did everything in style.

She saw him and hurried across the moon-washed floor. "Thank goodness you've come."

"What is this all about? You know, all you had to do was knock on the door and I'd have asked you into the parlor."

"No, no! I mustn't take a chance on being seen. You know how servants gossip."

"Old Jeremiah is the only one left. Besides, if you want to avoid gossip, why did you come?"

"I had to come." She looked over her shoulder again, her eyes large and frightened. "I thought I saw someone a minute ago."

"Just shadows. Why are you here, anyway? You've done a foolish thing in coming over. What if your husband finds out?"

"I had to warn you." Unexpectedly she threw herself into his arms.

Logan caught his balance and his arms automatically went around her.

Upstairs Abigail had just come to the window, hoping to cauterize her love by seeing Logan with Marie-Claude. Her hand knotted on the curtain as she saw them embrace. Quickly she turned away.

Logan disentangled Marie-Claude's arms from around his neck and stepped back. "Don't do that. You force me to say things that will hurt you. There will never be anything between us. Never. Now, go home."

Marie-Claude looked around. "Did you hear something?"

"No. Go home."

"Logan, listen to me! I've come to warn you." She gazed imploringly up at his face.

"About what?"

"This afternoon, just after you left, we had an unexpected visitor. He's staying at my house. Logan, he says he's chasing a dangerous war criminal, and when he catches him, he'll hang him."

"What's his name?" Logan demanded with a sick dread.

"Major Owen Chandler. He and my husband are old friends."

"What does this have to do with me?"

"It's you he's after, Logan. I know it. From all he said, it has to be. He even described the scar on your hand."

Logan glanced down at the familiar mark. "Damn!" he muttered.

"Then it is true! You are Nighthawk! You have to leave," she urged, "and take me with you. He doesn't know you're here, but when he starts asking questions around town, he'll find you."

"Take you with me?"

"Of course! If Amos finds out I've warned you, I could be arrested!"

"He won't find out. I remember you used to slip out regularly to meet Andrew, and your parents never suspected."

"He told you about that?" she flared indignantly.

"I can't take you. We'll be riding hard. I'm going inside now and rouse the others. I appreciate what you've done, but you can't come with us."

"I want to!"

"You don't get everything in the world just because you set your heart on it. I've told you that before."

She pouted. "I risked my life to come here to warn you, and now you're going without me. That's not fair, Logan."

He turned her gently around and led her down the gazebo steps. "I'll never forget what you've done."

"If you don't take me, I'll tell Major Chandler that Nighthawk's name is Logan Sorrell," she threatened.

"No you won't." He hoped he was right. With Marie-Claude's temperament and flair for drama, he couldn't be positive.

Her horse had wandered out of the yard and

into the wide lane of live oaks, where it grazed on the silky grasses as if such late-night rides were not uncommon. Marie-Claude frowned. The horse was a willful one and might be hard to catch. She should have taken the time to tie it. Chasing after a horse in the dark would waste precious time, not to mention making her look foolish.

"You go home now," Logan was telling her. "Get in as quietly as possible and no one will ever know you were here."

"Logan, you know I love you. Don't leave me. I hate Amos. It's you I want to be with." She put her arms around him and buried her face against his chest.

Logan gave her a brotherly hug, then pulled back. He doubted Marie-Claude's motivation was anything more than self-preservation, but somehow he couldn't blame her. Her selfishness would never change. "Thank you for warning me. Now, go home before you're missed." He turned her toward her horse and gave her a gentle push.

Dejectedly Marie-Claude walked toward the animal as it moved away. Logan watched her. She was his last living tie with Rosehaven and the life he had known. For all her melodrama and selfish profession of love, she had braved danger to come warn him. Logan would always be grateful to her for that.

Marie-Claude was almost under the reaching arms of the live oaks. Several yards separated her from Logan. Suddenly she jerked her head up and began to run toward the deep shadows. Her horse bolted away, but she ran with her arms outspread entreatingly.

A shot rang out, and to Logan's horror, Marie-Claude crumpled into the grass. Almost at once an agonized cry rang out from beside the tree trunk.

Logan took a step forward but stopped when Amos Smith staggered out into the moonlight. The man's shoulders were slumped, and a revolver dangled from his hand. With wooden steps he walked to his wife's still form. Logan saw him drop to his knees and turn her over. Marie-Claude's arm fell back lifelessly, a large splotch of blood staining her expensive ivory-and-gold gown.

"Why?" Amos cried out to her body. "Why did you step in front of him? Why did you do that?" He lifted her and cradled her in his arms. Her head lolled on her swanlike neck as if even in death she rejected his caresses. Amos glared at Logan. "I'll see that you hang for this!" he bellowed. "I'll see to that—Nighthawk!"

Logan had seen enough of death to know Marie-Claude was beyond his help. He turned and hurried up the steps and into the porch's shadow. Once inside, he locked the door and leaned against it. A wave of nausea gripped him, and he fought to clear his head. Nothing about the last few minutes seemed real.

How could Marie-Claude have been shot on the lawn behind his home, when only moments before she had been in his arms? How could she be dead when she had just pouted at him and threatened him and demanded to have her way? Marie-Claude was made for cotillions and teas and dresses with flounces of lace, not for bullets and a violent death on a dark lawn.

Logan knew he had to hurry. He had to get away from here before Amos collected his own wits and went for Chandler. Marie-Claude was beyond help, and allowing himself to be captured would make her death meaningless.

He shook his head as if cobwebs clouded his brain. Had she deliberately ran into the bullet meant for him? Or was she only chasing her horse? She could even have seen Amos and been running to him to lie her way out of being there on his lawn in such incriminating circumstances. Logan would never know.

He pushed open the door to his room and found Abigail throwing his belongings into his worn saddlebags. In this night of unreality, what she was doing was as difficult for him to comprehend as everything else had been.

"Get the others," she ordered. "We have to get out of here." Through the window she watched as Amos lifted Marie-Claude and stepped back into the shadows where he must have left his own horse. "Hurry!" she commanded when she noticed that Logan hadn't moved. "We must go. Now!"

Logan jerked his head toward her in recognition, then hefted his saddlebags over his shoulder and rushed out with her to tell the others.

Jeremiah heard the commotion and came up the stairs as Martin was hurrying down, his gear over one shoulder. "What's going on here?" the old man asked. "Where y'all going? Was that a shot I heard?"

"We're leaving," Martin answered over his shoulder. "Go wake up Travis."

Jeremiah went to do as he was told, wondering aloud as he did so.

Harley rushed down the hall, Tobe right behind him. After years of being prepared to ride at a moment's notice, both were ready to go. Abigail ran to her room and tied her money belt around her waist. Amos Smith was out of sight and probably riding hard toward Fair Oaks to get help. She grabbed her saddlebag and bedroll and raced after Tobe.

Logan and Jeremiah slapped Travis into a state of semiconsciousness. He cursed them liberally as Logan pulled him over his shoulder to carry him out.

Jeremiah ran behind Logan, keeping up as well as he could. "What's going on, Master Logan? Is the Yankees come after us?"

Logan paused on the landing and fished two sacks of gold coins from his saddlebag. "Jeremiah, take this. Tomorrow I want you to hitch up the mare and go into town. She's yours now. Find Lige and Mamie and use this money to buy a place of your own. Understand?"

"No, sir."

"I can't explain. Don't let anyone know you've got all this gold or they'll charge you more than a farm is worth. Get Lige to help you find a good one."

"Yes, sir."

"And you might as well dig up the silver over at Magnolias and sell it. That money will be yours too. I'd rather you have it than whoever buys these places at auction."

"But that silver belongs to Master Travis!"

"We won't be back this way." Logan went quickly down the stairs. "Take care of yourself, Jeremiah."

"Yes, sir." The old man stared after Logan, then at the bag of gold. He still didn't know what was going on.

His upside-down position and the night air cleared Travis' head and he twisted off Logan's shoulder. "What the hell are you doing?" he roared.

"We have to leave," Logan answered shortly. "Marie-Claude has been killed."

"What?" Travis stumbled after Logan to the barn. "What did you say?"

"She came to warn us. Owen Chandler is at Fair Oaks. By this time tomorrow we would have been in jail if she hadn't come."

"So why is she dead?"

"Her husband followed her. He said he was aiming at me, but he shot her."

Travis stared at Logan. "She's dead?"

"Yes. He's gone after Chandler."

"I'm not leaving."

"What!"

"Those damned Yankees have taken everything that was good and destroyed it! Now they've killed Marie-Claude!" The angry voices that never seemed to leave Travis anymore shrieked in his head. "Let's stay here and shoot it out!"

"Are you out of your mind? Chandler has an entire company at his beck and call."

Travis' eyes glittered in the moonlight. "We can take them. I'll bet we can even kill Chandler." He grinned, and in the dim light his face resembled a death's-head.

"You don't know what you're saying," Logan snapped as Tobe led his horse out of the barn and mounted.

"I know Marie-Claude is dead! We can't just ride off!"

"We can't do anything else. Our hanging won't bring her back to life. Get your horse."

"I'm staying. I'm going to kill as many of those bastards as I can. They can't take me!"

Logan didn't bother to argue. He drew back and hit Travis as hard as he could just beneath the jaw. Travis dropped like a felled ox. Logan lifted him onto Tobe's saddle, and Tobe supported him.

Harley had his own horse saddled and was tightening the cinch on Abigail's horse. Martin had almost finished with Caliban. Logan tightened his own saddle and mounted. The big horse half-reared in token protest, but Logan brought him under control. "Martin, you and the others head for the docks. Get passage for Jefferson. I'll follow and meet you there."

"I'm coming with you," Abigail said quickly.

"That's not as safe. Go with them."

"Chandler isn't looking for a man and a woman. If I go with you, everyone will be safer."

Logan frowned, but she had a point.

Martin finished saddling Travis' horse and mounted his own, leading the other behind him. "We're ready."

"Good. Be careful, and look for us at the hotel in Jefferson. I think it's called the Excelsior. Got that?"

Martin nodded. "Take care of yourselves." He and Harley spurred their horses into a lope and were joined by Tobe, still balancing Travis.

Logan looked at Abigail in the moonlight. Her face was pale and frightened. Protectiveness surged within him and he vowed silently that no harm would come to her.

Without a word they rode away in the opposite direction from the others, their horses' hooves leaving a clear trail on the driveway's dirt.

18

They rode hard through the moonlit fields, their horses' iron-shod hooves tearing through clods of grass and earth, leaving a trail even a fool could follow. Abigail rode hard to keep up with Logan. She knotted her fingers in Gypsy's dark mane with one hand and gripped the leather reins with the other. She dared not chance a fall at this speed, for they couldn't afford any delay.

After a while Logan slowed the pace. Gypsy gratefully matched Caliban's easier trot and breathed great gulps of air. Abigail patted his sweaty neck and spoke soothingly to him. To Logan she said, "Gypsy hasn't Caliban's strength, nor his endurance."

"I know. That's why we've slowed down. I didn't want to wind him." He turned in the saddle and looked back. "Even a blind man could follow that trail. Chandler will have no difficulty."

Abigail glanced back fearfully. "Do you think we'll get out of this safely?"

"There's a good chance." He grinned, his teeth gleaming white in the moonlight.

"I hope you know what you're doing." Her voice held shadings of doubt.

"So do I."

Abigail stared at him. She couldn't voice the fact that they had been unable to shake Chandler every time he had been hot on their trail.

Logan measured the ascending glow to the east.

"The sun will be up soon. When the horses are more rested, we have to pick up the pace again."

She nodded. Her body ached from fatigue, but she wasn't about to complain. After they had ridden another mile she asked, "What about Jeremiah? Will he be all right?"

"He'll find Mamie without any trouble. They have enough sense and enough money to buy a place and wait for the country to regain its sanity."

"That's what it's like, isn't it?" she mused in a low voice. "The country has gone insane. Brothers killing brothers, families torn apart, homes laid to waste."

"It's war," he said simply. "You would never believe the things I've seen in the course of this war. All those good men," he said with deep regret, "gone and buried."

"War is no bowl of peaches and cream for women, either," Abigail reminded him tartly. "At least you could fight back and not have to stand helplessly by and see your land picked clean."

"I never thought of that," Logan admitted.

They turned away from another boggy area and headed onto a carriage path that led through a woods. Occasionally Logan slowed even more so he could snap a twig to indicate their passage.

Abigail shivered. She had grown accustomed to trying to elude Chandler, and this business of leaving a clear trail for him was unnerving.

Dawn arrived in a pale lemon sky and countless birds sang in celebration. Abigail wished she felt as exuberant. She wanted only to be able to rest.

Up ahead a rangy farmer was walking out to his field, a hoe balanced over his shoulder and hooked nonchalantly beneath his wrist. Logan rode to the rail fence surrounding his field and called out, "Which way to Bogalusa?"

The farmer paused and pointed roughly in the direction of the squat orange sun. "Yonder. You've got quite a few miles to go yet."

Logan smiled and tugged at the brim of his hat. "Much obliged." They rode away at a gallop. Over his shoulder Logan told Abigail, "He will remember and tell Chandler we went to Bogalusa."

"I gathered that. Then what?"

"He won't find us." They had reached a thick woods bisected by a broad stream. This time Logan made no effort to break twigs and he kept Caliban to a walk in the leafy sod of many seasons.

At the stream they waded out into the clear water and let their horses drink. The lemon sky had turned an opalescent blue and the birds were singing less heartily. When Caliban lifted his head with a stream of water droplets beading like diamonds from his velvety black lips, Logan moved him downstream. Gypsy followed obediently, splashing through the swift-flowing water.

"We aren't going to Bogalusa?" Abigail asked.

"No, this is far enough." Logan pointed south. "We'll circle around and head back now. By late afternoon we should be on a riverboat headed for Jefferson."

She was silent for a few minutes. "Where's Jefferson?"

"You haven't heard of it?" he asked in surprise.

"Well, of course I've heard of it," she lied. "Who hasn't? But where is it?"

"Deep in East Texas. We'll leave New Orleans by riverboat, travel up the Mississippi, and branch off onto the Red River. That will take us all the way to Big Cypress and then to Caddo Lake. Jefferson is just west of there. It's the second-largest port in the South."

"I knew that," she said hastily. "I just didn't know it was west of the lake."

Logan grinned but didn't answer.

They rode at a steady pace, slowing only to work their way around and sometimes through a marsh. Abigail ached from head to toe, and by the time New Orleans was in sight, she hoped never to see a saddle again. After skirting to the north of the city to avoid contact with people as much as possible, they rode directly into the bustling cacophony of the wharves.

Abigail slid gratefully from the saddle and stroked Gypsy's nose as Logan bargained with a boat captain for transportation. The man waved his hands at the large boat, then at Logan, then at the river. Logan shook his head and gestured toward Abigail, who already looked as tired as a woman could and still move at all.

At last they shook hands and Logan came back to Abigail. "Damned pirates, every one of them," he grumbled. Then he smiled. "We have passage. The captain finally admitted he had one room left."

"One?" she asked weakly. Traveling with Logan to escape the Yankee major was a matter of necessity. Their lives were all in jeopardy. Having to share a bedroom with him after all that had happened was asking too much of her. But what else could she do?

"We were lucky to get that. Let's take the horses on board and get them settled." He didn't seem upset with the arrangement. She was hardly surprised.

They walked across the gangplank that had been

designated for livestock and led their reluctant horses onto the deck. Their hooves clopped with a hollow sound on the wood, and Caliban flicked his ears back in distaste. Logan soothed him, and the horse calmed. Abigail appreciatively patted Gypsy's red neck. She had no energy left to handle a nervous horse, and luckily Gypsy was too tired to care about the odd noise of hooves on wood.

They led the animals across a narrow strip of deck and down a ramp that led into the hold of the boat. A few other horses were tied there in stalls, along with the passengers' larger baggage and the boat's cargo. As a man directed them to a couple of empty stalls, Gypsy's lagging feet picked up as he scented oats and hay.

After unsaddling the two horses, they brushed them as the animals ate from the individual feed troughs. Abigail watched Logan and wondered how he could seem so tireless when she thought each brush stroke would surely be her last. He was actually whistling as he tossed their saddles over the top rail and spread the horses' blankets over them, hairy-side-up, to dry. Abigail reflected yet again that she wasn't cut out for this kind of life.

Satisfied that the horses were dry and cared for, Logan secured the stall doors and escorted Abigail up the stairway that led to the main deck. "I know you must be exhausted," he said contritely. "I apologize for the hard ride."

"I'm all right." He was gazing down at her in a way that made her pulse flutter in spite of her fatigue. She looked away and tried to harden her heart. "I'm sorry about Marie-Claude," she said, hoping her rival's name would conjure some degree of willpower.

A tired expression crossed Logan's face. "So am I," he sighed. "So am I."

Although this was the response she had sought, Abigail felt much worse. She didn't want Logan on the rebound, but on the other hand, she yearned for him at any cost.

"She risked her life to warn me," Logan said thoughtfully. "I wouldn't have ever guessed Marie-Claude was so unselfish."

"Perhaps she wanted a way out for herself," Abigail said sharply. At his startled expression she knew she had guessed right. She pushed the door open and walked out onto the deck.

Logan left her at the rail while he went to pay for their passage and get the key to their room. Abigail leaned on the polished band of mahogany and watched the throng of people that clotted the dock. Black and white, old and young, they formed an ever-shifting pattern between the bales of burlap-bound cotton, wooden crates, and coops of squawking chickens. Three boys raced through the adults, a spotted dog yapping at their heels. A turbaned black woman pushed a cart of fruit, singing out the chant of her wares. A well-dressed man flanked by a dark-skinned youth rested his thumb in his brocaded vest as he consulted his gold watch against the slant of the sun. Abigail wondered if he were a carpetbagger or one of the riverboat gamblers that she had heard William speak of.

A bevy of women dressed in red taffeta and gaudy yellow satin strolled through the crowd, their bold eyes meeting the men's with unveiled challenge. Abigail looked away. She knew exactly what their profession was. Curiosity overcame the teachings of her youth, however, so she studied them from the corner of her eye while she pretended to watch the cotton being loaded on the far end of the deck.

In spite of herself, Abigail was enjoying seeing new places and people such as would never have come down the dusty road by her farm. The gaily bedecked women alone were an education. The man she had decided was a gambler gave the women an appraising glance, but the fine pair of gentlemen beside him ignored them completely. A man wearing a houndstooth vest gave an almost imperceptible nod and one of the women veered off to join him. Abigail was staring in earnest by now.

She jumped when she heard Logan's velvety chuckle just behind her. "I was watching the men load the cotton," she defended herself automatically.

"Of course you were." He was grinning at her in a way that provoked her ire. His dark eyes flicked to the gaudy trollops and back again.

Color blazed in her cheeks and she lifted her chin defiantly. No lady would ever even admit that prostitutes existed, but as usual her tongue was faster than her discretion. "I thought perhaps you might know them. Sally Hankins, I believe was the name," she said haughtily.

Logan burst out in laughter. "Sally in that bunch of tarts? Never! Sally's ... establishment ... is way over there. That elegant house with the iron-work on the balcony. Those are just crib girls."

Abigail's mouth parted in amazement. She had expected him to be a gentleman and claim ignorance. Against her will, she glanced at the building he had indicated. Nothing about it set it apart from its genteel neighbors. And that was almost as shocking as the way the colorful women had almost all paired off and were strolling away on strange men's arms.

"Disgraceful!" Abigail said.

"Then why are you wondering about them?" he countered.

A melodious cry rang out as the last cotton bale was jockeyed into place and the loading ramp was pulled aboard. As if the call had been anticipated, a tremor ran through the boat and a billow of black smoke puffed from the red-and-black smokestack. The ropes had been cast off, and slowly the gap between boat and dock widened.

"Aren't they going to put the cotton below?" Abigail asked stiffly. She wished Logan hadn't seen her watching the women soliciting their trade. Uneasily she realized she wasn't nearly as embarrassed by what she had seen as she was that Logan had caught her observing it.

"Cotton is too heavy to move any more than is necessary. It rides on the deck." He tried to hide his smile. She was still blushing and he knew exactly why. Ladies just didn't discuss such things.

"If you don't mind," Abigail said with cool aloofness, "I would like to go to the room and rest." She tossed him a warning look. "Alone."

"Whatever you say. I've arranged for a washbasin, if you'd like to freshen up." His eyes still teased her, but his tone was that of a gentleman to a lady.

"Thank you," Abigail said as graciously as possible.

He showed her to a door on the promenade deck and unlocked it for her. "We were lucky. Boarding so late, we might have been lodged nearer the horse stalls."

Abigail looked in. "It's so tiny!" she exclaimed.

"All the cabins are small."

"In such a grand boat, I thought the rooms would be more . . . well, elegant."

"Some are, but only the captain's is larger. He all but lives on the boat, however. Go inside."

"Are you sure there's room?" she asked, only half-joking. "You can't possibly fit in as well."

"We'll manage." He smiled.

Abigail averted her eyes. Logan had spoken to her with such gentleness and with such a respectful tone that she wanted to agree with him that they would manage. She had had no time to evaluate the effect Marie-Claude's death might have on her relationship with Logan. She wanted to set aside the past and love him without reservation, but could he do the same? Only time would tell.

"Look back," Logan said, taking her arm. "We're leaving."

She turned to watch New Orleans sliding away beyond the rail. Logan walked over and rested his hand on the mahogany strip. Nostalgia was pooled in his dark eyes as the home he had yearned for again eluded him.

Abigail went to him and compassionately laid her hand on his arm. "You'll be back," she said gently.

He slowly shook his head. "No. All I came back to find is gone. My family is all dead, Magnolias is burned to the ground, Fair Oaks belongs to a Yankee. Soon Rosehaven will be sold to the sort of person I wouldn't hire on as overseer." A muscle clenched in his tanned jaw. "I'll never be back."

"Perhaps in a few years everything will change again," she soothed. "In so much turmoil, who knows what will come of it?"

"No, this much I do know. That part of my life

is gone forever." He watched as the city slid from view. "But no life will ever be as easy as that one, nor as sweet."

Abigail put her arm around him and held him as the trees along the Mississippi riverbank blocked his view of all he had known and loved. "Come inside," she urged softly. "You'll feel better for having rested."

Logan suddenly felt tired to the bone. He hadn't admitted even to himself how much he had counted on finding at least a remnant of his former life. He eased his arm around Abigail and held her close. He wanted her. He longed to bury his face in the warm curve of her neck and hold her until his strength and courage returned. Big as he was, he wasn't invincible, and at the moment he wanted nothing so much as to be cherished by the woman he loved. Unfortunately, she didn't love him in return.

Reluctantly Logan released Abigail and stepped away. "I won't intrude on you," he said formally. "After such a long ride, I know you'll want some privacy."

A cold knot formed in Abigail's middle, and she abruptly dropped her hand. "Yes," she said numbly. "I do."

He looked away as if he found the bales of cotton far more interesting than her. "I'll take a few turns on deck. You'll find everything you need in the room."

Not trusting herself to speak, Abigail turned and went into the cabin. Shutting the door, she leaned on it and squeezed her eyes tight to keep the hot tears from falling. She had reached out to him and he had rejected her. Never again! Pain and humiliating anger made a choking sob rise in her throat. As much as she hated to cry, she sobbed brokenly as she poured water into the china washbasin so she could rinse away the day's dust and heat.

Between tears and exhaustion, Abigail slept all night and well into the next day. When she finally awoke, she rolled to her back and stared at the wood grain on the low ceiling. A steady chug of muffled engines sounded all around her. Gradually she realized where she was and sat up.

She was alone in the room and she felt disoriented, unsure of how much time had passed. If Logan had come back to the cabin, she hadn't heard him. Her muscles were sore, but not as tender as she had expected. Gingerly she swung her feet to the floor and stood up.

Beyond the small window she saw cypress trees and a bank of tall greenery thick with trailing gray-green moss. The water lapped over the smooth river's surface and calmed among the jet-black pools that surrounded the cypress knees. Even the blue of the sky seemed to be swallowed rather than reflected in the swampy forest. A tall white bird with a thick tuft of feathers like those of a lady's hat stood motionless beside a fallen log as the riverboat chugged past.

Abigail had never seen a swamp like this, and she stared until the marsh was gradually replaced by more solid ground. The ever-present cypress still turned the water to ink and seemed to contradict the feathery lace of their bright green leaves; but on the firmer ground, weeds abounded instead of treacherous spear grass.

Unable to be still any longer, Abigail went out onto the deck. At once she saw Logan sitting in a deck chair. His morose expression as he stared at the passing scenery made her wonder if he had actually sat there all night.

Several people strolled along the deck, while others sat, but all seemed more interested in the lush woods than in the red-and-white confection of the steamboat that carried them so swiftly through the water. Abigail tried to assume an expression of well-traveled boredom as she crossed to the rail.

"Did you sleep well?" Logan asked without looking at her.

"Quite well. And you?" She could be as coolly polite as he was.

"No. This chair is damned uncomfortable."

She stared at him. "You sat there all night?"

He continued watching the passing trees. "You were taking up all the bed."

"The bed was overly small," she snapped, "but you could have asked me to move over." She stared sightlessly at the river. How foolish she had been to assume he might have wanted to share a room with her, and that she had secretly hoped that he might. "Lovely day," she commented in a garden-party tone.

"Too hot," he contradicted.

"You might go lie down if you like. It's warmer inside, but you could rest more comfortably."

He frowned at her as if wondering if she meant more than the offer of her empty bed.

"I won't disturb you," she said haughtily.

Logan looked away and started to uncoil his long body from the chair. He must have been tireder than he thought, to have read more than impersonal kindness in her words.

Abigail looked toward the front of the boat and

watched the people that mingled on the sun-washed deck. Suddenly her breath caught in her throat and she gasped as a tall man in a blue uniform rounded the corner. She shoved Logan back into the chair and tipped his hat to hide his face, as if from the sun.

"What—" he demanded, trying to sit up.

"Be still!" she hissed. In almost the same breath she said, "Good day, sir. Are you enjoying the journey?"

"Indeed I am. I'm on my way to Shreveport. On business," the man observed, his Minnesota accent unmistakable. "I don't believe I've had the pleasure. Major Owen Chandler, ma'am, at your service."

At the mention of the man's name, Logan eased lower in the chair, tilting his head so his hat brim obscured his face.

"I'm glad to meet you, Major Chandler," Abigail said, a Scottish burr dripping from her voice. "Miss Fiona McDougal." She bobbed a curtsy. "I'm journeying with my uncle here." She patted Logan's shoulder as if he were not only infirm but deaf as well. "I'm afraid he has dozed off. The sunshine puts him to sleep, you know."

Chandler nodded. The man looked rather well-built to be so old as to sleep in the sun, but with the hat at such an angle, he couldn't tell for sure. "Elderly, is he?"

"Aye. My great-uncle, as a matter of fact. On my father's side."

"Your accent intrigues me," Chandler said charmingly. "You couldn't be a Rebel girl."

"Me?" Abigail asked with delighted innocence. "Mercy no. Me uncle and I have only recently arrived from Scotland."

"If you had tried to come earlier, I'm afraid you would have been stopped by the blockade." Chandler smiled. "The war, you know."

"Blockade?"

"The British sided with the Rebels. For a while we had to shut off trade."

"Saints preserve us," Abigail murmured, as if she hadn't known.

Chandler studied her with interest. She was a lovely woman. That sunbonnet hid her hair, but he was willing to bet it was blond, as pale as her skin. And those eyes! Such an unusual color. "I don't wish to seem presumptive, Miss McDougal, but would you care to dine with me this evening?"

"I couldn't!" Abigail gasped. Then: "I mean, my uncle prefers a quieter company. His age and all, you understand."

"Does he retire early?" Chandler licked his lips. Aged uncles were easily sidestepped. But something about her eyes . . .

"Aye, that he does. Perhaps I could meet you in the dining room?" Her fingers bit nervously into Logan's shoulder. How would she ever get out of this?

"I'd be delighted. Say, at eight?"

"Lovely."

"Until tonight." He made a half-bow. Something about her seemed familiar, though of course that was impossible. "I have just left a good friend who was unexpectedly bereaved. I would welcome such charming company." He saw her pale to the hue of chalk and smiled. He liked frail women. And he knew all such women loved to cosset and cuddle a man beset by sadness. "Such a dear wife he lost," Chandler added. "I've been burdened greatly by her untimely death."

"My deepest sympathy," Abigail murmured. "Until tonight, then. At eight." She curtsied again so he would have no choice but to leave.

As soon as he turned the other corner, she yanked Logan to his feet. "He's here!" she hissed unnecessarily. "He never followed us at all!"

Logan growled an oath she had never heard before and dragged her sideways into their cabin.

"All that riding," she moaned, "for nothing! He never followed us!"

Logan was stuffing their belongings into the saddlebags. "You didn't have to stop him and pass the time of day!"

"He was looking right at me! What else could I do? If I had turned and ducked in here, he would have known something was wrong. And you! He would have known your face at a glance!"

"You didn't have to agree to have dinner with him!" Logan argued.

"What else could I do?"

Logan opened the door and warily peeped out. Chandler was nowhere in sight. "Come on."

She grabbed his hand and hurried behind him, glancing fearfully over her shoulder. They dodged into the narrow stairway and she held her skirt away from her feet as she shadowed Logan down the steep steps.

"What are we going to do?" she demanded.

"Just be quiet and come on," he snapped.

They emerged in the dim cargo area and she ran to keep up as Logan went to their horses. He hastily saddled Gypsy and moved to Caliban.

"What are you doing?" she asked again. "I didn't see a port. Are we about to dock?"

"I have a plan." He tightened Caliban's cinch and tossed the reins over the horse's head.

"What? What are we doing?"

"Be quiet. Do you want someone to know we're down here?" He put his hands on her waist and hoisted her onto Gypsy's back.

"Logan!" she protested, recovering her balance with difficulty.

He swung up onto Caliban and leaned over to catch Gypsy's reins. As they rode to the ramp he turned back to her. As if his question were an afterthought, he asked, "Can you swim?"

"Yes, but—"

"Good. Hang on!" He clapped his heels against Caliban's barreled ribs and the horse bolted forward, taking Gypsy and Abigail with him.

They clattered up the ramp and onto the deck, scattering passengers before them like a flock of chickens. Abigail's mouth was open in a silent cry and her eyes were round as she realized what Logan planned to do. She saw Chandler standing in shocked amazement as they rode by, but he was gone in an instant as she felt Gypsy's muscles bunch and hurl up and out over the water.

"Oh, no!" she shrieked as she flew through space and down to the opaque water below. Seizing the horse's mane, she buried her face against his neck. They hit the water with a huge splash and she nearly lost her grip as the saddle horn gouged at her stomach.

Water filled her nose, mouth, and eyes and she clung with terror to the only solid object she could find. All at once her head bobbed to the surface and she gulped in as much air as her lungs could hold.

Only Gypsy's head showed and his eyes rolled back at her as Logan pulled him after Caliban. The black horse was swimming easily; the tree-studded bank was drawing nearer. "I'll get you for this, Logan Sorrell," she cried out as water from the riverboat's wake nearly swamped her.

She came up to hear his laughter as he guided her to safety. Behind them the riverboat and its load of startled passengers chugged on upriver.

19

The campfire burned with a low, steady flame, making the surrounding earth warm. Abigail sat huddled in a blanket, her clothes spread to dry, as she glared across the fire at Logan. She wasn't nearly as angry as she pretended, but without the protective armor of clothing, she didn't trust herself to smile at him.

Logan was also wrapped in a blanket. He wanted to sit beside Abigail, but she had firmly put the campfire between them. Every time he caught her eye, she frowned. "I had to do it," he reminded her again.

"You could have warned me," she retorted as she had on the other occasions. "We were nearly in the water before you asked if I could swim."

"Well, it just never occurred to me that you couldn't."

"Logan, how many women do you know who can swim?" she demanded. "Could your sisters? Could Marie-Claude? Women don't go skinny-dipping, Logan, and nobody can swim in heavy skirts."

"I thought since you were a farmgirl . . ."

"That I was shameless enough to strip down and go swimming? Thank you."

"Well, you *did* know how. Why are you so mad?" He paused thoughtfully. "Now that you mention it, how did you learn?"

She lifted her chin defiantly. "William taught me."

The unexpected introduction of the gone but not forgotten William made Logan wince with jealousy. All too clearly he could picture Abigail's slender body and shapely limbs bobbing in crystal-clear water beside another man. That William had been her husband made the thought even worse. Logan knew what *he* would have done in that situation. "Are you cold?" he asked gruffly.

"No more than could be expected," she answered loftily.

"I'll tell you what," Logan suggested. "Next time I'll leave you behind where you'll be decorous and dry and let Chandler have you."

She recalled the night she had gone to Chandler's room and shivered. "I would have followed you anyway. It just seems like you could have warned me."

"Next time I will."

He reached out of the blanket and fed another log to the fire. As the flames engulfed the new wood, it crackled and threw sparks toward the sky. The fire's light burnished Abigail's skin to topaz and made her dusky eyes mysteriously dark. Her hair was dry now and fell in unbound waves over her shoulder. The blanket had parted, revealing the faint line of her collarbone and the suggestion of a curving breast. Logan looked away.

After a strained silence she asked, "We didn't lose the gold, did we?"

"Is that all you ever think about?" he snapped edgily.

"No, but I can see *you're* here. Is the gold?"

"It's safe." He frowned at her. "Do you want to count it?"

"I believe you." She bared her arm to run her fingers through her hair to loosen the tangles. "The gold is important to me."

"Obviously," he said with sarcasm.

She ignored him. "Without it I couldn't buy a farm. Then what would I do?"

His frown deepened. She could marry him, for one thing, he thought. She might not love him, but marriages that had started on less sometimes worked out quite well. Besides, he loved her enough for them both.

Satisfied that her hair was smooth, Abigail pulled her arm back inside the concealing blanket. "I hope your clothes dry by morning."

He made no comment.

"Do you know where we are?"

"Yes."

After a pause she said tartly, "Well?"

"We're downstream from Jefferson."

"We've been downstream from Jefferson ever since we left New Orleans."

"Then why did you ask?"

"Will we be able to find Tobe and the others?"

"Sure we will. We found them at the turtle rock, didn't we?"

"More or less."

"We'll find them."

"I hope so. I want to see Texas."

He studied her for a minute. "About that farm of yours . . ."

"Yes?"

"I think you ought to go in with me, and us get one together."

"Why would I want to do that?"

"Convenience. Some of that land out there has

never seen a plow. Farming is too hard for a woman alone."

"I've done it before."

"Did you enjoy it?"

She frowned. At times she had doubted she would ever get enough crops planted to last through the winter. "I'll manage."

"What if you get sick?"

"Are you trying to scare me?"

"No, just trying to get you to listen to reason."

"What if I buy a farm with you and you decide you want me off your land?"

"I would never do that."

"You say that now, but what if you marry?"

Logan gazed at her through the film of pale smoke. "It looks like I won't ever marry. If I can't have the woman I love, I don't want anyone else."

Abigail looked away. If he had been a true love, she would have been very happy. Especially now that they were out of New Orleans and more in her own element. "I think I'll raise sheep," she said to change the subject. "I'll plant only what I need for my own table, and earn a living by selling wool and mutton."

Logan stood, rearranging his blanket to keep himself covered, and walked over to her side of the fire. "You have it all figured out, don't you?"

"I didn't say you could come over here. This is my side," she objected as her heart beat a wild tattoo. The only two things that separated her from his warm flesh were the woolen blankets.

"I didn't ask."

She fixed her gaze on the fire to avoid the midnight of his eyes. "Sheep are easy to raise. All you really need is a good pasture and still water."

"Abigail . . ." he said softly as he knelt beside her.

"They won't drink from running water. They are afraid of drowning."

"Abigail, look at me." He gently drew her face around and waited until she raised her eyes. "I want you," he said softly. "I want you so badly I ache. There was no way I could stay all the way over there with you over here."

"It wasn't so terribly far," she whispered.

"Any distance from you is too far." He cupped her chin and rubbed his thumb over the velvet of her skin.

"I don't . . ." Abigail couldn't think straight when he was so near. Especially not with that look in his eyes and his hand sending delight through all her nerves.

"I know you don't love me," he said, "but do you want me?"

To say yes would have been a gross understatement, but she couldn't possibly admit it. Surges of need melted through her and she found she couldn't speak at all. Not when her words would, by necessity, end the magic that was spinning between them. She found herself drifting toward him as if she were drawn to a lodestone. Unable to stop herself, Abigail tilted her head up toward him and her rosy lips parted in anticipation of his kiss.

Logan lowered his head, his thick black hair tumbling forward on his forehead. A breath away from her lips he paused as her long eyelashes swept down to her cheeks. Her breath was sweet upon his lips, and he suppressed a groan for fear of breaking the spell.

Abigail crossed the remaining distance and found his lips. Firm, yet soft, they yielded to her kiss and she swayed nearer until their bodies touched. Lo-

gan ran his fingers through the skein of her hair
and guided her in a kiss that began sweetly, then
quickly merged into passion. He let his blanket
fall to his lap and took her into his arms. Teasing
her inner lips with his tongue, he drank of the
nectar of her mouth. Then Logan brushed the
scratchy blanket from between them, and Abigail
moaned softly as she let him gather her even
closer. As if she had been waiting for this, she put
her arms around him, and he thrilled at the touch
of her small hands upon his back. Her breasts first
teased his chest, then mounded against him in
desire. Logan felt as if he would explode from
loving and wanting her.

Abigail tried to control herself, remembering
that he might want her body, but that he had
loved Marie-Claude. She didn't want to be a substitute for another woman, yet at the moment she
couldn't stop herself. As long as Logan's arms
held her tight and his breath was warm against
her cheek, his magnificent body would call unbri-
dled passion from her.

She stroked the hard sheath of muscles that
covered his ribs and flexed in his powerful shoulders. He was so strong! One squeeze could break
her in half, yet he was so gentle she had no fear.
His hair was thick and silky and smelled faintly of
wood smoke. Abigail inhaled his clean scent as if it
were an aphrodisiac.

His hands circled her waist, measuring in love
spans the smooth flesh. Upward they moved, making her melt inside. As he supported her with one
strong arm, Logan's other hand found her breast.
Abigail murmured and shifted to give him easier
access to her proud nipple. Her flesh pouted beneath his fingers, wanting him to take her and

please her at once, yet desiring to draw out each sensuous caress to the utmost moment.

Logan felt her breast swell to fill his palm, and blood pounded in his temples. This was his woman; the mate he had been created to fulfill. How could she not love him when she so obviously desired him? He decided she didn't know her own mind, and that if she didn't love him now, he would win her. But the doubt that he might not and that this might be the last time he would ever hold her, caress her, please her, haunted him. He resolved that this night would be one they would never forget.

He flicked the blanket back and gently laid her down. His sinewy body stretched out beside hers and the firelight gilded them in a warm glow. He raised up on one elbow and gazed down at the woman he loved above all else. Her hair tumbled in a cape of waves that seemed full of dark flames; her eyes were deep amethyst and held all the mysteries of a Circe. Twin nipples of dusky coral peaked toward him, inviting his touch, and her waist narrowed gracefully as her hips swelled outward in a curve, partially hiding the curly nest of her womanhood. Long, well-shaped legs curved delicately to her slender ankles and small feet.

"You're perfect," he managed to say hoarsely. "I never knew anyone could be so beautiful."

She lay quietly, her lips slightly parted to reveal her glistening teeth. She made no move to cover herself or to pretend a modesty that she didn't feel.

"You were made to be loved," he whispered as he lowered his lips to hers.

His fingers stroked the underside of her breast, then finally the enticing crown. Gently he rolled the jewel between his thumb and forefinger until she arched toward him.

Leaving a trail of hot kisses over her throat and chest, he neared the prize and claimed it with his lips. She cried out as his tongue lathed her nipple, drawing it into his mouth.

She entwined her fingers in his hair, holding him to her breast and showing him how to love her. He treasured first one, then the other, and seemed to enjoy the sensation almost as much as she did.

"Logan," she murmured, "I want you. Make love with me. Please take me." When he smiled and teasingly nipped her tender breast between his lips, she sighed, "I want you so much."

"Not as much as you're going to," he promised.

His hands slipped lower, drawing fire from her hips and buttocks until she writhed at his touch. Only then did he caress her rounded thighs and run his palm up the sensitive inner curve toward her femininity. When his knowing fingers touched her moist warmth, Abigail moaned in an ecstasy that was near pain, then tried to press her body even closer to his.

Logan continued his slow exploration, finding the nerve endings that made her almost explode with desire, learning new ways to urge her to ever-greater passion. When she begged him to become one with her, he lowered his head and loved her in a way she had never known before.

She felt her fires rising beyond control; then his lips were replaced by his tumid maleness. Abigail cried out as fireflies seemed to flare up and fill her. Wave after pounding wave of love thundered through her and she almost sobbed as she clung to his muscled body.

Gradually the pulsating ecstasy subsided, and she could breathe more easily. Still he moved within her, urging her to join him in a soaring flight of passion. Her willing body quickened to the pace he set, and again Abigail felt the earth spin away from her. Nothing existed in her universe except Logan and her love for him. He was finished with teasing her and was thoroughly immersed in pleasing her to the depths and heights of her soul.

Skillfully he loved her, letting his own love tell him her needs. For as long as possible he kept them both on the brink of complete fulfillment, then both plunged to a mutual completion. Their murmurs of love blended into a single note as their souls met, entwined, and glided free.

After a long time, Abigail opened her eyes dreamily and found Logan watching her. His lips curved upward in a satisfied smile and his eyes were warm with an emotion she dared not define. She could think of no words great enough to convey what she was feeling, so she lay quietly in his arms. Some part of her being still seemed to be held and intertwined with his, and she floated in the enchantment.

Lovingly Logan brushed a tendril from her temple, and his smile broadened. "You're one hell of a woman," he whispered.

Abigail smiled and snuggled into the curve of his embrace. She never wanted to leave, and refused to think of the time when she would.

Abigail twisted in the saddle to check the angle of the sun and river. "Are you sure you know where we're going?" she asked. "I think we're heading south, not north."

"That's right."

"But we just came from this direction. Jefferson is north of here."

"I know."

Abigail frowned as she nudged Gypsy to a trot to close the distance between them. She had tried to say as little as possible to Logan that morning. In the clear light of day she could scarcely believe she had let her passions overrule her good sense. She didn't want to be second choice, whether her rival was alive or dead. While she cooked breakfast, she had almost convinced herself that Logan had made love with her only because he ached for Marie-Claude. By the time she had washed up and was ready to mount Gypsy, she was sure of it. Logan had tried to be friendly, affectionate even, but she had squelched that. She couldn't chance a recurrence of her mistake the night before.

After a few minutes she asked, "Then why are we heading south?"

"Because that's the way Chandler won't expect us to go. If I was after someone and they jumped ship on the west bank of the river, I would assume they were heading for Texas. I would get off at the next port and start searching west of here."

"Then he'll find us!"

"No, he won't. The boat won't stop until it reaches Alexandria. Chandler has no way to get off until then unless he and his men do what we did. That's pretty unlikely. I figure they are about ten miles behind us."

"What should we do?"

"I've been up and down this river all my life. I know it almost as well as I know Saint Charles Parish. There's a man who lives along the river near Effie who will ferry us across the river. Chandler won't know about him, and he will assume we are still on this side."

"Effie?"

"That's the next town. Look. You can see smoke from his sawmill."

They cantered down a low rise; then Logan led the way to a small farmhouse on the bank of the river. Behind the barn a conical tin roof spouted smoke and a large pyramid of sawdust was towering in the yard beside stacks of felled pine trees.

A middle-aged woman in a gray dress and faded pink checkered sunbonnet was hoeing weeds from a garden. She didn't speak but nodded a greeting. Logan tipped his hat and Abigail returned the nod. A bandy-legged man in old pants and a long-john undershirt came out of the sawmill. The air was rent by the shriek of a pine tree being ripped into planks by a saw.

" 'Morning," the man greeted, wiping the sawdust from his palms and offering his hand to Logan.

"Good morning," Logan said, glad to see no flicker of recognition in the man's open face. "I understand you run a ferry?"

"Yeah," the man drawled, scratching his head and looking over at the river. "I have a ferryboat. Don't take it out much these days."

"My wife and I need to cross the river," Logan said. "I'd make it worth your while."

"It's me poor old mother," Abigail urged in a Scottish burr. "She's ailing bad and we've got to reach her. Can you not help us?"

The man drew a reluctant breath and looked back to where his workers were hauling another tree into place. "Do you have to go now? I'm pretty busy."

Abigail buried her face in her hands as if in grief. "We've traveled so far, and she's just beyond the river. A few hours may be all she has left on this earth."

"Now, don't cry, darlin'," Logan comforted.

The man shifted his weight from one foot to the other. "I can't stand to see a woman cry."

Abigail managed a realistic sob.

"All right. I'll take you across." Over his shoulder he yelled, "Jeb! You keep working in there. I'll be back directly."

Abigail and Logan followed him to the river and led their horses onto a large raft, a crude affair with only a single low rail to fence it. They tied the horses to a hitching post in the center of the platform and Abigail waited nervously as Logan helped the man shove away from the mud. The water lapped mere inches from the surface boards and the entire contraption looked as if it might sink at any moment. The man stoked the small boiler, then cursorily inspected the engine. After making several adjustments, he threw a lever and the contraption vibrated to life.

"My name's Clive Dumaine," he said amiably to Logan over the engine's roar. The last of the mud released the logs of the ferry with a sucking sound.

Logan smiled. "Glad to meet you."

"I don't believe I caught you folks' name."

"Lee," Logan lied.

"McFarland," Abigail said simultaneously. They frowned at each other.

"Lee McFarland," Clive mused. "I don't believe I've heard tell of any McFarlands around here."

"We're from Texas," Logan said.

"Her ma was took sick sudden, was she?"

"Yes." Logan hated to lie and wanted to tell as small a one as possible.

"Whereabouts in Texas?"

Logan racked his brain for the name of a Texas town. "Jasper." He had once met a man from there, but he wasn't sure where Jasper was located.

Clive nodded. "Jasper's a good town. You know the Fred Willis family?"

"Not well," he hedged.

"Let's see. Who else do I know from Jasper." Clive Dumaine poled them away from the bank as he spoke, then bent over the motor and made a small adjustment as the shore slowly receded. "How about Nathan Armstrong?"

"I'm afraid not."

"Can't see how you wouldn't know old Nathan. He runs the feed store. You having animals and all, you ought to know Nathan." He scratched what looked to be at least a three-day beard stubble.

"Oh, yes," Abigail spoke up. "I know his wife. We belong to the same sewing circle."

"Nathan remarried?" Clive asked in amazement. "I sure wouldn't have expected it at his age. He must be nigh onto seventy years old."

"It was a May-December romance," Abigail said faintly. "It was the talk of the town for months."

Logan grimaced at her.

Clive steered them out into the middle of the river before he said, "What's ailing your ma?"

"Yellow jack," Abigail said.

"Typhoid," Logan said at the same time.

Clive shook his head. "She must be in real bad shape, poor woman."

"Sounds like it," Logan said grimly.

"Never knew anybody to get both at once."

"That's why we're in a hurry," Abigail said.

"I hadn't heard of an outbreak lately. Where does she live?"

Logan silenced Abigail with a warning glare. "She lives on a farm in the back of nowhere. It's not likely to spread."

"It's these damned swamps," Clive commiserated. "Begging your pardon, ma'am. The air gets back in them trees and backwaters and it sours. It's a miracle we ain't all dead."

Logan made no comment.

The dull red water eddied around the ferry as the far shore drew closer. Logan wanted to hurry the man in his painstakingly slow progress, but he didn't dare risk rousing the man's suspicions. If Chandler should question Clive by coincidence, Logan wanted the man to have no reason to connect them with the fugitive Chandler sought.

At last the ferry nudged against the ruddy mud of the opposite bank. Logan counted out the ferry fee and smiled at Clive. "Much obliged," he said.

"Glad to do it. You and the missus be real careful, now, you hear? Typhoid and yellow jack is mighty dangerous."

"We will."

After they had led the horses off the platform, Clive Dumaine started to maneuver the raft back across. When he looked back, Logan and Abigail waved farewell. Then Logan motioned for Abigail to follow him into a thicket of haw bushes nearby, where they could wait out of sight of the river.

"Why are we staying here?" she asked.

"I want to see that he gets back to shore. Nobody could miss seeing him out there on the river. If Chandler notices the ferry, I want to know."

"Do you think he's that close?" she asked anxiously.

"No," he said, but his eyes continued to search the trees on the far bank.

When the ferry operator reached the shore, he moored his unwieldy boat against the bank amid a mass of bushes so that it was all but invisible. He then walked back to his sawmill with the unhurried gait of a man with a clear conscience.

Logan held Gypsy while Abigail mounted, then got up on Caliban. They rode north at a steady pace, following the meandering Red River.

By afternoon they reached the busy port of Alexandria and crossed the bridge into town.

"Where are we going?" Abigail asked as the boats came into view.

"We're going to take a cabin on a riverboat. Jefferson is just a two-day journey by river. Much longer by land."

"Are you out of your senses!" Abigail said as she grabbed his arm. "We could run into Chandler here!"

"The way I figure it, he left the boat early this morning and headed toward Effie. Since that's the way he saw us heading, that's the most logical thing for him to do."

"But what if he didn't?"

"If you were chasing someone, wouldn't you look where you expected them to be? The least likely spot is the one where you already looked. Right?"

"But . . ."

"He saw us leave a riverboat. He won't think to look for us on the river. If I were Chandler, I'd get reinforcements from Marksville and fan out from the river to the west. By the time he realizes we aren't there, we'll be in Texas and long gone."

"I hope you're right," she said uncertainly.

"Trust me. I know about military strategy."

"Then how is it that Chandler didn't follow us toward Bogalusa, but was on that boat to Shreveport?"

"He must have figured that since we weren't in Shreveport when you said we would be, we had headed there this time. That's military strategy. See?"

Abigail made a noncommittal sound.

"And while I'm thinking of it, let's get our stories straight this time. You nearly gave us away with Clive Dumaine."

"*I* did? You're the one who told him we were from Jasper. He seemed to know that place like the back of his hand!"

"How was I to know that? He caught me off guard. You're the one who told him your mother was down with yellow fever *and* typhoid."

"No, I didn't. You gave her the typhoid. Not me."

"And don't you know any names that aren't Scottish?"

"McFarland is a fine old name. My Aunt Bess married into the McFarland clan and she never regretted it."

"That's fine for you, but I'm about as Scottish as my horse is. Can't you come up with an American name for once?"

"Like what? Pocahontas?"

"You know what I mean."

Abigail lifted her chin disdainfully. "You mean a British name. Never!"

Logan sighed. "Okay. I'll take care of it. You stay here and hold my horse. The office is right over there and I doubt there will be many people passing by this alleyway. If you see Chandler, hide."

"What about you?"

"I can take care of myself." He took some gold coins from his saddlebags to pay their fare. "I'm going to book us as the Jensons. Any objections?"

"Not as long as you tell them we're brother and sister and that you need separate cabins." She couldn't maintain her distance if they shared a cabin again.

"We don't look anything alike and your accent is as obvious as a bouquet of shamrocks."

"Cousins, then. Distant ones. But not man and wife." She glared at him stubbornly.

Logan growled as he stalked away. He couldn't understand her at all. She could make love with him as if her heart were overflowing with love, and turn right around and be cold as ice. He was better off without her. He only wished he believed that.

20

Chandler left his tired horse at the livery stable and walked down the boardwalk of downtown Alexandria. He had spent two fruitless days searching south and west for Nighthawk and his female accomplice. Finally he had given up and returned to town. His men were tired and growing disgruntled. Most of them were overdue to muster out and the others were ready for their long-delayed furloughs to visit families back home. He grimaced. Soldiers today weren't of the same caliber they once were. When he was a young soldier he would have followed his commanding officer through hell if asked to.

He went to the telegraph office and wrote out a message to his colonel in Washington. He had recently been reprimanded for not keeping closer touch. Colonel Dearborn was as bad as an old maiden aunt when it came to keeping tabs on a man. As if he wasn't on army business.

The man behind the counter took the message and tapped the code onto the telegraph key. Chandler watched him with the unblinking gaze that made most men squirm nervously. He didn't do that on purpose, though he would have if he had realized the effect his pale stare generated. Chandler wasn't given to noticing such subtleties.

The telegraph clerk looked up at him. "Do you expect a reply?"

"Maybe. If there is one, I'll be over at the saloon. You'll bring it over, won't you?"

"Sure thing, Major."

Chandler sauntered back outside. Several hours of daylight still remained, and he regretted giving up so soon. His men could have held up a little longer. He wouldn't have asked them to do anything he wasn't willing to do himself.

Crossing over to the saloon, he elbowed through the swinging doors. A number of men and several daringly dressed saloon girls were in the smoky room. Chandler went to a scarred table and sat down, motioning for the man behind the bar to bring him a whiskey.

Thoughtfully he ran over all he knew about Nighthawk. His name was Logan Sorrell, though Chandler had thought of him by his code name so long that the real name seemed false. He was of Creole blood and had owned the plantation adjoining Amos Smith's.

For a fleeting moment Chandler remembered Amos' lovely wife. Marie-Claude. That was her name. A beautiful woman and just the sort Chandler most admired. He doubted he would ever have taken her as a lover, since Amos was his friend, but he knew he could have. She had had that look about her. What a pity she was dead. From Amos' garbled account Chandler doubted Nighthawk had shot her, even though Amos said he had. If she and Nighthawk had been lovers, he surely wouldn't have shot her, and if they hadn't been, he would have had even less reason. No, he suspected the bullet in Marie-Claude's lovely breast had belonged to her husband.

That didn't really matter, because Amos was

willing to swear he saw Logan shoot her, and that was enough to ensure that Logan Sorrell would hang if he could catch him. *When* he caught him, Chandler amended.

The bartender brought the whiskey and Chandler tossed him a coin. The cool liquid slid like fire down his throat. No man was lucky forever, he mused. Eventually Nighthawk would be his captive.

Chandler toyed with the glass as he thought about the woman who had been with Sorrell on the riverboat. Who was she? A lover? A wife perhaps. Whoever she was, she was a beauty. He would rather take her to the woods than hang her. Something about her, however, seemed very familiar.

Her eyes. They were such an odd color. Almost the shade of a sky bruised by sunset. Sort of a violet. He had seen eyes that color before.

As he began to remember, his gaze became colder. That young whore in the saloon in Mississippi had had violet eyes. His fingers tightened on the glass. And so did the lady who had fainted dead away just as he had caught a glimpse of Nighthawk. He had no doubts at all that they were all the same woman. He slammed the glass down hard on the table. He felt like a fool not to have noticed this sooner. Chandler hated few things more than incompetence, especially his own.

The doors behind him parted and a man entered, spotted Chandler, and gave him a telegraph message.

Chandler grunted his thanks. Slowly he unfolded the thick paper and read the terse words:

Washington, D.C., July 9, 1865
To Maj. Owen Chandler, Alexandria, La.

Received your message from Alexandria STOP *You have violated my direct orders* STOP *You are ordered to return to Washington* STOP *Do not range further afield* STOP *Do not continue pursuit of Nighthawk* STOP *Am awaiting your acknowledgment* STOP

B. W. Dearborn, Col.

Chandler read the telegram again. Then he methodically tore it into small pieces and tossed it onto the table.

Nighthawk was headed for Texas and Chandler knew it. In a few days he could surely apprehend him. In fact he had to or Nighthawk would reach the less-populated regions where law was generally overlooked, and then he would be gone forever. Chandler couldn't let that happen.

Almost gently he brushed the shredded paper off the table. As far as he was concerned, the telegram had never been delivered.

Turning, he motioned to the messenger, who still waited by the door. "Do you have some paper?"

"Yes, sir." The man handed him a folded sheet.

"Good." Chandler took it and wrote out a description of Logan Sorrell, known also as Nighthawk, and his female companion. After a pause, Chandler added that a five-hundred-dollar reward would be paid for their capture. He gave the paper to the messenger. "I want this telegraphed to all the U.S. marshals in western Louisiana and eastern Texas. Can you do that?"

"Yes, sir." The man's eyes widened. "We can get right on it."

"That's good. Send me the bill when it's done. I'm staying here."

"I'll do that." The man hurried away.

Chandler raised his pale eyes to the youngest of the saloon girls. He let his eyes travel appraisingly over her slender body, then motioned for her with a quick jerk of his chin. He could use a female, and she wasn't the worst he had ever seen.

Reluctantly the girl went to him.

Logan frowned at Travis over the rim of his coffee cup. "I still don't see how you and Martin got separated from the others." He glanced accusingly at the older man. "We've waited a day and a half for you."

Martin looked uncomfortable, but Travis merely smiled and shrugged. "We got lost."

"But you were all supposed to be on the same boat. How do you get lost on a riverboat, Travis?"

"I told you. Martin and I got off the boat in Shreveport. We were just going to stretch our legs and see a few sights. Martin had never seen Shreveport before."

"That's true, Captain," Martin agreed. "I never had." He avoided Logan's eyes.

"Why do I get the feeling you aren't telling me everything?" Logan asked suspiciously.

"I have no idea." Travis motioned for the waiter to bring more coffee.

"We didn't know where they went," Tobe explained again as Harley nodded in agreement. "We thought they were in their cabins until after it was too late and the boat had left. So when we arrived here, we got a room at the Excelsior Hotel, like you said, and waited for you and them to show up."

"You didn't run into Major Chandler, did you?" Abigail asked in concern. "There wasn't trouble?"

"We never saw any sign of Chandler."

"From now on we either stay together or split up for good," Logan said. "And you two confine your sightseeing jaunts to safer territory."

"You worry too much," Travis drawled. "Always have."

"What a pity it's not a family trait," Logan responded. "You could use more discretion yourself."

Travis didn't reply, but smiled across the table at Abigail. She quickly averted her eyes. He looked at her as if she were an apple ready for plucking, and she didn't like that at all. Even with the others present, she felt uneasy around Travis. And she too thought their story was unlikely. Especially since Martin seemed so nervous.

"Well, we're together and safe," Logan said. "Where do we go from here?"

"My farm is southwest, about a day's ride. If we get separated again, I live in Laneville, just south of Henderson."

"We won't get separated again," Logan warned Travis. To Harley he said, "What about you? As I recall, you're from around Opelousas. Are you going back to your parents or ahead with us?"

"I reckon I'll stay with you." Harley shoved his lank blond hair off his forehead in a characteristic gesture. "A man can't go back home. Not and it be the same. When we get settled, I'll write them."

Logan nodded. "Martin?"

"I'm staying too. Tobe might get lost without me." Somehow his attempt at banter came across flat.

"Good. Then I guess we should get on the road. I know I, for one, am looking forward to finding a place to settle down. I'll tell the desk clerk we're leaving, and I'll meet you at the livery stable."

"I'm staying here," Abigail announced quietly.

Logan whipped his head around. "What?"

"I said, I'm staying here. Jefferson is a fine town and I like the looks of it."

"You're staying?" he repeated.

She nodded. "I'll buy a place at the edge of town. That way I won't be so lonely."

"You can't do that."

"Yes I can. Yesterday while you were pacing and worrying, I asked the desk clerk about farms for sale. He said there's a lovely one a mile out. It will be perfect for sheep," he said.

"I won't let you."

"You can't stop me. It even has a pond."

"You can't stay here."

"And a house. Nothing grand, but I don't need much room."

"Dammit, Abigail, listen to me!"

"You're saying nothing I want to hear. I've told you all along that I plan to buy a place and raise sheep. It's a life I know."

"You said you were going to do it closer to Tobe's farm!"

"I changed my mind." She kept her features calm and tried to still the turmoil in her mind and the longings of her body.

"Maybe we ought to go and leave you two to work this out," Tobe suggested.

Logan ignored him. "Are you doing this because I said I'm going to settle by Tobe?"

"Yes."

Tobe cleared his throat. "We're going to go up and pack now."

"If you're staying, then so am I!" Logan announced.

"No you're not!"

"I'll tell the desk clerk we're leaving," Tobe volunteered. "All but Miss Abigail."

"I'm not leaving her!" Logan snapped.

"If you're not going, I am." She glanced at the others. "Tell him Mr. Sorrell is staying."

"You're not leaving me behind, either!" he informed her heatedly.

"I reckon I'll let you tell him yourselves, once you work out the details," Tobe suggested as the men backed away.

"Abigail McGee, you're the stubbornest damned woman I ever met," Logan ground out.

"I'm not stubborn! I'm practical. We can't all settle in Laneville. How big could a town be that's named Laneville?"

"We aren't all buying land. Once we get there, Martin will move on. Harley won't do more than visit awhile. I imagine Travis will travel to Houston. He always has preferred cities to the country. That just leaves you and me."

"That's still two farms. I doubt there will be two for sale if it's so small a town."

"You don't know that. And if you weren't so damned mule-headed, we wouldn't need but one farm."

She lifted her chin. "I've said I'll not marry you."

Logan drew a deep breath. Every time she said those words, he felt as if someone had kicked him in the groin. Suddenly he felt tired and much older than his years. "All right. Stay here. To hell with you anyway. I don't need you."

Abigail frowned. He needn't be quite so definite about it. "I'll be perfectly all right, I assure you."

"Oh, I have no doubts about that," he answered sarcastically. "Your kind always lands on her feet."

"My kind? What do you mean by that?" she gasped.

"You, my dear, are a survivor. The country has been torn apart by war, thousands are homeless, even more are hungry and penniless, but here you sit. You have a saddlebag full of gold—"

"Hush!" she hissed, glancing about.

"—and you look as pretty as a peach blossom. If you run out of money, all you'll have to do is bat those eyelashes and half the men in town will trip over themselves in their haste to take care of you." As he spoke he had leaned forward threateningly.

She did the same. "Do you think for a minute that I'm like that? That I need someone to take care of me? Abigail McGee sees to herself!"

"Abigail McGee is going to wake up some fine morning and realize she threw away something that doesn't come down the road every day!"

"Will I, now? You've a fine opinion of yourself, Captain Sorrell!"

"Indeed I do, Mrs. McGee. And not every woman would push me away like you have."

"Is that so! Then maybe I had better step aside so the line can form. I wouldn't want to impede your progress in breaking hearts."

"What would you know of a broken heart?" he snarled. "I don't think you even have one!"

She told herself that the tears that stung her eyes were from anger, not pain. "Very well. You take your sterling character and haul it to Texas for all I care."

"This *is* Texas."

Abigail stood up. "Jefferson isn't big enough for

both of us," she said with high drama. "Are you leaving or must I?"

"No. You stay here and raise those blasted sheep. I wouldn't want to deprive you, since you've already found a farm and all." He rose to his feet too, and glared down at her.

Abigail studied his face, trying to memorize it for all the lonely years ahead. "What will you do?" she asked in a softer tone.

"That doesn't matter to you. Remember? You don't care one way or another." He turned and strode away.

Abigail felt worse than she had expected, and she had been prepared for a catastrophe. All the life seemed to drain from her as she watched him walk away. Had his eyes, too, seemed curiously moist? No, it must have been her own unshed tears that deceived her.

Instead of going to her room, which was near Logan's, she went out to the sheltered courtyard. Masses of greenery and rows of flowers bloomed beneath the shady trees, but she saw none of it. The whitewashed wall on the far side of the courtyard shimmered through her veil of tears; and in spite of her struggle, two slid past her lashes and down her pale cheek.

She was angry at herself for loving Logan. He was a cad and a rounder, and she was better off without him. Again she dredged up the memory that he had expected to marry her as a convenience to cover his affair with Marie-Claude. And earlier he had tried to steal all her gold and leave her penniless. But the worst was that he had made love with her when his mind was on Marie-Claude.

Despite all her grievances, the thing she hated most was losing him. And that made her angry indeed. She had grown up poor and had never expected to be anything else, but she had always had her pride. Love for Logan seemed to have robbed her of that, for she had to lock her knees to keep from running after him.

She stayed in the seclusion of the small garden for what seemed to be an eternity. She dared not chance running into him in the lobby or hallway, for with her pride gone, she had only her Scottish stubbornness to fall back on, and she doubted her strength there.

Had his eyes been wet? No! She couldn't think such a thing or she would run shamelessly after him. Instead, she forced herself to plan her day. First she would ride out to see that farm. If it was at all acceptable, she would buy it. Next, she would set about buying a modest herd of sheep. Next year she could hire a couple of men to help with the lambing and later with the shearing. Once she again started handling the sheep, her hands would become soft as they once had been, and she looked forward to that. The lanolin from the wool would smooth away the hard years on the farm.

But Logan wouldn't be there to hold her hand and admire its softness.

Deciding that she had to move before she melted down in a puddle of tears, Abigail walked briskly into the lobby, paused for a moment at the registration desk, then breezed out the front door.

Jefferson's houses lined the quiet streets like a regiment of fine ladies decked in Sunday lace. Gingerbread as graceful as cake decorations adorned deep porches that promised shady rest. Yardmen were busy here and there trimming shrubs and weeding flowerbeds.

But the evidence of normal, everyday living only

served as a backdrop for her misery. With each step she was putting distance between herself and the man she loved.

The advertisement about the farm was posted on a wall near the post office, exactly where the desk clerk had said it would be, along with several similar notices. One described a house for sale, another a team of mules, and another a child's pony.

Her eyes skipped over a wanted poster, then riveted back.

"Logan Sorrell," it read, "Alias 'Nighthawk.' White male, dark hair and eyes, over six feet tall. Rides a black horse. Wanted for murder and robbery. Was seen traveling with white female with long auburn hair and dark blue eyes. $500 reward for his capture."

Abigail glanced around anxiously. Had anyone else seen this? No one else was near.

As nonchalantly as she could, Abigail pulled the poster from the wall and crumpled it into her reticule. Chandler was behind this! He was trying to blame Marie-Claude's death on Logan! Abigail's heart raced. He was innocent and she knew it, but if he was caught now, he could be hung!

Walking as quickly as she could without appearing suspicious, Abigail went back to the Excelsior. With a seemingly calm demeanor she checked out of the hotel and went to the livery stable. One glance showed her the others' horses were gone.

As the stableboy saddled Gypsy, she tried to look bored. She had to look as though she was merely a lady out for a morning's ride. He led her horse to the mounting block and held him while Abigail got into the saddle.

She checked to be sure the saddlebag was tied

securely behind the saddle, then smiled sweetly at the boy. "I was just wondering. Do you know the way to Laneville? I have cousins there."

"Never heard of it."

She struggled to recall the other town Tobe had mentioned. "Henderson? Is there a place named that?"

"Oh, sure. It's southwest of here. You'd take the road past the Baptist church and turn left at the big yellow house. It's a long way, though. Maybe forty miles or more."

"Goodness. I wasn't planning to ride there," she laughed. "I only wondered. Thank you for saddling my horse."

"Yes, ma'am." The boy stepped aside for her to ride out of the stableyard.

For good measure Abigail started off in the opposite direction from the one she wanted. After circling the block, she eased her horse to a trot and found her way out of town. Once she was out of anyone's sight, she kicked Gypsy into a run. With any luck at all, she expected to overtake Logan within the hour.

21

Logan Sorrell couldn't remember a time when he had felt more miserable. Leaving Abigail behind had been like amputating a part of himself. More than once he had started to go back to her rather than pack, but each time he had stopped himself. She had turned away from him, had said she didn't love him, and had been firm that she wanted him out of her life. She couldn't have made it any plainer.

When he had gathered his belongings and joined the others in the lobby, he had weakened again. He saw her in the courtyard; her back was turned and she seemed to be contemplating the variety of flowers. He ached with the thought that he meant so little to her—his heart was breaking and she was looking at flowers. Again he almost weakened and went to her, but he restrained himself. A man had to have some pride, and his love for her had already shredded most of his. Instead, he memorized the set of her shoulders, the graceful line of her waist, the way her auburn hair seemed too heavy for her delicate neck.

Then Logan had resolutely turned away. She was cold and heartless to promise him so much and leave him with nothing. He should thank her for sparing him a lifetime with a woman who didn't love him. Someday he hoped to convince himself that he was better off without her.

In a numbed haze he had followed his men to the livery stable, saddled Caliban, and ridden out of town. Tobe had cast him commiserating glances, which Logan ignored, but the others seemed more anxious to reach the end of their journey than to sympathize with his separation from Abigail. But then, he reflected, only Tobe had known love.

Every clop of his horse's hooves on the packed dirt road took him farther from Abigail. Would she be all right? Times were hard, especially for a woman alone. A shyster might try to cheat her over the farm she was buying. Even if the sale went through, she would be out there all alone. What if she got sick or hurt? Where would she go for help? What if a renegade happened by? Abigail was a beautiful woman. Any man would want her. She could be raped out there on a farm, or killed, and no one would ever know.

"I'm going back," Logan announced decisively. "You go on to Tobe's house. If Abigail and I are staying in Jefferson, I'll send you a telegram."

Tobe grinned and saluted Logan jauntily. "Good luck, Captain."

Logan smiled and wheeled Caliban around. The horse flattened his ears on being separated from the others, but obeyed.

Somehow he would convince Abigail that she shouldn't be alone. If she insisted, he would buy a place close by and check on her periodically. She might be the most stubborn woman he had ever known, but she wasn't invincible. Abigail would just have to get used to the idea.

When he rounded a curve and saw Abigail riding straight at him at a hard run, Logan couldn't believe his eyes. He pulled his horse to a stop and stared at her. Abigail halted Gypsy and stared back.

"Why are you riding back toward town?" she accused.

"I was coming after you. Why are you out here?"

She looked uneasy, as if she expected him to make fun of her for following. "I found out something this morning. Something you need to know."

"Well?" He was half-afraid that she might turn and run if he came nearer.

Abigail fumbled with her reticule and pulled out the wanted poster. "Here. Look at this."

Logan rode closer and took the paper. His eyes skimmed the words and he cursed in a low voice. "Where did you get this?"

"I found it on the board where people post public announcements."

"Were there any more?"

"I left the rest," she responded acidly. "Of course not, or I would have taken them too."

Logan cocked his head to one side in puzzlement. "You were coming to warn me?"

"Isn't that obvious? I don't want you to be captured."

"Or were you just trying to save your own neck?"

Abigail paled as if he had slapped her, and her dark pansy eyes reproached him. Logan tried to force himself to harden his heart. He must have hit on the truth. She hadn't even denied it.

"Come on," he said gruffly. "Let's catch up with the others."

Wounded by Logan's attack, Abigail didn't trust herself to speak. She hadn't had to warn him! She could just as easily have ridden off in another direction. A lot of women had auburn hair and blue eyes. That wasn't *her* name on the wanted poster. As anger replaced the hurt, she promised herself that she would leave him again at the next opportunity.

Logan and Abigail easily overtook the others, who were riding at a comfortable pace. At the unexpected sight of the pair riding up behind them, they reined in.

"Miss Abigail?" Harley said in surprise. "What are you doing out here?"

Tobe beamed as if their reunion had been his own idea.

"Look at this," Logan said with a frown. He shoved the paper at Travis. "Chandler has a reward out for us."

Travis read it, then handed it to Martin, who looked considerably more worried. "I guess I had better be extra careful, cousin. You and I always have been mistaken for each other."

"Five hundred dollars." Harley whistled. "That's a lot of money."

"You and Abigail are the only ones mentioned," Travis pointed out. "Why do you suppose that is?"

"How should I know?" Logan growled.

"I guess he thinks we split up," Tobe suggested. "That's in our favor. He won't be looking for six people."

"What do you think we ought to do, Captain?" Harley asked.

Logan's black eyes swept the trees as if pursuers might already be on their trail. He wished, for once, someone else was the leader, because he was fast running out of ideas. "Tobe's right. Chandler must be looking for only Abigail and me. What about this farm of yours, Tobe? Is it off the road?"

"Nobody goes to Laneville unless they live there," Tobe assured them. "We don't have any close neighbors, either."

"How big is this farm?" Martin asked. "I never saw one with no neighbors."

"Average size. About a thousand acres," Tobe replied seriously. "My house is smack dab in the middle."

Martin snorted derisively. "That's not a farm, it's a kingdom!"

"Outside of East Texas, I guess it would be called a ranch," Tobe conceded. "Around here they're called farms."

"It sounds big enough to hide us." Logan grinned. To Abigail he barked, "What about you? Are you coming with us?"

"I might as well," she said coolly. "Thanks to you, my description is on wanted posters who-knows-where. Someone may have seen us together." She was still furious at his insinuation that she was only trying to save herself.

Logan's scowl deepened. So he was right. She had only ridden after them for her own protection. "I hardly planned it that way," he reminded her.

"When we get there," Tobe said, "don't mention this to Rosa. There's no point in worrying her. I'll tell her we were in the same company and all of you had nowhere else to go. That's the truth, mostly."

"As for Miss Abigail . . . She can be my cousin," Harley added helpfully. "If that's all right with her." He looked to Abigail for confirmation.

"Why not?" Abigail replied with a frown at Logan.

"That's all well and good, but will Rosa let us stay awhile?" Logan asked.

"Sure she will. Rosa always welcomes company. And I can use some extra hands to get the farm back in shape. If you don't mind, that is. After being gone for four years, I imagine there's plenty to keep us all busy."

"Somehow I never fancied myself as a farmer," Travis drawled.

"I'd be willing," Harley spoke up. "I grew up on a farm. Just tell me what you want done and I can do it."

"I reckon I could put up with farmwork for a while," Martin grumbled. "But no pigs. I just purely can't stand pigs."

"I'll take care of the pigs," Tobe reassured him.

"With so many extra mouths to feed, I guess Rosa will welcome my help," Abigail said hopefully. "Some women don't like having another woman under their roof."

"Not my Rosa. You couldn't find a better-tempered woman."

"Some men are luckier than others," Logan observed with a glance at Abigail.

"So are some women," she retorted, having accurately interpreted his snipe.

"Well, I for one am not only willing to do farmwork," Logan said, "I'm looking forward to it. I've seen all the traveling I want for a while. I feel like I must have been born under a wandering star."

Abigail heartily agreed that settling down for a while would be very welcome, but she was too proud to admit it. She only hoped Rosa would be openminded about so many unexpected guests, and one of them an unmarried woman. Since leaving Rosehaven, she hadn't given much thought to what people might think about her traveling alone with a band of men. Rosa might not look on it too favorably, however.

Late that afternoon when they rode into Tobe's yard, Abigail was pleasantly surprised. The Tanner homeplace wasn't at all what she had expected. The house was two stories tall and had three chimneys that rose above the roof. Victorian gingerbread trim adorned the peaked gables. The porch ceiling had been painted a bright blue, and all the windows had red shutters contrasting against the white clapboard walls. No lights shone in the windows but she could see the pale lace of curtains. A porch swing hung at the front corner of the wraparound veranda. And the screen doors, also painted red, boasted the same gingerbread design as the gables. "This is much grander than I ever expected!" Abigail murmured.

Tobe was frowning at the dark windows and the weeds that grew in the yard. He dismounted and tied his horse to the picket fence. "Something's wrong. By this time of day there ought to be lights in the house."

"Maybe she's out back," Harley suggested. "There's still light outside."

"No dogs came out to meet us. There's no chickens." He squinted at the feed lot. "I don't even see any cows. And look at the yard. Rosa always scraped the yard. She wouldn't let a blade of grass grow inside the fence. Just the flowers she planted."

Logan and Abigail exchanged a look. "Maybe we ought to look inside," he suggested.

After they all dismounted, Harley, Martin, and Travis went to search the backyard and barns. Tobe slowly climbed the wooden steps to the porch.

"This surely don't look right," he repeated. "My house is full of younguns. Rosa might be outside, but we ought to be hearing the *niños*. The place is too quiet."

Logan stepped up to the door and knocked loudly. "Rosa?" he called out. "We shouldn't all burst in on her and scare her to death," he said. "Give her some warning."

"She ought to have heard that. I don't hear anybody moving about." Tobe opened the screen and tried the door. "It's locked," he said in surprise. "I don't recollect the door ever being locked." He pounded on it with his open palm. "Rosa, it's me. Let us in."

His words did nothing to disturb the house's silence.

Without further ado, Tobe put his shoulder to the door, and on the second shove, it burst open. Abigail peeped into the shadowy room. She could make out dark bulks of furniture, but the room had the feel of having been vacant for quite some time.

With a worried curse, Tobe felt his way along the mantel, barking his shin on the wood box. The lamp stood in its usual place, along with a box of matches. He struck one and glanced around the room before putting the flame to the wick.

Abigail followed Logan inside and looked around. They were in the parlor. Two rockers sat before the cold hearth and several ladder-back chairs with cowhide seats stood against the walls. An oak secretary filled with books on home medicine, veterinary skills, and a novel or two stood to one side. A sewing machine was on the opposite wall beneath a calendar.

Tobe went to the far door, where Abigail saw the lines of a staircase. "Rosa?" he called again, with even less expectation. No one answered.

He crossed the landing and checked the front bedroom first, then passed the stairs to the central dining room. "Rosa!" he bellowed. Two other bed-rooms opened off the dining room, as did the kitchen and the enclosed porch that housed the well.

"There's nobody here," Logan said needlessly. "Maybe she's visiting neighbors."

"I don't think so," Abigail said slowly. She went back to the sewing machine and looked at the calendar. "This says July 1862. And look—there's a thick layer of dust on everything. Even the chair seats." She patted at the cushions of the nearest rocker. "I don't think she's been here for a while."

"Well, dammit, where else would she be?" Tobe thundered. "Where are my babies?"

"Does she have relatives nearby?" Logan asked. "Maybe she moved in with them until the war was over."

"Her nearest relatives are in Mexico."

"Did she write anything about leaving?" Abigail asked.

"We didn't write." To Logan he said, "You don't reckon anything's happened to her, do you?"

"Wait a minute," Abigail said as she stopped. "You say you didn't write? Tobe, you've been gone four years!"

He moved uneasily. "I know it."

"You haven't written in *four years*!"

"Rosa speaks English pretty good, but she can't read or write it. I can't write Spanish."

"You could have written and a neighbor could have translated it." She stared at him in disbelief.

Tobe averted his eyes. "A man don't want a neighbor reading what he says to his wife."

Abigail made a strangled sound and threw up her hands in exasperation.

"Well, she could have written me, too!" he defended himself.

"Look, she must be all right," Logan said. "If anything bad had happened, the neighbors would have boarded the house up against vandals. This looks as if she walked out planning to come back."

"I guess it does, doesn't it?" Tobe said hopefully.

"Four years!" Abigail repeated in disgust. "If I hadn't heard from my husband in four years, I'd leave too."

"I'll bet that's it," Tobe agreed. "I'll bet she went to stay in Henderson. It's a bigger town, and she could have found work there. Farming is hard on a woman. Especially one with little children."

Abigail shook her head in exasperation.

"That's probably it," Logan agreed. "Tomorrow morning you can ride to town and find her."

Abigail drew her fingers through the powdery dust on the mantel. "In the meantime, we're going to clean this house." Abigail knew the work would help her occupy her mind, but she wasn't going to do all the labor herself.

"We?" Logan asked.

"You heard me. It's bad enough to drop six visitors in unexpectedly. We can at least straighten up for her."

Logan sighed. He was tired and would have preferred to sit by the fire while someone cooked his supper. In all fairness, though, Abigail was as tired as he was and there was no faithful old Jeremiah to prepare the meal. "You cook. I'll clean," he offered.

"All right." Abigail had fully expected all the men to balk at doing housework, and was pleased that Logan had so readily offered his help. "Thank you," she added, letting her eyes meet his for a long moment.

The door opened and the other three men entered. "She's not out there," Harley said. "We looked everywhere."

"We think she may have moved to town," Tobe told them. "That must be what happened."

Logan edged closer to Travis. In a low voice he said, "You looked . . . everywhere?"

Travis nodded.

"No graves?"

"Not a one."

Logan exhaled with relief. Since they had arrived at the empty house, he had been afraid they would discover Tobe's entire family dead. "Abigail, you go see about finding food. Harley, get Tobe to show you the linen press, and you two put sheets on the beds. Martin, you and Travis can dust and sweep."

"Dust!" Martin exploded.

"Sweep!" Travis echoed. "Me?"

Logan grimaced. "Someone has to do it."

All the men's eyes traveled to Abigail. "Not me. I'm the cook." She threw them a smile as she took the matches from the mantel. "Let's just hope Rosa left some food behind."

She found another lamp in the kitchen and lit it carefully. In the yellow glow she noted a pine press cupboard, a roll-front cabinet, a wood stove, and a countertop with a sink. A kitchen table covered with a checkered oilcloth stood in the center of the room. A tray of eating utensils was at one end, along with jars of pickled peppers, vinegar, and salt and pepper. Although an examination showed that the larder was almost bare, she found a few cans and jars of Rosa's produce.

Abigail dusted the jars and automatically checked for swollen lids that would indicate that the food inside had spoiled. They seemed to be good, so she found some saucepans and started to work.

The kindling she needed was already next to the stove, and on the service porch off the kitchen she found a stack of short logs for the fire. Using a sliver of pine heart to ignite the kindling, Abigail soon had the oven hot.

She stepped into the adjoining room to draw water from the well. After folding the hinged wooden cover back, she lowered the oak bucket down with the creaking pulley. This certainly beat hauling water from a stream. In fact, she hadn't had such luxury in her own home, where she had had to brave the elements day or night to get water from her exposed well. She was amazed any woman would willingly leave such a perfect house behind.

Overhead she heard Harley moving around in the bedrooms. She smiled at the way Logan had rapped out cleaning orders as if they were military commands. Even Travis had obeyed. She decided to tell Logan later that she was grateful. After riding all day, she was tired to the bone. The dust she could have ignored, but she simply couldn't have slept on sheets that hadn't been changed in three years.

Martin wandered through in search of the broom. She directed him to the porch, where she had seen some dust rags as well. Through the open doorway she watched Logan in the bedroom across the dining room. He had stripped off the sheets and was turning the feather mattress. As he plumped it on the rope frame, she smiled. Except for his abominable temper, he would be so easy to live with. Resolutely she turned back to her work, trying to keep such thoughts out of her mind.

In spite of having neither flour nor cornmeal to make bread, Abigail considered her efforts a success. Although she had found no meat, she had prepared bowls of steaming vegetables and canned fruit, and was sure she had enough of everything to fill them.

Logan, his face and hands fresh from washing, looked at Abigail as they sat down to eat. Her cheeks were rosy from the heat of the cook stove and stray tendrils of hair floated about her face, but she looked contented, maybe even happy. She had rolled up the sleeves of her blouse and had tied a bleached cotton-sack apron around her waist. As he studied her, it occurred to him that she hadn't looked this satisfied at Rosehaven. A frown creased his brow because that didn't make sense. Rosehaven had all the elegance a woman could ever want, yet she seemed to prefer this farmhouse.

"Why are you frowning?" Abigail asked, interrupting his thoughts. "Did I forget something?"

"No, no. I was just remembering Rosehaven."

And Marie-Claude, she thought. "Oh," she said shortly, and sat down at the table. She immediately felt like a poor comparison to anything Logan was remembering about his old home. She knew Marie-Claude's cheeks would never have glowed red from working over an oven.

Logan served his plate and glanced surreptitiously at Abigail. How could she look so enticing after such a hard day? Her skin glowed, and the loose curls about her face dared him to reach out to touch them. He had never seen so desirable a woman.

After supper Abigail washed and dried the dishes

as she listened to wisps of conversation from the men in the parlor. This was exactly the sort of life she wanted, she mused. A house with airy rooms and the convenience of a built-in well. And Logan in the next room. She recognized his laugh at some joke of Martin's, and a warm glow spread through her. For a tiny, forbidden moment she pretended he was her husband and that soon they would go upstairs to their room and love the night away.

Her hands stilled in the act of drying the last plate as she indulged her fantasy. Logan's wife. The words had a magical sound. Taking a deep breath, she pulled herself back to reality. She could never be his wife. Not and live with the knowledge that he had preferred Marie-Claude rather than her.

Abigail reminded herself that Marie-Claude was dead, but she also remembered that Logan had said she had given her life to save him. Such an act might cause Logan to immortalize her, and Abigail could never compete with that sainted memory.

Abigail put away the plate and poured the wash water and the rinse water down the drain. She might never have Logan, but with her share of the gold she might have a nice house like this one.

She joined the men, and Harley got up to offer her one of the rockers. She thanked him with a smile as he sat on the brick hearth. All these men were becoming so dear to her. She looked on Harley and Tobe as if they were her brothers, and she had cast Martin as an uncle or maybe a grandfather. Only Travis struck a sour note. She still avoided him when possible and made certain she was never alone with him.

The male voices rose and fell as they discussed the best farming methods and how to train a horse. The night was warm and the windows were open to let in a cool breeze. Abigail watched the lacy curtains billow gently to the katydid chorus beyond the porch. For the first time in years she felt a measure of stability and peaceful security. She was surrounded by strong, able men who had become her family and who she was sure would protect her safety. With the possible exception of Travis. The security she felt was triggered by an intuition older than civilization.

She glanced at Travis and saw him watching her. Self-consciously she straightened so that her blouse didn't hug her breasts so snugly. As he continued to stare, she was reminded of a cat toying with a captured mouse. All her feelings of security vanished and she looked away.

"Where is everyone sleeping?" he asked in the voice that was so similar to Logan's.

"There's plenty of room," Tobe answered. "The front bedroom is mine and Rosa's. You can have any of the others. There's two downstairs and two up."

"Abigail, why don't you take the front room upstairs. It has a view of the little creek," Logan said to his boots rather than to her.

Tobe nodded. "That's my girl's room. You'll be comfortable there."

"Where will you be, Logan?" Travis asked silkily.

Abigail held her breath.

"Right across the hall from her door, cousin," Logan replied in a steady voice.

Had she imagined it, or had Logan's voice held a warning note for Travis?

At any rate, Travis chuckled softly. "Martin,

how about you sharing that back room downstairs with me?" he asked.

"I'll take that small one," Harley said, nodding at the door to his left. He ran his bony fingers through his lank hair. He was relieved that Martin was to share Travis' room and not himself.

Abigail stood and said, "I'm going to turn in, I believe. This has been a long day."

"I put water for you in the pitcher, and I lit your lamp," Harley said.

"Thank you." She smiled. "That was very thoughtful."

"He put water in all the pitchers," Travis informed her.

Abigail watched Harley deflate before her eyes. Travis was always deriding the boy and it made her mad. "Thank you, Harley," she repeated firmly. "I appreciate your kindness." She was rewarded by the boy's open grin.

"I'm going up too," Logan said. He stood and stretched lithely.

Travis glanced from Abigail to Logan and smirked. Lifting her head arrogantly, she said good night to the others.

As Logan followed her up the stairs, she was again struck by the sensation of hominess. They could well be a married couple going to bed. She tried to put the thought out of her head.

The stairs ended in a broad hallway that doubled back into an open sitting area. To each side of the landing was an open door.

Logan nodded to the one on the left. "That's the room I thought you'd like. I brought your saddlebags and bedroll up earlier."

She looked at him in surprise. He had evidently spent some time planning where she would sleep, and that he would sleep across the hall. "What if one of the others had claimed this room?"

"That's unlikely. It's obviously meant for Tobe's girl. If one of them had, I would have talked him out of it."

"What if Travis, say, had wanted that room?" she asked, nodding toward the opposite door.

"We would have shared it."

Abigail tilted her head curiously. "You don't trust him either?"

"Travis? Sure I do."

She thought his response sounded a little forced. "I don't. There's something about the way he looks at me. Makes me uneasy."

"He's not a man to tease and lead on," Logan observed, "but I've never known him to rape a woman. That's what you're saying, isn't it?"

"Not quite so bluntly, I wasn't," she replied stiffly. "And I'm not teasing or trying to lead anyone on."

Logan gave her a long steady look, then smiled. "In that case, you've nothing to worry about."

Abigail knew she should turn and go into her room, but her feet seemed rooted in the hallway. "Tobe's worried sick about Rosa," she said.

"He has every right to be. It seems strange that she would go without leaving a message or a note."

"Maybe she sent him a letter and it never reached him."

"Could be. Things were awfully confusing toward the end of the war, and even more so afterward. Especially if the envelope was written in Spanish."

"You don't think anything really bad happened, do you?"

"Travis didn't see any graves. Of course, that doesn't mean that they're not buried in a community cemetery around here. We passed one on the way in today. I'll go there tomorrow and check while Tobe is in town. There's no need for him to know I looked, unless I find something."

"You're very thoughtful," she said softly.

"They're my men. You don't eat and sleep and fight beside men for four years and not become part of them."

Logan seemed to be lingering, and Abigail was thankful. This way she could be with him and talk to him without having to make the move herself. "I understand. Back on my farm I helped my friend Mattie in childbirth. I sat beside her all night while we waited; and when the baby was born, I bathed it and gave it to her. My hands were the first to touch it. I feel a bond to both Mattie and that baby." She looked away. "Unfortunately, the baby died the next year."

"That's a shame." His voice was low and husky, as it was when they were sharing an intimacy. After a pause he said, "Abigail, did you ever have a baby?"

"No," she answered. "I didn't."

He nodded and reached out to touch her cheek. "If you were to, I'd be there for you."

Her startled eyes raised to his.

"Don't look so surprised. We have been ... intimate. These things happen."

"I never thought of that!" Since leaving her farm, there had been a gauze of unreality over everything. Silently she tried to count back to her last monthly course at Rosehaven. Unless something had come of that night on the river ...

"Don't look so stricken. I'd marry you and make an honest woman of you."

"I'm already an honest woman!" she retorted. "And I'll thank you to remember it!" Turning on her heel, she retreated to her room and shut the door firmly behind her.

Still the thought illumined her. If there were a baby, Logan would be there for her. Most men would be terrified at the prospect, not to mention being offended. But not Logan. He had actually looked as if the prospect would please him.

But of course she had imagined that.

Abigail began to remove her clothes as her thoughts flew to the intriguing man just across the hall. She was completely safe with Logan there. Safe from everyone but herself. She bent and blew out the light.

22

The next morning Logan waited until the other men left, then went to the barn to saddle Caliban. Abigail followed him and watched as he tightened the cinch and swung into the saddle. The early sun struck fire in her ruddy hair and gave an apricot glow to her cheeks. Logan thought he had never seen such a beautiful woman, so he kept his back turned to her as much as possible.

"You're going to the graveyard?" Abigail asked, though she knew he was. She wanted to hear his voice.

"Yes. First I'll check the one here in Laneville that we passed on the way in. If I don't find Rosa there, I'll try the one in town."

"Surely she's not dead. That would be too terrible." Her voice trailed away.

"I hope she isn't. Tobe loves her a great deal." He too was thinking of the children, though neither of them could even suggest such a catastrophe as for them all to be dead.

Abigail put her hand on Caliban's arching neck and blinked up at him against the sunlight. "Be careful," she said softly. "I don't know how far those wanted posters were spread."

"I won't do anything to draw attention to myself," he reassured her.

She nodded but looked doubtful. In her eyes

Logan's authoritarian carriage and unrestrained virility would make him noticeable in any crowd.

"Are you afraid to stay here alone?" he asked as an excuse to talk with her a bit longer.

"Afraid? Why would I be?"

"I just thought you might." Most of the women he had known would have quailed at the idea of being left alone in a strange house in the middle of acres of empty land, with no servants for company and protection.

"As a matter of fact, I'm looking forward to the privacy. I had grown accustomed to being alone back on my farm, and for weeks now I've been with someone constantly." That sounded as if she disliked his company, so she lowered her eyes, not knowing how to correct that misconception without admitting to more than she dared.

"I see." Logan's voice was cool. "Well, I'll leave you to your privacy. I doubt I'll be back before midafternoon. The others are buying stock and seeds, so they probably will be gone all day as well."

Abigail nodded, then stepped back. Her only concern was that Travis might come home first. She resolved to keep an eye on the road, and head for the woods, if necessary, to avoid him.

Logan rode past her and waved as she swung the lot gate shut after him, then looped the chain fastener over the nail. She didn't acknowledge his gesture of farewell. He had hoped she might have softened somewhat, but her words and actions seemed to prove otherwise. Although she appeared more content than he had ever seen her, her feelings seemed to vacillate between indifference and anger. The anger he could handle. The indifference greatly concerned him.

He rode the mile or so to the crossroads that made up the small town, then continued north to the cemetery that lay on the slope of a low hill.

Tying his horse to the fence, Logan entered by way of the metal turnstile beside the closed lychgate. The graveyard, like the town, was sparsely populated. He wandered among the stones, reading the names.

A boy of about twelve, who was trimming grass along the far fence, looked up as Logan neared. Resting his trimming shears, he said, "Can I help you, mister?"

Logan nodded. "Is there a Rosa Tanner buried here? It could have been as long as three years ago."

The boy pushed back his straw hat and scratched his head thoughtfully. "I don't recollect it."

"Do you work here?" Logan asked. The boy looked too young to hold down a job.

He nodded. "My pa is the caretaker but he's teaching me how to do it. I know all the graves and there's not a Tanner among them. At least I know all but one, and don't nobody know who he was." He pointed toward the only brick crypt above ground. "He come riding through years ago, got sick, and died. Nobody knew where he'd come from or where he was headed, so they buried him here. After a while other people started using this hill for a cemetery, but he was the first one here." He shook his head in what was clearly a copy of his father's gesture. "No Tanner, though."

"That's good news," Logan said. "Much obliged." If his luck held, he would find the same was true at the cemetery in Henderson. With a lighter step he went back to his horse.

*   *   *

Martin narrowed his eyes and rubbed his whiskers on his chin. "I don't know, Travis. I just don't know."

Travis frowned at his companion. "I'm telling you, it would be easy. This isn't a big city like New Orleans or Shreveport. If we come on a weekday, we won't be seen by a crowd."

The older man again surveyed the brick-and-marble bank building. "There's bound to be a guard. Maybe more than one."

"There was a guard in the bank in Shreveport," Travis reminded him. "He was more afraid than anybody else in the room."

"He was for a fact." Martin grinned.

"Remember how it felt?" Travis continued in an excited, hypnotic voice. "We talked about it, remember? You said holding up that bank was as thrilling as going over a waterfall in a barrel."

"I did say that."

"Those damned Yankees don't need the money half as much as we do."

"But somehow this don't seem as much like Yankee money. Nearly everybody in town grew up here. There's not a passel of carpetbaggers like there was in New Orleans. I'm not so sure we're not taking Rebel money."

"Somehow I never figured you for a quitter, Martin. Next thing I know, you'll be stodgy as Logan and Tobe. I had you sized up as the sort of man that would always get what he wanted."

"Now, there's no need to mean-mouth me," Martin objected. "I just don't want to rush into things."

"Besides, Tobe said Rusk County had troops go to the North *and* South. This is bound to be Yankee gold. Tell you what. Let's go inside the bank and look around."

"Inside?"

"Sure. No harm in going inside a public building." A surge of the daredevil excitement Travis had felt when they robbed the bank in Shreveport coursed through him. He knew Martin could be talked into going along with his plan. He just needed to phrase his words correctly.

"I guess we could look around."

They shouldered through the doors and entered the building. Directly ahead was a dark gray marble wall of tellers' cages. Behind that stood a huge green-and-brass wall safe.

"I see two ways out," Travis said in a low voice. "The front door and that one over there."

Martin glanced at the side door that led to the street. "What kind of money would you find in a town this size?" he scoffed. But his eyes were watching the busy tellers and the enticing safe beyond.

"With all the cattle around here? There's money. Otherwise they wouldn't have a bank. And this isn't a small one, either."

"Let's go back outside."

Once they were in the fresh air again, Martin rubbed his nose thoughtfully. "I didn't see a guard."

"Neither did I."

"There weren't but three tellers, and two of them were old."

"You're right." Travis waited patiently for Martin to work his way around to agreeing with him. The sun was giving him a headache, but the usual chorus of angry roars deep in his brain wasn't bothering him and hadn't since he had decided to lash out at the world and crush it as it had smashed his own life.

"You really reckon there's gold there?" Martin asked again.

"Has to be. Think what you could do with a fortune like we're going to have. There's not a woman in the world that would refuse your attentions. Money is power. Real power!"

"You're right about that. Nothing talks as loud as gold."

"A few banks, and you could be as rich as Croesus."

"Who?"

"You can find you a town where no one ever saw you, marry a young wife, and be set for life."

Martin grinned. "If there's enough gold in my pocket, I won't have to marry her."

"That's the way to think. Bed them and forget them. You could have a steady stream of beauties."

Martin looked back at the doors to the bank. "Ain't we taking a chance, though? This is awfully close to Tobe's place."

"Afterward we'll move on. You and I didn't plan to stay around here anyway. Farming isn't for men of our caliber."

"That's a fact." Martin felt a surge of youth and a sense of . . . class. He was secretly flattered that a man of Travis Dunn's distinction had sought him out as a friend. He had never seen Travis' home, but he knew it must have been comparable to Logan's Rosehaven, which was the finest house he had ever entered. Living hand to mouth as he had all his life, Martin was amazed Travis treated him as an equal.

He thought a minute. "What about the others?"

Travis shrugged. "They had their chance to go in with us and turned it down."

"Will they get in trouble, do you think?"

"Why should they? You and I are the only ones involved. After it's done, we just ride out of town and keep going."

"Sounds mighty simple."

"It is. Like picking plums." Travis grinned. "Are you with me?"

Martin nodded. When Travis put it that way, it was an adventure. All his life Martin had loved the surge of adrenaline he got when he launched out into some foolhardy or even dangerous stunt. That push of excitement was the main reason he had volunteered to be a member of Nighthawk's sabotage operations. "I'm with you. When should we do it?"

"Not yet. We need to study the bank for a while. See when things seem to be quietest and whether a payroll of any kind comes through here on a regular basis."

"You can count on me." Martin grinned broadly, exposing his tobacco-stained teeth.

"Good." Travis clapped him on the shoulder and shook his hand.

Harley strolled down the boardwalk and watched the traffic in the rutted streets. Tobe had said this wasn't a market day, but nevertheless the town seemed to bustle with activity. Although Harley had grown up on a farm, he preferred to mix and mingle with people.

He stuck his hands deep into his pockets and made his step as jaunty as any man who had money. In spite of his youth, he had seen most of the country over the last four years and thought of himself as a man.

He was so busy conducting himself as an adult, he didn't see the girl until he ran into her. Later he wondered how he could have ever been so blind.

She gave a startled cry as her two packages flew out of her arms and she stumbled backward to catch her balance.

When Harley reached out to steady her, he found himself looking down into the greenest eyes he had ever seen. Harley had only recently started to gain what would be his full-grown height, and this sensation of towering over a woman was heady in itself. That she was a very pretty one with pink cheeks and pouting, rosy lips was an added bonus. Her hair was as brown and glossy as a sparrow's wing and was pulled back in a cascade of sausage curls beneath a rosebud-trimmed bonnet. Her pink dress molded her pert breasts like a second skin, then flared beneath the sash and bow at her tiny waist into flounces of ruffles. Her small hands, clad in snowy gloves with pearl buttons at the wrist, rested on his upper arms.

Harley fell in love at first sight.

"Oh my," the girl breathed.

"Did I hurt you?"

"Not at all."

Further words failed him as he stared in dumb rapture.

"I don't believe we've met," she said, moving a demure step away. "My name is Nell Overmyer."

A silly grin crossed Harley's face. Nell Overmyer was suddenly the most beautiful name in the world.

"Who are you?" she prompted.

"Begging your pardon, ma'am," Harley stammered. "I'm Harley Dobson."

She too smiled, and a coquettish dimple appeared in one cheek. "I'm glad to meet you, Mr. Dobson."

"Please call me Harley." He was thankful that his voice had more or less settled into a manly baritone and no longer squeaked up at unexpected moments.

As her long lashes swept her cheeks, she said, "If I'm to call you Harley, I guess it's only proper for you to call me Nell."

"I guess so." He seemed to be all hands and elbows and didn't quite know what to do with them, so he stuck his hands back into his pockets.

Nell glanced down at her packages. "Dear me. I seem to have dropped my parcels."

"I'll get them." Harley made a dive to retrieve the two boxes.

"Thank you. How clumsy of me."

"You, clumsy? Never. It was my fault." He was proud of that sally. The captain couldn't have done better himself. "Can I carry them for you?"

"That would be an imposition," she said, but she made no effort to take the packages.

"Not at all." He cleared his throat importantly. "I came to town to do some business, but it's all taken care of now. I'm at my leisure, so to speak." That gambit was another to be proud of.

"My goodness! You're a businessman?"

She was gazing up at him with such rapt attention that he almost forgot to breathe. "In a manner of speaking." This was somewhat true. Tobe had asked him to see about buying several chickens and a cow and the feed for them.

"I don't believe I've seen you around here before," Nell purred, letting his wrist brush against her bare forearm.

Harley swallowed at the unexpected contact of flesh upon flesh. "I'm staying with Tobe Tanner. We fought together. The war, you know."

"A soldier? Oh my." Again she moved so that his hand grazed her arm. "How exciting. I find a soldier's company so . . . protective."

"You do? I mean, that's right. We're real protective."

She paused beside a buggy. "We can put the packages in here."

He stacked them neatly in the built-in box behind the seat, then closed the lid. "Do you live far from here?" Without the packages he was again at a loss as to what to do with his hands.

"No. I live on East Main. In that small white house with the blue shutters." She began walking and he fell into step beside her. "I suppose I could have walked to the store, but Papa was driving in so I rode with him. It was silly of me. I just love to walk." She cast a hinting glance at him from under her lashes.

"Me too. I mean, there's not much I like better than to take a walk."

"There's a little park a couple of blocks over. Would you like to walk over there?"

"Sure I would." He tried to see her out of the corner of his eye, but he found her looking up at him, so he jerked his head forward.

After a few steps he said, "Have you lived here long, Miss Nell?"

"Goodness yes. All my life."

"I'm from Louisiana myself. Of course, I've been about everywhere there is to go. The war and all."

"How exciting. I think it would be simply wonderful to travel. Not in wartime, naturally. Heavens, the sights you must have seen!"

Harley wasn't sure if she was referring to the atrocities of war or to the amount of country he had observed, so he played it safe by saying,

"There's been a mess of them, for a fact." He gathered his courage and said, "I ain't seen nothing to equal you, though."

"Harley! You'll turn my head." She blushed prettily.

Pride swelled Harley's chest. No boy could pass a compliment with enough finesse to make a girl blush—that took a man. "It's the honest truth. I believe you're the prettiest girl in this town."

"Nonsense! You mustn't say that." Nell's face was wreathed in smiles and dimples.

"I'm sorry, ma'am." He hadn't meant to overstep the boundaries. What would the captain say at this point? "I didn't mean to offend you."

"I'm not offended. Not at all. In fact," she said as she looked down demurely, "I think you're awfully handsome yourself."

"You do?" His palms grew moist, and he wondered if his voice had creaked or if that was only his imagination.

They had reached the park, which was no more than a vacant lot shaded by trees, before he remembered to shorten his stride for her. As they slowed, he could tell that she was thankful, although she had not complained. Harley filed that away in his memory. A man walked with a woman, not the other way around.

"I guess you'll be coming to the church social," she said.

"When is it?" He hadn't been inside a church in four years and he fervently hoped neither Nell nor his ma ever found out.

"Next Saturday. I guess you'll be bringing your best girl."

"I don't have a best girl. That is, I only got in town yesterday."

"Oh, really? Well, if you're a stranger, I guess you won't think me forward if I ask if I could introduce you to my friends?"

"No, ma'am. I'd never think that." A bank of bushes ahead separated the path they were on from view of the town. Nell strolled behind them, her face seemingly intent on the progress of a pale blue butterfly. Harley took a deep breath. "Would it be all right if I was to call for you at your house? That is, if you don't have a favorite beau."

"No, I don't have a favorite. But if you don't mind, I would rather meet you, say, by the bank. I know it's silly, but my papa is protective of me. He doesn't like for me to walk out with boys unless he knows their parents."

"I can understand that. A girl as pretty as you needs protecting."

"Harley Dobson! You stop that!" She swatted his arm with her gloved fingers.

He grinned. She was like a playful kitten. That blow was no more than a pat on his arm. "Being a soldier and all, I can protect you."

"I know. But my papa is awfully strict. Ever since Mama died, he's been like a hen with one chick. Not that I don't appreciate it," she added.

"I know what you mean. If you think it's best, I'll meet you at the bank. I saw it when we rode into town."

"Lovely. About noon, say?"

"Sure."

Nell looked past him and leaned forward so that her firm breasts brushed against Harley's arm. "Over there! See the butterfly? Isn't that beautiful?"

"Yes, ma'am. It sure is." He was staring awestruck

at her compact bosom. She didn't seem to realize what she had done.

Nell sighed guilelessly, causing her breasts to strain against the tight bodice of her dress. "I think butterflies are so adorable."

"Yes, ma'am. For a fact."

"I'll tell you what. Just so everyone accepts you right away, let's tell everyone this Saturday that you're my beau!"

"Sure!" He glanced down at the hand she had unconsciously rested on his chest.

"What a lovely idea." She dimpled. "Then everyone will know you're with me." Before he knew what she was about to do, Nell tiptoed up and kissed his cheek. "I've got to go now, Harley. I see Papa looking for me."

He stared at her in amazement. She had actually kissed him! A wide grin spread over his face. "I'll see you Saturday." He knew he should walk her over to her papa's buggy, but for reasons he hoped she hadn't noticed, he thought it best to stay behind the bushes for a while. Besides, she was already running away, as light and colorful as the butterflies she had admired.

Nell tripped across the grass to where her father waited impatiently in the buggy. She hoped Harley would be smart enough to stay out of sight until they were gone. When it came to young men, her father had been completely unreasonable ever since that episode the summer before.

With an angelic smile, Nell greeted her father. A glance told her that Harley was still out of sight. He was discreet. That was good. The boy last summer hadn't been, and she had been confined to the house until just the last few weeks. Her papa could be so unreasonable.

She thought of the way Harley's lips curled up so adorably when he smiled. He looked as if he could kiss quite expertly. Nell hoped so. She liked to kiss. For starters.

"I'm sorry I kept you waiting, Papa," she said sweetly. "I was looking at some butterflies."

He grunted his disapproval and slapped the reins on the horse's rump. As they drove away, sunlight glinted on his sheriff's badge.

23

Shreveport, La., August 3, 1865
To Col. B. W. Dearborn, Washington, D.C.:

Believe Nighthawk involved in bank robbery here
STOP *Am investigating* STOP

Owen Chandler, Maj.

Abigail moved through the barn in search of eggs. After three weeks, the hens Harley had bought were finally starting to lay. As she passed her, the new milk cow regarded Abigail with bovine interest as she lazily chewed a mouthful of hay from the manger.

Abigail enjoyed the fresh hay scent of the barn mingled with the slightly musty smell of feed and the aroma of newly sawed pine lumber where Tobe had repaired a stall. Summer was waning but the first bite of autumn was still several weeks away. The slightly cooler days made her feel too energetic to stay inside the house. Had she had less to do, she would have given in to the urge to saddle Gypsy and go for a ride.

A row of square cubbyhole boxes built into the tack-room wall had been half-filled with new hay, and already the hens had rounded out comfortable hollows. To encourage them to lay eggs, Abigail had put a china doorknob in each nest. The hens, seeing one "egg" already there, would lay others beside it. In three of the four nests she discovered pale brown eggs.

Placing them carefully on the cup towel in her basket, she continued her search as she moved down the line of stalls, because sometimes a foolish hen would nest in the cow's manger. Sure enough, she found a large white one in the stall beside the cow.

From out in the barnyard she heard the young rooster crow, even though the sun was well up in the sky. As if in answer, a hen clucked the slow drawling sound of a chicken contented with sunshine and plentiful feed. The cow lowed softly and in the back woods a mockingbird was singing his heart out. Abigail hummed under her breath. She enjoyed the sounds and smells of a well-run farm.

A noise above her head startled her and she looked up as wisps of straw sifted through the floorboards of the loft. She had thought she was alone.

For a minute she paused to consider who it might be. She had seen Martin and Travis ride south toward Cushing on one of their mysterious outings. Harley had gone to town, as he often did these days. Tobe had ridden to Laneville to get a sack of flour from the general store. Logan was the only one unaccounted for.

She wandered to the steep steps that led to the hayloft, speculating whether she might find eggs up there as well. After all, the chickens' ways weren't set as yet, and she had found eggs in far more unlikely places than that. Convincing herself that this was the only reason she wanted to go up there, Abigail gathered her skirts and climbed the stairs.

With no handrail and only one free hand for balance, she picked her way carefully. Once her head and shoulders were through the square opening in the upper floor, she reached out to the security of a roof support before taking the last steps.

As she had thought, Logan was there, standing beside the open hay door that took up a good portion of the back wall. He was busy repairing the rope on the hay pulley and didn't hear her arrival, so Abigail had a moment to study him.

Because of the contrast between the dimly lighted interior and the bright sunlight outside, he was almost in silhouette. Strong rays of sunbeams spread to either side of him, and dust motes floated in the still air. His legs were slightly parted and his pants were tightly molded to his powerful thighs and narrow hips. His pale blue workshirt hugged his lean ribs and stretched across the expanse of his shoulders. His head was bent slightly forward in his concentration, and his thick hair was tumbled over his forehead like a black thatch of silk. Abigail realized that Logan too was thriving on farm life. Perhaps it was only due to the relief that the chase was ended, at least for a while, but for whatever reason, he seemed more contented. He now bore little resemblance to the Creole aristocrat who had ruled Rosehaven.

Unfortunately, that thought triggered a reminder of Marie-Claude, and she stiffened. She had no business being up here alone with Logan. If there were any eggs, they could wait until he had repaired the rope and had gone on to another chore. She turned to leave, but his deeply resonant voice stopped her.

"Don't go," he said quietly.

She turned to find his unsettling gaze upon her. "I was just looking for eggs. There aren't any here," she said, as if her presence needed an explanation.

"You must have excellent vision if you can stand on the steps and see if there are nests way over here." He smiled. "Most people would have to take a closer look."

She blushed. "I didn't want to disturb you."

"I'm just mending this rope. Come on up."

Reluctantly she stepped onto the plank floor. The hay had been swept away from the openings over the stairs and mangers for safety's sake, but a soft billowing of straw covered the rest of the floor. To her right were several rectangular bales, each tied with jute. She walked along beside them, peering into every crack and crevice for a cache of eggs.

Her back was turned to Logan, but she was intensely aware of his movements. The hair on the back of her neck prickled as she realized he was watching her. All her senses thrummed in response and her movements felt awkward. "No eggs here," she said with assumed cheerfulness. "I guess I'll go back to the house."

"Don't leave yet."

She turned to face him. His dark eyes searched her face, and although he hadn't moved, he seemed so close. She gripped her basket handle tightly, as if that could keep her from going to him.

"Unless I'm interrupting you," he said.

"I wasn't doing anything in particular," she heard herself say.

He tested the strength of the rope he had spliced. "I've missed talking to you. You've been avoiding me."

"I'm not avoiding you at all," she denied. "I've just been busy."

His eyes told her he didn't believe her. "There's a lot to do on a farm."

"I don't mind. I enjoy it." Her fingers were starting to go numb from her grip on the basket handle, so she relaxed a little.

"You seem to like it better than you did Rosehaven," he observed.

Abigail turned her head away from his provocative eyes. "I didn't fit there. I'm a farmgirl. That's all I'll ever be. It's all I want to be."

"I wasn't faulting you for it."

She risked looking back at him. "Do you miss Rosehaven very much?"

"Sure I do. It was the only home I ever knew, Rosehaven and Fair Oaks. At times I still dream about being there." He studied her thoughtfully. "I've been considering going back."

Abigail's lips parted in surprise. "You can't do that!"

When he didn't reply, she put down the basket and closed the space between them. "Why would you want to do such a thing? Rosehaven is gone by now. The auction was to have taken place two weeks ago. Why, you're wanted for murder in New Orleans!"

"That's why I ought to go back."

"Are you out of your mind?" she exclaimed.

"My name has been dragged through the dirt for something I didn't do. Amos Smith shot and killed Marie-Claude. I saw him."

"So did I."

He raised his brows in question.

"I was watching from my window," she had to admit. "I saw . . . everything."

Logan paused for a moment. "Ever since that night I've been haunted by something. Did Marie-Claude do it deliberately?" His eyes begged her to tell him the truth.

"I honestly don't know," she finally answered. "He was in the shadows. She was trying to catch her horse. I don't know if she saw him or not."

He shook his head. "Neither do I. Sometimes I think she did, and at others ... well, I don't know. At any rate, *I* didn't kill her. I ought to go back and prove it."

"You should do no such thing! Amos Smith would have you lynched before the matter ever came before a judge. You wouldn't have a fair trial and you know it."

"I know you're right, but—"

"But your damned chivalry forces you to! Logan, the woman you love is dead! Getting yourself hung won't change that."

"What?" he asked in astonishment.

"If you go back to New Orleans, you're as good as dead."

"What did you say about the woman I love?"

"Don't deny it," Abigail said scathingly. "I know all about you and Marie-Claude. At least give me that much credit."

"I have no idea what you're talking about," he said with a frown, "but you're sure as hell going to tell me before you leave this loft." He caught her arm as she turned to leave.

Her smoky violet eyes dared him to deny it as she said, "Marie-Claude told me all about you two. How you were having an affair and all."

"I was doing no such thing!"

"Come, now, Logan. Do you take me for a fool? A lady would never admit to such a shameful thing unless it was true. She told me since you two couldn't marry, you were going to wed me for appearance' sake. Then the two of you could carry on and no one would suspect."

"You believed a pack of lies like that?" he thundered. "Abigail!"

She took a wary step back. "She told me so herself!"

"Marie-Claude was the biggest liar in Saint Charles Parish!" he roared. "Everybody knows that!"

"I don't know it. And that's a fine way to talk about the dead!" Abigail's superstitions had deep roots.

Logan stared at her. "You thought I loved Marie-Claude?" he demanded.

"Of course. She said you did."

"But I told you I loved you!"

Abigail lifted her chin in silent accusation.

"You took her word over mine? Abigail!" he sputtered.

"She was quite convincing."

"Most liars are. Otherwise they give it up. I never loved Marie-Claude."

Abigail stared up at him. "What?"

"Is that why you called off our wedding?" he asked incredulously.

"I could hardly marry a man knowing he loved another," she answered stiffly. Thoughts and emotions were jumbling together in her head.

"Why in hell didn't you confront me with this?" he roared. "You've confronted me with everything else!"

"You would only deny it," she said with dignity. "It's a man's way."

"A man's . . . Don't hand me that drivel!"

"Well, you *are* denying it!" she pointed out heatedly.

"I'm denying it because it isn't true!" he yelled. "She was my sister-in-law, dammit!"

"There's no need to shout. I can hear you quite well."

"Abigail, listen to me." He took a deep breath and tried to speak reasonably. "Marie-Claude . . . liked . . . men. She chased after every pair of trousers in the parish. Everyone knew it. Even Andrew. When I told her I'd have nothing to do with her, that galled her. Just before I left for the war, she found me in the garden at Fair Oaks. She threw herself at me and demanded that I run away with her instead of going to war. I think she expected Andrew to divorce her and for her to take over Rosehaven. It's larger than Fair Oaks and has more land attached.

"I would have had nothing to do with her even if I hadn't known of her reputation, because she was my brother's wife! I sent her back to the house in tears. I only hope Andrew never found out what happened."

"I never knew all this," Abigail said in a small voice. "You never told me. You always treated her so politely."

"I may be a lot of things," he told her, "but at the bottom of them all, I am a gentleman."

She gazed at him in wonder. "You don't love her?"

"I didn't then and I never have." He stepped forward and put his hands on her arms. "Abigail, I've never loved anyone but you."

Her world dipped and spun about as she met his eyes. Words failed her.

"Is that why you stopped loving me?" he asked softly.

She slowly shook her head. "I never stopped loving you, Logan."

He frowned. "You said you did."

"I tried, but I couldn't."

He stared at her for what seemed to be an eternity. Then he gently pulled her into his embrace. "Then you do love me?" he asked doubtfully, not daring to hope.

"I couldn't stop loving you, Logan. Not as long as I draw breath." She buried her face against his chest. Hearing the thud of his heartbeat filled her with joy. Taking a deep breath, she gloried in his uniquely masculine scent.

He held her tighter and nuzzled into her hair. "I love you, Abigail. God, I love you."

"You do?"

"You're enough to drive a man crazy, but yes, I do." He held her so tightly she could hardly breathe. "When I think of all we could have missed! What if you hadn't come looking for those eggs?"

"I would have gone to you eventually," she confessed. "I almost have for several nights. Whether you loved me or not, I wanted you."

"My darlin' Abigail," he murmured. "Don't ever pull away from me again. If you have any further doubts, promise me you'll come and ask me about them. Don't let this happen again."

"Is it likely to?" she queried. "There's not another Marie-Claude lurking in your past, is there?" Her voice was filled with anxiety.

Logan had to laugh. "No, thank God. There was only one Marie-Claude."

He kept his arm around her as he led her back from the open doorway. "Sit down in the hay," he said. "I can't bear for you to leave me yet."

"I wasn't going to leave." She smiled mistily. She still couldn't quite believe what was happening.

He guided her down to the loose hay and sat

beside her. "When I think of all you must have gone through—" he began.

She silenced him by putting her fingers to his lips. "It's over now. Let's bury the past."

His eyes searched hers as he cupped her cheek in his palm. "I love you," he whispered.

"I love you too." Her words were so faint he heard them mostly with his heart.

Moving as if in a dream, Logan leaned forward and tasted her lips. Abigail tilted her head to kiss him and felt his lips brush hers, then return with greater assurance. As his kiss became more passionate, she wrapped her arms around his neck and lay back, pulling him on top of her.

Without pausing, Logan slid his arms beneath her in the rustling hay and arched her body against his own. As their lengths met and their legs intertwined, Abigail murmured with pleasure. Lying in his arms was like a cool drink to a person dying of thirst. She kissed him deeply to slake her need of him.

Logan rolled to his back, bringing her to lie upon his chest. His fingers deftly untied the bow of her apron strings; then he pressed his palms against her back, moving them up and down as if he couldn't get her close enough.

When Abigail lifted her head, she smiled the way he had never expected he would see again. Her lips were pink and dewy from his kisses and a faint blush of excitement bloomed in her cheeks. Logan eased her legs around until she straddled his midsection. Still gazing into her eyes, he began to unbutton her dress.

"Someone might come up here," she said in token protest.

"No one else is home." He smiled sexily, his eyes daring her to let him love her there and then.

"We really shouldn't," she murmured, sitting up so he could reach the rest of her buttons.

A pale wedge of creamy skin was revealed beneath the opening bodice. Logan ran his fingertips lightly beneath the fabric and over the swell of her breast. "Do you want me to stop?"

"No."

She opened his shirt buttons and ran her hands over his furred chest. The hair was silky, the muscles beneath firm and warm. "Don't stop."

He brushed the dress off her shoulders, and as he untied the string of her camisole, it loosened obligingly, spilling her full breasts into his gaze. Logan restrained himself from ripping away the filmy material and instead eased it down to lie around her hips. Her breasts were proud and her pouting nipples begged to be touched. Logan obliged. He stroked the velvety flesh beneath the twin globes and measured their fullness in his palms.

When his thumbs and forefingers trapped the coral buds, Abigail moaned in pleasure. Gently he rolled her nipples, making them blush deeper and harden into centers of pure pleasure. His fingers urged her forward, and she bent over him, letting him take first one tempting beauty into his mouth, then the other.

Logan sucked her nipple gently, tasting the rough bud encircled by the incredibly soft areola. His nose rubbed against the full swell of her breast as he kissed her hungrily while his hand loved the other one.

Abigail felt a shortness of breath as his hot tongue lit fires that soared straight to the center of her being. She was all too aware of him between her widespread knees and of the insistent bulge in his pants. All the weeks of wanting him and not being able to have him culminated, and she felt as if she would explode if she didn't have all of him.

Sitting erect, Abigail gazed down at him. Logan's sensuous eyes flicked from her lips to her love-moistened nipples. She drew away from him and pressed him back into the hay. Her shoes were easily removed, and as she rolled down her stockings, she watched him. Logan rested his head on his bent arm and eagerly feasted his eyes.

She stood to let her clothes slide down to the straw, and felt dizzy from passion. Not taking her eyes from him, she removed her lace-trimmed bloomers and stood naked before him, her clothing puddling around her feet. Seductively she raised her arms and pulled the pins from her hair. The waves of dark fire tumbled over her shoulders and down below her waist to brush against her hips. By the expression on Logan's face she knew he thoroughly approved.

She knelt beside him, but when he reached for her, she gently pushed him back. For weeks she had wanted him, and she wasn't going to rush this. Moving to his feet, she removed his boots, the effort making her breasts sway most sensuously. Then his socks joined the pile of clothes. She sat on her bent legs between his thighs and slowly unbuttoned the fly of his pants.

Logan's eyes widened at her assertiveness. He had never known a lady to do anything like Abigail was doing. As she exposed his skin, she let the back of her fingers graze him. He wished she would hurry, because he was aching for her already. But she continued to move slowly, enticingly. When all his buttons were freed, she ran her hands under his buttocks, signaling him to raise himself. When he did, she pulled his clothes away and off over his legs. Logan watched her closely, but she gave no sign of apprehension over his obviously eager body. Instead, she smiled and cupped her hands around his swollen manhood. Logan groaned in an effort of self-control. If she kept stroking him like that . . .

Abigail moved upward until she was again astride his body. Logan felt the searing fire of her womanhood against him and had to struggle with the almost overwhelming desire to take her as hard and as fast as he could.

As if she had all the time in the world, Abigail reached down and unbuttoned his cuffs. He had forgotten he still wore his shirt. Trembling with restraint, he helped her remove it, each movement a torment as he rubbed against her open body.

Bracing her palms on his chest, Abigail shifted and he closed his eyes and moaned as he felt himself slide into her. Sweat moistened his forehead as he tried to hold off. To wait until she too could be fulfilled.

Abigail rocked experimentally. His rapt gaze was fixed on her breasts as they moved tantalizingly. He dared not think of the hot recesses he assailed. One hand closed over her succulent breast as his other hand caressed lower over her supple moving waist and still lower to the enticing curls that met his skin.

Parting her lips of femininity, Logan found the center of her desire. Gently he massaged it as she cried out in delight. He increased his tempo and suddenly she moaned in ecstasy and leaned forward. A hot pulsing surrounded his staff as she reached her climax of passion. Logan clenched his teeth to restrain himself and managed to bank his own flood.

When she could breathe again, he lifted his hand and swept her hair back from her breasts. Wrapping the soft skein around his palm, Logan pulled her down for his kiss. Her peaked breasts grazed his chest, then mounded against him as she lay forward.

Still encased in her sweet warmth, Logan rolled over so that she lay beneath him. He spread her hair over the hay and gazed deep into the mysterious violet depths of her eyes. She was Woman. Elemental, desirable, seductive.

Slowly he began to move within her. Abigail quickened to meet his passion and closed her eyes to shut out everything but the delicious sensation of his flesh moving as one with hers.

"I love you," he whispered as she tossed her head restlessly. "I'll never be away from you again."

"Love me," she murmured. "Love me always."

"Always," he confirmed. "And then some."

He changed his pace and she arched toward him, her hands stroking the hard planes and ridges of his arms and torso. Still he built upon her passion until she called his name almost desperately. Then he lay upon her, his elbows taking his weight and his body drinking all of her charms. Abigail cried out hoarsely and he again felt the rhythmic pulsing of her love. This time he couldn't hold back, and he moaned as his body released with hers.

For long moments they lay side by side in the hay, minds and bodies still linked. Neither spoke, for there was no need. Their eyes, gentled by love, expressed feelings too deep for mere words.

Logan traced the curve of her cheek, and she smiled at his look of wonder. She kissed him lightly and felt her heart expand with love for him.

"Marry me," he said at last, not as a question but as a statement of fact.

Abigail recalled the other time he had proposed, and she grinned. Then he had refused to make love with her and had insisted upon keeping everything proper. He had come a long way. "Aye," she answered.

"I don't think Laneville has a priest."

"There is one in Nacogdoches. Or at least there was."

"How do you know that?"

"I heard Tobe say so." She paused. "Logan, we can't get married right away. You're wanted for murder. If you give your name, you'll be arrested."

He frowned. "That would give them your name as well. I can't put you in danger." He pulled a straw from her hair. "I spend a lot of time worrying about your safety."

"Do you?" He had never let her know.

"Yes. The rest of the time is spent in loving you."

She smiled the smile of a recently loved woman. "We can't let the others know just how thoroughly we've made up."

"I suspect they'll guess. That smile of yours is a dead giveaway."

"Luckily for us, your room is just across the hall from mine."

"Luckily." He was smiling the same way she was.

"Do you think they will guess?"

"Do you care?"

"Not really."

"Tobe will be overjoyed. Next to locating Rosa,

there's nothing he wants more than for us to get back together."

"He certainly got his wish." She smoothed the night wing of his thick hair.

"I doubt the others will notice. Travis and Martin seem to have some project of their own going. Harley has all the earmarks of puppy love."

"He does?" she asked in surprise.

"I think he has his eye on a girl in Henderson. Every time I turn around, he's headed for town."

"You don't think he would let it slip that you're here?"

"No. Even if he did, who would care? As far as I can tell, there are no wanted posters in Henderson yet." He stroked the pulse in her neck. "Maybe there aren't in Nacogdoches either, and we can get married."

"I hope so," she sighed happily. "I love you very dearly."

Suddenly they heard the clatter of footsteps on the stairs. Logan jumped and swept an armful of hay over their naked bodies.

An instant later Tobe's grinning face bobbed up through the stairwell. "I thought I heard you up here," he said exuberantly. "I found out where Rosa is! She's with her parents in Mexico!" He ducked back and disappeared. A loud Rebel yell reverberated throughout the barn and Tobe raced for the house.

Logan looked at Abigail and she gazed back wide-eyed. "I guess we won't have to tell Tobe about our reunion," he said with a grin.

Abigail pulled the hay over her head.

24

> *Jefferson, Tex., August 6, 1865*
> *To Col. B. W. Dearborn, Washington, D.C.:*
>
> *Have evidence that Nighthawk is here in Texas* STOP *Cannot wait for your reply* STOP *Will keep you advised* STOP
>
> *Owen Chandler, Maj.*

Abigail sat in the porch swing beside Logan. His arm lay along the back, and out of sight of the others, his thumb caressed the nape of her neck in rhythm with the swinging motion. Dark had come early due to a sky full of heavy clouds, and the katydids sang for rain in the thick rye grass beyond the fence. Abigail was glad for the cover of darkness because she couldn't treat Logan with nonchalance no matter how she tried.

Tobe sat in one of the ladder-backed porch chairs, leaning back precariously against the chimney. His face was hidden by deep shadow, but his voice was eager. "I still can't believe it. When I was in town today I ran into Lupe Cardanas—she's Rosa's best friend."

"Looks to me like you'd have checked with her first," Martin observed. He was being unusually quiet tonight and his normal banter was missing. Instead, he kept glancing nervously into the night.

"I tried to, but she had moved. I thought she

had left town, but turns out she had remarried. That's why I couldn't find her. Name's Carpenter now."

"Get on with it," Martin muttered.

Tobe turned his head toward the old man. He had told them the entire story at the dinner table. "Anyhow, I saw Lupe and asked her about Rosa. It seems the farm was too much for her to handle and she was uneasy out here so far from town. She sold all our livestock, locked the house, and caught a coach to Mexico, *niños* and all. Lupe said she wrote and said they all got there just fine."

"Amazing," Travis said in a bored voice. In contrast to Martin, he had been full of biting humor all evening.

Tobe ignored him. "I asked Lupe to write Rosa and tell her I'm home and safe." Concern crossed his face. "I can't decide if I ought to go after her or whether she should catch another coach home."

Abigail looked at him with sudden understanding. Tobe hadn't written Rosa because he couldn't write. Spanish or English. "Maybe you should go after her," she suggested. "Traveling with bairns can be taxing."

"Yeah, and she has the younguns to look after." Tobe hadn't understood the Scottish word, but he didn't want Travis or Martin to know. "But there's the farm to see to. I just bought a cow, and there's the chickens to feed."

Abigail glanced out to a low-branched apple tree where plump round balls of feather were asleep for the night, the chickens' heads all tucked beneath their wings. "We could stay here and look after your farm," she offered. "Couldn't we, Logan?" She enjoyed the feel of his name on her tongue.

"We'd be glad to," Logan agreed amiably.

Tobe's teeth flashed in a grin. He hadn't mentioned to anyone the scene he had accidentally interrupted in the loft, but he had smiled whenever he saw Logan and Abigail together. "I appreciate the offer. I'll give it some thought."

Logan toyed with a curl on Abigail's neck. Although they had loved so long and thoroughly in the barn that morning, he was hungry for her again. All afternoon he had made plans to go to her room that night. His room would never have done, since it was over the one shared by Travis and Martin, and he didn't want to be overheard.

Again he wondered whether it was prudent for them to go to the priest in Nacogdoches. He wanted to marry her before anything else came between them, but he didn't know if the wanted posters had been distributed there. Thinking about it, he recalled that Abigail had mentioned that Martin and Travis had ridden off in that direction. He said, "Travis, did you go to Nacogdoches today?"

"No, why?"

Martin leaned forward, and when the light from the parlor window fell on his face, Logan could see his apprehension.

"Abigail saw you two heading in that direction this morning, and I was wondering if any of those wanted posters had shown up there."

"I wasn't there, and I haven't seen any."

Martin leaned back. "Neither have I."

Logan was silent for a minute. Martin was certainly acting strangely. "Anybody know when Harley will be getting home?"

"Don't know, don't care," Travis answered. "I'm not the boy's father."

"Neither am I, but I care about him," Logan

responded with an edge to his voice. Travis was odd tonight too.

"He's gone courting," Tobe said. "He told me he would be in pretty late. After dark."

"It's after dark now," Abigail mentioned. She too worried about Harley.

"Then I guess he'll be along anytime now," Travis observed. "He can take care of himself."

"What girl is he courting?" Logan asked Tobe.

"He didn't say. I might not know her anyway. She lives in Henderson, not Laneville."

"He rode all that way to see a girl?" Logan grinned. "Looks as if he could have found one closer to home. That's twelve to fifteen miles, isn't it?"

"Yeah. That's why he said he wouldn't be home until after dark."

Travis looked to Martin and grinned. "Maybe tomorrow we ought to ride over to Nacogdoches to look for those wanted posters."

"Maybe," Martin said after a long pause.

"While you're in town, will you check to see if the priest is still there?" Logan requested.

"You aren't planning on confessing anything, are you?" Travis teased. "If you are, I want a head start down the road."

"I was planning on getting married," Logan said, looking lovingly at Abigail.

"Anybody we know?" Martin grinned and winked at Abigail.

She blushed and was glad the shadows hid her.

"Abigail is going to make an honest man out of me." Logan laughed. "Finally."

"That'll take some doing," Travis put in.

"Well, I'm real happy for both of you," Tobe said, as if he had had no idea.

"There's cupids flapping around all over this place," Martin grumbled with some of his old spirit. "First Tobe and the Remarkable Rosa, then Harley and this girl he fancies, now you two." To Travis he said, "I guess you and me had better watch our step."

"I may chase a skirt, but never down an aisle," Travis confirmed.

"You just never met the right woman," Logan informed him.

Abigail's cheeks felt as if they were on fire, but she couldn't help smiling.

Footsteps sounded unexpectedly on the drive and Martin abruptly leaned forward. His eyes narrowed and he cocked his head to one side in an effort to pierce the darkness. "Who's there?" he demanded.

Travis didn't speak, but his wiry body tensed and his hand drifted toward the knife he wore strapped to his belt.

"It's just me," Harley's voice answered. "You sound like you could bite the head off a bear."

Martin and Travis relaxed visibly.

Logan made no comment, but he studied them carefully. After living with them for four years, he knew them as well as they knew themselves. They were nervous about something, but he couldn't figure out what it might be. He had seen Martin prepare for a battle with less show of nerves.

"How's that sweet girl doing?" Tobe asked as Harley sat on the edge of the porch.

"She's sweet, all right." He grinned. Leaning back on a porch support, he bent one knee under his elbow and swung the other leg carelessly. Tonight Nell had not only kissed him until his ears buzzed, but she had let him unbutton her dress and play with her breasts. His loins ached at the memory.

"Don't you go rushing into anything," Martin warned. "We've already got one new-wedded couple on the way."

Harley looked up in surprise at Logan and Abigail and grinned.

"It didn't take him long to figure out who, did it?" Tobe chuckled.

"I'm real glad to hear it's back on. I can't say I'm much surprised." He picked at the seam on his pants leg and added offhandedly, "I heard the Cushing bank was robbed."

"It was?" Tobe said. "When?"

"Sometime today was all I heard."

"Did they catch whoever did it?" Abigail asked.

"No, ma'am. They got clean away."

She shivered. "I hope they keep on going. We have more gold here than the bank probably did."

"You wouldn't want to have that stolen gold get stolen, would you?" Logan teased her.

"That was entirely different."

"I think I'll turn in," Martin said abruptly.

"Me too," Logan agreed, giving Abigail's neck a signaling squeeze that no one else could see.

Tobe stood and stretched. "Yeah, seems like the nights are sure a lot shorter than the days on a farm." He preceded the others into the house. "At least I can quit worrying about Rosa." He waved them a good-night and went to his room.

Martin seemed even more uneasy than he'd been, and after mumbling something about being sleepy, he hurried from the room.

Travis rested his forearm on the mantel and watched Harley go to his bedroom and close the door. "That boy is as randy as a billy goat. You think that girl of his is putting out?"

Abigail's head snapped toward him in astonishment. His tone was that of a man discussing the weather.

Logan's head jerked toward Travis. "I'm surprised at you, Travis. We were brought up knowing better than to talk like that in front of a lady."

A wicked sneer split Travis' face as his eyes met Abigail's for a long, disconcerting moment. "You're right, cousin." He made no offer of apology, however.

Logan decided the incident wasn't worth causing a scene. "Tomorrow I would like for you to ride down to the pond in the back forty. Tobe says the spring is clogged up. You may need to hoe it out."

"Not me. I'm not hoeing out a spring for anybody. Let Tobe do it. This is his land."

"He's giving us room and board in exchange for our work," Logan reminded him. "All too often you either aren't around when there is work to be done or you refuse to do it."

Travis shrugged. "I wasn't meant to be a farmer."

"Neither was I, but I'm willing to learn."

"I'm not."

"You might come to like it. I have. The plantation days are over, Travis. We have to turn to a new way of life or become as extinct as the dodo bird."

"Oh, I'm learning a new life, all right," Travis replied with a maddening grin.

Logan stepped nearer. "I don't know what you mean by that, but as long as you're living on Tobe's farm, you're going to work like everybody else."

"Don't push me too far," Travis warned. "After all, it's your fault we're in this mess. If you hadn't killed Marie-Claude, we would still be in New Orleans."

"I didn't kill her!" Logan snapped as he advanced warningly. "Her husband did!"

"So I hear. But I think it's a lot more likely you shot her to keep her from telling him about the two of you."

"Don't do this, Travis," Logan warned.

"You mean don't mention sex in front of Abigail? She's just Scots-Irish trash. Do you think you're the first man that came along the turnpike?"

Instantly a red haze washed over Logan and he struck out with his fist, solidly smashing Travis' jaw and sending him reeling across the room.

In one smooth motion Travis drew his knife and pointed it menacingly at Logan.

Abigail had jumped out of the way when Logan lunged forward, and she grabbed Tobe's rifle off the mantel. "Drop it, Travis!" she ordered as she pointed the rifle at his head.

Travis grinned tauntingly. "Do you expect me to believe you would be able to shoot and kill me?"

She lowered the gun until it was pointed squarely at the fly of his pants. "I don't intend to kill you," she stated.

Travis blinked, then slowly returned his knife to its scabbard. "Can't you see I was only teasing? I wouldn't hurt Logan. He's my cousin." Travis spread his hands innocently.

"Get out of here," Logan commanded in a low voice that was not to be disobeyed. As Travis left the room, Logan added, "I still expect you to open that spring."

Travis made no reply.

When he was gone, Abigail slowly lowered the heavy rifle. Her arms were shaking and her hands were cold as ice.

Logan put his head to one side and grinned at her. "I've never had a woman gunslinger protect me before."

She glared at him, still too nervous to appreciate his humor, then took a deep breath and smiled back.

Logan took the rifle from her and laid it back on the mantel. "Come on, darlin'. Let's go to bed." He held out his arm and took her into his embrace. Arm in arm they started up the stairs.

They reached her bedroom door and Logan paused. Abigail took his hand and drew him inside. "Stay the night with me," she said.

Pushing the door shut, he took her in his arms. "Abigail, what I'm about to say is very difficult, but what happened downstairs has convinced me that I'm right."

"I already don't like the tone of your voice." Her words were muffled against his shirt.

"This place isn't safe for you. I think you should leave."

"No."

"In a few months all this will have settled down and I'll join you."

"No." Her voice was firmer.

"You're not being reasonable. What if Chandler tracks us here?"

"You may need me to rescue you."

"Be serious. I'm trying to keep you safe."

"I'm quite serious. I won't leave you." She smiled up at his frowning face. "There's really no need to discuss it, Logan. My mind is made up."

"Is anything more stubborn than a Scotswoman?"

"Not that I know of," she answered cheerfully. "I'm going to stay with you, and that's that." She kissed his cheek before turning to her dresser.

After loosening her hair, she brushed the auburn waves. Logan was so dear. Especially when he was so determined to protect her. No one had ever offered to do that before, and she liked the way it felt.

Logan sat on the bed and leaned back on his elbow as he watched her. "Do you think Travis really believes I killed Marie-Claude?" he asked in a worried voice.

Her brush strokes faltered and their eyes met in the mirror before she resumed. "No, of course not."

"You don't sound very convincing."

"*I* know you didn't. But then, I saw what happened," she reminded him. "I don't think any of the other men would believe you shot her."

"Then why would he say that? He must have known how that accusation would hurt me."

"Perhaps that's the reason," she suggested. "I see him baiting Harley all day long. Tobe avoids speaking to Travis when he can. Only Martin is close to him."

Logan shook his head in bewilderment. "And Martin is the last man I would have expected Travis to befriend. You know, sometimes I look at Travis and it's like I'm seeing a stranger. There's a certain look he gets in his eyes. I saw it down there in the parlor. It's as if somebody else is looking out at me. That's silly, isn't it?"

"No, I've noticed the same thing." She put down her brush and came to sit beside Logan on the bed. "I haven't known him very long, but he's changed just in that length of time."

"He hates farming," Logan said in a halfhearted effort to be loyal. "Travis was born to manage a big plantation. It's all he was ever trained to do other than to sabotage the Yankees."

"The same is true of you."

"But Travis hates manual labor."

She refrained from pointing out that most lazy people did. In her opinion, Travis' arrogance lay at the heart of his rift with Tobe. "I saw someone change like this once," she said thoughtfully. "She was married to one of William's cousins. She had a high fever that lasted for days, then after she was well, at times she seemed driven to provoke arguments. Was Travis sick before I met him?"

"No. No, I think he was just more affected by the war than the rest of us." He sat up and pulled a lock of hair over her shoulder and fingered it. "I feel sorry for him."

"I don't trust him," she stated flatly.

Logan paused. "He wouldn't touch you. If I thought there was a chance of that, I'd send him away."

Abigail wasn't at all sure that he wouldn't try to attack her someday, but she didn't say so.

"Give him time to adjust to this new life. He'll come around."

She wasn't convinced of that either, but there was no point in disagreeing. When it came to his cousin, Logan tended to be closed-minded and stubborn. Besides, Abigail had no intention of giving Travis an opportunity to take liberties with her.

Instead she said, "Someday all this will be over, won't it? Running from Chandler, I mean? We'll be able to settle down on land of our own and live a peaceful life?"

"Someday, sweetheart," he promised. "Soon, I hope. Chandler can't follow us forever."

She smiled and leaned forward for the pleasure of his kisses.

Owen Chandler sat back in his chair and surveyed his companions over the poker table in the smoke-hazed back room. His pale eyes, coupled with the fact that he seldom blinked, had affected the concentration of the other players. A large pile of chips was jumbled in front of him. "Two cards," he said conversationally.

The dealer gave him two and he took them without a flicker of emotion. To the man opposite he said, "You say you know a man that rides a black horse like I described?"

"Don't know him," the man drawled as he arranged and rearranged his cards. "I seen him, though."

Chandler tossed two red chips into the pot. After a pause he said, "Was he around here?" In his best investigative manner, he pretended that he couldn't care less.

"What was it you wanted with him?"

"He's my brother-in-law. Owes me a hundred dollars. My sister, his wife, was she with him?"

"Not when I seen him. Of course, he was at a feed store, and a lady wouldn't have call to be there."

"When was this?"

"I guess about a week, ten days ago." He turned to one of the other men. "When was it we were in Henderson, Charley?"

"A week to ten days ago. I fold." Charley tossed his cards facedown on the table.

"Henderson? Not here in Marshall?" Chandler's eyes drilled into his opponent.

The man shifted. "I've got a cousin over in Henderson and I was over there visiting him. I ain't seen nobody like that in Marshall."

Chandler added three chips to the pot and waited for the man to call his bet. "You don't know where he's staying, do you?"

"Now, you've got me there. I don't have any idea. There's a hotel and a boardinghouse there. Or he might have just been passing through. I had no call to talk to him."

Chandler spread his cards on the table faceup and drew in his winnings. "I appreciate the information."

The man looked at his own cards and tossed them down. "Don't mention it."

25

Harley dismounted and tied his horse to a bush as he looked around Henderson. The town was silent. No one walked the dark streets. As he paced impatiently, he studied the rectangles of lamplight that shone from the windows of the homes at the far side of the park. Most families, he guessed, had finished their suppers by now and were settling down for the peaceful hours before bedtime. A dog yapped from a yard down the street, then was quiet.

Suddenly Nell was on the path, waving at him in joyous reunion. With a broad grin, Harley hurried to her and hugged her exuberantly. "I was wondering if you were going to come."

"Me not show up? After you riding all this way?" Nell pouted prettily and struck his arm in mock severity. "Shame on you, Harley."

Manliness spread over him like warm butter. She was so frail, so ladylike, so kittenish. Best of all, she enjoyed kissing and always allowed him to touch her firm young breasts. He was fairly sure that no one else's hand had ever been there before. No, he corrected in a gush of love, he was positive! And he was also very grateful. Visions of her pretty breasts with their pale pink nipples had tortured him all day.

"It's late," he pointed out. "I was afraid your

papa wouldn't let you out to go 'visit your friend.' Does he ever ask who you go to see?"

"Of course he does. I just tell him I'm going to see Alice or Janie or Mary Sue. That satisfies him."

"I sure hope they don't let it slip that you weren't over there. I'd hate to see you get into trouble."

"You would?" She batted her long eyelashes. "Would you protect me?"

"Sure I would. In a flash." He squared his shoulders as if he might be called to do battle at any moment.

"Oh, Harley," she sighed. "You soldiers are so brave."

His grin broadened as he started to draw her expectantly into his embrace.

Nell stopped him by putting her hands on his chest. "Guess what?" she said with delight. "I have a surprise for you."

"You do?" He always liked Nell's surprises. Like the time she had come to meet him wearing only her dress and no undergarments. He had been afraid to touch her below the waist, but the idea that she was naked beneath her skirt had almost driven him crazy.

"Papa's not home." Her dimple danced in her cheek and her eyes were mischievous.

"He's not? Where is he?"

"There is a meeting down at city hall." She wrinkled her nose. Once a month all the county deputies met to receive the latest wanted posters and news of who had or hadn't been captured since the last meeting. Nell found it tediously boring when her father's friends talked shop, but these meetings guaranteed her one totally free evening each month.

"How long do these meetings last?" Harley asked as his hand traveled up her arm.

"He always hangs around and talks to friends afterwards. He won't be home until *very* late." She waited for Harley's response, and when he didn't speak, she said, "We could go to my house and not have to be out here in the park with all the mosquitoes."

"Your house?" he repeated. "Alone? Together?"

She lowered her lashes demurely. "I'd like to show you my room."

He swallowed convulsively. "Your bedroom?"

"Come on," she said, taking his hand decisively.

"What about my horse?"

She thought a minute. Slipping Harley inside without notice would be easy, but the neighbors might notice a horse. "Leave him here. No one ever comes here after dark."

"Nobody but lovers," he amended daringly.

She giggled and pulled him after her. Harley followed quite willingly.

Nell's house sat behind an immense stretch of lawn in shadowed dignity on one of Henderson's main streets. Although it wasn't as large as Tobe's house, it had elegance and charm. Carefully tended flowerbeds bordered the trim lawn, and although it was hard to tell in the dark, the clapboard siding appeared to be wearing a new coat of paint. Harley suddenly realized he knew very little about Nell. This house looked like the home of a prominent citizen.

"What does your father do for a living?" Harley asked.

"You don't want to talk about him." She smiled as she drew Harley into the house. In the past she had noticed a definite trepidation in her beaux whenever they learned about her father's occupation. "My room is this way."

Harley followed her through the maze of furniture and doilies that made up the parlor, and down a short hall.

"The house isn't new," she chattered cheerfully. "When downtown burned a few years back, we were scared silly our house would catch fire too. Mama was still alive then, and she and I sat on the porch and watched the men running to put out the fire. It was arson." She added, "When they caught the man who set the fire, they dragged him behind a horse all around town, then hung him. There was a black woman who helped him, and they caught her too. But since she was in the family way, they waited until her baby was born before they hung her."

Harley gulped. He had noticed that most of the stores looked new, but he hadn't guessed that the people he had met here in town would be capable of lynching someone. "Was he a local man?"

"Goodness no. He was a Yankee. Some said he was hiding out here from the law, but after him almost burning down our whole town, it didn't matter much."

"Oh." Unwillingly Harley recalled that he too was a wanted man.

"Here's my bedroom," Nell said in happy discovery. She pushed open the door and practically pulled Harley across the threshold.

He looked around at the frilly pink curtains and rose-patterned wallpaper. The bed had a lacy canopy and a spread of nubby candlewicking. The furniture was pale bird's-eye maple, and a hooked rug in pink and green covered the floor. This room was blatantly feminine, and Harley felt awkward in it. "Very nice," he said. That bed seemed to be growing larger every moment, and he found himself wondering if he could perform in a manly fashion when the time came.

Nell plopped herself down on her bed and smiled at him beguilingly. "Do you really like it? This is my pillow," she said as she patted it, "where I dream about you. I expect my dreams will be even more exciting after tonight."

Harley tried not to blush as he thrust his hands nervously into his pockets. Somehow he had pictured himself as the hunter and Nell as the pursued. Instead, he felt like a trapped rabbit. "Nell, I don't know if this is such a good idea," he mumbled. "If your papa comes home . . ."

"He won't. These meetings drag on forever. Then he stands around gossiping with his friends."

"Still, if he came home early . . ."

"Harley! Are you afraid to be in my room?" She got off the bed and came to him, her lips pouting sultrily.

"No! Not afraid, just . . ."

"It's just a tiny little room," she murmured as she unbuttoned his shirt. "It can't hurt you any." She stroked his bare chest. Suddenly her eyes widened. "Harley, have you ever done this before?"

"Well, sure I have," he blustered in embarrassment. "Dozens of times. Hundreds, maybe. It's just . . ." He fumbled for a plausible excuse. "It's you! I mean, a man shouldn't take a woman in her own bedroom. It's not . . . chivalrous. You being a virgin and all," he ended lamely.

Amusement lit Nell's eyes, and she unbuttoned her dress front. "But, Harley, we might not ever get this chance again. Papa isn't gone very often."

She exposed the small globes of her breasts and brushed them against his chest.

Harley felt as if he would faint dead away. He wanted to throw her on the bed and rid them both of their virginity, but he had never felt less like dalliance in his entire life. Here he was in her room, and they were both half-undressed. With a woman rubbing her bare breasts all over a man's chest, Harley suspected there wasn't but one thing a man could do and not shame himself.

Harley fumbled with his suspenders, and prayed he would be able to do it, and do it right.

Nell helped him undress with anxious anticipation for what was to come next. No man had been in this room for months. "Hurry, Harley," she encouraged.

He glanced at her as he bent to step out of his pants. She sure was ready and willing. He had always heard that virgins were very reluctant, but that just proved that not everything a person heard was true. As he tried to shake his pants legs over his boot, his eyes were on a level with a framed daguerreotype on Nell's bedside table.

He froze, his pants around his ankles and his loose shirttail shrouding his summer long johns. "Who's that?" he demanded, staring at the photograph of a burly man, and the six-pointed badge on the man's shirt.

Nell had finished removing her dress, and stood there wearing only her petticoats. Following Harley's gaze, she said, "That's Papa."

Harley grabbed the picture and straightened, his pants pooling at his ankles. "What's that on his shirt?"

She glanced at the familiar picture. "I guess it's his badge." She shrugged.

"Badge! Is your papa the sheriff?" he demanded.

"Of course. Everybody knows that."

"Oh, shit!" Harley jerked up his pants and frantically shoved the buttons back into the holes. Then he haphazardly stuffed one side of his shirt into the waistband of his trousers.

"Harley!" Nell exclaimed. "What are you doing?"

"I've gotta leave," he yelled as he bolted for the door. "You never told me your daddy is the sheriff!"

"Harley!" she wailed as he disappeared down the hall.

He barely slowed to dodge around the chairs and tables and bric-a-brac. The sheriff's daughter! Of all the damned luck! Nell *would* have to be the sheriff's daughter! He burst out of the house and cleared the porch steps, his shirttail flapping and his suspenders flying behind him.

The stocky man from the photograph was just coming up the walk. Harley let out a whoop of fear and barreled past at high speed. The startled man yelled after him, but Harley just ran faster. His heart was beating as if it would burst, but he slowed down only long enough to get his horse.

Logan tested the buckles on the harness and frowned. It hadn't been stored properly, and the weather had been at it since it was last used. He doubted it would stand the weight of a dogcart, let alone the bulky harvester. "I don't know, Tobe," he said, shaking his head. "It's pretty well rotted. I think we need some new straps."

Tobe fingered the cracked leather and nodded. "I reckon you're right. This harness wasn't new before the rain got to it. Was there more strapping in the tack room?"

"No, Martin used the last of it to mend a bridle. We'll have to go into town for it."

"It means a trip all the way into Henderson. The Laneville general store won't have this in stock." He glanced over at the stalls where Harley was mucking out the old straw. "I'll bet I know somebody that wouldn't mind going in."

"He's there half the time as it is." Logan said with a grin. "He might as well pick up some leather while he's there."

"Harley," Tobe called as they strolled over to him, "how would you like a chance to see that girl of yours?"

At Tobe's question, Harley flinched.

"We need some straps to mend this harness, and I imagine Abigail needs a few things for the kitchen. Why don't you take the buggy in?" He knew Harley had been trying to find an excuse to go in by buggy so he could drive his girl around town.

"I'm real busy," Harley mumbled as he continued shoveling out the stall.

"We really need this," Tobe said. "There's enough hay to bale if we get after it before the rains start. We won't need much, since we don't have much livestock, but I don't want to pick it by hand." He grinned at the boy to include him in his levity.

"I haven't been feeling too good today," Harley said. He avoided their eyes. "I got a stomachache."

"You have been acting sort of odd today," Tobe agreed. "Real quiet-like."

"Maybe you should go in and have Abigail tonic you," Logan suggested. "Sometimes a change in seasons can make a person feel sickly. A dose of tonic should do the trick."

Harley scowled. He hated tonic, but he couldn't

admit he wasn't sick—not and have to go into town. By now the sheriff was probably searching all over for him. The thought actually did make him feel sick. "Maybe I should," he admitted.

"The boy must be feeling poorly," Tobe said. "Nobody would take tonic unless he really needed it. That stuff tastes awful."

Logan looked at Harley skeptically. "Did you and your girlfriend have an argument?"

"I've got a bellyache! All right?" Harley threw down the shovel and stalked from the barn.

Tobe and Logan watched him in surprise. When Harley kicked savagely at a clump of bitterweed as he passed, Tobe observed, "I believe you figured it right."

"Young love," Logan laughed. "Why should it go any easier for them than it does for us?"

"You're right about that. Well, we still need the harness leathers. I guess I'll saddle up and ride in."

"Where's Travis? He hasn't done much else around here. We can send him, and you and I can work on that back fence."

"I don't know where he is, nor Martin either."

"They sure are gone a lot these days," Logan said thoughtfully. "Where do you suppose they go?"

"Got me. Maybe they've set up a whorehouse around here somewhere." He grinned at Logan.

"Maybe so," he laughed. "I'll sure be glad when they settle down, so we can get some work out of them." He glanced at the house as Harley was going through the kitchen door. "Do you want me to go in?"

"No, just to be on the safe side, you ought to stay out of sight until this whole thing blows over.

Just because there aren't any wanted posters here doesn't mean somebody might not have seen one somewhere else."

"While you're in town, go by the post office and check out the board."

Tobe nodded solemnly. "I always do."

After Tobe had gone, Logan resumed his chores. One of the yearling calves Tobe had bought looked as if she were sick, so Logan set about to doctor her. He took a small bottle of magnesia laced with oil of peppermint and laudanum and went out to the pen.

As before, the half-grown cow was standing a little apart from the others. Her legs were bunched under her and her back was bowed. As Logan approached her, she moved away a few steps, then stood still while he put a rope around her neck. He checked her gums and eyes as he would have a horse, and frowned at her. At a year old, all these animals should be weaned, but she acted as if the food wasn't agreeing with her. He patted her rangy neck and noticed her hair was coarse. Another sign of ill health.

Logan had never had much experience with cows, but they didn't seem to be very different from the horses he had raised. Looping his arm around her neck, he put the bottle neck behind her teeth, raised her head, and poured in the medicine. The calf rolled her eyes and bellowed, but he held her firm until she swallowed the dose.

"You do that very well."

Logan turned to see Abigail watching him over the fence. "I didn't hear you walk up."

"Is the calf ailing? What's wrong?"

"I'm not sure. But that medicine will make her

feel better. Now we have to wait until she either gets well or develops more symptoms."

Abigail nodded. "It's the same with sheep. I've heard my father say more than once that his doctoring would either kill them or cure them." She held out a cup towel she had tied into a bag. "I thought you might be hungry."

A slow grin lit Logan's face as he took the rope off the calf. "You're spoiling me," he told her. "And I like it."

"You had better get used to it, because you have a lifetime of pampering ahead."

He opened the gate for her. "Let's go down by the stream." Taking the improvised bag, he said, "It smells good."

"I made a pound cake. There's also some sausage and biscuits that were left from dinner."

"I get the first slice of pound cake? Before Harley has a chance to finish it off?"

"He's a growing boy," Abigail defended him. "Besides, I like seeing a man with an appetite."

"Do you, now?" Logan grinned and hugged her affectionately.

"I was talking about food!"

"Why, Abigail, you shock me," Logan said in pretended protest. "So was I."

She pinched his buttocks and smiled up at him. "To be sure you were."

They sat in the deep grass on the bank of the stream, holding hands and enjoying the view. Though the stream wasn't broad, it was deep and clear, and the water flowed sedately. A large fish basked in a sun-warmed spot, facing upstream in search of any food that might float or swim by with the current.

Logan unknotted the corners of the cup towel and spread it on the grass. "Boiled eggs too?"

"I wasn't sure how hungry you would be."

He offered her the first bite of a biscuit with a sausage patty in the middle. "You take good care of me."

She smiled demurely. "I want you to keep your strength up." Her laughing eyes met his.

"Shameless hussy." He grinned. "You keep this up and you won't get any sleep at all."

"As long as you don't either, I won't complain." She peeled a boiled egg and held it to his lips. "Oh, I nearly forgot." With a flourish she pulled a mason jar of milk from her deep apron pocket.

A cool breeze ruffled Logan's hair as he looked around. They seemed to be alone. Maybe Abigail wouldn't be averse to making love. The tall rye grass waved sensuously and the water murmured a lulling song. "Where is everybody?" Logan asked as he finished the biscuit sandwich.

"I haven't seen Martin and Travis since breakfast. Harley is mending the gate on the chicken yard."

"Is Tobe still in town?"

"I think so." She smiled. "I guess it's just the two of us." Her glance flicked over him and she met his eyes.

Logan had the sensation of floating down into her soul when he gazed into her eyes. The green of the tree leaves was reflected in the violet depths, making them pools in which a man could drown and never regret it.

Logan unpinned her hair and let it cascade over her shoulder. "I like it down," he said as he stroked the auburn masses. "Why don't you leave it loose?"

"That would be about as proper as me running around in my chemise."

"I'd like that too."

Her tinkling laughter rivaled the birdsong as she put her arms around him and lay back in the grass.

"You aren't like anyone I've ever known," Logan marveled.

"You're right. At Rosehaven you knew only ladies. I'm a woman." She pulled his head down for her kiss.

As always, Logan could sense sparks igniting as their lips touched. She was all woman; no doubt about it. "You're a lady too," he growled into the curve of her neck. "The best kind."

She squealed ticklishly. "What kind is that?"

"The kind that loves her man and nobody else."

She smiled up at him. "After knowing you, I could never love anyone else. I've given all my love to you, and as fast as I make more love, I'll give that to you as well."

"I adore you, Abigail," he said with a sigh. "I just wish you would be reasonable and go away."

"Go away? What a constant lover you are," she teased.

"You know what I mean. I want you to be safe."

"I'm safer here with you than I would be anywhere else," she pointed out. "Besides, I won't leave you, so there's no use in you scowling at me." She smiled beguilingly. "Make love to me instead."

He was already unbuttoning her blouse, and as he pulled it loose, he slipped his hand in to cover her breast. "Didn't anyone ever tell you that you're supposed to dislike this?"

"No. Am I?"

"You're supposed to call it 'your duty' and never refer to it outside of the bedroom." He noticed her nipple was already peaking against his palm.

"Is it your 'duty' too?" she asked as she trailed the very tip of her tongue along the faintly salty skin at the base of his throat.

"No, it's my 'right and privilege.' "

"It's my privilege too," she announced. "And my pleasure."

He pulled up her skirts and cupped her firm buttocks in his hand. "Abigail!" he gasped. "Where are your underclothes?"

"In the wardrobe," she answered blithely. "Surprised?"

He laughed and hugged her to him. "Continually!"

With an easy motion he rolled her under him and loosened the fastenings of his pants. Letting them slide to his knees, he knelt between her thighs. His fingers told him she was already eager for him, and he entered her.

Abigail closed her eyes in pleasure as she felt him moving within her. "Logan," she whispered, "I love you so."

As easily and naturally as a blooming wildflower, he brought her to her completion and rode with her in love's golden triumph. As the world slowly reformed around them, Logan murmured, "There's never been anyone like you, love. Never."

"Do you still want me to leave you?" Her voice was drowsy with contentment.

"I never wanted you to leave me. I want you to be safe."

"I am," she sighed, nuzzling into his shoulder. "Together we can take on the world."

"Spoken like an Irishwoman," he grumbled good-naturedly. "Always looking for a fight."

For the rest of the day Abigail sang as she went about her chores. Her notes weren't always true, but her spirit was lilting. She loved Logan and he loved her. In a short time they would be married and would find a place of their own. She had never been happier.

Before supper, Tobe rode up, but instead of going first to the barn to put away his horse, he came into the yard. Abigail looked up in surprise. Dusting the flour from her hands and wiping them on her apron, she stepped out onto the tiny kitchen porch.

Logan was standing in the yard talking to Tobe. By their stances and the white lather of sweat on the horse's neck, Abigail knew something was wrong. Fear gripped her heart in its icy fingers. She went out to them in time to hear Logan say, "Are you sure?"

"I'm telling you, the wanted posters are all over town. Only these have a drawing of you and Abigail!"

"A drawing?" she gasped. "Of us?"

"We've got to get out of here," Logan stated. "I appreciate your hospitality, but Abigail and I have to leave."

"I'm coming too," Tobe said.

"Your name isn't on the posters, Tobe. This is your farm."

"How long do you think it would take to trace you here? My neighbors are very loyal, and I'm sure they'd be more than pleased to overlook us stealing the Yankee gold, but those posters . . . I know you didn't kill anybody, but my neighbors don't."

"You're right. And by association you'll be figured guilty." Logan ran his fingers through his hair. "I'm sorry to bring trouble to your door, Tobe."

"Don't dwell on it. I'll be ready to ride when you are."

Abigail was speechless as she stared at the men. She had a full meal in the oven. That afternoon she had made love with Logan there by the fishing hole of the creek. How could this be happening?

"Harley is feeding the calves," Logan was saying. "I'll tell him when he comes to the house."

"I'll turn the calves loose to roam when we leave, as well as the chickens and cow. My neighbors will claim them and we won't have to answer any questions. Where are Travis and Martin?"

"Didn't you see them in town? They never came home."

"Damn! Of all the times for them to be gone."

"We can't leave without them," Logan said. "They might get caught waiting around here or looking for us in town."

"Well, we can't write them a note, or everybody will know where we went," Abigail pointed out.

"They're bound to show up by suppertime," Tobe put in.

But they didn't.

26

"Where in hell could they be?" Logan growled menacingly.

Abigail dipped her hand into the bucket of chicken feed and broadcast the grain in an arc. The hens and rooster ran greedily to peck at the yellow corn. "I have no idea, but they couldn't have picked a worse time to disappear."

"Are you sure their beds weren't slept in? Maybe they came in late and left early."

"Martin never misses breakfast. Besides, we were all up very late last night preparing to leave."

"You're ready? When they come back, we should leave right away."

"I'm ready. All I have to do is saddle my horse." Abigail tossed the last of the chicken feed and watched the plump feathered bodies scramble for it. "What do you suppose Mexico is like?"

"I've never been there." He shaded his eyes against the sun and gazed down the dirt road. "Maybe I ought to ride out and look for them."

"I've heard it's hot in Mexico," Abigail mused as she wiped the feed dust on the tail of her apron. "I wonder if it's good land for sheep."

Logan wasn't listening. He paced a few yards and looked back at the road.

"I'll bet it is," Abigail continued. "Sheep are very hardy and will thrive almost anywhere."

"What?" Logan asked impatiently.

"Never mind." She had learned that men were remarkably single-minded, and if Logan was busy fretting over the absence of his friends, he probably wouldn't be receptive to her ideas for their sheep ranch.

"I'm going to look for them," he stated.

"And you'll get yourself arrested," she scolded. "You'll do no such thing. Send Tobe and Harley."

"I can't send someone to do something I can't do myself."

"Their pictures aren't plastered all over the county. You stay here."

He hated to admit it, but Abigail was right. Nobody suspected the others. "I can't just stand around and wait," he protested anyway.

"You could get Tobe's map and plot our route to Mexico," she suggested. "Or you could help me in the kitchen. I'm cooking as much food as possible to take with us."

About that time Tobe came around the corner of the house, closely followed by Harley. "Any sign of them?" Tobe asked.

"None. I think it's time to go looking for them," Logan replied.

"I was just fixing to suggest that. You ought to stay here, though, and let Harley and me go. You might be recognized."

Logan glanced at Abigail, who gave him an I-told-you-so look.

"We'll probably meet them on the road," Harley suggested. "They'll likely ride up at any minute."

"We can't wait around to see."

"I'll take Cushing," Harley said quickly. He was afraid of running into Nell and her papa in the larger town.

"All right," Tobe agreed. "Let's meet back here as soon as possible."

They agreed and went to saddle their horses.

Abigail left Logan pacing in the yard while she went inside to look after her cooking. Most of the meat was salted and cured, but she was baking as much bread as she could stack in a flour sack. Weeks might pass before she had a proper stove again. She tried not to think about it.

After a brief planning session, she decided potatoes would also travel well. She had both Irish and sweet potatoes in the root cellar out back. Taking the bread from the oven, she went out the back door.

At the same moment, Logan's eyes narrowed at the sight of a lone horseman coming through the woods by the creek. The horse looked like Martin's, but it was foamed with sweat and staggering from exhaustion. The man on its back was bent low over its neck and wobbled in the saddle.

"Martin?" Logan called doubtfully. Then he cried out, "Martin!" as he ran to meet the man.

He intercepted the horse on the broad sloping meadow that separated the house from the creek. "Martin! What happened?"

The old man raised his bleary eyes and blinked to focus. "Logan?" He fell forward and the horse shied away.

Logan caught the man and eased him to the ground in the shade of a big black walnut tree. "What—?" His question was interrupted as Martin uncurled and Logan saw the blood.

His right pants leg was sodden and the front of his shirt was red and sticky. Logan stared at the wounds as if he couldn't comprehend what he was seeing.

"We robbed the bank in Henderson," the old man wheezed. A thin trickle of blood from the corner of his mouth stained his gray beard.

"Robbed a bank?" Logan repeated dumbly. "Where's Travis?"

"He got away. Last I seen him, he was headin' north. I wasn't that lucky. They shot me."

Logan ripped open Martin's shirt. A cursory glance told him the man was as good as dead. He gently covered the wound again.

Martin half-grinned. "I remember we always said if we had to go by gunfire, we didn't want it to be a gut shot." He coughed and his body twitched spasmodically. "Takes too long to die."

"Lie still." Logan glanced at the woods. Had he heard a sound?

"Want to know the bad part?" Martin gasped. "They didn't have but two hundred dollars in the safe. We thought they would have thousands. Cushing bank did."

Logan looked at him sharply. Harley had told him about the bank being robbed in Cushing. "Did Travis talk you into this?" he demanded.

Slowly Martin nodded. "Don't blame him. I knew better." He coughed again and his eyes began to glaze. "Logan," he whispered. "Want you to know ... Name's Cyrus E. Martin. From ... Kansas City ..."

A long rattle sounded deep in his throat and Martin's head lolled limply on his neck. The pupils of his eyes widened as if to take in as much of life as he could, even while slipping into death.

Just at that moment, a band of riders burst out of the woods, but Logan scarcely glanced at them. As he sat there supporting Martin's body, he numbly tried to piece together what had happened.

The posse quickly surrounded Logan and Martin. "So," one of the men said almost pleasantly, "this is where you've been."

At the sound of the familiar voice, Logan's head snapped up. "Chandler," he said at last.

"Hello, Nighthawk." He turned to the sheriff. "This man is wanted for robbery in Mississippi, and for murder in Louisiana as well. Arrest him." To Logan he said, "When I heard about the bank robberies in Cushing and Nacogdoches, I wondered if it might be you. Turns out I was right."

"Not this time. Here's the man you want. I'm afraid he's beyond arrest, however."

"There were two men," Chandler said with keen enjoyment. "Him. And you."

"Not me. I've been here all day. The man you're looking for resembles me." He was through shielding Travis. "We're cousins."

"Sure you are." There wasn't a shred of belief in Chandler's voice. "This time you made too many mistakes. You killed once too often."

"What?" Logan stared up at him.

"The bank teller you shot. He's dead." To the other man in uniform Chandler motioned toward the barn. "Go get his horse. A big black one." Chandler grinned maliciously. "After we hang you, I think I'll keep the horse for my own."

Logan pushed Martin aside and stood up. "I never shot anybody. Not Marie-Claude and not this bank teller! I told you, I've been here all day. I didn't have any idea they were robbing banks!"

Chandler leaned forward and rested his forearm on the pommel of his saddle. "Can you prove it?"

Words caught in Logan's throat. He could, but

not without implicating Abigail and the others. "I'm telling you, I'm innocent."

Chandler nodded. "Exactly what I would say in your place. Where's the woman?"

"She stayed in Jefferson. She has family there." The lie came easily to Logan's tongue.

"Search the house," Chandler told the other soldier. "Sheriff, this is the man I've trailed for months. He has a woman accomplice, like the warrant says. I'll be taking them both back to face federal charges."

"No you won't," the sheriff spoke up. "He gunned down Pete Dryden. Everybody in town liked old Pete. No, we're going to hang him here."

Chandler's eyes narrowed coldly. He hadn't expected the sheriff to speak against him. On the other hand, Logan was sure to be hung here, and in a federal court where emotions weren't involved, he might be merely imprisoned. Chandler wanted to see him hung. "All right, Sheriff. He's yours. But he owes the federal government fifty-five thousand, eight hundred dollars."

The soldier came running back to Chandler. "The house is empty, sir."

Logan hid his surprise. Abigail must have heard them and hidden.

"Are you sure?" Chandler rapped out.

"Yes, sir. I looked all over."

Chandler again eyed Logan. "Where's the money?"

"I spent it." Logan smiled. "Every last dime of it."

Chandler's boot lashed out, kicking Logan in the jaw. He fell back as bright lights spangled his vision. Shaking his head, Logan regained his feet and lunged at the major. At once two of the sheriff's deputies were upon him, along with the soldier. Logan felt himself being overpowered, but he struggled furiously. He struck a blow that sent the soldier reeling, but one of the deputies hit him with the butt of his gun as the other produced a pair of handcuffs.

Logan was hardly aware of Caliban being led up and of being thrown onto the saddle. By sheer reflex he balanced and the deputies tied him to the horse. He tried to look back at the house to see if he could see Abigail; but as they led his horse forward, Logan needed all his attention to stay upright in the saddle.

Abigail had gone to the root cellar, a stone building with a rounded top, whose walls were half-buried in the dirt. She seldom went there because she viewed it as a probable sanctuary for snakes and spiders of all kinds. And Abigail wasn't fond of either.

Holding her skirt close about her, she ventured down the two wooden steps and blinked to adjust her eyes to the gloom. A tiny window near the ceiling in one side allowed a flicker of light, but most of the room was in deep shadow.

After waiting for her eyes to adjust to the darkness, she picked her way carefully across the floor. The potatoes she sought were in the low bin on the back wall. Gingerly she picked through them, choosing only the potatoes that felt firm and discarding the others out the window. When her basket was at last full, she looked around to see what else might be of use.

On the shelves to her right were canned tomatoes and preserves that had turned dark from age. She wouldn't trust those. A bag stood in one cor-

ner. Carefully she untied the rope that closed the
burlap and found it was full of dried beans. She
scooped up a handful and carried them to the
window to see if they were still good.

A movement in one of the windows drew her
attention, but by the time she raised her head,
whoever it was had gone. She shrugged. It could
only be Logan.

The beans seemed sound enough, so she looked
around for something to carry them in. Across the
room was a neat stack of flour and meal sacks. She
took one for each of them and started to fill them
with beans.

When that was done, she tied the necks with
strips torn from another sack, and started stacking
them in the doorway. As she placed the basket of
potatoes by them, she heard the sound of voices.
Her head tilted to one side, she went up one step.
The thick walls of the root cellar blocked almost
all sound from the outside.

Yes, those were men's voices. Travis and Martin
must have arrived at last. Abigail climbed into the
sunshine and crossed the narrow yard to the enclosed porch that contained the well. They could
leave at once if Harley and Tobe were back. She
was suddenly feeling very uneasy and was eager to
ride away.

By the time she rounded the corner, the band
of men was riding away, Logan handcuffed in
their midst. Abigail smothered a cry and ducked
back behind the house. As she did, she saw Logan
glance back, but she couldn't tell whether he saw
her or not.

Fearfully she peeped around the corner. Three
of the men wore Union uniforms, and the tallest
one she recognized as Owen Chandler. A sick

feeling gripped her stomach. She had to save Logan! But how?

To run recklessly after them would only mean her own capture, and alone she couldn't free him. Tobe! Tobe would return soon and he would know what to do.

Her fingers were pressed tightly against her lips, and her eyes were wide and frightened. Several minutes passed before she realized there was something lying in the meadow.

Slowly she neared, keeping her skirts gathered so she could run away without tripping over them. She noticed a horse was grazing off to one side; then her eyes darted back to the still shape. Her mind balked and refused to accept what she saw.

Then she was running forward. "Martin!" she cried. Little sound escaped her lips, but it seemed to echo over and over in her brain. "Martin!"

She dropped down by the prone figure and drew back in shock. Blood was everywhere, clotting the shirt she had washed for him only two days before. How could it be bloody, and soaking one leg of his trousers? Already it was darkening and losing its brilliant red. "Martin?" she whispered.

He was dead. She knew it inside before she could admit it consciously.

In total confusion she looked down the now deserted road.

"What . . . ?" she stammered aloud.

With no one to explain, she sat in stunned silence, keeping watch over her friend until Tobe or Harley should come home to help her move him.

Tobe was the first to arrive. She saw him riding hell-for-leather down the road, his horse's hooves gouging clots of dirt from the sandy road. Abigail had not moved from the spot where she had first knelt beside Martin. Her eyes followed Tobe as he cut across the meadow and churned to a stop only yards away.

"Martin!" he exclaimed.

"He's dead." Abigail's voice was flat. Shock had mercifully blanketed her emotions. "I don't know how or why."

Tobe pushed back his hat and rubbed his eyes fiercely. "Damn him! Why did he have to go and pull such a damned fool stunt!"

Abigail raised her eyes to his in silent question.

"He and Travis robbed the bank! In Henderson!" he added as if that compounded the crime. "They robbed the damned bank and killed one of the tellers. A man named Pete Dryden. Another man was wounded. Hell! I grew up with Pete's sons!" Tobe looked as if he would like to kill Martin himself.

"They came and took Logan away," she said, as if the words had been carefully rehearsed.

Tobe looked away. "They're saying in town that Nighthawk was the leader. He was the one that shot Pete."

"Logan didn't do that. He was here all day."

Tobe made an angry sound. "It was Travis! You know as well as I do how much he looks like Logan."

"Travis?" she repeated as if the name were unfamiliar. Then she said, "He'll have to confess. To tell them he did it. Not Logan."

"He's gone. Travis rode off one way, Martin the other. He's out of the county and gone by now."

Abigail struggled to gather her thoughts. "Chandler was with the men. He has Logan."

Tobe's eyes met hers and spoke the words they dared not voice.

Finally he said, "Go clear off the kitchen table and lay out the old oilcloth. I'll bring Martin in."

Abigail forced herself to stand, then unsteadily backed away. Necessity gave her the willpower to turn toward the house.

They buried Martin in the pasture behind the barn, near the orchard. With no time to build a coffin, nor with any materials readily at hand, Harley and Abigail had no choice but to stitch him into one of Rosa's quilts. Then Harley and Tobe laid Martin in his grave.

No one wanted to speak. They were all too stricken with grief. Martin was dead and Logan was in danger of hanging.

At last Tobe said, "Either of you know his full name?" When they both shook their heads, he said, "Do you know where he's from? If he has any people?"

"You knew him better than we did," Harley answered. "Martin never talked about himself."

"I don't suppose he was a religious man," Abigail added. "Not if he robbed banks."

"I reckon not." Tobe gazed down at the quilted shroud. "But he was a friend to me for four years, and there were a couple of times when Martin saved my skin."

"That's true," Harley agreed. "More than once he kept me out of a jam."

"I used to pretend he was my grandfather," Abigail murmured. "I never knew another one."

Tobe bent and picked up a handful of dirt. After a long pause, he tossed it into the grave.

"Dust to dust," he said in a grieving voice. "Rest easy, old friend."

Silently Harley and Abigail did the same, and she crossed herself before turning away. Not looking back, she returned to the house, leaving Tobe and Harley to fill in the grave.

27

"What do you mean, we're leaving for Mexico?" Abigail demanded. "I can't leave Logan behind to hang!"

"Miss Abigail, calm down," Tobe soothed. "Nobody feels worse about this than I do. But those were the captain's orders. He told me that if anything should happen to him, I was to be sure you're safe. I gave him my word."

"Damn your word!" she cried out. "I'll not leave him."

"If there was anything we could do, we would," Harley insisted. "You know me and Tobe rode out looking for Travis all day yesterday. If we can't find him, we can't clear Logan."

"Surely if we went to the judge . . ."

"You're a wanted woman," Tobe reminded her. "All that would do is put you in jail. It wouldn't do Logan any good."

"But he's innocent!" She paced the room in frustrated anger.

"The way I figure it, we have to head for Mexico. Chandler's authority won't reach across the border. I wouldn't mind settling there, and I suspect Rosa would prefer it. You can still get that sheep farm. Maybe Harley will help you run it."

"I'd be glad to, Miss Abigail," Harley volunteered. "You'll have to teach me, but I learn real quick."

Abigail looked from one to the other. "I can't leave Logan."

"It's what he wants! Dad-gum-it, be reasonable," Tobe said in exasperation.

She lifted her head. "His trial is tomorrow. Perhaps he will be freed."

Tobe dropped his eyes and Harley looked steadily at the floor. They both knew Logan didn't have a chance, and though it chafed them raw, they could do nothing about it.

"Well, he *could* be," she insisted. When neither answered, she said, "I'll not go until I know for sure."

"Miss Abigail—" Tobe began.

"What if Logan is set free and he can't find us?"

"It's a wonder someone hasn't come out here before now," Harley said. "They know you were with him."

"I guess Logan sent them on a false chase."

"The point is, the sheriff could ride up at any minute. We need to leave."

"Tomorrow. After the trial," she repeated stubbornly.

"All right," Tobe reluctantly agreed. "But we leave right after that."

"With Logan," Abigail amended. Not waiting for them to correct her, she left the room.

She had very little to do. If they were leaving the next day, dusting again or mending the small tear in the tablecloth would be pointless, so she went upstairs and sat in one of the chairs in the little sitting area in the wide hall. Beyond the window were the walnut tree that had sheltered Martin in his last moments and the road where Logan had been taken away. Travis and Martin had used that same road to go on their hell-raising ventures that had led to Logan's capture and Martin's death. The road lay like a faded red ribbon, its dusty surface giving no clue to the part it had played in her misery.

She had to see Logan. Reason told her that he would never be freed, and she had to see him, touch him, one last time. A single tear escaped her control, and she angrily wiped it from her cheek. She had to be strong, for him.

Running her hands over her skirt, she pondered how she could manage to see him. Without a doubt the sheriff and his deputies would be looking for any woman that came to visit him. But a boy might get through.

She glanced at Logan's room. His clothes would never fit her. But Harley's might.

Before she had time to back out, Abigail went downstairs. The men had gone out to the back porch and were discussing the best route to Mexico. Abigail went into Harley's room and found his saddlebags. His extra shirt and pants were folded with military precision. With very little compunction, Abigail took them and ran back upstairs.

Shucking off her dress, she surveyed herself critically. Her breasts were too large. Taking a pillowcase, she ripped it into strips. Carefully she wound it around her ribs, flattening her breasts beneath the bandage. Then she pulled on Harley's blue chambray shirt. Once it was buttoned, it fell straight down her front. Next she put on his pants. They were tight over her hips, and it felt strange indeed to have fabric wrapped around her legs, but they fit. Boots would be the problem. Harley was wearing his only pair, and her own shoes were out of the question.

Reluctantly she decided there was only one solution. She would have to use Martin's. He had been buried without them, and they were the only ones available.

Slowly she eased down the stairs. If either Harley or Tobe saw her, she would never be able to get into town. Fortunately, they were still on the porch, and she had no problem slipping into the room Martin had shared with Travis. The boots, along with his other belongings, were stacked neatly at the foot of the bed.

Abigail put on two pairs of socks and hesitantly pulled on the first boot, trying hard to forget that Tobe had pulled them off Martin's dead body. Martin had been her friend, but her Gaelic superstitions were deep-seated. And there was that dark red-brown splotch on the right one. She tried to pretend it was a mud stain.

Cautiously she tried walking. The boots were still too large, but she found that in her struggle to keep them on, her stride became more like a man's. She also tried moving her shoulders more than her hips. If she were careful, she thought as she picked up Martin's battered old hat, she could pull it off.

Keeping the house between her and the men, Abigail hurried to the barn. Soon she had Gypsy saddled and ready to go. She dared not chance the open drive, so she rode out into the feed lot and left by way of the back pasture.

Abigail had been to Henderson only once, but the road was clearly marked. She felt oddly alone on the road by herself, especially dressed so scandalously. The miles to town gave her plenty of time to wonder if she had again done something foolish.

The jail was easy to find, as it was the only

building behind the courthouse. Abigail pulled Martin's hat low over her eyes, praying that the bundle of her hair would stay beneath it. Remembering to slouch in the saddle, she rode to the square building.

At the hitching rail she dismounted, then sauntered inside. To the right of the door was a battered desk, behind which sat a large man.

"Can I help you, boy?" he asked with casual friendliness.

Abigail tried to keep her voice as deep as possible. "I heard you have the man here that robbed the bank." She reminded herself to avoid rolling her R's.

"I sure do."

"Can I see him?" She tried to talk as much like Harley as possible. "I ain't never seen a bank robber before."

The sheriff thought for a minute.

"I was hoping to be a sheriff when I grow up," Abigail said in sudden inspiration.

"In that case, I reckon I could bend the rules a mite. Don't you ever tell anybody, though. This is a dangerous man. A killer twice over. Don't get near the bars."

Abigail nodded.

The sheriff led her through a back door and down a short aisle of cells. The last one held a man who sat dejectedly on the bare cot, his elbows resting on his knees. "Look up, Sorrell," the sheriff greeted. "Here's a young lad to see you. Mind you behave yourself."

Logan glanced up with a scowl and did a doubletake as Abigail winked at him.

The sheriff nodded at her and said, "I've got

work to do. Just stay back and he can't hurt you." He strolled away with a rolling gait.

When the wooden door shut, Abigail hurried to the bars. "Logan, darling. Are you all right?" she whispered.

"Abigail, what in hell are you doing here? Have you lost your mind?"

"Hush! He'll hear you." She reached up to touch his cheek. "You've a bruise! What have they done to you?"

"Don't worry about that. Where are Tobe and Harley? Did Travis come back?"

"Not a sign of him. I'm afraid he's left you to take his place."

"He wouldn't . . ." Logan stopped and a muscle moved in his jaw. The old Travis he had known might not have done that, but the new Travis would.

"How can I help you?" Abigail pleaded. "There must be some way of getting you out."

"Are Harley and Tobe here too?"

"No, they would never have let me come. I stole Harley's extra clothes and slipped out. We're all ready to go to Mexico."

Logan covered her small hands with his and gazed lovingly into her eyes. "I want you to go back to the farm and leave now. Tell Tobe I said to get you to safety."

Her eyes flashed. "I'm not a parcel that needs transporting, Logan. I'm here to break you out of jail."

His grip tightened on her hand. "You'll do nothing of the sort! Promise me you won't!"

"But I don't think you can get a fair trial here," she protested. "Especially since I can't testify and say where you really were."

"Abigail, listen to me. You can't possibly get me out of here. If you try, you'll only make matters worse." He tried to speak calmly and sway her with logic. "Now, you turn around and walk out of here. Get on your horse and go home."

"Don't you dare talk to me as if I were simple-minded," she hissed. "I've come to save you."

"I can prove my innocence somehow, and they'll turn me loose." His own anger was rising from the strain of being falsely arrested. "I can't prepare my defense and worry about you. Now, get out of here!"

"Have you no lawyer?" she gasped.

"Yes, I do. But I have to tell him what to say. He was the only one available."

The wooden door opened and Abigail barely had time to jump back from the bars. The sheriff entered, followed by a reedy little man with one arm in a sling. "Is this the man?" the sheriff asked.

Abigail shrank back as the man came forward, a fanatical look in his eyes.

"That's him! That's the man that killed Pete and shot me."

"You're wrong!" Logan growled, lunging at the bars. "I never shot anyone. You've got the wrong man!"

"I'd know him anywhere," the man said. "I was as close to him as this during the whole robbery. That's him."

The sheriff smiled. "Good news, Sorrell. Your trial has been moved up to today. We were just waiting for Dobb Cadenhead here to recover enough to testify. No need now to wait another day."

Abigail pressed her back against the bars of the empty cell behind her. Slowly she shook her head.

Logan's eyes met hers. He knew she was dangerously close to breaking down. "Get these people out of here," he demanded of the sheriff. "This is a jail, not a zoo." Once more he dared glance at Abigail, and wished he hadn't. She was trembling with fright and he ached to hold her and soothe that haunted look from her eyes. By the time they left, he found that he too was trembling.

Abigail managed to squeeze into the crowded courtroom, where the trial was already in progress. She held her hat firmly in place to hide her hair and hoped that no one would demand that she remove it. Two matrons gave her a displeased look and one remarked to the other that boys were being allowed to grow up any which way these days.

Abigail ignored them and nudged her way closer. By standing on tiptoe she could see over the shoulders of the people ahead of her. As a woman, she was accustomed to having men part a way for her convenience; as a boy she was shown no courtesy whatsoever.

In the time it took for her to compose herself and find the courtroom, it had filled to overflowing and the trial had started. Abigail dared not draw attention to herself, but she had to hear what was being said, and that meant weaving her way through the crowd. The packed bodies jostled against her and she dodged, afraid that her breasts might not be well enough concealed. Between the press of the crowd and the snugness of the binding around her chest, she could hardly breathe.

The judge rapped for quiet and Abigail leaned forward expectantly.

"Mr. Cadenhead, can you identify the man that shot you and murdered Pete Dryden?" the prosecuting attorney said as he turned to glare at Logan.

"Yes, sir. That's him there," Cadenhead accused. "I seen him plain."

"Your witness," the prosecutor said.

Logan's lawyer stood up and went to the witness box. "Mr. Cadenhead, we've just heard Miss Ellie Sykes say she wasn't sure, and she's the other eyewitness. Couldn't you be mistaken?"

"I can't help what Miss Ellie saw or what she didn't see. Everybody knows she has weak eyes."

"Objection!" Logan burst out.

The judge banged his gavel. "You can't object. Your lawyer has to do that."

Logan glared at his lawyer, who shook his head. "I can't object when everybody knows it's true. Miss Ellie is shortsighted."

With a groan, Logan dropped back in the chair. He would have done better to defend himself, he realized too late. The lawyer was young and acted as though he was afraid of the judge. Logan suspected the man believed him to be guilty.

Cadenhead was dismissed and Owen Chandler smoothly took the oath and sat down. His pale green eyes locked with Logan's and he smiled.

The prosecuting attorney said, "Major Chandler, tell the jury why you're here in Henderson."

Chandler faced the twelve men in the jury box and stated, "Logan Sorrell there, also called by the military code name Nighthawk, is wanted for stealing a military payroll from one of our trains."

The men, all of whom had fought for the South, exchanged glances. Clearly they saw no crime there.

"I tracked him and his band to New Orleans," Chandler continued. "There he killed a woman named Marie-Claude Smith. He shot her down in cold blood in front of her husband."

This was a different matter entirely, and twelve pairs of accusing eyes riveted upon Logan.

"It's a lie," Logan hissed to his lawyer. "Say it's a lie! Amos Smith killed his own wife!"

His lawyer nodded. "Objection," he said in a mild tone.

"I can prove it," Chandler disputed. "There are wanted posters out for Sorrell and his female accomplice. I followed them most of the way to Jefferson, then lost the trail. Only recently did I realize they must be near or in Henderson. I don't think there can be any doubt that they robbed the banks at Cushing and Nacogdoches as well."

"All of that is irrelevant," Logan hissed. "I'm on trial for the killing of the bank teller."

"Are you a lawyer?" his attorney asked. "You never told me that."

Logan groaned.

Chandler glanced at the prisoner. "After those banks were robbed, I figured the next target would be here in Henderson. So my men and I have been watching the bank. On the morning in question, we saw two men come out of the bank, shooting behind them. Sorrell was one of those men. The other was a Cyrus Martin, who died of wounds received when my men opened fire."

Again Logan leapt up. "I'm telling you that I'm the wrong man! Martin was guilty, but the other man is my cousin, Travis Dunn!"

A murmur swept the courtroom and the members of the jury exchanged looks with one another.

"Sit down, Mr. Sorrell!" the judge demanded. "It will go worse for you if you keep interrupting."

"Can I get another attorney?" Logan asked.

"Now? With your trial in progress? No!"

Logan sat down under the glare of his lawyer.

"Your honor," Chandler said, "I've trailed this man across three states. If I say I saw Logan Sorrell rob a bank, there is no doubt about it."

The jurors nodded to each other sagely.

"Put me on the stand," Logan growled to his lawyer.

As Chandler stepped down, Logan passed him. They paused for a moment, eye to eye. Then Logan stepped up to the witness stand.

"First of all," Logan said when his lawyer asked that he speak in his defense, "the robbery of that gold was on orders from my commanding officer. 'Nighthawk' was a code name for our entire company. What Chandler can't abide is that I not only accomplished my mission, I made him look like a fool in the process.

"Marie-Claude was shot by her husband, Amos Smith, not by me. But he and Chandler are friends, so Chandler believes Smith's story. Or he sees it as a chance to put a noose around my neck.

"As for the robberies and the shootings here, I didn't do them. I've told you the man responsible is Travis Dunn. My cousin. We greatly resemble each other." He glanced around. "That's all I have to say. Martin is dead and Travis is getting farther away even as we sit here, but I'm innocent."

The judge motioned for Logan to step down and then nodded to the lawyers to make their final summations. When they were finished, the judge motioned to the foreman of the jury. The twelve men stood and filed out.

Abigail was clenching her fists so tight that her nails cut into her palms, but she didn't notice. Every prayer she had ever known had flown from her, and she could only repeat over and over in her mind: Not Logan. Please, not Logan.

In a matter of minutes the jury returned and the foreman handed the judge a square of paper.

The judge moved his spectacles down his nose, then read, "Guilty." Glancing at Logan, he added, "I sentence you to hang by the neck until dead. Sentence to be carried out at noon tomorrow." He slapped his gavel down and rose to leave.

Abigail felt physically sick. Even from this distance she saw Logan's face tinge with gray, then red as he lunged toward his cowering attorney. Feeling as if she would faint, Abigail watched as two deputies dragged him back from the man and toward the rear of the courtroom.

Guilty! Guilty! Her pulse pounded the dreaded words through her brain as the crowd swept her out the door. On the steps, she let herself be moved along with the crowd. Guilty! How could they have found Logan guilty when he had even given them Travis' name?

She made her way back to the jail. By the time the deputies returned Logan to his cell, she was by his window.

Silently she reached out, her hands easily entering the bars. His cold hands gripped hers and she returned the pressure. This was no time for her to give way to the terror that beat at her. Now Logan needed her strength.

When she thought she could speak without crying, she said simply, "I love you."

"Abigail," he whispered, "I told you to leave. I could have spared you that scene in there."

"I had to know."

His grip tightened until her fingers numbed as he said, "Promise me something, Abigail. This is the last thing I'll ever ask of you." He waited until she nodded. "Don't come to town tomorrow." His dark eyes pierced hers. "I couldn't bear thinking that you might be in the crowd."

She licked her dry lips and tried to swallow the lump in her throat. "Logan, I—"

"Promise me!" his voice grated harshly.

Her chin tilted up and she said levelly, "I promise I'll not see you hang," she said. The word almost choked her.

Logan kissed her hands. For a long time he gazed at her. Finally he released her fingers, and kissing his fingertips, placed them on her lips. "I'll always love you," he said. "I always have."

Not trusting herself to speak, Abigail turned and ran, tears streaming down her face. She didn't care if anyone saw and wondered what could cause so large a "boy" to cry.

As she was riding out of town, a girl about Harley's age called out to her, then looked at her in confusion. Abigail paid no attention. She had far more on her mind.

And by the time she reached Tobe's house, she had a plan.

28

Tobe watched Abigail as he saddled his horse. She was several yards away, pacing in the feed lot and looking toward town. "I'm real worried about her," he commented in a low voice to Harley.

The boy brushed his hair out of his eyes and peered over his horse's rump toward the woman. "She's taking it hard. We all are."

"Yeah, but she's not thinking straight. Last night when we divided Martin's gold, she made me count out Logan's share. Kept it separate, just like he was coming with us." His brow furrowed in worry.

"Maybe she'll snap out of it once we get on the trail to Mexico." Harley's voice reflected his doubts. "She sure is grieving."

Tobe glanced at the pale sky. "Sun's up. We'd better get started." He led his horse and Abigail's out to the lot.

Harley mounted in the barn and rode over to the gate. Unlatching it, he drove the yearling calves out onto the drive and started them down toward the road.

"Miss Abigail," Tobe said in a solicitous voice, "we'd better get started. Mexico is a long way from here."

Her eyes were stormy and troubled but her voice was steady as she said, "We're going to town first."

Tobe stared at her. "No, we're not going to do

any such thing. You know what's happening in town today. You don't want to see Logan hung."

"I'm going. With or without you."

"You promised Logan you wouldn't. You told me so yesterday."

"I told him I wouldn't see him hang, and I won't. But I have to see him once more."

"What's going on?" Harley called back.

"She says she's going to town," Tobe answered.

"Miss Abigail! You can't even think that!" Harley said as he rode back.

Abigail got onto her horse and looked from one to the other. "I'm going."

Tobe and Harley exchanged a long look and Tobe shrugged. "I can't let you go alone. Harley?"

"If you two are going, so am I."

Abigail turned her horse toward town.

Chandler had stayed at the jail all night. After the long chase, he wasn't about to let Nighthawk out of his sight. He still wasn't convinced the entire band had split up, and he had expected a jailbreak attempt during the night.

He awoke early and rolled to a sitting position on the narrow cot in an open cell. Through the bars of the several cells in between them he saw Logan. Chandler's mirthless grin widened his lips. No one had attempted to free him, nor had his woman companion even tried to see him. The saying was true that there was no honor among thieves, Chandler surmised. Maybe he hadn't been lying about them all going their separate ways.

Logan felt Chandler's eyes on him, and he swung his gaze from the window to the soldier, but made no sound.

Chandler's grin broadened. The sun was well

up. Soon he would see Nighthawk swing from the gallows. Or, to be more exact, the tree, for Henderson had no regular hangings.

He stretched and rubbed his lean belly. The cot hadn't been uncomfortable compared to some beds he had slept in. From the office he could smell the aroma of coffee. Throwing another smirk at his prisoner, Chandler left the open cell and strolled in to join the sheriff.

A young woman was there pouring coffee into the sheriff's cup. Chandler's eyes narrowed appreciatively. She was little more than a girl, yet her figure was rounded and her breasts pressed snugly against her bodice. Pale brown hair curled in ringlets around her innocent face, and when she glanced at him, her eyes were as green as clover. Her rosebud lips lifted slightly and Chandler correctly interpreted the message. Here was a girl-woman who enjoyed bed sport.

The sheriff saw Chandler and nodded in greeting. " 'Morning. This is my daughter, Nell. That's Major Chandler."

The girl bobbed a slight curtsy, as if she weren't quite accustomed to being an adult. "I'm happy to meet you, Major." Her tones were sweet and still held the ring of girlhood.

Chandler couldn't take his eyes off her. Being the sheriff's daughter might pose a problem, but nothing he couldn't work his way around. "I'm pleased to meet you, too, ma'am."

Nell smiled and blushed prettily, lowering her eyelashes.

Suddenly Chandler realized he was going to have to shift his thoughts or give himself away. His pants were beginning to feel inordinately tight. "Do you have some extra coffee there?"

"Sure," the sheriff said. "Pull up a chair."

Chandler drew up a battered ladder-back chair with a furry deerhide seat. He knew the girl was watching his every move, though she was pretending not to, and he was glad he had maintained his lean physique. Not many men who were about to retire could boast of wearing the same size uniform as they had when they enlisted. He let his shoulders roll a little as he sat down and took the coffee cup.

He was about to take a sip, when the door opened and several soldiers entered. His eyes flicked over them until he found the senior officer. As the man nodded perfunctorily to the sheriff and Nell, Chandler rose.

"Are you Major Owen Chandler?" the army officer asked briskly.

"That's right," Chandler said warily. None of these were his men.

"I'm Captain O. D. Blair, U.S. Cavalry. I have orders here for your arrest from Colonel B. W. Dearborn."

All the blood drained from Chandler's face and he put down the coffee cup. "Arrest! What for?"

"Disobeying a direct order and for ordering the men under your command to duties contrary to those assigned them. I'm to take you into custody and escort you immediately to Colonel Dearborn, where you will face a court-martial." All this was delivered in a clipped, machinelike manner.

Chandler stared coldly at the man. He had known this kind before. They rose in the ranks like hot-air balloons. "There must be some mistake," he bluffed. "I never received orders contrary to my actions."

"Yes, sir, you did. We've already talked to the

telegraph operator at Alexandria. The message was delivered."

A scowl crossed Chandler's face. "You're making a mistake, Captain."

"No, sir." The man's eyes never wavered and he was alert, ready to signal his men to forcefully restrain the older man if necessary.

To the goggled-eyed sheriff and Nell, Chandler said, "There's been a misunderstanding. Nothing I can't clear up, I assure you."

"Sir," said Captain Blair, "I have orders to take you to headquarters. Will you come peacefully?"

Chandler restrained himself from punching the man's expressionless face. "I'll come, but first I have something I must do. There's a man back there that I've chased through three states. He's going to be hung"—he glanced at his pocket watch—"within the hour. As soon as the hanging is over, I'll go with you."

The officer nodded decisively. "I can wait that long, sir."

Chandler growled and glanced back at the row of cells. Logan was listening to all that was going on, and he had a smile on his face.

Abigail and the two men rode to the shady, parklike lawn beside the courthouse. Her heart felt like a stone in her throat as she saw the platform beneath one of the big oaks. Keeping her eyes averted, she rode past it.

Tobe led them to an alley near the jail, where Abigail could get a glimpse of Logan as they took him past. A crowd had already gathered, and children were rolling on the grass and chasing each other in a game of tag while their parents talked in low tones to various friends as they awaited the big event. Hangings were rare in Henderson, and most of the town had turned out to see justice done.

Once more Abigail turned her plan over in her mind. She hadn't dared tell Tobe or Harley for fear they would try to stop her. Carefully she gauged the distance from the alley to the gallows. Several yards beyond was the road out of town. Tobe and Harley were talking in terse, nervous sentences and not paying any attention to Abigail. Quietly she untied her saddlebags from behind the saddle and laid them over Gypsy's neck, within easy reach. She tied them in place and unbuckled the straps that secured the flaps.

Suddenly the door to the jail opened and an expectant murmur swept through the crowd. Abigail leaned forward. Her hands were cold, yet her body had a sheen of nervous perspiration.

First Chandler stepped out, followed by several Union soldiers. Abigail saw him mount Caliban, who was saddled with a Union cavalry saddle and a blue blanket with "U.S." in gold letters. The horse tossed his head and stamped, but Chandler controlled him with a firm hand. The other soldiers mounted their horses for the short ride.

Then the sheriff came out, his hand firmly clamped on Logan's arm. For a moment Logan's steps faltered as he saw the platform for the first time. Then he lifted his chin and strode toward it as if he were heading into battle, even though his hands were tied behind him.

Abigail was quivering as he passed. Tobe touched her arm and she jumped as he said, "You've seen him. Let's go."

She shook off his hand and kept her eyes on Logan. This had to be planned exactly right.

The soldiers reached the platform and Chandler dismounted, as did the others. He started up the steps, closely followed by the other officer and a soldier. After a contemptuous glance, Chandler seemed to ignore his fellow soldiers.

Next, Logan and the sheriff mounted the steps, and Abigail lifted her reins in expectation. He stood with his legs slightly spread, his shoulders seeming incredibly broad beneath his shirt. A breeze tousled his black hair over his forehead. Chandler caught the end of the rope that was tied in a hangman's knot and looped it over a thick limb.

Abigail kicked Gypsy's ribs and gave a fair imitation of a Rebel yell as the horse plunged forward. Tobe and Harley cried out in surprise as their horses sprang after Gypsy. As she rode, Abigail dipped her hand into the saddlebag and strewed gold coins, spinning and glittering over the heads of the people and onto the grass.

The crowd was instantly in chaos as they scrambled for the gold, and no one tried to stop her as she thundered toward the platform, showering it with gold as well. Bending from the saddle, she grabbed Caliban's reins. "Jump, Logan!" she yelled as they galloped past.

Because the sheriff had bent to pick up some gold, Logan was able to run to the edge of the platform, leap into the air, and straddle Caliban. Gripping the horse with his knees, he leaned low to keep his balance as Harley rode near enough to cut the rope that bound his wrists.

Chandler bellowed like a wounded bull and would have jumped after him, but the captain and corporal each grabbed one of his arms and restrained him.

As the four rode hard for the deserted street,

Logan reached forward to take the reins from Abigail's hand. No one tried to stop them as Abigail kept throwing gold from side to side. All their would-be captors were on their knees clambering for personal gain.

"Are you crazy?" Logan yelled at her when they were away from the green. "Are you out of your mind?"

"I couldn't let you hang," she called back. "And it worked!"

"You could have been killed!" He nudged Caliban to keep pace with Gypsy, and none of them slacked their speed.

"My life wouldn't have been worth living without you. I love you too much. By the way, I threw my own gold," she told him as the wind whipped her face. "Yours is on Tobe's saddle."

"I don't care about the gold! I'm worrying about you right now." He risked a glance back to see that only Harley and Tobe were behind them.

"We're going to Mexico," she informed him. "Chandler can't get us there. We can buy a sheep farm and settle down."

Logan stared at her. "I can't go live in Mexico! I have to clear my name!"

"And get hung? We're going to Mexico."

"I can't let Travis get off like this!"

"And we'll raise sheep," she added against the tug of the wind. "You'll love it."

"I hate sheep," he called over to her. "We'll raise cattle."

"Sheep!" she argued.

"You're a damned stubborn woman, Abigail McGee," he shouted back.

"That's right, and I love you, too."

EPILOGUE

Logan leaned back in his porch chair and let the back rest against the adobe wall of Casa Rosehaven. Within the house he could hear Abigail singing a lilting Irish song that contrasted oddly with the Mexican surroundings. Yellow strips of sunlight filtered through the gaps between the cedar-post sunshade over the porch. Long strings of dried red peppers turned lazily in the breeze.

Just beyond the yard was the road that led to Tobe and Rosa's rancho. After siesta he planned to ride over with Abigail to see their new baby. Harley, the proud godfather, had ridden over the night before with news of the baby's arrival. He had been too excited to remember if it was a boy or a girl.

Past the road, as far as Logan could see, lay rolling pasture dotted with longhorn cattle. All his. In the distance a mountain range spread in blue-gray splendor against the azure sky. Logan sighed with deep contentment. In only two years, he had not done badly.

Nor had Caliban. Logan had a pasture of fine mares, many with colts sired by the big black. Already his horses were becoming well-known, and within the next few years would make him wealthier than the first Rosehaven ever would have.

The screen door opened and Abigail came out to join him, their son balanced on her hip. Logan held up his hands and the toddler all but leapt toward him. Logan tossed him in the air and the boy squealed with delight. Abigail smiled indulgently.

Logan hugged the boy and made hungry-bear sounds in the warm curve of his neck. The boy giggled and did the same to his father.

The love Abigail felt for them both expanded inside her every time she saw them playing. Little Rowan was the spitting image of his father, as Abigail's mother would have said. The same black hair so thick it hid his scalp and defied a comb, his features a softer version of the man he would be in adulthood. Only his violet eyes suggested that Logan wasn't his sole creator.

She ran her hand over the faint curve of her stomach and the sunlight glinted off the wide gold band that was her wedding ring. By spring they would have another child. A girl, Logan said, because she was carrying lower this time. Somehow she sensed it would be—and Logan wanted a daughter.

"Have you heard how Rosa is doing today?" she asked as Logan let Rowan wrestle him to a standstill.

"Elena Montoya came by a little while ago and she said Rosa is fine."

"And the baby? Is it a boy or a girl?"

Logan looked at her blankly. "I forgot to ask."

She gave him an exasperated look, but smiled as she pulled up a chair. "It's nice out here today. I've always liked autumn."

His eyes took in the gray-green mesquite trees and the flowers that still bloomed in red and gold profusion beside the front walk. "This looks just like summer to me."

"Nonsense. Can't you feel the change in the air? Winter is coming."

Logan smiled at her humoringly. "I think pregnancy has affected your mind," he observed in a conversational tone.

"Soon we must have Juan and Sancho bring the sheep down from the far pastures. Winter comes quickly on the mountain." He glanced at her. The pastures behind the house were Abigail's, as was the large herd of sheep. She had hired two local boys as shepherds, and he had to admit she was a good manager. Her mutton and wool brought in as much as his cattle profit. Still he kept up the pretense of disliking the sheep. It was a point of honor.

She glanced at him. "I went to town yesterday."

"I know."

"While I was there, I heard some news." She had been trying to break it to him ever since she returned home. "First we heard Rosa was having her baby, then I got busy making supper. I didn't get a chance to tell you what else I learned." She watched Logan smile fondly at Rowan, who was trying, with deep concentration, to unbutton his father's shirt.

"There was news from the States. Consuelo Martinez told me about it. There was a bank robbery. The robber was killed."

Logan's eyes grew wary as he waited for her to finish.

"It was Travis, Logan."

He looked at her. "Are you sure? How do you know?"

"The Laredo paper had a big write-up. He was robbing the Laredo bank."

"So Travis is dead." His voice was thoughtful,

showing no grief for his boyhood companion, nor relief over the death of the man who had left him to die in his place.

"The article said he confessed to several robberies and killings before he died. Including the one in Henderson." She met his eyes. "Your name is clear."

"Except for Marie-Claude's death," he reminded her.

"Tempers have cooled over the years. We could prove your innocence now."

"Does that mean you want to go back?"

"I wanted you to know that we can now. If we want to."

Logan looked down at his son, who was babbling babyishly in a singsong mixture of Spanish and English. Then he looked at the shady comfort of the porch and the cool adobe house behind him, and at the yellow road that led to the hacienda where their friends lived. "This is home," he said at last. "Are you happy here?"

She nodded. "Happier than I ever thought to be."

He stood decisively, shouldering his son, and reached out to Abigail. "Then why would we want to leave? I have my cattle and horses, you have those damned sheep. Let's stay right here."

"I was hoping you would say that." She let him pull her up, and she hugged him, the boy between them.

He held her close, breathing in the sweet scent of her hair, mingled with the warm baby smell of Rowan. His heart expanded with love and his eyes smarted with tears of happiness. "Let's go over and see that baby," he suggested. "Rowan can take a nap there with Tobe's brood."

Abigail linked her arm around Logan's waist as they walked toward the barn. "I think Rowan is Scots-Irish at heart," she commented. "This morning he looked at me and said, 'Let's go see sheep.' That's his first sentence in English."

Logan snorted. "That's nothing. Yesterday he told me he wanted to brand cattle—in Spanish."

Abigail sighed and smoothed her hand over her middle. "Maybe his little brother will be the shepherd."

"Sister," Logan corrected automatically.

Abigail smiled.

About the Authors

Lynda Trent is actually the award-winning husband-and-wife writing team of Dan and Lynda Trent. Not only is it unusual for a husband and wife to become coauthors, but Dan and Lynda are living the kind of romance they write about. After dating for only a short time, they were married in 1977, and then began together a new career for them both.

Formerly a professional artist, Lynda actually began writing a few months before she met Dan, when she put down her brush and picked up a pen to describe a scene she couldn't get onto the canvas. The paints dried and the picture was never completed, but Lynda continued to write.

Dan, also a native Texan from Grand Prairie, worked for seventeen years for NASA in Houston before turning to writing full-time. The Trents have written a total of ten novels, and when asked how they manage to write together, Lynda says, "We only use one pencil."